VALLEY VERSUS VECTOR

FOLK HORROR OF THE WILLAMETTE VALLEY

JAHAN BRIAN IHSAN

TEASEL HOUSE

Valley Versus Vector

By Jahan Brian Ihsan

Valley Versus Vector

Folk Horror of the Willamette Valley

Book cover art by Zubrick7

Interior book design by Jahan Brian Ihsan

1st edition 2025

ISBN: 9798990494220 (hardcover)

ISBN: 9798990494237 (ebook)

Library of Congress Control Number: 2025918609

Published by Teasel House, Corvallis, OR

United States of America

CONTENTS

DE(A)DICATION

This book is for the outsiders.
And in memory of Paul Laffoley.
To Jennifer Ihsan, my dark mirror in the trench:
As Maldoror saw himself in the shark.
A true love does not cling to surface meanings.
Such a bond is in the gaps;
The space where language frays, as silence thickens,
And the sacred stirs beneath contradictions.

1

THE GOSPEL OF THE BODY BAG

Here I am, Ellis Horning, RN, now living in Benton County; more precisely, a small city named Corvallis, Oregon. It feels more like a quaint town than a city here. Still... I have big city news to share. When our hospital's doctors diagnosed me with what they thought was an emerging new STD specific to the Willamette Valley, they were right in a way I couldn't have imagined. This is sexually transmitted... divinity. This is how gods are born: through the mingling of fluids, the exchange of microscopic messengers, the colonization of one body by another. The Christ Contagion isn't a disease; it's an awakening. So, you see, it is not about her. No, after death, she is the object where the living subject goes for expression before crossing over into the fields between life and death, and lingering awhile. I didn't know she was a carrier, and frankly, I didn't realize the contagion was even a real thing. I dedicate this journal to you, Dear M. I'd like to share my journey with you, a steadfast dedication that reveals what I couldn't share with anyone else. I'll start by telling you about her and how I unknowingly welcomed the vector within her into my body so that you can understand my meaning.

Her gown was all rucked up around her pelvis. A disposable adult diaper cupped her hips; I eased it back, noting the blood trickle from the groin, where the Foley catheter had been roughly pulled. And here, between the pale of her thighs, was the nexus; the gospel of it all. The body was no longer merely clinical, but symbolic. A mother. An engine of generation. Even dead, her flesh invoked generations of veneration and taboo.

The dead were not meant to be beautiful, but she had died so quickly, so violently, that the rot had no time to efface her sexuality. Instead, it had amplified it. The corpse is thirty-five, status post MVA (motor vehicle accident), she passed away on the table two hours after admission for what should have been a routine spleen repair. Her name is M., or so says the chart attached to her sheet-wrapped ankle, but by the time I sign her out on the service floor and swipe my badge on the secure door, that's already an abstraction. Her face is obscured by the plastic of the body bag, dew already condensing inside it, a faint cloud of exhaled mystery pooled against the vinyl. Somewhere three floors up, her husband is in full collapse the last I saw him, he was fighting off the chaplain, his daughters on either side, both clutching the same child-sized plush animal anime-thing and matching in every visible gesture of panic and denial.

But there is something about the dead that compels me in ways the living cannot. When the elevator doors close on me and the dead, we descend to the service floor as the world above becomes theory and memory. Down here, the cold isn't just environmental; it's metaphysical, with a pressure that pushes the self to the edges, until even my breath feels borrowed.

I wheel the body into one of the two bays of the walk-in cooler, and I am careful with the turns. Rigor has already set in, as it does to even good-looking mothers, and her arms are now locked at her sides like she's sleeping off a bender in an airport terminal. I leave her zipped and tagged for a moment, eyes tracing the long stainless slab of the gurney. The single-bulb light comes out of the wall horizontally and lights the space in forty calm watts. I can see my reflection in the gloss of the cabinet: thin, unshaven but manicured, hands steady but already betraying a faint tremor of nerves. I catch myself running a tongue over my canine, acting like an animal at times.

I unclip the chart, double-check the cause and time of death, and start the protocol. The first step is to verify. I roll back the zipper and pull aside the bag just enough to see her face. In life, she would have registered as an entire history of decisions, a complex of loves and anxieties and indulgences, but now, in death, she is just a set of features. The mouth is slightly parted, tongue receded like a dog's, lips pale and bloodless but still plush. Her cheeks are beginning to settle into the hollows of the jaw, and her eyes are glazed, half-lidded, unfocused. They seem more like lenses than organs. There's a cut above her left eyebrow, stitched but leaking a little, a maroon crust at the seam. Her hair is damp from either sweat or postmortem secretions, but still manages a certain radiance, a golden sheen even the morgue's light can't kill.

I attach the toe tag and note the time. With every step, I attempt to summon the reassurance of my nursing protocol, searching for a calming rhythm of routines: "Verify ID, note distinguishing features, document the chain of custody, preserve the dignity of the remains." Yet, a part of me seems to have different intentions. As I adjust the sheet, a scent escapes the bag: a chemical sweetness that I taste through my nose as sharp with a foreign nature. And yet somehow, through grace, it ignites not disgust but a tingling pleasure across my palate and down my torso. But I know the pleasure is not solely chemical. It feels as though something within me acknowledges the taste, embraces it, and yearns for it, waiting for me to discover it all along. I instinctively go in for a kiss, and it's sweeter than I could have ever imagined. How long we kissed is unknown, a duration outside of calculations.

I have never spoken to a therapist about these sensations. Even my fellow nurses would call it a pathology. Oh, who am I fooling regarding such judgment by my fellow person, as it is always brutal, especially from my fellow nurses! I unwrap her arms from the shroud. Her skin is cold, of course, but not yet fully transformed by death; I can see the subtle blush of blood pooled under the surface. Her hands are beautiful in their feminine way. Her fingers are long and almost delicate, nails painted a conservative blush, one knuckle bruised from the accident or perhaps another unresolved trauma. I press my own palm to hers, compare the size of our fingers, the shapes of our bones beneath flesh. For a moment, I imagine her alive, these little manicured fingers tracing a steering wheel on the way to church, or stroking on her husband's chest for comfort, or the downy arm of one of those devastated little blonde girls upstairs.

I want to experience disgust, yet all I can feel, for lack of better terms, is hunger. For the first time in my life, I sense spirits speaking to me now; their voice is so gentle, a persistent sensation at the base of my spine, energizing my thoughts as though granting them swift passage. I understand that it's not something others can relate to. Their voice lacks a language. But it's insistent like an inmost light, and it conveys a structure that I am soon to comprehend: *She belongs to you, she is a part of history, it's embedded in her matriarchal DNA, she is a vessel.* These words blend with the pulsing rhythms of my own blood, making it difficult to discern whether the hallucination is a symptom or an epiphany. Such an inmost light would be categorized as madness or evil by those who do not hear these seductive angels. I attempt to ground myself, reciting the names of the bones in the arm in Latin, anything to remind me that I am made of flesh and more than a dream: humerus, radius, ulna, carpus, metacarpus, phalanges. Yet the room's silence consumes the sound, and the voice only intensifies.

I lean closer, examining her eyelids. There's a faint shimmer beneath them; some residue of soul or consciousness persists in the eyes' luminosity. I know this is impossible. At least for cold science and the tangible, after death, the essence of a person, the soul, is an unknowable story, a loss of meaning, a fracture, the ultimate mystery for those living with broken hearts. Surely, the soul is a story that we tell ourselves to endure the certainty of decay. But still, I feel it, a pulse of otherness radiating outward. I imagine, suddenly, that her eyes are open, fixed not on me but through me, she can see the spirits writhing in my own blood, because they are the ones that brought me to her in such a greeting. I know they're sensing the secret kinship between us. For a moment I'm convinced she will speak; that she will tell me my own fate in the voice of Marys River, the voice of the water that the zealots in this hospital hold as sacred, the river's motion offers a persistence of the sacred that is now feeding the community baptisms with vitality, the essence of Marys River's power has shaped the community, and now it is right here in this woman, or perhaps it is in me alone. She is the triangulation, the amplifier of energy; it is hard to articulate, as it is channeled into thought forms, a silent voice that communicates without audible language, saying that we humans are limited beings. It communicates through her, flirts with me, or perhaps I am mistaken and she's the one who's flirting from the other side.

Instead of an ongoing flirtation, an invitation of the sacred ignites, her lips part a little further, and a thin string of saliva stretches between her teeth. Again, I am overtaken by the urge to kiss her. I want to keep tasting the residue of the sudden end, to see what the kiss of death might communicate. I catch myself in the act, lips an inch from hers, and recoil with a bashfulness so pure it burns. What the hell am I doing?

The moment is fleeting, replaced by a second wave of desire. It is hotter than my previously staunch morals, more insistent than a conscious duration of a bashful experience, where one goes from being thrown into the world, to transcending death. My hands move on their own, tracing the line of her clavicle, mapping the nodes of lymph and the subtle indentations of trauma. I want to unzip the bag completely, to see the bruising along her abdomen, the surgical staples glinting like jewelry above the pubic bone. It isn't the normal allure for a lady to look this good in a body bag. The chart says status post laparotomy; I want to see the evidence, unzip the bag a bit more, and follow the path of the scalpel and the hands that opened her. I can see they did a loving job. So I unzip the bag further, slowly to enjoy the audacity, slowly while exposing her torso, the sternal notch appears, but isn't a stopping point as I make my way ever so slowly down to the iliac crest. Her breasts are remarkable for a mother of two, or for any woman, and the left one bears a light scar above the large areola, a relic of some childhood accident, perhaps. I thumb it gently, marveling at the resilience of tissue, the way the body carries its history in layers both visible and secret.

I am beyond turned on. I can't pretend otherwise. The sensation is not sexual in the ordinary sense; it is hunger, it is prophecy, it is the call of the higher mind manifested through flesh. I want to take her, yes, but more than that, I want to understand her, to merge with her, to become with her.

I slide a gloved hand across her torso, feeling the chill of her belly and the puckered line of the surgical incision. I feel ridiculous using such caution, so I remove my gloves to be closer to her essence. I feel down her torso again. The stitches are fresh, the skin around them angry and purpled, but there is an odd serenity to the violence. I trace the wound with my fingertip, then press down, just enough to feel the give of the tissue beneath. In my mind's eye, I see the entire procedure in reverse: the abdomen re-knitting, the organs restoring themselves to wholeness, the blood drawing back from the wound in a red tide. I see the moment of impact, the car spinning, her body absorbing the force, the beautiful inevitability of physics and biology entwined. I see her last breath, the oxygen saturating her cells, the mitochondria firing one last desperate shot at immortality.

The vision overtakes me, and I have to steady myself against the table. I think of all the times I could have touched the dead in secret, the way their bodies have always seemed to whisper to me, to invite my gaze and my reverence. It is not a perversion; it is a sacrament.

The dead are not objects, not completely, now I understand this: they are portals, and I am their priest. It took me my whole life to discover this. It took something I cannot yet name. Something completely *other* is speaking to me beyond language.

I slide my hand further down, past the curve of her hip to the cleft between her thighs. The chart says she was menstruating at the time of death; I want to see if this is true, to see if the flow persists in death as it does in life. I part her labia and am met with a trickle of old blood, dark and viscous, pooled in the vaginal canal. The smell is metallic, intoxicating. I inhale deeply, letting the air fill my lungs, and for a moment I am both inside and outside her, the boundary between self and other dissolving in the chemical fog.

My other hand goes to my zipper.

Where is she now?

I position myself between her legs, lowering my face to the wound. I kiss the incision, tasting the bitterness of iodine and the sweetness of death. I run my tongue along the stitches. The voice in my head is chanting now, a liturgy of vibratory hymns. I unbuckle my belt, pull down my scrubs, and press myself against her, not entering yet but resting, feeling the chill seep into me, the last remaining pulsations that came from her beating heart now evaporating in the space between us.

I am crying my eyes out with gratitude. Loneliness has a cure. The voice of the otherness has claimed me, and in this moment, I understand the new gospel that death is an illusion of transformation. I thrust softly, rubbing myself against her labia, smearing her blood across my cock and inner thigh. I want to come inside her, to join our lineages in the final embrace. I stroke myself, slow and deliberate, savoring the friction of her cold skin, the slippery ecstasy of the blood.

When the little death arrives, it is like being dissolved. My vision goes blurred, then a riot of colors of the past: myself as a child, sick and feverish in a basement full of candles, my mother whispering the secrets of the old faith into my ear. I see the future of the world overrun, the living and the dead merging in a chorus of endless appetite. I find my future with dead homosapiens, where the human ceases and becomes a host for another consciousness, and it is here alone where I take liberties with the pleasure of an embrace for an emerging new consciousness.

2

CORVALLIS, OREGON

I cannot believe it's already spring, or that I turn forty-one this year, or that it's 2037. All this quickening of time makes me feel old. My new apartment in Corvallis is located on the second floor of the Witham Hill apartment complex, facing north towards a dense cluster of trees that seem more conjured than planted. My view is of an ever-dreaming wood of heritage gnarled white oaks, modest (but invasive) cherry trees, and the towering gangs of Douglas firs with branches that sometimes appear unnaturally still, untouched by the wind. The sunlight barely reaches the room before retreating behind the forest, pushed back. I leave the curtains open, even though I sleep in daytime hours after the night shift, to keep track of time and observe any changes in the stillness of the trees. I try to hack the circadian rhythm and adjust to the nightlife.

Already, humidity has taken hold inside my apartment. Witham Hill is a seductive place to land when you're new to Corvallis, but once you're settled in, the problems come out of hiding. These apartments, nestled on the forested hill, need to be torn down and replaced due to the infestation of mold (which they paint over to fool you as a newcomer). My books have already begun to warp, and black mold is creeping in under my front door, slowly making its way upward. I'm uncertain if I should be concerned about the mold at Witham, because I want to enjoy living here, across from an Odd Fellows Pioneer cemetery. I am "settled in," though the phrase feels anatomical, like tissue settling after death. The apartment resists warmth. My bedroom walls especially retain a chill, and at night, the trees seem to press closer, and on occasion, wild turkeys sleep in the branches, making odd noises and casting shadows that move as I lie in bed. There's a hush here otherwise; life is hiding from an impending storm, waiting just beyond the window, or beyond the trees, preparing to make its entrance.

I maintain a journal for the sake of posterity. If anyone ever discovers what remains of me, they'll have something to examine, to analyze, if they even care to (mis)understand me. I cannot say that I completely understand what is happening to my body and mind. Honestly, I hope no one ever finds these pages; the thought of my private musings being archived and scrutinized by future generations fills me with an indescribable dread. Still, there is merit in attempting to explain the reasons behind my departure from Greenville, even though the tale is far from heroic.

For generations, my family practiced medicine on Paris Mountain in Greenville, located on the edge of South Carolina, where Georgia and North Carolina lie just beyond the horizon, and where the land itself seems aware of its own scars. Our home, known locally as "Devil's Castle," was a Victorian maze, painted black on the exterior with an interior full of folklore. There were rooms I was forbidden to enter until I turned of age; rooms containing more than just surgical instruments and medical equipment. Some held bones and talismans arranged like a museum; one held a large oak table that bore blood stains from my father's research. The rooms were not to be discussed at the dinner table or any other comfortable time unless prompted by my parents.

Looking back on the years, I struggle to distinguish between what was rumor, what was memory, and what was merely a dream. My father, a surgical legend in the Upstate, presided over it all with the detachment of a mortician. His eyes were a cold, luminous gray, often like the belly of an unfed tick.

When I told him I'd chosen nursing school, he looked at me as though I'd confessed to a murder: "Ellis," he said, voice sharp, "you dishonor our legacy with a servant's job." I laughed, unconvincingly. It was precisely the point to venture on my own and make something of myself without standing on his shoulders.

Years ago, the curriculum at Charleston School of Nursing had been rigorous but finite, the way drowning is finite. I had already learned, from home, how bodies fail; how systems collapse, how to maintain a mental distance while performing duties that would horrify the uninitiated. The only real surprise was how little the instructors knew compared to what I'd learned from my father before puberty. They commented on my "natural aptitude," but I had the sense they'd have used different language had they watched me dissect our naturally deceased family dog at age eleven, under my grandfather's tutelage, with nothing but garden shears and a ball-peen hammer. I could easily have been a surgeon had I chosen that career path.

After my father's death last year, I applied to other hospitals across the country. I desperately wanted to go anywhere far from South Carolina. I was at the midpoint of life, and sought deeper discovery. I fantasized about the anonymity of the West Coast, where people seemed less likely to care about your genealogy or the skeletons inside your walls. This was how naive I was! The Corvallis offer arrived with the hospital's salary 15% higher than the market rate. The name gave me pause. Christ Hospital. But need outweighed my intuition, and I signed the contract. I was intrigued by this hospital, reportedly founded in 2035 by an Episcopal bishop with a noted interest in bird watching, presenting an unusual intersection of religion and ecological curiosity. I was hoping that two years of Christ Hospital's operations were enough time to iron out the kinks and still allow me the full experience of a newer pristine building.

For weeks, I only did the bare minimum research on my new city, focusing on things like climate, population density, and average rent. However, as my move-in date neared, I felt a growing compulsion similar to the early stages of obsession to learn more about the hospital and its bishop CEO. One article led to another, and I lost hours in a web of open tabs. I guess this is called fun when you're nerdy in your forties! Before long, I was sketching out the genealogy of Corvallis's medical system on the backs of grocery receipts. I tried to convince myself it was just thorough research, but that was a lie. I recognized the pattern in my intense focus, morbid curiosity, and the comfort of organizing the uncontrollable. After all, it's a family trait.

My obsessive focus produced interesting results that led me down the rabbit hole of Benton County history and its subtle power struggles with healthcare. Initially, Corvallis General Hospital was housed in a brick building on Harrison Boulevard. After World War II, the hospital went bankrupt, barely operational; doctors went without pay for months, and rumors circulated that entire wards had to be shut down due to a lack of supplies, not to mention staff. The board minutes from 1947 read like a goddamn suicide note. I spent a night sipping some cheap Trader Joe's pinot that I picked up on 9th street, while transcribing the notes from grocery receipts into my journal, chuckling each time the language of finance clashed with the terminology of medical crisis. It's the same story everywhere: lives are lost due to a lack of funds, and money vanishes in the process of saving lives.

The "salvation" arrived when the Episcopal Diocese assumed control, and the language in the *Gazette Times* took on a reverent tone. Words like "resurrection" and "divine intervention" began appearing. The photographs shifted as well, featuring bishops and vestrymen at the ribbon-cutting ceremony, their hands folded in a gesture that signified both blessing and ownership. The press didn't seem to question why a religious authority was now managing triage, or if patients were concerned whether their morphine was administered by the devout or the secular.

The hospital was renamed Good Samaritan, and we all know that Christians are not the first committee that mistook virtue for branding, but they are an excellent example. The parable of radical mercy might illuminate the ailments of a town where suffering is politely scheduled, and empathy wears a fleece Patagonia vest, speaking in tongues was the next step. Corvallis is a place where diversity is a seasonal garnish sprinkled on the myth of charity, which arrives, cruising with a clipboard and a grant proposal, and the only beaten travelers are posh joggers who forgot their electrolytes. The board of directors had more clergy than medical professionals, so I assumed it was some kind of orgy behind the scenes, especially when correspondence adopted the tone of a religious decree. Staff were instructed to start each shift with a moment of silent prayer, regardless of whether their workload allowed it. The hospital plays a recording of three women weeping when someone passes away, as well as a lullaby for babies born. I was on the toilet the other day while two babies were born, and I was thinking of how messy birth is. Later, when I asked a fellow nurse about whether we would be required to pray if we're not religious, she merely laughed and said, "Oh, honey, that's been phased out. But we all pray over the budget."

Later, I had to give an enema to a patient I just met, and then run straight to lunch right after midnight. The kitchen was having stuffed potatoes on special. I saw them under the warmer before the start of my shift at 7 p.m. The shift's twelve hours would have been better had I brought my lunch, but when off work, I went on a walkabout of the town to digest and prepare myself for sleep.

I strolled by where the original hospital once stood on NW Harrison, hoping to find a plaque or at least some trace of the building among the overgrowth. But there was nothing but the bland design of a student apartment complex and a chain-link fence covered in lichen. It was as if the old hospital had never existed; the lives and deaths it once housed had been reduced to an extinguished memory. Fortunately, the essence of the old hospital has been seamlessly integrated into the new one: the same records and philosophies remain, though the world around us has changed by the decade. I tend to believe that history and the dead remain in the present. I often think of the term I heard from my first and last visit with a psychiatrist, that I had a "necrophilic assimilation," even though I know it's not an official diagnosis. My dreams have started to follow a similar theme. Every night, I wander the corridors of Christ Hospital, trying to find the body of a deceased patient whose name escapes me, only to end up in a chapel instead of a patient ward.

The building stretches into an infinite corridor of chapels, each one diminishing in size until I have to crawl on all fours. Every doctor wears the same mask, featuring a benevolent, unchanging smile, with eyes as dark as cavities. The air is thick with the scent of incense and infection. I continue to crawl, shrinking down until I'm nearly microscopic. Each time, I wake up sweaty on twisted bedsheets. I've realized now that I haven't truly left my family's legacy; I've merely followed the path, evolving into a different version. I'm beginning to think there is no clear line between the medical and the spiritual here. It's all one persistent wound, attempting to heal but failing, where each scab is merely the start of another infection.

I spent last Sunday reviewing our hospital's CEO, Bishop Elijah Ashworth's career, assembling a curriculum vitae of his public life. He's always in the background of the photos: at charity luncheons, hospital fundraisers, blessing new ambulance purchases. His hair is salt-and-pepper, meticulously maintained. His hands are the most striking feature: long, delicate, nearly translucent, the bones appearing bleached before being wrapped in skin. He has the demeanor of a man who can quote both Leviticus and the prose of William Blake from memory, and probably does.

The records I uncovered indicate that Ashworth is exceptionally skilled at navigating his way through both church and hospital systems, advancing sideways until he suddenly reaches the top. There is a three-year gap in his biography, which the diocesan website labels as a "private sabbatical." During this period, he co-authored two academic papers filled with such complex jargon that I needed to use both Wikipedia and a German metaphysics dictionary to understand them. The first paper is titled "Spiritual Responses to Gram-Negative Bacterial Infection," and the second is "Theological Implications of Microbial Consciousness." Both are nearly impossible to read, yet their main message is unmistakable: Ashworth seems to believe that bacteria possess souls, or something akin to souls that is significant.

The concept isn't as crazy as it seems. I recall my grandfather once explaining, while carving a Thanksgiving turkey with the precision of a surgeon, that every living creature is driven by an urge to survive. "It's all about appetites," he said, "even in the smallest among us. Especially in the smallest." The following day, he passed away from a hemorrhagic stroke, and my father called it poetic justice.

By 2035, a majority of modern hospitals across the globe had artificial intelligence as infrastructure, using algorithms assessing pain, touch screen machines dictating treatment. Then, Bishop Ashworth pursued a radically different vision. Christ Hospital, nestled at the edge of the William L. Finley Wildlife Refuge, stood as a deliberate inversion: a sanctuary where the full spectrum of human sensation was restored to the center of care. No automation. No synthetic mediation. Just bodies, breath, and the timeless rhythm of the land.

Ashworth was building more than a medical facility; he was constructing a theology of embodiment. A mechanism of longing. Christ Hospital was a liturgy of actual suffering, where healing itself became a sacrament supporting his vision. During his presentation to the city council, his words rang with ecclesiastical conviction:

"Corvallis deserves healthcare that nourishes both body and soul. These must move in unison—like the wings of the birds that rise above our Valley." He didn't have to elaborate. The implication was clear.

The choice of site disturbed me more than it should have. The refuge is a place where the artificial and natural bleed together with unusual speed. Even the map of it looks like an ulcer, gnawed at the edges by encroaching farmland. Indigenous stories, I read from pamphlets at the Benton County Library, speak of the area as a liminal zone, a haunt of ghosts and animal doubles. I wasn't raised on Pacific Northwest folklore, but I recognize an infection site when I see one. This land evolved into the grass capital of the world, where allergy medication is hawked on the street corner.

The deeper I delve into the architecture of Corvallis's healthcare crisis, the more I perceive a larger, looming presence beneath the surface. The departure of each CEO feels less like a symptom and more like a shedding of skin; each new initiative seems like a growth. I am convinced the hospital is on the brink of an event, a transformation that will demand an unnamed sacrifice. This may be why I accepted the job. Maybe I am attracted to decay. Perhaps I have inherited a craving I can't identify or resist. A refusal to let anything remain buried. It is a fascination with unearthing, with the persistence of flesh against time and reason. I am frightened. The dreams are becoming more frequent and changing. In a recent dream, I found myself not in a chapel but a morgue, kneeling before a woman's body covered with my own changing skin, but I feared she was pieced together from memories and regrets. The body's hands reached up to touch my face, and the contact was so cold that I awoke shivering.

Tomorrow, I'm back on shift, so I will visit my patient, Harold Gideon, once more. I'll listen to his wild talks about the Willamette Valley's soil, consciousness, and the revival of bacteria. I'll jot down his words, pretending it's for his benefit, though deep down, I know I'm really documenting my own issues. And oddly enough, that brings me some comfort. We can never fully escape what we're born into; we merely change the way our desires manifest. In this devilish garden, something is emerging, something that uses human concerns as both disguise and vehicle.

I fear that the people of the Valley, in blindness, not only allow it —they thank it for coming.

3
GREENVILLE, SOUTH CAROLINA

I tried hard not to disconnect from reality. Within my family, pain created power struggles that would linger far after my removal of self into the new landscape of adulthood, and the stain of childhood was surrounded by lives in turmoil. I chose to stay quiet amidst the chaos. Life's secret seems to be letting things pass by rather than letting them pierce you. I'm not a savior for others, and I'm uncertain if I'd ever need redemption myself. I unapologetically turned away from the life of wealth and generational damnation that I was born into. Even though I turn away, I sometimes turn back, I sometimes side-glance back without willing to. I do this in daydream, and in sleep. I look back on it and see the horror of my own life, especially to note that, yes, it lingers behind, yet is more ahead of my steps than behind. Somebody call for an exorcism; someone get the wretched Bishop Ashworth to do a holy thing, or two, if we are talking miracles!

So, my past awaits. People in Greenville have called our generational family home the "Devil's Castle" for decades, and cross the street on Altamont Road to avoid walking past our private gated drive. At school, I've heard them whisper that Igor is my real name, like Ellis isn't bad enough. I've seen these types, their heads huddling together, walking under the shadow of downtown's tallest structure, the Daniel Building, or in coffee shops, gossiping that every Halloween my family takes a child to offer up to the Devil. The leaves on Paris Mountain burn bright as blood every autumn, and they come up here and take one leaf as a trophy and tell stories about approaching the house, although the majority are too afraid. They say the estate is haunted. I let them say what they want.

The stone tower and cold German architecture closely resemble the Rhine castle they were inspired by, lending credence to the rumors. If I had lived in the Rhine castle, perhaps I would have found peace by a moat, and I might have been amused if people called me "Igor." Moss and ivy freely cover the exterior walls in certain areas, giving it an abandoned appearance; only the past remains to blend with the elements. The carefully maintained gardens and sculpted bushes indicate it is well cared for, with mazes where lovers once frolicked like a scene from a Botticelli painting. Local Greenville residents often fabricate stories, with daring teenagers claiming they sneak up the long private drive to the large circular driveway around the house to observe the harsh way light filters through our stained glass windows, displaying chilling images of angels being slaughtered and violated. They say the light from our bedroom windows projects explicit scenes across vast rooms with oak floors, where giant candelabras cast shadows from one room to another. They say our statue of Pan is the devil. If I didn't know better, I would say these storytellers sound like they share my father's distasteful imagination mixed with a taste for sacred art. How fascinating to know that the explicit nature of sacred art and holy literature comes from revealing man at his most intimate—falling apart.

They tell stories that scream like the Greenville News headlines want to but cannot, the kind that keeps neighbors from knocking at the door: Signs of Satanic Behavior on Paris Mtn! Devil Worshippers in the Upstate?! The truth of those stained glass windows is less sensational. They simply depict pagan scenes: fertility rites, Pan dancing with nymphs, the worship of nature, a Pre-Raphaelite embrace of form. But people see what they want to see, or better yet, what they *need* to see to keep their reality afloat. They need to believe we are evil.

The estate had been in my family for four generations, built by my great-grandfather, who made a fortune in medicine before he was 35. His eccentricity was tolerated because of his money. Ours is not, despite the family fortune remaining intact. My father tells stories of our family in Greenville. He remembers being seven years old, walking with his mother through McAlister Square Mall. The way conversation stopped when they entered a store. The way mothers pulled their children closer, such happened to him as it did to me decades later, as though our family carried disease. I learned to recognize the look—part fear, part disgust, part fascination. I used to think they hated us because they didn't understand. Now I know better. They hated us because we represented everything they were afraid to admit existed in themselves.

At school, teachers watched me with wary eyes, as though waiting for me to scratch pentagrams into my desk or recruit a classmate to Satanism during recess. Children can be cruel, but they're also honest. "My mom says your family drinks blood," one kid told me in third grade. I didn't know how to respond. We didn't drink blood. We drank expensive wine that my father imported from France and Germany. But denial only makes people believe the rumors more.

Midnight ceremonies on the observation deck overlooking the city below—these were real. My parents and their friends, dressed in ceremonial robes, chanting in languages I didn't understand. But there were no sacrifices, no blood, no demonic summonings. There were just adults playing at being special, at being connected to something ancient and powerful. I watched from my bedroom window sometimes, more bored than frightened.

I grew up in the aftermath of Greenville's transformation. For my parents, the late eighties and early nineties downtown was caught between decay and rebirth. Abandoned buildings stood like hollow skeletons just blocks away from coffee shops or other hang-out spots. Their teenage years unfolded in that space, drawn to places others avoided, fascinated by the remnants of what once was and what might emerge from its remains. The Poinsett Hotel was my father's cathedral, the downtown streets his playground, and the strange rituals I witnessed in our home came from my parents learning ritual magick in abandoned Greenville spaces; this lineage became the first pages in my lifelong study of transformation.

My father told me of his life, and I later verified all the facts. The Poinsett Hotel had closed in 1987, an unceremonious death by foreclosure and fire code violations. Father was an emerging teen then, already drifting toward the margins of Greenville society, black clothing and pale face marking him as something other than what the Southern town expected from a rich youth. When the hotel's grand doors were shut, it wasn't an ending but a beginning for those who found beauty in abandonment.

By 1990, the twelve-story building had become a vertical playground for the dispossessed. The homeless claimed the lower floors, while he, a rich black-clad teenager with a solid platinum ankh and twenty-eye Doc Martens, ascended to the higher levels. The stairwells smelled of urine and spray paint, but he climbed past the fifth floor each time, a space where the air changed, carrying the scent of dust and forgotten opulence.

"Watch for nails and holes in the floor," he would warn a small group of friends, his eyes already trained to spot hazards with the precision that would later serve him in his medical profession. The floors were littered with debris. They navigated the dark while stepping over chunks of plaster, broken furniture, shattered chandeliers. He told me of lighting the way sometimes with just a cigarette lighter; his fingers would brush against peeling wallpaper, feeling the texture of decay, cataloging it all.

The ninth floor became their regular haunt. An empty ballroom where crystal fragments from a fallen chandelier caught the thin shafts of light that penetrated the boards over the windows. One of his close friends was a girl he described as always wearing an oversized gothy Cure t-shirt with dyed hot pink hair. She once cut her finger on one of these crystals. Father said they watched, transfixed on LSD, as a perfect sphere of blood formed on her pale skin as another friend lit the scene with a cigarette lighter. He collected that crystal, as she used the blood to draw on the Poinsett walls, and decades later, it became the first item in what I would later call my inherited archive. Like my father, I am a keeper of things, a documentarian of the transformation of moments into a past and present tension.

The upper floors of the Poinsett revealed evidence of rituals that stirred something in my father. It was a recognition he couldn't articulate to me fully. In a former guest room, he found a crude altar constructed from broken furniture. He photographed it. Dead pigeons arranged in a pattern that suggested sadistic sociopathic intention. Candle wax had dripped and hardened on the dusty floor.

The homeless men who occasionally occupied those spaces watched my father and his friends with wary eyes. One man with a drunken face weathered like eroded sandstone, so the story goes, once told him, "This place remembers what it was like. I remember what I used to be. Buildings have memories in their bones."

I nodded when my father told me these stories, dismissing them as fanciful tales from his teenage years. Now, of course, I have begun to know better. Everything remembers. And I have friends who are nihilists, they think the world will forget them and everyone else. But unlike the hobo, they don't drink to forget; they consume to adapt and return.

Father said he was drawn most often to the Poinsett Hotel, due to that sense of memory lingering, the history in its abandonment. He never told anyone when he went alone. He'd slip through a gate in the back and then a broken service door and climb the stairs in silence, listening to the building breathe. The settling pipes and creaking wood became a language he strained to understand. One solitary visit on the third floor changed him.

He never wrote about it, but I found the drawing years later, tucked between pages of one of his notebooks: a man in a long black coat, standing in front of a window, his face obscured by shadow. The coat was drawn twice. Once on the man, and once lying on the floor, left behind. Father had annotated the sketch with a single phrase: “He removed it before vanishing.”

Some of my father’s friends say they heard knocks on walls. Some say he is Pan, or the Old One, as they say. Some say he’s a phantom of one of the homeless who died in the building during its vacancy. I don’t know.

But I do know this: my father saw him before anyone else did. And he never went back.

This was my young father who resembled who I am now, and not the stranger he became at the end of his life.

In the same year Father saw the phantom, beyond the Poinsett, in the heart of downtown Greenville was Mother’s teenage theater of operations. The 200 block of Main Street housed the gothic and alternative subcultures, a collection of outsiders drawn to the aesthetics and promise of something beyond Greenville’s conservative surface. A corner store on Main Street, the Uptown Downtown, was Mother’s wardrobe department. She would always talk about how the shop smelled of incense and leather, racks of gypsy florals and black clothing waiting like shed skins for new bodies. She saved for weeks to buy her first pair of creepers—thick-soled shoes that elevated her little body physically, as she also felt elevated mentally from her peers. The owner knew all the teens by their preferences rather than their names.

“Your Doc Martens came in,” she told Mother one afternoon, reaching beneath the counter for a box. “The ones with the extra buckles.” Mother thanked her with the awkward formality that characterized her interactions then. Mother’s communication style was already developing into what would later be described as cold, using very few words and always precise, minimal emotional content, observations rather than expressions.

Next block up towards the largest building in Greenville (the Daniel Building, later named the BB&T bank building), the neo-pagan shop Rainbows and Moonbeams offered different transformative tools. Crystals, tarot cards, books on witchcraft, and alternative spirituality lined the shelves. Both mother and Father spent hours there, reading texts on herbalism and folk medicine, drawn to the intersection of healing and the mysterious. Father purchased his first anatomy book there: an illustrated volume from the 1930s with detailed hand-drawn plates. Grandfather had a library with volumes like this, but held onto them until he passed, and such was dispersed in the family. My father's first anatomy book sat alongside occult texts in his collection, both approaches to understanding the mysteries of flesh and spirit. This and the crystal from the Poinsett are now in my collection since my father passed.

For sustenance, my dating parents gathered at Bistro Europa in the afternoons or Fuddruckers in the evenings. I remember their smiles when they made the contrast between the Bistro's attempt at European sophistication in tiny cups of espresso and plates of unfamiliar cheese, and Fuddruckers' aggressive Americanness, with its hamburgers and self-serve condiment bars. The subcultures of the various teens of Greenville moved between these spaces like amphibious creatures, adapting to each environment while remaining fundamentally themselves.

The crown jewel of downtown, however, was the Hyatt. Unlike the abandoned decay of the Poinsett, the Hyatt represented sleek corporate prosperity, yet it offered unexpected public space for many of my father's friends with no money to spend. The fountain outside created a constant soundtrack of falling water, white noise that made conversations feel private even in the open air. Mother told me stories of how they would sit on the edge, black clothing absorbing the South Carolina heat, discussing bands and books and the crushing limitations of physical existence in the politics of the South.

But it was the interior that provided a true sanctuary. The lobby between the office and hotel towers was technically romantic-goth property, a fact mother guarded jealously among her memories of courting Father. They traded hickies back there, in what they described as "the cave under the fountain", and he played with her punk Chelsea-style haircut endlessly. As long as they maintained a minimum standard of no overtly antisocial behavior, no visible drug use, nothing that would cause the staff to call security, they thought they could occupy the space indefinitely. Eventually, they grew up, and then others, such as my friends, replaced them and did the same.

Water ran throughout the atrium in designed channels, creating an artificial river system that fascinated onlookers. In my teen years, I would go there and trace the flow patterns with my eyes, noting how the water was both contained and free, following predetermined paths while retaining its essential fluidity. Sometimes I'd place a leaf or small object at one end and track its journey through the system, timing its progress between sections. I sat and read where my parents' small group claimed a corner of the atrium, where the ambient noise created a pocket of acoustic privacy. My parents would sit in this spot and share headphones connected to portable Walkman cassette players. I listened to some music from my parents' time as well as my own. Skinny Puppy, Sisters of Mercy, and 4AD Bands—an alternative soundtrack overlapped in our lives, full of references to death and transformation that resonated with something already present within us.

In the early '90s, the Greenville News published a series of articles about "occult activity" in the Upstate. Although they never mentioned our family by name due to libel laws, the insinuation was evident. The articles included photos of our gates and quotes from "anonymous sources familiar with the family." My mother collected every article, framed them, and displayed them in her study. "Publicity and fond memories with your father," she would say with a smile that never reached her icy eyes. "All publicity is beneficial for those who understand its worth." My father was always more pragmatic. "Let them talk," he would say. "Their fear keeps them always at bay, and that's how we like it." In a sense, he was right, and we found it amusing. The rumors created a barrier around us that lasted into my teens, proving more effective than the wrought iron fence or trespassing signs surrounding our property. Although the rumors were far less attractive than our beautiful fence, they were more enduring.

I carried the weight of our family name through school, through adolescence. I learned to keep my head down, to speak softly, to reveal nothing, a ghost in my own life, observing but never participating. It prepared me well for nursing, for watching people in their most vulnerable moments without becoming involved. My family's position in Greenville wasn't unlike the region itself; it is what locals call the Dark Corner. There's a reason it earned that name. After the Revolution, while the rest of South Carolina developed and connected, that northeastern corner remained isolated, a realm unto itself. The people there are fiercely independent subsistence farmers who kept to themselves and developed their own ways.

During the Civil War, the Dark Corner became a haven for Confederate deserters. Later, it gained notoriety for moonshining, beyond a bathtub hobby, as an economic means for survival. They transformed a bushel of corn into three gallons of whiskey worth far more than the raw crop. My grandfather used to joke that our family was just doing the same—alchemically transforming the raw materials of ancient beliefs into something potent that could sustain us within South Carolina. The Dark Corner's isolation bred tales from the good ole days of violence—gunfights, family feuds, battles with federal agents. In 1891, a government distiller was murdered near Mountain Hill Church, followed by a bloody gun battle. My grandfather spoke of his great-uncle, who participated in the gunfight. These stories cemented the region's reputation as dangerous and secretive. And so it went with us. One incident—a particularly raucous summer solstice celebration that prompted noise complaints—spawned a decade of rumors about human sacrifice.

In my lifetime, I saw how the improved roads connected my Dark Corner to the wider world. In the early '90s, as my parents were finishing high school, wealthy retirees and professionals began moving into the area, drawn by the mountain views and the mystique. The same began happening around our estate. The isolation that had defined us started to erode as expensive homes crept up Paris Mountain, closing in on our borders. New neighbors peered over our fences with curiosity rather than fear. But by the year 2020, after Covid-19, when I was 24, I was already planning my escape. I left the Dark Corner of South Carolina and my family's dark legacy behind me to work as a traveling nurse. I traveled for years working, until my father fell ill and I had to return to Greenville, where I remained until his death. Afterwards, I left for the last time. I left the tragedy I witnessed buried there, beneath the red autumn leaves on Paris Mountain.

Right now, here in Corvallis, I still feel the weight of that bygone past. I've exchanged one outsider status for another, one set of whispers for a different kind. But here, at least, the whispers aren't about my family. They're about what I'm becoming in my senior years. About the changes I can feel happening inside me, changes I'm documenting with the same clinical detachment I learned as a child watching from windows. The irony doesn't escape me. I fled from one form of transformation only to embrace another. But this time, the change comes from within. It is mine, not theirs. And that makes all the difference.

I wonder now if those early experiences prepared me for what's happening in Oregon. If perhaps I was always meant to find my way to the Marys River, to feel its unusual warmth against my skin, to notice the iridescent shimmer on its surface that others somehow fail to see. To welcome what lives in those waters into myself. The transformation began so slowly after my first contact with the deceased. A faint patch, a little dab under the skin of something glowing faintly, a new type of underlayer of veins on my genitals, which were often swollen as if erect, yet flaccid until I was turned on. When I am turned on, my penis grows more aggressively swollen than ever. When erect, the glow intensifies in the large veins, and I have strange, sensual dreams happening more frequently. At first, I made notes and observed these changes with a concerned scientific interest. I am a nurse, after all. But lately, the line between observer and observed has blurred.

As my hometown of Greenville rose from the shadows of the Dark Corner, its transgressive magnetism refashioned into prestige, its isolation traded for wealth. I, too, am undergoing a similar metamorphosis. I have become the stone the builders once cast aside, now revealed as the dark cornerstone. The voice of the inmost light tells me of what was feared. My presence, my vision, my unsettling clarity is now a foundation. They testify in their bacterial voices (which don't require ears to receive them) to all that was rejected—my difference, my decay, my signal—is now integral.

This bacterial consciousness moves as grace does without regard for pedigree or creed. It spreads, not in conquest, but in the sweetest non-linguistic communion. It builds no cathedral, yet it gathers the forsaken, it has no dogma, yet is unmistakable in righteousness, it knows no denomination, yet it speaks in tongues—it is shaped like a serpent of religion, yet is invisible to us until we fall into its microcosm like lightning. Where the old community asked for conformity, this one asks only for contact it seems. I feel it reaching out. I want a taste of their fruit, to share the history in their tree.

4
THE CHRIST CONTAGION

He lies there, caught in the slow spiral of decay. He is both what was and what will be for my new life in the Willamette Valley. He is a grotesque question of entropy that warps every line of the human form—yet here I am, charged with caring for him. His name is Harold: a frail, malformed man whose body trembles with anxiety under the murky light; mottled spots dot his patchy, testicular-looking bald head.

Yet, he represents more than just another flawed chapter of altruism draining strength from my body. He is a plot connecting meaning from the human to the cosmos, he is a folktale told in the failures of the flesh, and he is a microcosm showing the as below so above entanglement in our doomed non-profit hospital. And, as above so below, he embodies a fleeting moment of eternity, a mysterious lapse in memory where profound insights are only understood in retrospect, moments obscured by trauma's erasure. It's my moment to come into being, when the absolute void of existence turns into sharp illumination, when madness is driven by another's perversion, and when gods walk among us as us, showing themselves as the entities we once considered to be illnesses or demons.

It's when all you cherish collapses, when the earth consumes the future. This is the essence of living in the present and then falling into the future, meeting fate. Was I disillusioned that my own fate manifested as a grotesque figure, sitting in filth, slowly dying? I don't think so. Events in my relatively young years led me to believe that prophets have a disagreeable scent, an odor of a goat; it is their spiritual essence that fills the gap between the sacred words. Perhaps my own memory set by trauma understood his presence.

As soon as I enter, a strong smell of urine hits me, blending with the stale odor of weariness. I pause at the doorway to decipher the scent: dehydration, a neglected urinary tract infection, and the lingering residue of forgotten housekeeping. The air itself in the chilled room seems to rasp, a distress signal from his body, which has been at the mercy of bad luck.

"I have your night meds," I announce, my voice sounding a little brittle to my ears as it bounces off the bare patient room walls.

Harold turns his head slowly, his cracked, yellow fingernails tapping a tired rhythm on the worn food tray in front of him. He's wrapped in thin, paper-like gowns that cling to his frail skin. Each breath he takes feels like a transgression far greater than the rebellious acts of today's troubled youth—a quiet defiance that insists life must carry on in the shadow of death. His breaths seem to originate from a place disconnected from his body, each one collapsing space with a final wheeze. Yet, he endures. Much like an odor, he lingers.

I approach with two small paper cups in hand. "Take your pills," I insist. "Life is precious." And I genuinely mean it; such idealism is the most challenging part to lose from my fading youth. The cold meal on his tray remains uneaten, and more trash accumulates on the bedside table. He'll likely request food at odd hours, only to let it go bad. I see him as someone who is drawn to decay. And indeed, he is. A solitary stink bug lands amidst the clutter; yet even such grotesques are not alone, relatives of its stink-clan meander slowly toward the glaring lights above.

Earlier, the charge nurse identified them as box elder beetles.

However, they are indeed stink bugs—more specifically, brown marmorated stink bugs. They are flying and buzzing fecal flickers who disregard our transmission precautions. That's about as close as I get to swearing, speaking of these flying shit-bugs, though I'm not on a moral high ground, nor am I religious. I've spent time living in the South, surrounded by evangelical Christians, and now in Corvallis, Oregon, I've encountered religious groups that seem even more toxic than those in the Bible Belt.

Outside Harold's hospital window, a whisper of the wind stirs the oaks and grasses in an unruly chorus serenading the old man to beckon the bugs back out into the wild. The bugs heed the call, vanishing into the cracks where wild things inevitably go.

Even here, in this hospital, in every room and corridor, the wild endures. It breathes beyond the machines that strive to hold Corvallis's broken captive. Wildness is the opposite of walls: a reminder of the world before life's fierce, irreverent dance was confined to this graveyard for the dying.

Wildness spoke when I chose not to wear peppermint under my nose; I faced the stench in order to understand. I stand above him, medicine in hand, a carrier of mercies to nurse a carrier of MRSA. I count the slow rhythms of his chest as it moves with undisciplined persistence. For a long moment, we are a single constellation: a patient, a pill, and a nurse in the Oregon sky. In that suspended moment, I repeat myself, louder this time, so that he must hear, "I have your meds." My voice falls more sharply, perhaps coming off as impolite, though that's not what I intended.

He seems to hear. Maybe he did before. Maybe he is a trickster. A stutter of light outlines the warped movement of his awfully hollowed-out face. A bug in the light fixture flickers, and I see its shadow cast on the wall behind the man. I see the geometry of the wild's wings in the dark shadows of complex, layered angles. How interesting that Christ Hospital features the juxtaposition of angles versus angels, the layered shadows versus the stained glass crucifixion, all just a few floors away from each other. Shadows cast him in strange proportions also, distorting his old gargoyle-like face into the formless unknown. What lessons does a person learn in this world when they are hideous? I wouldn't know.

The spectacle of his body parts its lips. A sound begins to form. A new creation would emerge from his speech. A new concept that I didn't know would alter my understanding of what was happening to me and to the Valley. Like all new births, this carries the potential to obliterate what was once known; at the very least, it corrected my understanding of the link between science and religion. And it did obliterate all I had defined as good and evil. His hands imitate the sound of an unspoken word. I am uncertain if he can speak. The disfigured patient lifts a singular, accusing finger, extending its curse in my direction to cast the evil eye. At that moment, a lullaby plays over the intercom, signaling the birth of a child on the floor above us.

I struggle to navigate the social niceties in this setting. I meant to introduce myself.

One small act could disrupt the balance of our painfully awkward interaction and alter everything. I proceed to introduce myself. After all, this man is a human being, and I am here to care for him. This is my job, even if I lack charity today.

"I am Ellis Horning, your nurse again tonight."

A brief silence follows, then his unpleasant, long fingers preach of osteoarthritis, bony almond-shaped lumps on the first finger joints, fingernails caked with the filth of his own expulsion, and once again they tap out a slow, deliberate rhythm on the tray. I don't recognize the beat; for all I know, it could be Barry Manilow or Engelbert Humperdinck. One or the other, I think about this humorously and briefly, judging the age and look of the old man. I place the paper cups in front of him—one with his medication and the other with water. He takes them immediately, like a strategic opening chess move. He wipes his mouth and fixes his piercing pale eyes on me.

At the end of his reeking bed, I observed stains of gleaming whitish fluids, and then a slurred chant began—one that defied the normality I was accustomed to in my nursing duties. I've heard strange stories before, and I've told them a time or two myself, but this experience opened a door to something within me. I had moved across the country to find something, I wasn't sure what. Now here before me was the gate to the kingdom of Christ Hospital, or better yet, the key to greater depths of life in the Willamette Valley.

Harold leaned forward, his bloodshot hazel eyes narrowing, and in a voice that seemed to come from outside himself, he spoke, altering everything I thought could happen in this room. Like a poet or deranged prophet, he said, "Ellis Horning, your name means the Horned Jehovah is God. Interesting, so good to see you again, yes, let me tell you why. Jesus Christ is a Contagion, and we have a Contagion in the Valley. You recently caught it; I can smell the Contagion. It is entwined in the evolution of our souls. Yes. Accept the inevitable transformation or resist the relentless tide that consumes all." He lifted his hand, drawing my attention. I must have been lost in thought, as I watched his disfigured skin momentarily smooth before returning to its aged, blotchy state. He could speak after all and was notably articulate, pronouncing each word clearly in a deep, raspy voice.

His voice continued, asking himself a question to elaborate on his previous statement: "Why?" In response, his voice echoed from a realm beyond his physical form, much like his earlier breath, "Through the floods that shaped this sacred land, epochs have crumbled and been reborn. I understand that in your limited view, you see everything as a cosmic duality; in that framework, here is the truth of it all: the Devil is Christ exalted... crowned, what's in a name, Ellis Horning, and the lesser prophets are united to be greater, in astounding harmony, like geese flying together as a larger entity." Then poor, frail Harold, the man I am somehow tasked to care for, the grotesque schizophrenic, the compulsive pervert, puts his hands down his pants and begins to touch himself while he stares directly at me. He begins again. "Tonight, the geese fly over this hospital in the shape of extinct creatures their ancestors mimicked. Likewise, the ancients have gone, but others mimic their memory as instinct. Glory and praise, O infernal sovereign, Great Satan, you are the unmasked Lord Jesus, the Holy Spirit, Our Father and Mother in One, where darkness whispers in the vault of the void, in the depths where silence transforms like a woman screaming in the labors of childbirth. Such knowledge is forbidden for the safety of our young species. Just a taste of it is the original taboo, the sweetest fruit!" He seems comforted as his hand increases its rhythm. He is obviously a man of routines.

Harold tilts his head, owl-like but far less cute than any wild animal, and opens his mouth. His talk of the geese disturbs me for good reason, to which I will make plain soon enough. An unsettling choice of groans spills out. "It's here. The Christ Contagion." His face bends to an unsettling grin as he continues to fondle himself. I realize I am in his lair now, and he is in charge of the space. "The Missoula Floods awoke it," he says. A moment of silence falls between us, except that I can hear his hand rubbing away. "We fed it with murder." He chuckles and moves his hand more frantically. I squeeze my eyes shut to stop this sight. I see bright floaters in my eyes, swimming around an incoming headache. My eyes snap open to see him watching, perched like an albino crow staring soulless from his sickbed nest. He breathes with me as he leans forward. "In Marys River." A heaping of fear takes hold. "In the water," he hisses. "The rural towns outside Corvallis hold a flowing key."

He repeats it, softer now, almost speaking to himself. His words, whether big or small, are murkier than the filmy Willamette River, closer to the ramblings of a madman. "The Christ Contagion. That's what they call it." He pauses. "A fever for the Valley." He reaches out, grasping at empty air, his eyes meeting mine once more, unblinking. "Awake before the floods. Awake again." A tremor runs through his thin frame. "Awake and hungry." His whispers grow louder, yet echo in the room, while resonating in his throat. "Fed it with murder. Sacred murder." My hands tighten as he repeats, "We fed it." He mumbles something incomprehensible, talking to unseen guests. A tremor passes through his torso; it causes his yellow, almond-shaped fingertips to constrict suddenly. In the fraction of a moment as I grow concerned, he seems at peace, trailing off into a dry chuckle. I am relieved; he is an easy patient, all things considered.

A calculus textbook and Bible sit on the bedside table, surrounded by a half-full urinal and another empty one, drawing my attention to the disorder in the room. "A fever of memory that consumes everything." His eyes shine with an unsettling insight. "It will spread." He laughs again, making my skin crawl. I've never encountered a patient like him. The way his eyes seem to vibrate when he speaks. His speech is also unusually dense and frantic. I struggle to keep up. He expels a sharp breath. "Corvallis. Philomath. Monroe." My jaw clenches as tension rises. "You've seen it," he insists, repeating. "You've seen it." He lets out another laugh, sounding more like a sob. "In Marys River," he gasps. "They are baptized." His intensity is unsettling. He continues, breathless. "We know. You know."

I take a deep breath to steady myself. "What do you know, Harold?" My voice is louder and more detached than I'd intended for this intimate setting. The smell of the old man somehow becomes more pronounced, almost tangible, and in smelling him, I am actually eating a part of his filthy body through my nose. Suddenly, he falls quiet, and the silence is abrupt and unsettling, coupled with his heightened stench. Was that his gas, or did his soul bleed out a little? Have you ever met someone who gave you the feeling of dread, a stranger who shoved their unwashed dick in your face all of a sudden? Harold's oily head, those awful spots; some of his spots remind me of the iridescent patch I have on my groin. I feel my blood throbbing in my neck's carotid arteries. I am flooded by hawkish observation and the undercurrent of uneasy feelings of synchronicity between us. "We've observed," he says, his hand trembling, jerking under his gown. "Others can't perceive it. But we are aware." He releases a hoarse breath. "It's more than a plague. It's here, in the minerals, in the water. In me, in you." His eyes, once wild a moment ago, now focus intensely and almost gently. He lowers his voice to a whisper and leans in like it could be a secret. "You've witnessed it, you've *tasted it*."

I try to interrupt, but he plows ahead, and words spoke of something other than their symbolic fill-ins. It must be that my growing discomfort is solely with him or these theories. Surely it is his stench that has made me feel so peculiar. I listen when I can excuse myself—why? His face takes on a haunted expression. The stench is unbearable now, clinging to my nostrils and throat. A strange terror grips me; he knows things about me he shouldn't, he seems to thrive on my fear, feeding off it.

Suddenly, anxiety appears to close in on him, tightening around his frail frame, while I feel like an outsider standing too close. "You've witnessed it," he insists, his voice now quieter, almost reflective, as I approach closer with my stethoscope. "It spreads through our towns, once through Edmund Creffield's veins, through Ashworth's believers." He raises his heavily veined hand, his fingers shaking as he extends them. He inhales sharply, producing a harsh sound.

My heartbeat is erratic, its rhythm uneven, yet his heart remains steady and calm as I press the drum of the stethoscope to his chest. He runs his tongue over his dry, cracked lips, trying desperately to moisten them. The room seems to sway around me, yet he stays motionless. I back away.

My fingers twitch involuntarily as I abruptly reach for the door. I have other patients to tend to. His eyes shine with something ominous. "Nothing can be done," he concludes. A sense of relief washes over his expression and voice. "But watch."

5
GENERATIONAL CURSES

I had a memory of my old life in Greenville, Halloween, 2003. I had just turned seven. Some kids are actually brave enough to come around the neighborhood and ring the bell for trick-or-treat. I look out from our dining room and see a pink fairy and a cowboy sheriff standing near our front gate. They huddle close and start up the drive, staring at the windows, whispering, hoping for a glimpse of some phantom. A gaunt woman in a black turtleneck answers the door. Her celebratory witch wig is a black and white two-tone set against a high-cut Morticia Addams-inspired vampire dress. I call her Mother. My father calls her Mia. Her smile is all teeth. She drops dark chocolate bars in their bags. When they run away screaming, the sound chases them down the mountain. Mother enjoys their fear, I think. Not in a malicious way, but as an artist might enjoy the reaction to a provocative installation. She stands in the doorway after they've gone, watching the empty driveway, sipping from a glass of cabernet. The light from the hall catches the deep red liquid, making it gleam like blood. It's these small, accidental moments that feed the rumors.

She was beautiful, in the way of mega-fashion models from the glam 1990s: sharp cheekbones, ice-blue eyes, platinum hair, she wore long. In photographs from before I was born, she looks untouchable, standing beside my father at gallery openings, and even in the more casual Polaroid snapshots. Her expression is always slightly bored, slightly amused, as though she's privy to a joke no one else understands. By the time I was old enough to form memories, that beauty had hardened into something else. Never ugliness, but a kind of terrible perfection, like a carved ivory chess piece. She moved through our home like a ghost herself, trailing silk scarves and the scent of patchouli oil. She spoke rarely, and when she did, it was in odd riddles or poetry fragments that reflected her dark (possibly depressed) sentiments.

I can recite the fragments she favors: Sylvia Plath's "I am vertical but would rather be horizontal." Baudelaire's "Evil comes up softly like a flower." Sometimes, when the moon is full and the air is thick with incense, she recites William Blake: "The tygers of wrath are wiser than the horses of instruction."

My parents did hold their rites and rituals, oblivious to the horror stories spinning around them. Or, maybe, not caring. Maybe even pleased. But I've always wanted something else. I never belonged to the Cult of Pan, as it was called. They call it the Cult for short. The pentagrams, candles, and midnight rituals. Old. Unbending. Locked in time, but not dusty. That is what my childhood looks like.

The ceremonies were held on the new and full moons, and on the eight sabbats that divided the year into segments marked by solstices, equinoxes, and the midpoints between them. They had friends who were Wiccan due to similarities, but the Cult of Pan they represented was on a darker path, what they called "a neo-pagan left-hand-path magickal think-tank." My father would don robes embroidered with symbols I later learned were the Elder Futhark. My mother would be bare except for white, thin robes, her hair crowned with flowers in spring and summer, with dried wheat and berries in autumn and winter. Their friends would arrive at sunset, parking their expensive cars—Jaguars, Mercedes, the occasional Bentley—along our circular drive. They brought wine and elaborate dishes arranged on silver platters. Before the ceremony, they would dine in our cavernous dining room, laughing and talking about art exhibitions and opera performances. They seemed ordinary then, just wealthy, educated people with unusual spiritual interests.

It was only when they moved to the ritual space—a circular clearing in the woods behind our house, or in winter, the great hall with its vaulted ceiling—that they transformed. They would form a circle, holding hands, chanting the runes or sometimes Latin. My father, as the high priest, would stand in the center, raising a ceremonial knife toward the sky, calling down the spirit of Pan, the ancient god of wild places.

I grew up a ghost in their lives, not quite there. My toys were my ancestors', wooden horses and lead soldiers. They were always the same, hand-me-downs from before the world knew plastic. The soldiers had chipped paint, revealing the dull lead beneath. The horses were smooth from generations of small hands. I would arrange them on the Persian rug in my bedroom, creating battles based on historical ones my father had told me about, or pretend extended campaigns of Erik the Red.

While other children in Greenville played with new toys or hand-me-down Star Wars figures and Transformers purchased from McAlister Square Mall in their parents' childhood, I learned to make my own entertainment with hand-me-down artifacts from my great-grandfather's time. I've often wondered if this is why I became so observant, so analytical—having to extract maximum engagement from minimal antique stimuli. Antiques carry more than history; they hold projected consciousness, from their original crafting to those who hold and cherish them. Objects receive energies of mass and aesthetics; thought forms of consciousness are more powerful than the layman assumes. It is for good reasons that people see old toys as haunted. What childhood isn't waiting to return?

Although my parents definitely kept secrets, I was never

forbidden from watching the lesser magick rituals, but neither was I encouraged to participate. I would sometimes sit on the grand staircase, peering through the balusters at the adults in their robes, their faces transformed by candlelight and wine into something ancient and otherworldly. They didn't seem threatening or evil—just strange, like characters from a play being performed in our home.

"Are we Satan worshippers?" I asked once, as a child, standing next to my mother on the observation deck they had built for "big ceremonies." I can see Greenville spreading below us, framed by the distant line of blue mountains. The city sparkles like the stars they say are already dead by the time their light reaches us.

She looks at me, something of a pitying expression on her face, and cups my cheek with her palm. "We are servants of the Horned God," she says, and I see something in her eyes that's like nostalgia.

"But not Satan?" I press, thinking of what the children at school had said that day, of the pamphlet someone had left on my desk with horned demons torturing sinners in cartoonish, colored detail.

"Satan is a Christian invention," she says, her voice taking on the lecturing tone she uses when discussing art or literature. "A way to demonize the old gods, to make people fear what came before their church. Pan was worshipped for thousands of years before Christ was born. He is the god of wild places, of freedom, of the connection between human and animal nature. We don't worship Pan, but instead use him as the most potent symbol of our relation to the world and cosmos."

I remember nodding, not fully understanding, but relieved that we weren't the demons my classmates believed us to be. It was a small comfort, knowing we weren't evil—just different, honoring gods that had fallen out of fashion millennia ago.

"Why do people hate us, then?" I asked, watching the lights of cars moving along the highways below, like blood cells in veins.

"People fear what they don't understand," she replied, her hand cool against my face. "And they hate what they fear. It's easier than learning, than opening their minds to possibilities beyond their Sunday school lessons."

She turned me toward her then, kneeling to meet my eyes directly. "Never apologize for who you are, Ellis. Never let their fear become your shame."

It was perhaps the most profound maternal moment I ever shared with her, this woman who seemed more like a priestess or a stoic friend than a mother most days. For a brief moment, I felt seen, felt the connection that I watched other children share with their parents. The moment passed. She straightened, smoothed her skirt, and walked back into the house, leaving me alone on the deck with the city spread below me like a circuit board of lights and darkness.

I stood there until the evening chill drove me inside, wondering if it was possible to be neither the demon others saw nor the acolyte my parents wanted me to be. In the years that followed, I found my answer in books, in science, in the orderly progression of cause and effect that explained the world without recourse to horned gods or midnight ceremonies. I found comfort in biology textbooks, in the clean lines of anatomical drawings, in the predictable reactions of chemicals combining. I found a different kind of magic—one that could be proven, replicated, and understood.

In the youth of my parents, South Carolina was already steeped in a tradition of devils to banish and others to discover—sometimes even among your neighbors. The satanic panic was in full swing. My grandmother (Nana) spoke of Karla LaVey's visit to the private Wofford College in Spartanburg, and it still echoed in the whispers of churchgoing mothers in the Upstate. There was a teenage "warlock" from Greenville who was serving a life sentence for murder in Florida. I didn't know these stories until I heard them from Nana—my parents shielded me from local news, and I was uninterested in their social connections. But I've since pieced together the context in which my childhood unfolded in the shadow of theirs.

Greenville was constantly changing. The old downtown my grandparents glimpsed on rare shopping trips with little Mia, my mother, was hollowed out as department stores fled to McAlister Square and Haywood Mall. Main Street mainly stood empty until its late-90s revival, and the west end became synonymous with drugs, prostitution, and crime. My Nana avoided it, preferring the sanitized corridors of the malls. Occasionally, they would press their luck and drive down Wade Hampton Boulevard into the fortress of Fundamentalism: Bob Jones University. Nana and mother visited their extensive art museum until the BJU cult recognized them as outsiders and asked them to leave.

Among the museum's prized acquisitions was *St. Francis Receiving the Christ Child from the Virgin*, a large altarpiece by Denys Calvaert. But the Christ child's nudity proved too much for the institution's sensibilities. During restoration, a BJU-hired artist painted a wisp of fabric over the exposed genitals—a gesture of modesty that aligned with the expectations of Bob Jones Jr., the University's president and founder of the collection. To cover the genitals of Christ, one best hire an expert. He defended such alterations as necessary concessions to the Fundamentalist constituency. And this wasn't an isolated case. Other works in the collection—many by European Old Masters—were also believed to have been retouched to conceal nudity, especially when depicting sacred figures. Yet the museum's exhibits and publications remain silent on these interventions, erasing the tension between religious symbolism and bodily truth.

Mother and I discussed her visits with Nana. We also visited the BJU gallery together, where we discussed the body as a symbol in religious art—how nudity could signify vulnerability, incarnation, or divine humanity. But that kind of conversation didn't belong in the BJU galleries as many turned their heads in judgment. We returned home, buffered by privilege and our mountain isolation. Still, the bullshit of society reached us. We lived in Greenville, after all—through the wary glances of shopkeepers, the rumors that clung to our name, the quiet judgment that followed us wherever we went.

Last week, Mrs. Abernathy visited. She's an elderly woman who lives alone in a colonial revival estate just down the road on Altamont. She brought a bundt cake and an envelope of news clippings about satanic activity in the Upstate.

"I worry about your soul, Ellis," she said, her hands trembling slightly as she passed me the cake. "Your family... there's a darkness there. A generational curse."

I invited her in, like a boy playing with a poisonous snake, curious about what she might reveal. My parents were away at an art auction in Spartanburg, and I welcomed the company, even if it came with proselytizing.

"A generational curse is passed down from one generation to another due to rebellion against God," she explained, perched on the edge of our sofa as though afraid to sink too deeply into it. "If your family line is marked by divorce, incest, poverty, substance abuse, or other ungodly patterns, you're likely under a generational curse."

She opened her worn Bible to Deuteronomy 30:19 and read: "I call heaven and earth to record this day against you, that I have set before you life and death, blessing and cursing: therefore choose life, that both thou and thy seed may live."

"You have a choice, Ellis," she said, her watery blue eyes imploring. "You can choose life and blessing, or death and cursing. Your parents have chosen their path, but you don't have to follow it."

I thanked her for her concern, for the cake, and for the clippings. I walked her to the door and promised to consider her words. What I didn't tell her was that I'd already made my choice—not between God and Satan, not between blessing and cursing, but between superstition and science, between fear and understanding. I made a decision to shed the superstitions of witchcraft and Christian theology from my life.

The clippings she gave me were fascinating, though. Articles as old as my mother, about police departments across South Carolina establishing formal training on Satanic cults. Reports of "breeders" —women allegedly giving birth to infants who were off government records and meant for sacrifice. Accounts of teenage graffiti along I-26 are interpreted as demonic symbols. Reading these, I understood better why our family had been so feared, so isolated. We had become characters in a collective nightmare, embodiments of anxieties that had nothing to do with us and everything to do with a society grappling with change and uncertainty.

Tonight, as I watch Mother standing in the doorway after the last of the trick-or-treaters has fled, I wonder what she makes of it all. Does she understand the role she plays in their imagination? Does she care?

"They were saying in town, when your mother was your age, that a criminal justice course on Satanism was going to clean up Greenville," Nana told me. "Over three hundred officers took the field training program the first year it opened."

She takes another sip of wine, her lipstick leaving a perfect crescent on the rim of the glass. "Fear is a powerful industry," she says. "There's money in monsters. Your mother, Mia, is a little monster."

Mother laughed. Our fingers brush as I take the empty candy bowl from her, and I feel a spark of static from the dry air, but it jolts me nonetheless. For a moment, I see Mother, a priestess of Pan, the phantom that haunts my childhood memories, simply as a woman—barely aging (she passed these genes on to me), tired perhaps, but still carrying herself with the dignity of someone who has never apologized for who she is.

I wonder, as we stand there in the doorway looking out at the night, if I've been wrong to reject everything she represents. If somewhere between her devotion to ancient gods and my faith in science, there might be a truth we both miss. But these are thoughts for another time. For now, I close the door against the October chill, lock it, and follow her into the warm heart of our strange, haunted home.

6
INDIVIDUAL COLLECTIVISM

I am separate. I am their host.

The changes unfold slowly for my new life in the Valley—subtly. I keep this journal to track such things as otherwise the changes blend, though I pay little attention to numeric dates. Memory lives outside the calendar. Events build and accumulate like tides shifting beneath a placid surface. It begins with dreams so vivid, visceral, and unlike anything I've ever known. These visions intensify, pulling me into realms both terrifying and sublime, where the laws of nature twist to the whims of the beings that now share my form.

I just woke drenched in sweat, trembling, their desires still ringing through my mind. I try to dismiss these episodes as hallucinations, fragments of an overactive imagination. But I know the truth. Others occupy me; they are real, and they grow stronger by the day.

Each morning, my senses sharpen further. Colors vibrate with unnatural brilliance. Sounds take on a piercing clarity. A veil lifts, exposing a world pulsing with hidden meaning and invisible currents. The beings within me delight in these perceptions, urging me to dive deeper into this strange, unfolding reality.

With that awareness comes a toll. They twist through my thoughts with riddles and spectral imagery. I resist their siren calls, clinging to the fading remnants of normalcy. I see now, there was nothing mundane about reality to begin with. Even as I maintain this journal, I feel my grip slipping.

In desperate moments, I retreat to the only solace I know—my work. As a nurse, I witness human fragility on a daily basis. I watch bodies ravaged by disease and minds unraveled by trauma. But at Christ Hospital, I begin to see my patients through new eyes. Their suffering reveals spiritual dimensions I once missed. I gravitate toward the broken, the near-departed; their pain mirrors the chaos within me. I feel compelled to mend them, to hold together the splinters of their psyches.

Yet even here, transformation continues. The beings' influence saturates everything. I daydream of complex chemical structures and of places that I never studied. Occasionally, I lose time—blink and find myself somewhere unfamiliar, seeing through the eyes of someone else. My anxiety spikes during these episodes until I anchor myself again. It is in these moments that I sense it fully: I am no longer sovereign over my own existence.

Alone in my apartment, I sit paralyzed by dread. The beings stir constantly, reminding me of the distance between myself and humanity. I grow younger, a young-looking forty-something blending into a fit hybrid of youthful and mature, a timeless look. I am an alien within my own skin, torn between worlds. And yet, beneath the horror, I marvel. To serve as a vessel for something unfathomably vast is a fate few know.

So I endure. I am separate, and I am their host.

Rumors circulate through Christ Hospital again—whispers of another incident in Med Surg. I overhear bits of conversation; some staff even include me intentionally, though I continue eavesdropping. My mind races with implications. Harold, a recurring source of concern, now draws attention for his vulgar mouth and what dangles and lingers beneath it. He frequently fondles himself, removes his urinary catheter, and seeks female staff to rectify his undoing. But perversity isn't the core issue. What piggybacks on the treats he offers staff and passers-by escapes human sight.

His chart lists unusual bacterial strains in his urine, spreading through the catheter and prompting contact precautions. Whether his actions stem from his diagnosed schizophrenia or something darker, I cannot say. What I do know is this: *other* things cling to us here—things larger than ourselves. Sometimes, we become monsters through the eyes of another who sees identity in our affliction. Youth interprets age and disability as monstrous masks not only in the Willamette Valley but everywhere.

During rounds, I feel drawn to Harold's room, so compelled and damned. A respiratory therapist passes me, venting about burnout. He questions why he remains in healthcare, overwhelmed by human suffering. What he may not realize is that questioning the system itself is vital. Complacency corrodes. In his words, I find myself reflected and full of questions. I press on toward Harold's room.

Urine stench saturates the air, the abject lingering and impossible to ignore. I wonder if Harold, too, has been overtaken by what now resides in me. And then I see her—a little girl darting past me, radiant amidst the slow churn of hospital life. Her golden hair cascades like a sunlit river, her floral dress against our institutional creams and grays. She sprints room to room, drawn by invisible magnetism.

Harold waits in his wheelchair under the doorway, shadowed grotesquely. Lit from above, his face vanishes in darkness. He unfurls his thick, yellow-nailed fingers to offer her a piece of candy.

"It's a local candy made from Marys River and with all-natural ingredients. It's the sweetest thing—maybe not sweeter than you," he says with the practiced ease of a salesman.

She hesitates. *Good girl. Resist.* My thoughts race. I feel the crushing weight of knowledge no child should bear. I stand at a precipice—a place where disability wears the costume of normalcy, and within this null-space of horror, monsters wear the faces of men.

But who am I to judge Harold? Who am I to deny him dignity in a world that discards its wounded? Did he know what he offered? Is his obsession with the river a channel for kindness, however malformed? I'm frozen, captive to my thoughts as Harold sits with the grim majesty of a gargoyle.

The girl's presence lingers in my mind long after she disappears from view. Her innocence, her radiance—it is a stark contrast to the darkness that surrounds Harold and me. She embodies a purity I have lost, a reminder of the humanity I struggle to hold onto.

As I watch her move through the hospital, I see her as a beacon of hope and a harbinger of change. She is untouched by the beings that reside within me, yet her presence stirs my contemplation. In her, I see the path I could have taken, and the life I could have lived if not for the beings that now define me. She is a reflection of what I have lost and what I could become.

I am separate, and I am their host. But in the presence of the girl, I am reminded that I am also human. And I ask myself now if it is this humanity that will guide me through, toward whatever lies ahead. Then my thoughts were broken by her actions.

The girl gives in and reaches out, acting rather shy and shaken, her small hand hovering above the candy, a moment of hesitation that seems to stretch time. I hold my breath, my pulse pounding in my temples, as I silently will her to turn away, to run from this place and never look back. But it is too late. Her fingers close around the sweet, and in that instant, I know that her fate has changed. She has stepped into a world of shadows, a place where the rules of society no longer apply, and there is no turning back.

As she skips away, now eating the Marys River taffy candy, her hair bouncing with each step, I feel a profound sense of loss, a grief that seems to emanate from the very depths of my being. For I know that I have failed her, that I have stood by and watched as innocence was corrupted, as a young soul was drawn into a web from which there might be no escape. The creatures within me stir, their whispers rising to a crescendo, flooding my mind with images of transformation, of humanity remade in their image.

About an hour later, I badge into the break room and step into a tribunal I don't know is in session. I see their faces and feel like a defendant entering a courtroom, already judged before I can speak a word in my defense. Maria leans against the wooden breakroom table, arms crossed over her blouse that bears faint coffee stains from the morning's rush. Her dark hair is pulled back so tightly it seems to stretch her skin, accentuating the sharp angles of her face. Tommy perches on a worn chair with tennis balls cut and fitted to the legs to lessen the noise of movement—a Chet innovation, one of his many attempts to make our workspace more "civilized." And there stands Chet himself by the coffee machine, his domain, arms folded over his meticulously pressed scrubs, not a wrinkle in sight despite being eight hours into his shift.

The break room smells of burnt coffee and Maria's jasmine perfume, which is too strong for a hospital setting, but no one dares tell her that. The coffee machine in the corner hums an off-key melody, its internal workings struggling like the conversation about to unfold. A half-eaten muffin sits abandoned on the table, crumbs scattered like evidence at a crime scene. Maria's face tightens as I close the door behind me. She jabs a finger in my direction, eyes narrowing into slits of accusation.

"You could have stopped her," she snaps, her voice cutting through the stale air like a scalpel.

I freeze, my hand still on the door handle, a part of me wanting to retreat into the hallway. But there's nowhere to run from this confrontation. Chet uncrosses his arms and braces them against the counter.

"She could get sick," he says, his voice low and urgent. "Didn't you think of that? MRSA isn't just a minor inconvenience, Ellis."

The way he says my name—like it's a diagnosis, something to be charted and treated—makes my skin crawl. Chet, with his bald head set against his obsessive precision and coffee rituals, always finds the flaw in others while performing his own immaculate facade.

Tommy's lips curl in frustration as he adds, "Harold shouldn't be handing out candy—hell, he's contagious and has mystery shit doctors are still looking into." He adjusts his position on the chair, the tennis balls squeaking against the linoleum. "We all saw you standing there, watching it happen, Ellis. What's up, man?"

The accusation hangs in the air, impossible to ignore. I feel my pulse spike, my palms slick against my scrubs. My throat constricts, the same paralysis that held me earlier now prevents my defense.

"Yes, Tommy is right. Did you even read Harold's chart?" Chet presses, moving away from the coffee machine toward me. "Known and unknown Gram-negative bacterial colonizations. Contact precautions. Isolation protocols." He ticks each item off on his fingers, indicating I've never heard these terms before, belittling me as we spent years in the same training programs.

I open my mouth, but words catch in my throat until I manage a dry rasp: "I… I spaced out, I thought it was harmless."

The moment the words leave my lips, I know they're inadequate. Harold may be many things—disturbed, fascinating, possibly connected to something beyond our understanding—but harmless is not one of them. And we all know it.

Maria pushes herself off the table and steps closer, her tone sharp as broken glass: "Think harder next time. We're not just letting you off the hook. This isn't about you zoning out during rounds or forgetting to document something. This is a child, Ellis."

Her words strike like physical blows. Behind her professional outrage, I detect something else—fear, perhaps. Fear of what Harold represents, of the contamination he carries that has become the rumors all through Benton County. But she doesn't understand the true nature of that contamination, of what might be spreading through our hospital beyond bacterial colonies.

Chet presses: "Did you see how he looks at all the kids who pass by? The way he watches them? It's about the MRSA—it's about boundaries. Professional boundaries that we're all responsible for maintaining. The man is sick in the head."

He moves to his coffee pot, adjusting it with unnecessary precision, aligning the handle exactly parallel to the counter edge. His coffee obsession, the specific beans, the temperature control, all of it suddenly strikes me as a desperate attempt to impose order on a world spinning increasingly out of control. I am grateful for his nursing abilities, yet annoyed regardless.

"We're not condemning Harold," Maria chimes in, her voice softening slightly. "He is mentally ill, we get that. But we're protecting all our patients. That's our job." She tucks a strand of hair behind her ear, revealing a small scar I've never noticed before. "And it's your job too."

My stomach twists, and I grip the edge of the table, knuckles whitening, as heat rises to my cheeks. The room seems to contract around me, the air growing thinner. They're right, of course. On the surface level, where hospital protocols and medical ethics operate, they're absolutely right. But there's more happening here, layers they can't see, currents they can't feel.

"Did you at least tell the parents?" Tommy asks, his question hanging in the air like an indictment.

I shake my head, the simple motion feeling like a confession.

"Jesus, Ellis," he sighs, running a hand through his growing beard. "You have to report it now. Document the exposure."

The thought of documenting this by reducing it to clinical terminology, incident reports, exposure protocols seems absurdly inadequate. How do you document an exchange that might go beyond physical contagion, that might represent something metaphysical?

I swallow hard, my voice barely audible: "I'll talk to him... I'll make sure it doesn't happen again."

They exchange glances, unease flickering across their faces. There's something in their expressions—a subtle shift that makes me wonder if they sense more than they're saying. Do they feel it too, the currents of change running beneath the hospital?

"This isn't just about Harold," Chet says finally, turning back to his coffee preparation with deliberate movements. "It's about you, Ellis. You've been... different lately. Distracted. Not yourself."

The observation hits home.

"I'm fine," I lie, the words hollow even to my own ears. "Just tired. It won't happen again."

I slump back as the vending machine hums louder in the corner, the chastening weight of their words settling like lead in my chest. They return to their activities: Chet to his coffee, Maria to her paperwork, Tommy to his phone. Yet, the air remains charged with something unresolved. They've said their piece, delivered their professional rebuke, but none of us has addressed what truly happened in that hallway.

They've made it abundantly clear what is not welcome here, not in this breakroom, not in their lives. The mysterious Gram-negative bacteria co-opted by the heretical enclaves of our own administration, and out past the refuge, where scripture is twisted into feverish rites and bodies go missing. Whatever happened in that hallway, they won't name it. None of them calls it the Christ Contagion. They don't know that I carry it too, and perhaps some of my coworkers do also.

I remain in the break room after they leave, listening to the coffee machine drip as I now wait for a cup. My reflection in its chrome front looks distorted, stretched into a funhouse mirror version of the man I was just weeks ago. I press my palms against my eyes until colors appear in the darkness, trying to organize my thoughts into something resembling normal professional concerns.

I shook my head. The sickness is a part of me now, perhaps preventing me from stopping the transmission; it was as intrinsic as the blood that flowed through my veins. And yet, even as I struggled against their sway, a part of me couldn't help but know my gossiping coworkers were finally right about something that mattered. If, by allowing that child to be exposed to the same unholy bacterial communion that had claimed me, I had indeed set in motion a chain of events that would possibly lead to her demise, something beyond the scope of my coworkers' understanding.

With a fast double breath, I exhaled anxiety, squaring my shoulders as I prepared to face the world anew. I stepped out into the hallway, and the familiar sights and sounds of the hospital suddenly seemed like a thin veneer of normalcy masking the true nature that lurked beneath.

And as I made my way back to the urine-soaked confines of Harold's room, I couldn't shake the feeling that I was walking into a place within myself from which there might be no return.

7
THE GOD PAN

After being chastised by coworkers for my lack of care for the girl who accepted Harold's contaminated treat, I made another dreaded approach to his room, trying to hold my breath as the overpowering stench of his musky urine hit me. Peering through the small window beside the door, I saw him seated upright in his wheelchair, his hospital meal untouched in front of him. When our eyes met, I felt drawn into an abyss by the depth in his gaze. Some less observant coworkers murmured about seeing their childhood memories transform into unfamiliar landscapes under Harold's distant stare. Several CNAs, assigned to provide constant supervision for his safety, have fallen asleep and had vivid dreams while watching over him. These one-on-one assignments were recently canceled due to the workers' reaction to his strange behavior and the discomfort they felt around him.

Taking a deep breath, I opened the door and entered the room. His presence filled the air, heavy and oppressive, and I paused for a moment, caught by the intensity of his gaze. He sat in the wheelchair, clearly unbathed and so still, his eyes locked on me with a piercing intensity that made my skin tingle. “Have you seen them too?” he asked softly, breaking the silence. “The secrets of the world, revealed across the Valley?”

His words take me by surprise, but I maintain a professional demeanor. “I’m here to check your vitals,” I say, approaching him with a stethoscope. He watches me with a knowing smile; he sees right through my facade.

I fasten the blood pressure cuff around his thin arm, noticing how it struggles to grip his frail frame. He turns his eyes to the window, where sunlight slips through the blinds, casting long shadows on the floor.

“The Valley,” he begins, savoring each word, “is a vast land stretching 150 miles from north to south, bordered by the Coast Range to the west and the Cascades to the east.” His voice flows steadily like a river. “It starts at the Columbia River, a wide expanse of water, and ends at the Calapooya Divide, where the mountains rise like a wall.” He pauses, taking a shallow breath, his chest moving under a worn sweater. “But it wasn’t always like this,” he continues, his eyes narrowing with the weight of memory. “Once, towards the end of the Pleistocene, around 15,000 years ago, catastrophic floods swept through this land.”

He leans forward, seemingly eager to share his secret, his voice gaining in strength.

“Let’s focus on your health for now,” I respond, trying to steer clear of unsettling predictions. The sphygmomanometer’s needle dances as I pump it.

“Of course,” he concedes, his smile widening. He clearly knows about things that I don’t. “The Missoula Floods,” he says, ignoring my request, “came with a force that defies imagination. Water, released from a glacial dam, thundered across the land, carving the earth, sculpting the landscape.” His words are as relentless as floods, filling the room with their power. “The floodwaters scoured the Valley, leaving behind isolated buttes, like islands in a sea of grass.”

He gestures with those dreadful, thick nails almost theatrically with his trembling hand, marking their location or casting a spell. "It was a landscape of extremes, shaped by the fury of nature."

I listen, occasionally glancing over, because to see him entirely is to drift into his heightened sense of knowing worlds that I am unsure I want to visit, so I keep my hands busy with the tasks at hand, but my mind is caught in the current of his story. This man is like a riptide for my thoughts; never had I seen someone so utterly grotesque. He pauses again, letting the enormity of the event sink in. "But the floods were only the beginning," he says, his voice softening like a receding tide. "As the glaciers retreated, the climate changed, and the Valley began to transform." His hands, though unsteady, trace the lines of this transformation in the air. "Grasslands spread across the lowlands, and oak woodlands took root on the hills. The transformation made the Willamette Valley the new Garden of Eden. In the future, this land will be the holy land, the Valley is the fully realized Palestine."

I glance at him, unsure whether to admire his knowledge or dismiss it as the ramblings of a sick man. He pauses, a shadow crossing his face, and his next words come with a hint of sorrow.

"Have you been to Caesarea Philippi, Ellis?" Harold asks, watching my face with an intensity that makes the hair on my arms rise. "Not physically, of course. But in your studies?"

"I haven't," I say, noting his blood pressure—142/86, slightly elevated but not concerning given his age and condition. I move to check his temperature, sliding the digital thermometer into his ear.

"It was a remarkable place in antiquity," he continues, his tone shifting into something academic, professorial. "Located at the southwestern base of Mount Hermon, where a spring emerges from a large cave. The Greeks identified it as the birthplace of the god Pan, the site of his worship."

The thermometer beeps. 99.1—again, slightly elevated but not alarming. I make a note on the chart, keeping my movements deliberate and professional. Despite his unusual lucidity, something feels off, like the pressure change before a storm.

"The cave was called Panion," he continues, unperturbed by my clinical ministrations. "Later, it became known as Banias. The water that flowed from it formed one of the sources of the Jordan River." His voice has a rhythm to it now, a practiced cadence that suggests he's delivered this lecture many times before. "The ancients believed it was a gateway to the underworld—Hades, if you will."

I check his oxygen saturation, clipping the monitor to his index finger. 97 percent—normal. His skin feels cool and dry to the touch, not feverish despite the slight temperature elevation.

"The natural rock formation was quite imposing," Harold says, his gaze now fixed somewhere beyond me, beyond the room. "A massive red rock cliff with the cave at its base. The spring flowed out from darkness, from the very bowels of the earth. The pagans believed Pan resided there, guarding the gates to the underworld."

"Any pain tonight, Mr. Gideon?" I ask, deliberately using his surname, trying to maintain the professional barrier that feels increasingly thin.

He ignores my question, lost in his lecture. "Herod the Great built a temple there, dedicated to Augustus Caesar. Later, his son Philip expanded the site and renamed it Caesarea Philippi. It became a center of worship—for Pan, for nymphs, for nature spirits, for all manner of pagan devotion."

I check his IV, adjusting the flow rate slightly. The saline bag is half-empty, the line clear. As I lean across him, I notice his eyes have taken on a feverish glow, seeming to reflect more light than the dim room provides.

"The worship was... extensive," he says, his voice dropping lower, taking on a different quality. "They conducted rituals there, at the mouth of the cave, with the water flowing beneath their feet. Ecstatic rituals, Ellis. Sacred prostitution. Union with the divine through the body."

My hands are steady as I check the catheter bag hanging at the side of the bed—half full, clear amber, no signs of infection—but I feel a coldness spreading through my chest. Harold's gaze follows my movements with unnerving precision.

"They would bring goats, you know," he continues. "For sacrifice, yes, but also for the act itself. The god Pan was half-goat, after all. His worshippers believed they could commune with him through bestial union."

I step back from the bed, clipboard held like a shield. "Your vitals look good tonight, Mr. Gideon. Is there anything you need before I go?"

He doesn't acknowledge my question. His right hand has slipped beneath the sheet, and I watch with growing horror as it begins to move in slow, rhythmic motions once again. His expression doesn't change—no leering smile, no provocative glances—just the same scholarly intensity as he continues his lecture.

"The water was believed to have properties," he says, his hand moving steadily beneath the thin fabric. "Transformative properties. Those who bathed in it, who drank from it, who offered themselves beside it, they were changed. They became vessels for something greater than themselves."

I take another step back, my shoulder blades pressing against the cool wall. Harold's hand continues its motion, but his eyes remain fixed on mine, his academic discourse uninterrupted by what his body is doing. The disconnect is more disturbing than any of his previous, more overt sexual behaviors.

"Mr. Gideon—" I begin, but he cuts me off.

"The gates of the underworld," he says, his voice perfectly steady despite the movement beneath the sheets. "Where life meets death, where the divine touches the profane. That's where the real power resides, Ellis. Not in purity, but in the confluence of opposites."

My watch shows 3:17 a.m. Eight more minutes of required observation before I can leave. The room feels smaller now, the air thicker.

Harold's hand continues its rhythmic movement, but his face remains serene, detached; his body and mind are operating on separate tracks.

"Have you felt it yet?" he asks. "The change in the water? The change beneath your skin?"

Harold's hand moves beneath the sheet while his other hand gestures in the air, tracing invisible diagrams of ancient temple layouts. I fix my eyes on my clipboard, pretending to review notes I've already memorized. The hospital air suddenly feels insufficient. I breathe through my mouth, counting seconds between each inhalation—a technique I learned in med school for maintaining composure during autopsies and traumatic injuries. This is neither, and yet my body responds to witnessing violence.

"The ritual prostitution was quite elaborate," Harold continues, his tone shifting to something resembling a museum tour guide—detached, informative, educational. "Men and women would prepare for days, purifying themselves with special herbs and unguents before offering their bodies at the temple."

I take two measured steps to the small sink in the corner. The automatic soap dispenser whirs, depositing a dollop of antibacterial foam onto my palm. I work it between my fingers.

"The priests would select those deemed most suitable for divine communion." His voice changes then, becoming breathier, more excited. "Young men with unblemished skin. Women whose menstrual cycles aligned with the lunar calendar. They would be anointed with oil, dressed in garlands of spring flowers, and led to the cave entrance."

The water runs cold over my hands. I count to twenty, watching the soap spiral down the drain. In the mirror above the sink, I can see Harold's reflection, the rhythmic motion continuing unabated. His eyes are half-closed now, but his mouth continues to form words with scholarly precision.

"Earthquakes were common in the region," he says, his voice

returning to academic detachment. “The fault lines run deep there, you see. Each tremor was interpreted as Pan’s movement beneath the earth, his hooves striking the underworld’s ceiling.” He pauses, licks his lips. “During the most powerful quakes, the spring would temporarily stop flowing, then restart with greater force—further evidence, they believed, of the god’s presence and power.”

I dry my hands on a paper towel, folding it precisely before discarding it. Seven minutes remain on my mandatory observation period. I position myself at the foot of the bed, at maximum distance while still performing my duties, and check the monitors. Everything is normal. Everything is routine, as I pretend the old man isn’t pleasuring himself while discussing ancient fertility cults.

“Mr. Gideon,” I interject, my voice steady and neutral, “are you experiencing any discomfort tonight? Any pain we should address?”

He continues, ignoring that I had spoken. “The Romans adopted many of these practices, you know. They understood the power of these liminal spaces, these gateways.” His breath hitches slightly, the first crack in his scholarly facade. His hand moves faster beneath the sheet. “The mixing of bodily fluids—semen, blood, the waters of the spring—was believed to create a medium through which divine communication could occur.”

My jaw tightens, a dull ache spreading into my temples. I make a show of checking the IV line again, though I know it’s fine. My pulse ticks upward; I can feel it hammering in my throat.

“Mr. Gideon, I need to know if your medication is working properly. Are you feeling any side effects?” Another attempt at redirection.

His free hand gestures dismissively in my direction. “When the earth shook,” he continues, his voice now taking on a rhythmic quality that matches the movement beneath the sheet, “the worshippers would enter a state of ecstasy. Some would speak in tongues, others would collapse into visions. Many reported seeing the god himself emerge from the water, his pipes playing music that could only be heard by those in the throes of divine communion.”

I retrieve the hand sanitizer from my pocket and apply another liberal amount, working it into my skin until the alcohol evaporates completely. The smell centers me momentarily.

"The cave itself was shaped like a womb," he says, voice dropping to a near-whisper. "And the water, flowing from darkness into light, was seen as divine birth, an eternal emergence." His breathing becomes more labored, though he maintains the scholarly cadence. "Some devotees would submerge themselves completely, holding their breath until nearly unconscious, seeking visions between life and death."

My own breath feels shallow now.

"The earthquakes," Harold continues, his voice thickening, "would sometimes alter the course of the spring, creating new channels, new pathways for the water." His hand moves more vigorously now, the thin sheet tenting and shifting. "The ancient geographers noted how the water would occasionally take on unusual properties after such events—strange colors, unexpected healing qualities, or sometimes, a phosphorescence visible only at certain lunar cycles."

I check my watch—three minutes remaining.

"Pan's worship involved collective frenzy," Harold says, his academic tone now completely overtaken by breathless excitement. "Groups would gather, dancing to flute music that mimicked the god's own pipes. They would consume wine laced with psychoactive compounds that opened the mind to divine influence. As the music reached its peak, so would the worshippers."

He locks eyes with me suddenly, his pupils dilated, sweat beading on his forehead. The movement beneath the sheet becomes erratic, urgent.

"They called it *entheos*, the god within," he gasps. "The moment when human and divine occupy the same vessel. When the boundaries dissolve."

I sanitize my hands a third time. The plastic bottle crackles slightly as I squirt out the sanitizer. My tongue feels thick in my mouth, and my chest is tight.

"The river," Harold says, watching me closely, "is just the beginning, just as it was at Caesarea Philippi. First, the water changes, then those who touch it."

I feel a drop of sweat sliding down my spine. I think of the reports I've read, the letters to the editor of the *Gazette* describing transformative experiences at the riverside. I think of my own reluctance to go near the river. Although I know I have to.

"Did you know," Harold continues, his voice now a ragged whisper, "that when the Missoula Floods carved out the Valley, they deposited silt and minerals, and more importantly within that, did you know, mister nurse, there was microscopic life from hundreds of miles away? Ancient bacteria, carried like secrets in the water, waiting for the right conditions to awaken."

His free hand clutches at the sheet. The monitoring equipment beeps more rapidly now—120, 123, 125 beats per minute. The muscles in his neck stand out like cords.

"Some life forms can remain dormant for millennia," he says. "Waiting in perfect suspended animation. Not dead, just... paused. Until conditions are right for awakening."

I check my watch again. One minute left in this mandatory observation that feels increasingly like an imprisonment. Harold's eyes shine in the dim light, feverishly bright, focused on something beyond the hospital walls, beyond time itself.

"Jesus came to that very place," Harold says, his voice rising as his hand moves faster beneath the sheet. "To Caesarea Philippi—to a pagan shrine, the mouth of hell itself. He brought his disciples to the gateway of the underworld, stood before that cave with its flowing water and its history of ritual debauchery, and there—right there—he chose to establish his church." His back arches slightly, the thin hospital mattress creaking beneath his weight. I find myself frozen, a medical clipboard clutched in white-knuckled hands, watching a theological revelation and an orgasm converge in the dimly lit room.

"Matthew sixteen, verses thirteen through nineteen," Harold continues, his breathing shallow and rapid. The cardiac monitor beeps frantically now—130, 133, 136 beats per minute. "'Who do people say that the Son of Man is?' he asked them. And then: 'But who do you say that I am?'"

Harold's eyes roll back slightly, eyelids fluttering. His free hand grips the metal bed rail with such force that I worry he might bend it. The tendons in his neck stand out like roots beneath parched soil.

"Peter answered," he gasps, "'You are the Christ, the Son of the living God.' And Jesus replied, 'Blessed are you, Simon Bar-Jonah, for flesh and blood has not revealed this to you, but my Father in heaven.'"

I should intervene—offer a sedative, at a minimum, acknowledge what's happening. Instead, I stand transfixed, caught in the grotesque spectacle of divine ecstasy playing out before me. My training has not prepared me for this intersection of the sacred and profane.

"And then," Harold continues, his voice rising to a crescendo, "Jesus said to him, 'And I tell you that you are Peter, and on this rock I will build my church—'" His body tenses, trembling visibly beneath the thin hospital sheet. The monitors emit a sustained, urgent beep as his heart rate spikes to 140. "'—and the gates of Hell shall not prevail against it!'"

The words tear from his throat as his body arches. His face contorts—not in pleasure but in something closer to agony or revelation. Then, as suddenly as it began, it ends. Harold's body relaxes, sinking back into the mattress. His hand emerges from beneath the sheet, and without any sign of embarrassment or acknowledgment of what just occurred, he straightens his hospital gown with trembling fingers. The cardiac monitor settles back to a more normal rhythm—90, 87, 85 beats per minute.

"Do you understand the significance?" he asks, his voice returning to that of the scholar, the professor addressing a lecture hall. No trace remains of the breathless ecstasy of moments before. "Jesus didn't choose the Temple in Jerusalem. Didn't choose a synagogue or a mountaintop unsullied by pagan worship. He chose the most notorious site of ritual sex and pagan devotion in the region."

I swallow hard, my throat clicking in the quiet room. "Mr. Gideon, I need to finish your check." My voice sounds distant, belonging to someone else—someone who hasn't just witnessed what I have.

Harold continues, "The traditional interpretation is that Jesus was making a statement of opposition—standing at the gates of hell and declaring war. But that's simplistic. He wasn't rejecting Pan; he was absorbing him. Transforming him." His fingers smooth the blanket methodically, erasing all evidence of his recent activity. "Jesus understood something his followers didn't: you don't defeat primal forces by denying them. You incorporate them. You transform them through recognition. It's the alchemy of the world, of matter and spirit, bound by consciousness."

I move mechanically through my remaining tasks. Check the IV site for inflammation—none visible. Adjust the saline drip—flow rate normal. Empty the catheter bag and record output—500 milliliters, clear amber, no odor, which was unusual, all within normal limits. My hands perform these functions while my mind reels. I'm caught between professional detachment and existential dread.

"Christianity didn't defeat the varieties of paganism," Harold says, watching me work. "It consumed them. The old gods didn't die; they were baptized. The saints replaced the local deities, point for point, function for function." His voice has taken on a hypnotic quality, low and rhythmic. "What we're seeing now in the river is just another turning of the wheel. The old is becoming new again."

I make my final notations on the chart, signing my name with a hand that trembles almost imperceptibly. The room feels both too small and impossibly vast; the walls have become permeable, opening onto some older, wilder landscape.

"That will be all for tonight, Mr. Gideon," I say, the words stiff and formal. "Try to get some rest."

I turn to leave, relief flooding through me at the prospect of escape, of the mundane paperwork waiting at the nurses' station.

Harold's hand shoots out, impossibly fast for a man his age, and clamps around my wrist. His fingers are cold and dry, but the strength in them is startling—not the feeble grip of an elderly patient but the vise-like hold of someone in their prime. I feel the small bones in my wrist grind together.

"Ellis."

I turn back slowly, unwillingly. Harold's eyes have changed. His pupils have expanded until almost no iris remains; they are black pools reflecting the dim light of the monitors. His face is calm and serene, but his gaze holds me like a physical force. His grip tightens momentarily, then releases. I step back, rubbing my wrist where five distinct finger marks are already blooming into bruises, each centered on a point where his yellowed nails pressed into my skin. The marks glow faintly in the dim light.

Harold settles back against his pillows, eyes drifting closed. The monitors show his heart rate decreasing—75, 72, 68—as he slides toward sleep. His breathing becomes deep and regular, the chest rising and falling with the peaceful rhythm of a man unburdened by his revelations.

I back toward the door, unwilling to turn away from him entirely. My hand finds the door handle without looking, cool metal against overheated skin.

"They only remember half the verse," Harold murmurs, eyes still closed, voice fading. "The gates of hell shall not prevail against it. But for gates to not prevail... someone must be opening them first."

I slip through the door and pull it firmly shut behind me. In the harsh fluorescent light of the hallway, I examine my wrist. The bruises are there, five distinct points forming a pattern like a constellation. But the blue glow is gone—if it was ever there at all.

The medication cart waits patiently where I left it. My watch shows 3:31 a.m. The night shift continues, implacable as ever. I should document the incident and report Harold's inappropriate behavior. That's what hospital protocol demands.

Instead, I stand frozen in the empty corridor, Harold's words still in my mind. I think of my Nana's books hidden in the attic of my childhood home, of family rites and transformations, of the burden of knowledge I thought I'd left behind when I chose nursing over my family's legacy.

8

THE REMAINS OF ROMANCE

I lingered in the charting bay outside the break room, feigning interest in my patient census while the shift's real activity pulsed a few feet away. The first hints of the conversation drifted through the cracked door, wreathed in the dry heat of the microwave and the chemical perfume of single-serve coffee pods. At this hour, the Med Surg break room was a synaptic junction where gossip flowed in, was processed, and emerged transformed, electrified, incapable of returning to a prior state.

"—left her there, just fucking left her, like it was nothing—"

The voice belonged to Nurse Hannah, a tidy brunette with a fondness for pastel scrubs and an aversion to patient contact that bordered on phobia. She was speaking in a valley girl tone reserved for describing insect infestations and policy infractions, and she did not notice her hands were white-knuckling her thermos.

"It was the housekeeper Romas, I swear," replied a second voice, dry, deeper, with a faint PNW country drawl. Tommy. He was always in the breakroom watching sports broadcasters blather on. "I saw him by the pharmacy the day before, just loitering on the service floor. Real creep. Always had that little mop cart, like a shield he hid behind."

A third voice, precise and somewhat nasal, cut through the speculative fog. "No. The report said security found her in the tunnel, by the water pipes. The body was defiled. This isn't simple-brained janitor work. This is pathological."

That was Dr. Harkness, a hospitalist I rarely see; he floats by now and again, with the aura of a long-haul airline pilot: clipped, efficient, and clearly thrilled by turbulence. He had the eyes of a man who survived exclusively on nicotine patches and ambition. The inflection on "defiled" was just as surgical as one could expect of a doctor in the conversation, neither judgmental nor sensational, merely a statement of observed fact.

I angled my clipboard and pretended to chart, letting the LCD screen's glow bleach my face to neutrality. They had not yet noticed me. I could sense their conversation getting closer to the bone, and I wanted to hear how they would dissect it before I made my presence known.

"Do they know how long she was down there?" Hannah again, voice lowered to the frequency of confessions.

"A while. The coroner thinks she died shortly before oh-three-hundred, but wasn't found until another housekeeper walked in on it. Blood all over." Tommy's voice wavered.

A heavy silence. Even the vending machine paused, as though the fluorescent tubes themselves recoiled from the implications.

"Her name was Evelyn," Harkness said. "She was forty-one. Many thought she was in her early thirties. Lived alone on Walnut in the Timberhill neighborhood. Med Surg nurse. Quiet, but not unhappy. There was a wound in her chest—an actual knife, some kind of... ritual? Yes, it was some form of cult sex ritual. Full-blown. I read the report by forensics."

"I worked with her fairly often. She was a great nurse. That's so fucked up," said Tommy, but he said it in the same tone he would use for a difficult IV stick or a DNR patient with an inconvenient family.

Disgust was a flavor in short supply around here, but everyone craved a hit.

"People like that," Harkness began, "it's not about sex. It's about—"

I saw my window and opened the cracked door, making my entrance loud enough to announce myself but soft enough to seem apologetic for interrupting.

"About what?" I said, forcing a yawn into my voice. "I missed the beginning."

The room stilled. Harkness recovered first, eyes lighting on me with an intensity that was almost admiring.

"Come in. You may or may not appreciate this," he said, patting the spot next to him at the plastic table. "We were discussing the, ah, tunnel incident."

I played dumb, faked a slow nod. "The murder in the tunnels under the hospital? I saw the news, following up on it. I didn't realize they'd released the full details." I sat, careful to keep my back to the window. "So, who do you think did it? Was it the guy they prosecuted?"

Tommy coughed, uncomfortable. "It's got to be Romas, he was an outsider who tried to befriend Evelyn before she died. He seemed OCD about the history of the area and other weird shit. No one else who works here would do that."

It startled me, the realization that I had a distinct similarity with the murderer who killed the nurse I replaced. There had to be a connection, and in seconds, I tried to refocus on the conversation. Hannah had nodded vigorously, possibly thinking this alone could banish the possibility of who may have killed Evelyn.

Harkness shrugged. "You'd be surprised what the hospital brings out in people. This place is a crucible. You work here long enough, you see things you can't unsee. Some people can't handle it."

His words hung in the air, and I wondered who, exactly, he thought could handle it. If he suspected me, he gave no indication, but I saw his eyes dart to the backs of my hands, noting the faint webbing that had appeared in my skin over the last week, which is just visible enough to catch a glint from the overhead lights.

I looked down, flexed my fingers, and saw the faint blue-green shimmer that was becoming a constant feature. I covered it with my palm and asked, “What was the actual cause of death?”

Harkness’s lips curled. “Hypovolemic shock, per the preliminary. But the interesting part is the post-mortem activity. The body was... interacted with. More than the average sexually deviant would. There were bite marks. Human, yet rather aggressive. Like the teeth didn’t fit the jaw.”

I felt the hairs on my arms rise from a recognition that bordered on kinship.

Hannah recoiled. “Are you kidding? That’s like, actual cannibal shit.”

“Some cultures consider it a rite of passage for the dead,” Harkness said, and he was looking directly at me now. “Of course, in the West, it’s a sign of sociopathy or deep psychosis.”

Tommy shuddered and excused himself, mumbling about an overdue glucose check. Hannah followed, after a pause, leaving the break room’s heat and its trauma for the sterility of the hallway.

Harkness remained, fixing me with a gaze that was both dark and predatory. I recognized the hunger in it, the need to push boundaries for the sake of intellectual conquest.

“You find this interesting,” he said. It was not a question.

I nodded, opting for honesty. “I guess I do. People always talk about what they’d do to survive. No one talks about what they’d do if they didn’t have to survive anymore.”

I nodded again, feeling a pulse of something between admiration and dread.

“Do you think it’s contagious?” I asked.

Harkness tilted his head. “The urge? Or the event?”

“Either.”

He smiled. “The urge, maybe. People underestimate the power of suggestion. You see a line, and even if you never planned to cross it, you can't help but imagine what's on the other side. The event itself?" He spread his hands. "Well. Bodies change. People change—place changes. As a whole, the Willamette Valley isn't what it was even twenty years ago. I see it in my patients. I see it in myself and the land."

He tapped against his knee, then looked at me sidelong, his gaze equal parts confiding and conspiratorial. "I want to apologize if I come off... insensitive. I forgot not everyone finds this sort of thing stimulating."

I shrugged. "It's the most unusual conversation I've had today."

"Good," he said, then he followed up with a heart stopper: "Have you ever read reports on killers who have sex with dead bodies?"

I blinked, unsure if he was joking. He was not. I shook my head in shock, feeling exposed. I was beginning to wonder if he knew things about me.

"There are, classically, five categories," he said, shifting into didactic mode with the ease of a man who spent his off-hours annotating DSM revisions. "First, the reunification urge. The desperate need to reconnect with a beloved person who's gone. It's less sexual than you'd think, more about annihilating separation."

He ticked off a finger. "Second, passivity. Some people only want a partner who cannot refuse, cannot leave, cannot judge."

Another finger. "Third, pure aesthetics. The arousal isn't for the person but for the corpse itself—the color, the coldness, the perfection of stillness. An object of beauty made untouchable."

A fourth. "Another factor is loneliness. The overwhelming hunger for touch, even if it means touching death."

A fifth. "And finally, power. To possess a body so completely that nothing of them can resist."

He folded his hand, closing the taxonomy. "Most cases involve a blend. It's not a clean science. But you can learn a lot from the residue."

I felt so exposed, wondering where I am in such equations. Clenching my jaw again, harder this time.

He cleared his throat, then let the silence stretch. When he spoke again, his tone was softer, almost gentle. “Did you know Evelyn, the nurse murdered in the tunnels?” I shake my head. I didn’t work at the hospital when it happened, but I did not want to shut off the flow of information. A lie is in order. “Saw her once or twice. Quiet. Kept to herself.” He nods, but there’s a glint in his eye.

“She was one of the prettiest girls I’ve ever seen. More than pretty, dang it—perfect symmetry, porcelain skin, eyes like a goddamn Renaissance painting. I couldn’t look at her for too long. Made me feel—“ he hesitates, searching for the word “—jealous, maybe. Or envious. Her beauty was effortless. Makes you understand why someone would want to... possess it. Even after it’s gone, here, I have a picture of her. Check this out.”

He opens his phone and shows me his obsession. Pictures of Evelyn, taken from social media, including some from work meetings, as well as her funeral and gravestone. I recognize the location. She is buried at the cemetery across from my apartment complex. The edges of his description of her feel too practiced, like he’s rehearsed it. Either he is trying to hide that he is obsessed with Evelyn, or perhaps he is an undercover cop. I want to recoil and get out of here, but I make myself hold the line. I say nothing, let the discomfort register only as a tick in the muscle at the base of my neck.

He goes on, oblivious or pretending to be. “The wounds were fascinating, too, for a killing. There was reverence. The cuts were precise, almost surgical. If you didn’t know better, you’d think it was an art piece. And her body, even after—“ he trails off, eyes unfocused for a second. “It was beautiful. Cold, but beautiful.”

A silence settles between us that extends into the corridors. We’re like kids seeing images from some men’s magazines and getting our first glimpse at lust. I hear footsteps on the upper landing —two nurses passing by, their conversation dropping to a hush as they catch the shape of ours. One of them glances at me, then at Harkness, and I see the flicker of concern in her eyes.

Harkness looks at me, tilting his head. "Sorry. I get carried away sometimes."

"It's fine," I say, forcing a smile. "We all have our obsessions."

He seems satisfied, then straightens, closing his book with a snap. "Well. I should get back to rounds. You should try to sleep, Ellis. You look—" he pauses, really taking me in "—like you could use a little rest."

He leaves me there, alone on the landing, the silence thickening in his wake. I stare at my hands as I wonder what Evelyn's skin had felt like, and if the man who killed her had done so out of passion or necessity. If, in that moment, he had understood what it meant to be truly possessed.

9
MEMORY'S EARS

Hours later in the shift, at precisely 04:00, I perform my small act of ritual of entering Harold Gideon's cell—I mean his patient room. Clearly, they are different, right? I think I am starting to feel bad for him. But that's neither here nor there. I have noticed the corridor leading to the 3rd floor west unit is designed to frustrate memory with its walls in an institutional sameness, corridors at deliberate angles so the fluorescent hum rebounds unpredictably. The effect is like being inside a single, unbroken capillary loop, every turn erasing the previous. It is a design both deeply medical and deeply ecclesiastical: you circumambulate. I appreciate the metaphor. I do not appreciate the sound of the bulbs overhead that flicker more than they should on the night shift. It burrows into my scalp, like a superorganism of light and hum, a sound like invisible gnats above your head.

Harold is bent over a standard plastic bedside table, his hands tightly gripping a Bic pen and a sheet of thin, yellowed graph paper that seems like it's been in his possession for ages. The skin on the back of his neck is as delicate as the paper, spotted with age and lined with wrinkles. He doesn't lift his head when I walk in, as is typical, nor does he react to the sound of the lock clicking open behind me. I'm uncertain if he's aware of my arrival at first, but then I notice his right hand hesitating briefly as a silent acknowledgement.

I sit across from him, notebook open, ready to record. My notes on Harold are already ten times as long as any other patient's, most of them unfit for the electronic health record but perfect for my journaling. Harold stops drawing and finally meets my gaze. His eyes are incongruously bright, the blue so vivid it looks backlit. The rest of him is decomposing at a stately pace, but the eyes remain unblemished. He says, "They made the walls thin so you could hear the memory of the Valley." His voice is rough, but when he chooses to, he can modulate it to a near-whisper that resonates with a nasal whistle from the surrounding bones outward. "You understand, Ellis, you have the right kind of ears."

I suspect it is both an insult and a compliment, as I do have odd ears, and yes, I think they are silly-looking. But he intends a heavier meaning.

"Go on," I say, uncapping my pen. "Tell me about the memory of the Willamette Valley, and if you're able, tell me about the recent murder at the hospital. Did that affect you at all? Did it perhaps scare you?"

He licks his lips, and his tongue looks disgusting, like a grayish pink slug sensing sunlight. "The memory of the Valley is manifest. The Christ Contagion is outside of metaphor. Inside or outside, it is beyond metaphor," he repeats, this time as if reciting the Nicene Creed. "Example. Do you know what a lithotroph is? It eats the rock. It devours the marrow of mountains. It feeds on the bones of trilobites, on the calcified prayers of the dead. And what it excretes, what it leaves behind, is the future. Rock and bones remember. Every hand that ever wielded them. Every scream that ever echoed through the fault lines. The Valley metabolizes us, and all the little families."

He is teaching, although it sounds like a rant. I write: *lithotrophy =*

sacred recursion. If my psych rotation preceptor could see these notes, she'd have me sectioned alongside Harold. I keep writing anyway.

"You do not understand the nature of memory," Harold says. "People think it is encoded in the cells, in the spiral of the genes, or in the matter of the hippocampus. Not completely. Memory is soil, the layering of the landscape, the breath of the genius loci, the curse of a tutelary spirit. Memory is the aggregate of everything that has decomposed before you. When you eat, you consume history. When you rot, you become the future."

This is somewhat new. Harold has been steady for weeks, asserting that opposing religious themes are equivalent, and I've grown accustomed to his metaphysical style. However, today there's a hint of something new underlying his doctrine. He points to his paper, showing me a drawing he's done. I take a look. It's a cluster of intertwined circles, some open, others shaded to appear both concave and convex. There are arrows, along with notes written in a mix of English, Greek, and what seems to be electrical schematic symbols.

"Show me," I say, pointing to a particular motif, a circle within a circle, like an eye inside a socket.

He nods, pleased. "The Christ Contagion is the parasite that wears the host like a mask, but the host is neither you nor me, nor any single body. The host is the church. Not the brick and mortar one, the other one—the one made of language and blood and meal." He takes a breath, and the next words are so quiet I almost miss them. "They never buried her. Really. She persists in the unspeakable space before language."

I pause.

"Who is she, or do I know of 'her'?" I asked awkwardly.

Harold's face collapses in on itself, a slow-motion inversion that resembles neither sorrow nor rage, but something closer to the euphoria of nausea just before vomiting. "She is the mother of all infection," he says, "the matrix before the matrix, the mucosal river in which all souls ferment. She is the Virgin." His hands are trembling now, but he does not stop. "You must understand, nurse, that the Christ Contagion is the sacred perversion. It is a return. All flesh longs for reunion with the mother, even if it has to kill itself to get there."

I feel my own hands tightening on my notebook. I have heard this kind of rhetoric before, in the mouth of my mother, just before her death. She, too, spoke of the unspeakable, of a feminine principle that was neither goddess nor woman but something far more vast and cold. I had thought she was mad in the need to believe in something, and perhaps she was. But perhaps that is the only way to know life and oneself deeply: triangulating with the sacred.

I glance at the paper again. Now I see it—the circles are eyes that stand for other things too, wombs or tombs. Or both? There is a deliberate blurring of categories, a refusal to assign meaning where the only truth is in the rot. That was where I found the sacred, in the leftover matter, the excess.

"I was never allowed in the viewing room at my old hospital," I say, surprising myself. "My father said it was for the morticians and the priests. Not for the living." I do not know why I say this, only that it feels necessary to confess it now.

Harold smiles suddenly, and it's so jarring that I jump. "They don't want you to know what's really going on," he says. "But I saw something last year in this hospital. There was a janitor named Romas — he was Lithuanian. He always hung around, cleaning nearby and overhearing people's private conversations. He knew things, like when new bodies were brought in. One night, he told me he saw a man come in late. He was dressed like a bishop, but his hands looked strange, almost like they were glowing. The man opened a locked room on the service floor, and inside was a woman's body, perfectly preserved. She looked to be in peak physical shape. Romas said the bishop felt her body. He pressed on her, feeling the organs, and walked out."

"I don't understand. Was it Bishop Ashworth?" I ask.

He shrugs. "It is always him. It is always Edmund Creffield. They play out their roles because our cycles demand it. But the bacteria are above names. They only care for communion."

For the first time, madness seems like the smaller diagnosis. Harold has become an interface, a membrane where the old world leaks into the new.

"I heard a doctor talking about the tunnel incident, about the ritual murder," I say. "What would you say about this perversion? Why would Romas or anyone do this?"

Harold sits back, his bones creaking audibly. "You know what a saint is, nurse? A corpse that can resist the rot for a little while. Incorruptible. But eventually, even they break down. The difference is that some are chosen to become language, to be spoken into the mouths of others. The necromancer is just a priest who lives the script. Romas obsessively loved her. Something in her. Many did. There was something *beyond* her, more than just a body. More than an attractive body."

"But what about the rest of us?" I say. "What about those who are not saints, who are just—" I almost say "alive," but the word sticks. "What about the rest of us?"

He looks at me with what might be pity. "You become vessels. Containers for the language. You carry it until it needs to move on, and then you rot. But you get to be part of the memory. You get to be soil someday."

He taps his own head, then the table, then the diagram. "It is a privilege. Not everyone is chosen. Some are just food. The Contagion does not treat all alike."

I am unusually embarrassed, not even fully comprehending why, but Harold seems not to notice. He is staring at the far wall now, eyes unfocused.

"Will you come to see me tomorrow?" he asks. "Everything's going to be better with the right company."

I want to say no, but I say, "Yes. I'll be here at oh-four-hundred."

He smiles again, but the expression is brief, almost stroboscopic. "Thank you. Nurse Horning."

I gather my things and stand. For a moment, I consider touching his hand, just to see what it would feel like, to bridge the gap, what would be exchanged. The ever curious me wants to, but I stop myself. There is not enough membrane already on his broken complexion.

I exit the cell, locking the door behind me. The corridor seems even more convoluted than before, the light somehow yellower, as if the bulbs have been dipped in tea. I walk to the staff washroom and scrub my hands until they sting, but when I dry them, I see a streak of dark under the left thumbnail: dirt, or something like it. I scrape at it, but it holds tight.

The walk home from Christ Hospital takes eleven minutes. I have timed this three times on three different shifts, which tells me something I have not yet decided to know.

The pharmacy is dark. The bar on Monroe is just unlocking. In the parking structure doorway on Harrison, the sleeping man has arranged his bedding with the consistency of a patient on a skilled unit: sleeping bag folded under the cervical spine for neutral alignment, shoes placed parallel twelve inches from the curb. I don't know his name. I know the placement of his shoes. I cross at the green even when the street is empty, a habit from a house where certain performances were expected regardless of audience.

My apartment smells of the mold under the bathroom baseboard and the cedar insert I keep in the closet. I took it from Greenville the week after we buried my mother, while my father was still in the study accounting for his bourbon. I wrote *heirloom* in my inventory of what I removed from the house. I see now that the word was load-bearing.

I sit on the bed without removing my shoes.

My notes from the Harkness conversation are on the kitchen table where I left them. Three grocery receipts, both sides, the handwriting getting smaller toward the margins. I should not have written any of it down. I cross at the light. I note the placement of a stranger's shoes. I filled the backs of three grocery receipts with case details about a woman I have never met, whose grave I can see from my window. These belong to the same chart. I keep placing them in separate columns. They keep touching.

I read back through the receipts in the kitchen light, which I have been meaning to replace for three months because the tube hits somewhere behind the left eye. Harkness writes about Evelyn through photographs the way I write about symptoms that don't yet have a diagnosis: exhaustively, from multiple angles, with the slightly desperate precision of someone who suspects the picture will only make sense in retrospect. I am not Harkness. I note this without confidence.

She moves through the ward, and the ward holds the shape of her passage for a few minutes after. I have timed this. I have not told anyone I timed this.

That last line is mine. I wrote it after Harkness pocketed the phone. I don't know where it came from.

I fold the receipts, put them in the notebook, and leave it on the desk.

The window faces the cemetery. I have lived here for four months, fourteen days, across the street from the Odd Fellows Pioneer Cemetery. Evelyn is in there. Dr. Harkness showed me the grave location the way another man might show you a photograph he keeps returning to: the social media announcement, the funeral notice, the stone marker visible in the background of a candlelight vigil someone posted without intending it as documentation. I have not walked over there. I have stood at this window on seventeen separate mornings and looked toward the cemetery, and noted that I was looking toward the cemetery.

I would characterize this as data collection. I am aware this characterization may be imprecise.

I set an alarm for seven-fifteen. Sleep does not come at first. The ceiling has a water stain in the shape of nothing in particular. I have a differential for it anyway: roof fissure, plumbing failure, condensation migration through the subfloor. All three are consistent with the presentation. You cannot rule anything out from the morphology alone.

When sleep comes, it comes badly. In it, Evelyn is waiting.

Lying on the slab, eyes closed but mouth open. Romas stands at the foot of the table, mop in hand, but when he looks at me, his eyes are full of helplessness. I am allowed closer. The skin of her belly is translucent, a window into layers of coiled intestine and unidentifiable organs that appear tattooed with writings. "It's my journal," Romas says without using his mouth. Her hair floats in a slow-motion halo, even though there is no water.

Above her, the ceiling is a vault, a Gothic arch made not of stone but of living tissue, the veins and arteries stained the colors of church glass. In the spaces between ribs, tiny figures move: bacteria the color of amber, yes, but also angels, and also something that is neither. I try to speak, but my tongue is fused to the roof of my mouth. Harold stands behind me, hands folded, eyes luminous.

He says, "You see now. She is not dead. She is only language, waiting to be spoken. I wanted no one else, only her, from the moment we met."

I woke with the taste of soil in my teeth and checked my hands first, finding the dark still there under the left thumbnail, embedded past where scrubbing reaches. The notebook was on the nightstand. I do not remember moving it from the desk. I carried it back there and began to transcribe the dream, every image in order as I could recall, every word Harold had spoken. At some point, my own language ran out, and I found myself using his instead, borrowing his formulations.

At seven-fifteen, I turn off the alarm, put on yesterday's clothes, and go downstairs. The dark under my left thumbnail is still there from Harold's room. It is not coming out. I stop trying.

There is a decision I have apparently already made. I am in the process of finding out what it is.

You don't notice such a difference until you look at the handwriting.

10
BEATRIX DEPARTED

The morgue's new lightbulb is unkind to the living but somehow perfect for the dead. The harshness casts shadows on R, leaving no place to hide imperfections. Not that she had any. Her face emerged from the body bag more beautiful than when I saw her alive. Her lifeless face looked like a painting. I thought of *Beata Beatrix* from the Pre-Raphaelite Dante Rossetti. She was pale, an archetypal mysterious sorceress type, and the perfect corpse. I attempt, nervous like it's a first date, to risk everything in discovering whether R may be my soulmate. Here, I feel akin to Rossetti, who also admired Dante Alighieri's writing, and he thought of his wife Elizabeth Siddal as his own Beatrice; in other words, she became his knowledge of the sacred on the horizon for love, she became a mirror for the divine which can never be reached—except in its withdrawal and the revelation that would bring. Siddal was Rossetti's soulmate, and when love is true, it is divine, and when it is lost, it manifests in an ultimate heart-wrenching loss, but in such pain comes a great treasure of inspiration and vision. Suppose one can weave a reinvention of artistic vision around the madness of true love's withdrawal. I stand beside the stainless steel gurney, my gloved hands steady despite the butterflies I feel inside for this possibility for my life.

The lightbulb buzzes faintly in its protective cage, the sound emits from the bulb like a moth flittering wildly, most people tune it out after a few minutes. I never do. I register every detail of this environment—the cold thirty-nine-degree air maintained to slow decomposition, the faint chemical smell of her after-death cleanser. I know if she could smell my cologne, she would know that I am cultured on the subtlety of an underarm musk. She is the kind of woman who would appreciate that, and with that thought I let out a moan while smelling under her arms. Her stubbled axilla tickled my nose, and the scent of her living hormonal body odor still remained even after being washed. This indicated that we did not wash her completely, and to this, I must confess I am guilty. I put my nose in again and cannot help but respond with a growl, which seems to emanate from outside my body as I dwell in her heavenly odor. Sound seems to not have a location inside the refrigerated room.

In this space, R becomes something more than a former patient, and far more than a cadaver. She gives the impression of a folktale sleeping princess waiting to be saved by the notion of someone obsessed enough to kiss her comatose mouth. Some condense this into the word *love*. She has the feel of a banned book that I have never read, and I am now aching to read it. I observe her with the same focused intensity I've brought to my deepest fascinations over the years—the same intensity I once used to research my move to Corvallis, noting every detail (leading to my introduction to the historically nefarious Edmund Creffield); it might unlock a secret about why I ended up here.

Her dyed two-toned black and crimson hair framed her face in waves, styled in that distinctive Bettie Page cut—straight bangs across her forehead, the rest falling just past her shoulders. Even in death, it maintained its shape, the product still holding each strand in place. I resist the urge to touch it, to feel its texture between my fingers. Not yet. First, I observe. Twenty-two years old, according to her chart. I wonder about the age of the dead. If a younger woman that I fancy is half my age, but she is dead, then how old is she really when I am quite alive and healthy? Is death the *older* woman, regardless of its leftover form? She had been a college student at OSU, studying microbiology. We had discussed her studies briefly when we first met, and they seemed to excite her. I prefer her now as her quiet more mysterious feminine energy comes through. Her eyes had brightened as she described her research into how single-celled organisms could create complex communities with behaviors resembling animal-like intelligence.

"They talk to each other," she'd said, her voice soft and raspy. "Not with words, but with chemicals. They share information. They remember."

Ironic, considering what's happening to her now, at the cellular level. The bacteria that have always lived in harmony with her body are now taking over, breaking down tissues, generating gases, and returning her to the elemental components from which she was formed. The ultimate bacterial communion. I unzipped the body bag further, exposing her neck, shoulders, and the hospital gown we'd put her in after cleaning her body. Standard procedure. I'd been part of that, my hands and manners in work mode then. I was polite and professionally engaged in my role as a nurse, not like now. Now, I was someone else, or something else, entirely.

Her face demands my full attention. The bone structure has a European elegance, with perhaps something Slavic in the high cheekbones and slightly square angle where her jaw meets her ear. Her eyebrows are dark, natural, but shaped, and angled into perfect arches that give her a perpetually questioning expression. Her nose is small but strong, with a barely perceptible bump on the bridge that saves her from conventional modelesque beauty and pushes her into something more interesting. Her lips are full, the bottom one slightly larger than the top, creating a permanent kiss-inviting pout. Even without the makeup she must have worn in life—the winged eyeliner and red lipstick I can imagine perfectly—she is a striking punk rock *Beata Beatrix.*

Now, pleasantly stripped of the unnecessary adornments, she holds a kind of ceremonial stillness; her body retains the memory of life's anxious movements hiding inside of her. Her beauty reminds me of my evening walks during my half-hour work breaks. Usually, on those walks, I'm looking to reinforce pleasant memories of my mother, as I look in the sky at William Finley Wildlife Refuge. Sometimes, when I am lucky, the Canada geese pass through and offer me less painful glimpses of her memory. In their voice is her silence; in their departure, a severance of her from my sense of home. R, too, has made her final flight, but perhaps she is welcomed home in the fairytale of a loved one's heaven. Not northward she migrates, but inward—into whatever terrain the dead inhabit. Not all the dead are created equal in beauty, if I am to be the judge of aesthetics and a dead woman's aura, but they clearly inhabit an equally mysterious terrain to the general question: *Where is she now*? Could the dead take different routes of migration after death? I believe so. And like geese, she leaves behind a contour in the world, a space where presence once lived.

I often find my mind drifting back to the refuge, and it isn't only the geese I think of there—it's the wetlands themselves, how the ponds at Finley hold secrets beneath their still surfaces where darting life hides in microscopic worlds. And how the wetlands mirror the vast Oregon sky without revealing what stirs below, unless one considers the reflection of the sky a map of what is, in essence, under the water, where other micro-universes revolve and coordinate similarly. Her eyes remind me of those waters, glassy and veiled, the skin around them tinged blue like other worlds reflected in a winter pond.

The skin around her eyes shows the faintest blue tinge, like the shadows beneath shallow water. I lean closer, examining the delicate network of veins visible beneath the translucent skin of her eyelids, which are empty conduits or dried riverbeds. I trace the pale, branching pathways just beneath her skin and think of the hallways of Christ Hospital—the quiet ones that stretch toward the edge of Finley, where oncology patients look out the window to where the wetlands begin.

I recall assisting the other nurse earlier in preparing her body, washing it, and swapping the soiled green checkered hospital gown for a fresh one. We worked quickly; often, nurses and nursing assistants were uncomfortable with the dead, and we exchanged words only when essential, upholding the solemn quietness customary in these situations. There was no hint that I would come back later, standing here alone, examining her face that held a hidden message I needed to unravel. I gave no indication that my washing in certain areas had not been thorough enough in order to leave her natural scent. No one knew anything, and I only knew as an afterthought, although my actions prove my unconscious already planned the event. No one will know of this, I must make certain.

The security camera in the service hall has been "malfunctioning" for weeks. Like many work orders placed, select ones get priority; on the service floor, nobody bothers to fix much. Budget cuts are always in our emails. Or something else is happening on this floor. Given that the hospital morgue is located right by the pharmacy on the service floor, which occasionally experiences high volumes of deliveries, it is clear that more security is needed. Sometimes I wonder if others come here too, drawn by the same desires.

She came to us the other evening, barely conscious after a failed suicide attempt. She took an overdose of Klonopin, they said. Not enough to kill her, just enough to make her sick and land her in our psych unit. Under my care. I remember the first time I saw her, slumped in a wheelchair in the emergency department. I was the one who helped transfer her to the psychiatric unit after they pumped her stomach. I remember how light she felt as we moved her from the gurney to the bed, how her arm had flopped lifelessly over the side. I'd carefully repositioned it, noting the small tattoos that dotted her forearms. When she regained consciousness, I was checking her vitals. Her eyes fluttered open—green with flecks of amber, clouded with chemicals, but still with a sharp indication of a strong presence at home in her body. She knew or had seen things, I could tell by her eyes. She'd seen the bottom of the world and come back with heavy burdens of knowing while keeping her beauty freshly edged by the darkness.

"Ellis," she'd said, reading my name tag. Her voice had struggled more initially from the recently discontinued intubation. "Like the island?"

"Like the family name," I'd replied, adjusting her IV drip.

She offered her name. To this, I must only reveal her first initial.

I nodded without responding, recording her blood pressure in the chart. Names create connections. I prefer numbers, codes, and classifications. Except now, in these private moments, when I allow myself to see them completely.

"You've experienced it too, haven't you?" she'd asked, grabbing my wrist with surprising strength. "In the water. In the soil. I think it's everywhere now, spreading through the watershed."

I'd gently disengaged her hand, assuming she was still delirious from the drugs, but she struck a chord similar to Harold's ravings. "You need to rest. The doctor will be in to evaluate you in the morning."

"It's in you," she'd whispered as I turned to leave. "I see it, your eyes. The Christ Contagion."

Her words struck me with a deep sense of familiarity. The Christ Contagion was a new term I came across only after relocating to Corvallis. As mentioned in an earlier entry, Harold in the psychiatric unit of Med Surg made the term unforgettable. According to coworkers, he'd been raving about it for months, much earlier than others, insisting it was spreading and altering people internally for the coming new cycle of spiritual evolution. It was through Harold's passionate and intense manner of speaking that I realized this went beyond just local religious enthusiasm.

Her ears are small and close to her head, with delicate lobes that were never pierced. I note this as a curious detail. Most women her age have multiple piercings, but R has none—no holes in her ears, no studs in her nose or eyebrow, no rings through her lips. Her body remained unpunctured by decorative metal, though now it bears the marks of medical intervention—the small bruises in the crooks of her elbows where IV needles entered, the slightly discolored patch on her chest where we performed CPR, trying to force her heart back into rhythm.

I think about how the geese carry stories of their migrations in their bodies to pass on to future generations. I think of the matter that constitutes the living: the food, the soil, the fat deposits that fuel journeys, the muscle memory that guides us and guides them along traditional flyways. R's body carries different stories and the tale of her suicide, needle marks and bruises, and a life of missed flight patterns into brighter sunsets. And now, my own story is being written onto her as well, my presence altering her posthumous narrative in ways that violate every ethical principle I was taught to uphold.

My hand hovers above her face, hesitating. I am a professional, and I have ethics; a large part of me always knows that touching a deceased patient outside of necessary procedural contact is unprofessional as well as unethical. The other part that drives my actions without regard for any outside morality is the part that brought me here after hours, the part that's fascinated by the perfect architecture of her features, which have been cast into stillness, and that part of me doesn't give a damn about professional boundaries or ethical considerations.

The fluorescent light flickers slightly, creating a momentary illusion of movement across her features. But it's just an unstable electrical current, the problematic infrastructure of Christ Hospital asserting itself even here, in this quiet sanctuary of the dead. I reach out, allowing my fingertips to graze her cheek. Cold, of course. The skin is firm but with the peculiar texture that sets in after death. A touch reveals neither object nor subject lingers in full.

She'd managed to smuggle fentanyl into the psych ward. We found the empty packet tucked into the binding of the journal they'd given her for therapy. By then, it was too late. I was the one who found her, slumped in the bathroom, pulse already fading beneath my fingers. I called the code, and we performed CPR for eighteen minutes before the doctor called it final.

My hands remember the feeling of her ribs yielding under my compressions. It's always so strange to break someone in an attempt to save them. I'd been back in the rotations of compressions when I felt the precise moment she was truly gone—the subtle shift from a body fighting for life to one surrendering to death. Even as the doctor called time of death, I continued compressions for several seconds, assuming my hands could force life back into her.

Now those same hands move with different purposes. I stroke her hair, feeling its texture—slightly brittle from the dye but still soft. I trace the perfect curve of her ear, the hollow beneath her cheekbone. My finger runs along her jawline, firm and elegant, before coming to rest at the corner of her mouth.

Without thinking, I press gently, parting her lips. Her teeth are perfect—strong, white, even. The kind of teeth that speak of good genes and expensive orthodontics. I slip my ungloved finger between them, feeling their smooth enamel, the ridges on the backs where they curve toward her gums. Her mouth is dry but not unpleasantly so. I trace the sharp edge of an incisor with my fingertip, feeling a small thrill when it nearly breaks my skin as I press harder.

Canada geese mate for life. I learned this watching them at Finley, seeing how they move in pairs, how they guard each other, and protect each other. They're monogamous creatures with a fierce loyalty to their chosen partners. When a goose dies, its mate sometimes refuses to leave the body, standing guard over it even as it decays, even as predators circle. A loyalty that transcends reason, that defies the imperative of survival.

I never had the chance to be loyal to anyone in life. R was simply my patient, and our interactions were bound by professional ethics and hospital protocols. But in death, I find a different kind of loyalty emerging—this compulsion to see her, to touch her, to know her in ways forbidden to me when her heart still beat beneath her ribs.

The neck of a Canada goose is black and slender, designed for reaching into depths, for stretching toward what sustains it. I let my hand drift to R's neck, feeling the firm column of her trachea beneath the skin. In life, her throat would have vibrated with speech, with laughter, with breath. Now it's silent, a hollow passage. I press gently, feeling the cartilaginous rings beneath my fingertips.

Geese have hollow bones to make them light enough for flight. Humans don't share this adaptation, but in death, R seems lighter somehow, already taken flight, leaving behind this beautiful, empty vessel. I prefer her like this, in between, like the geese at twilight when they're neither fully of the day nor fully of the night. I withdraw my finger from her mouth, wiping it absently on my scrubs. There's little moisture there, just the faint impression of having touched something intimate.

That's when I noticed it—the smell. Not decomposition, it was far too early for that. Not the typical hospital smells either. It was water. River water, specifically. Murky and mineral-rich, with that distinctive organic quality that comes from a living ecosystem. I knew that smell from childhood, from summers spent wading in South Carolina rivers, from the rituals my family performed at their banks.

The scent triggered memories I'd tried to bury—my father teaching me to recognize the plants that grew only in places where the veil between worlds was thin. My mother's hands preparing poultices from roots that bled milk-white sap. The smell of river water had always accompanied their rituals, their communions with what they called "the greater body."

I looked around, confused. The morgue has no windows, no connection to the outside world. The smell couldn't be coming from outside. It seemed to be emanating from her skin, as though she'd been swimming in a river just before death. But that had to be before she had been admitted. She'd been in our care for nearly twenty-four hours before she died, and then she was given a bed bath. It made no sense. Bodies don't develop new smells after clinical cleaning. They don't transform in refrigerated rooms.

I pulled the gown lower, exposing her breasts. They were so pale with large pink nipples, already showing the beginning of livor mortis, the blood pooling on the side of her body that had been pressed against the drawer. I cupped one in my hand, feeling its weight, its unnatural coolness. My other hand moved lower, skimming over her stomach, feeling the slight softness there. I pushed the gown down lower, exposing her thighs, the dark groomed triangle between them. The smell of river water was overwhelming now, making me dizzy, and it emanated from between her thighs. I removed the gown from her smooth legs and folded it, setting it aside. Now, I could hear something alongside the buzzing of the light, a noise which I could not locate the source—a faint rushing sound, like water over stones. If I had to speculate its location, my senses suggested it was coming from inside her, or somehow connected to her body in unknown metaphysical ways, as though her veins still flowed with something other than congealed blood.

The contrast between my warm, living flesh and her cold, dead tissue was electric; a tantric circuit was flowing. My thumb brushed across her nipple, noting how it remained soft, unresponsive. In life, it would have hardened at my touch. In death, it merely accepted contact without reaction. I took a moment to take her all in, to really look at her from head to toe. Her body was full-figured, lush even in death. Her breasts were large and heavy, her waist narrowing before flaring to rounded hips. In life, she must have drawn stares, her appearance a carefully crafted homage to a bygone era of femininity. In death, she transcended even this, becoming something timeless and iconic.

I touched her between her legs, my fingers exploring the cold folds of flesh. The geography of female anatomy is rendered strange by death's transformation. Yet as I touched her, I felt a connection—

a bridge between living and dead, between present and past. I unzipped the body bag completely, exposing her legs down to her feet; her precious bare feet with their chipped black nail polish. I noted the small tattoo on her ankle—a DNA helix, another nod to her studies. The double spiral wrapped around her delicate ankle bone, the nucleotide pairs rendered with scientific accuracy. I traced it with my finger, following the curve of the genetic code inked into her skin. Did she understand when she chose this design that DNA itself is merely a vehicle, a puppet structure controlled by worlds within which we have yet to penetrate?

The morgue air is perpetually cold, but I was sweating and believed my body temperature was making the room considerably warmer. My scrubs felt too tight, too rough against my skin. I positioned myself between her legs, which were stiff but manageable. The initial contact—my living heat against her deathly cold—made me gasp as it felt so intense. It was like plunging into ice water —a shock that radiated through every nerve ending, leaving an amazing and clean feeling.

As I pushed inside her, I began to kiss her neck, the smell of river water was also reinforced as a taste in my mouth, and I nibbled at it. It wasn't unpleasant but mineral-rich, musky, with undertones of algae and soil. It tasted ancient, primordial, like drinking from the source of life itself. I moved within her, feeling a resistance that wasn't physical but something else—as though I were pushing against the membrane between two worlds. With each thrust, the barrier seemed to thin, allowing something to flow between us. Not life returning to her, but something else transferring from her to me. Knowledge, perhaps. Or bacterial consciousness, spreading through fluid exchange, colonizing new territory.

I'm not sure how long it lasted, but after a while, I began to sweat even more profusely, similar to my experience in cardio training. Time behaves differently in the morgue. Minutes stretch and contract like living tissue. The rushing sound in my ears grew louder, drowning out the hum of the refrigeration units, the distant hospital sounds. It was a roar now, like standing beside a waterfall, like being submerged in a flood.

I remembered suddenly, vividly, the Missoula Floods that Harold Gideon ranted about—cataclysmic events that had shaped the Willamette Valley thousands of years ago. Walls of water hundreds of feet high, carrying soil and microorganisms from distant places, depositing them in new environments where they would evolve and adapt. Was something similar happening now, on a microscopic scale? Were ancient bacterial communities being transported from one host to another, reshaping the landscape of my body as the floods had reshaped the Valley?

The rushing sound surrounded me completely now. I could feel the water—not physically, but in some other sense, as though my consciousness had expanded beyond my skin. I could feel the bacterial networks spreading through my body, communicating with each other through chemical signals, restructuring my awareness from the cellular level outward. Eventually, my movements grew more desperate. I buried my face in her neck, inhaling that impossible river scent, my hands gripping her hips hard enough to bruise—though there would be no bruises, not anymore. No blood would rush to the surface in response to trauma. No capillaries would break. She was beyond harm, and I could grab her hips as hard as I chose to.

The light continued to flicker erratically, but now faster, as the rocking gurney hit the wall in rhythm with my accelerating movements. In the increased flickering came a strobing effect that cast the bulb's metal cage bars as wild shadows thrown. I saw changes in her face in this movement of light—subtle shifts in her features that couldn't be explained completely by the play of just light and shadow. Her lips seemed fuller, her cheekbones more pronounced, her entire countenance somehow more sensual and irresistible than before. It occurred to me that the bacteria were reshaping her even in death, returning her to some template of humanity either rewritten by them or already present in her genetic code.

When it ended, the rushing sound in my ears crescendoed, then stopped abruptly. The light stabilized. The smell receded, though it didn't disappear entirely. I looked down at her face and, for just a moment, thought I saw something move behind her eyelids. A trick of the light, surely. Or my unconscious mind creating phantoms. But the movement was too real to be imagined like something watching from behind the curtain of her eyelids.

I pulled away from her body, suddenly aware of the cold air against my skin, of the harsh exposed bulb highlighting the obscenity of what I'd done. My seed glistened on her belly where it had spilled, pearlescent against her pale skin. I stared at her belly and thought of the geese, how they migrate between Alaska and the Willamette Valley, carrying microorganisms in their gut flora, in the mud clinging to their feet. Unwitting vectors for bacterial communities seeking new territories. Was I such a vector? Was R's death merely a transition in her role as carrier for these ancient consciousnesses? Her eyes remained closed, but I could swear I saw movement moments ago, like dreams continuing beyond death.

I looked down at her face again, at the perfect crimson waves of her hair, at the full lips now slightly parted as though in mid-sentence. What would she say if she could speak? Would she thank me for adoring her in this state when no one else will? For allowing the bacterial communion to spread beyond her physical boundaries? Or would she scream at the violation of her body, her dignity, her transition? I would never know. The dead keep their secrets. Most of the living can't. But perhaps I was beginning to understand their chemical whispers, their electrochemical conversations. Maybe the dead do reveal their secrets when we learn how to listen. Perhaps that's what R had recognized in me from the beginning—a potential translator for messages that can only come through after death.

I cleaned her obsessively, I wiped my seed from her belly and chest as well as the pre-ejaculate fluids that would be detectable inside her or on the floor or gurney. Evidence must be removed. Traces eliminated. The body returned to its official state of documentation. The alcohol wipes left brief streaks on her skin that quickly evaporated in the cold air. I checked her fingernails for any tissue that might have been scraped from my skin during our contact, though I knew this was impossible. The dead don't scratch. They don't resist. They accept whatever is done to them with perfect equanimity.

I smoothed her gown, arranging the thin fabric to cover her completely, erasing the evidence of my intrusion. Her face remained serene, unchanged. If something had moved behind her eyelids, it was still now. Patient. Waiting. R may have known we were connected. She'd seen it starting in me before I recognized it fully in myself. The Christ Contagion, spreading through contact, through exchange of fluids, through bacterial communion. She obviously was unaware when she sensed I carried the Contagion that I had received from another who lay as she would—cold and dead. Tomorrow, her family would claim her, bury her in soil where the bacterial communities in her tissues would merge with those in the earth. The cycle would continue, with or without human awareness.

As for me, I will continue my shift tonight at Christ Hospital. Perhaps I would visit the refuge on break or my next day off. For right now, though, I simply replace the cover of the gurney with R's body inside. Then I removed my gloves, used the lotion hand sanitizer until I could wash my hands at a sink, and prepared to exit the little morgue and return to the world of the living, carrying something of my new love within me.

11

BLOOD AND FROST

I left Greenville, changed my name, and never looked back. That's the simple version, which leaves everything truly personal out. The truth crawls beneath the surface like the luminescence now moving under my skin, which is noticeable throughout my groin when I am alone in bed trying to relieve myself. I haven't written about this before. Some things you lock away, hoping they'll dissolve like sutures in a healing wound. But they don't dissolve. They become encapsulated, walled off by scar tissue, but still present, still there.

It happened when I was thirteen, during my father's annual hunting trip. We went every November; it was a tradition he insisted on despite my lack of enthusiasm. "Connecting with nature," he called it, though it seemed contradictory to kill what you claimed to honor. But my father contained multitudes of contradictions, all of them existing in perfect harmony within his mind. Memories surface unbidden, the return of the repressed, vivid as hallucinations, as real as organic vine-ripened home-grown tragedy. Perhaps journaling this will help me understand how my past connects to what I'm becoming. Perhaps there's a reason the Contagion found me, specifically.

We had a cabin near Lake Jocassee, in the mountainous northwestern corner of South Carolina. Nothing fancy, it was just two rooms, a fireplace, and an outdoor shower rigged to a propane water heater. No electricity, no plumbing beyond a hand pump for well water. My father loved the primitive conditions, and he said it brought us closer to our "primal selves."

The lake itself felt veiled, hidden in intent as much as location, accessible only through Devils Fork State Park. My parents liked the name—they said it had a certain edge, a charming deviance. "It suits us," my mother had once said, a wry smile on her lips. They both had an affinity for the liminal and the esoteric, and there was something about crossing a place so starkly named that felt—if not sacred, then at least properly aligned. It was like passing through a threshold not everyone would choose, or even notice.

That year, my father was focused on hunting Canada geese. The rolling farmland of the Upstate, particularly around Anderson County, had become home to resident populations of them. Fields with leftover corn and soybeans attracted feeding geese, making the region ideal for hunting.

"Canada geese are the most abundant," he explained as we set up blinds near a recently harvested cornfield. "But we might see snow geese or even brant, though those are rare this far inland."

He spoke with the precise tone of a professor giving a lecture, the same voice he used during rituals. Everything was a ceremony to him—loading the shotguns, arranging the decoys, positioning ourselves in the blinds. He wore no hunting camouflage, only his usual dark attire, claiming the geese responded to energy more than visual cues.

"They're intelligent birds," he said, his breath visible in the predawn chill. "They recognize patterns. They remember."

My mother had come with us that year, unusual as she typically stayed behind during these trips. "I need to reconnect," she had said cryptically before we left. She spent most of her time at the cabin, reading or writing in her journal, occasionally walking to the edge of the lake to sit and stare at the water—as though the lake, too, carried some hidden correspondence she was waiting to decipher.

That morning, November 15th, I still remember the date with perfect clarity—we left before sunrise. The air was cold enough to burn the lungs, frost crunching beneath our boots as we walked to the blinds. We settled in to wait, my father occasionally using a caller to mimic the sounds of geese.

Around mid-morning, after several hours of nothing, he decided we should move to a different location. "They're not flying this way today," he said, gathering his equipment. "We'll try the south field."

We returned to the cabin to get the truck. As we approached, I saw movement through the trees. Some white movement into the cold air. Looking back after the tragedy, I recognize this as steam from our solar-heated outdoor shower.

My father stopped suddenly, raising his hand for me to do the same. He pointed silently toward the tree line near the camp, where a lone Canada goose had landed, its black neck and white chinstrap distinctive against the brown undergrowth.

He raised his shotgun slowly, motioning for me to do the same. I hesitated—we were too close to the camp, surely. But he gave me a sharp look, and I complied, lifting my 12-gauge and sighting along the barrel as he had taught me.

"Together," he whispered. "On three."

I aimed for the movement, the white movement. We fired simultaneously, the shots deafening in the quiet forest. The goose took flight, unharmed. But there was another sound. Wailing from the direction of the outdoor shower.

The twelve-gauge shotgun pellets had pierced the plastic curtain of the shower stall. My mother fell to the ground, naked, wet, her chest blossoming red where the shot had torn through her heart and lungs. She collapsed onto the frost-covered ground, steam still rising from her skin, mingling with the blood that pumped from the wounds.

Her eyes found mine as we ran toward her. There was no accusation in them, only surprise, as though this outcome was unexpected but not entirely implausible. She tried to speak, her lips moving around words that wouldn't form. Then the light went out of those ice-blue eyes, leaving them flat and empty as the late autumn and early winter sky above. My father made a sound I had never heard before and hope never to hear again—not quite human, more like something torn from deep inside an animal. He gathered her into his arms, heedless of the blood soaking into his clothes, rocking her like a child.

The week-long investigation finally ruled it a hunting accident. No charges were filed. The Greenville News ran a small story on page six a few days before the funeral: "Local Woman Killed in Hunting Accident." A final bit of publicity that even my mother couldn't have orchestrated. Locals thought it was something devil worship-related. My hometown instantly went from uncomfortable to completely toxic for my present and bleak future.

12
HAROLD'S THEOLOGY

After attending to other patients, I knew I had to conduct a final follow-up with Harold before the shift ended. So, I stall and wash and dry my hands longer than usual, and finally make my way back into Harold's foul-smelling hellhole, where the stink bugs now fly like believers around his body. Those awful bugs find a way in through the walls or a permanently closed window of his room, all the staff speak about when they are exterminated, they return worse than before. At this point, I am both fascinated and horrified by the way he attracts creeping creatures and scents. The moment I cross into the room, I'm assaulted by his creeping aroma of body odor, which seems worse today. I pause in the stench. I think simultaneously about the chaotic threads of belief that my upbringing wound around me, and how meeting Harold has jarred me in ways I have yet to fathom.

I find myself drowning in the cloying embrace of death that drips from the frail figure curled beneath tattered sheets in the corner of a Med Surg third-floor patient room. What truly awaits me here? I wonder, as I brace myself against the intrusion of all that is putrid and wrong. I've encountered despair many times before in patient rooms. Yet, the specific horror of Harold, a man who is a deranged oracle lost in his own maze of twisted theology, provokes an unsettling curiosity in my veins, a spark ignited by my own strange upbringing. He is a conundrum I cannot easily resolve. I have entered a place where reverence mingles dangerously with madness. His delusions spill over, and I am merely an observer.

I approach the bed. I can see the thin outlines of his form half-buried beneath layers of fabric. Oh, the sickly sheen of his skin, the wasted husk that shudders with the labor of every shallow breath. I count his respirations on my watch. Each movement of the nasty sheet reveals more of his shattered frame, reminding me that even in this land of misery, he clings tenaciously to life. When I last visited, he spoke of shaken dualities, of angels and demons, intertwining their fates. The words stirred something dormant within me of my own childhood, steeped in mysticism, shadows, and alternate deities.

"Harold," I call softly, hoping to penetrate the shroud that envelops him. He rolls his head lazily toward me, his hand moving under the sheet; however, those hollow eyes reflect something beyond mere recognition. "Just here for your catheter. We both know what needs to be done." There's an uncomfortable weight to my words, a confession laid bare in this unholy sanctuary. I offer a semblance of solace, knowing it is my duty to ease his suffering.

I maneuver the catheter bag into position, ensuring it hangs lower than his bladder, then turn my attention to the drainage valve. As I pull the valve open, an amber stream flows out, its sickly sheen glistening in the dim light. It smells infected and foul, as it has since our introduction.

I glance at Harold, whose sunken features glisten with sweat as he relentlessly rubs his genital area with his eyes closed. I am between a moment of thinking they don't pay me enough for this shit, and realizing my work has gotten far more interesting on a knife's edge between reverence and repulsion, for I know that I have come to witness the essence of existence dwindle into the margins.

The stench of his piss that invades my senses is a reminder, a testament to mortality wrapped around the certainty of my duty. To drain his catheter was an act once routine in its necessity, now an act transfigured. Each drop of this man's filtered voided essence pulses with a quiet apocalypse, a sacrament of absence. In this ritual of release, I witness the body's waste, and the residue of Harold's Christian god who has died into flesh, who bleeds not from a cross above but from the hollow below. Here, under the fluorescent buzz of Christ Hospital, heaven and hell no longer oppose as they collapse into one another, bridged by the slow drip of a man's fluids. I am beginning to shift, to believe that the sacred has emptied itself into history, and I hold its daily crucifixion in a plastic bag of colonized urine. I think of those relentless stink bugs watching me, creeping who knows where. They are the only angels who bear witness.

"Let's talk while I do this," I say, attempting to mask the discomfort coiling within me. "Tell me, what have you been thinking about in here? I've read in your chart that you don't care for visitors, you do not want to speak to physical therapy, or even a chaplain. Are you doing okay alone?" The question lingers in the air, a moment of silence.

He then chuckles. "Oh, I have the company of the morning star and then the evening's cries. I am never alone. You know, Protestant theologian John Calvin rejected the identification of Lucifer with Satan or the Devil. He said that when it referred to Satan, such has arisen from ignorance; it must be understood as the king of the Babylonians. I have discovered that it means the king of fallen kings, which is an undoing of power through belief, and belief forged into the will to power." The cloudy fluid continues to escape into the measuring cup with aroma curling upwards.

I close my eyes for a moment, trying to understand his words within the alternate landscapes of my consciousness. "An undoing of power through belief, and belief *itself* into the will to power." I recognize that his words dance over the edge, twisting the foundations of what is defined as light and darkness.

"Why do they share the title of the morning star?" He asks questions only he can answer as his gaze pierces through my layers. I'm reluctant to explore his eyes too deeply. "Look closely, nurse... Ellis. In the eyes of their followers, in the depths of their faith, you will find the truth of both. Both fell when bound to this world, and both carried the weight of despair, navigating the same sacred truths." My hands seal the valve, yearning to contain the flood of thoughts that threaten to wash away my own grasp on sanity.

As I clean the area, swabbing at the remnants that cling to the edges of our exchange, I contemplate Harold's fractured soul. "And what of you, Harold? Have you found the truth?" The air grows thick, charged with an intensity that swirls like fog in the void.

He lets out a cackling laugh.

With the last of his catheter output contained, I notice the gloves are torn on my left hand above my palm. I dispose of the gloves and sanitation materials, the remnants cast in the waste bin kept by his bedside. The waste basket is nearly full with wadded tissues and unopened pieces of mail. As I step back, I think about how the path of truth often lies obscured, and the discarded vestiges of our beliefs seep like shadows into every crevice of belief. As I wash my hands, the feel of water over my skin cleanses my mind a bit and reminds me of the delicate line we tread—a line that wavers between absolution and despair. I glance back at Harold.

As I turn to leave, Harold's voice reverberates. "Remember, Ellis, the path to truth is often lined with deceit; embrace it all. The Abrahamic god confuses himself with the origin of all things and deceives his fellow demons, also known as human beings, into believing that he is the ultimate Creator. One of Satan's names is Jesus Christ. Angels are like sharp angles of light; they have no free will or any agency, unlike Satan and unlike humanity with the ability to choose and to truly speak. The 'morning star' is known as 'Lucifer, son of the morning.' The book of Isaiah refers to Satan's fall from heaven. The morning star refers to Satan through the evolution of our understanding. In Revelation, Jesus unmistakably identifies Himself as the morning star. Watch closely."

I should have pawned him off on someone else after our first session. They say his memory is weak from hunger, dementia, anemia, and pain, but Harold forgets nothing. And yet the smell, the disarray, the crumbling of his body resulted from self-neglect. How can one claim to have insight into things eternal when one cannot even master themself on basic upkeep? How can I resist listening? Well, I don't believe what I hear, but maybe I want to. He does not soothe his own external sores by speaking; rather, he soothes my soul's wounds while he speaks. Where is this man's power? That is a question that puzzles me.

"Watch closely," he said one last time, more a command than advice. "Look into their eyes, the followers. If you're brave, if you really want to know, that's where you'll find the truth." I think of Harold's words as maps to lead me from my past or back into it. I am collecting them like a fountain full of wishes.

I left the room, hoping the remainder of my shift might be as amusing, even if I was slightly nauseated, thanks to the eccentric old man. Yet, the rest of my shift passed without any notable events, allowing me to enjoy three peaceful days off. On the last day of my break, I treated myself to some extra rest and eventually got up to enjoy some coffee and catch up on the news. Everything changed dramatically when I read the headlines, which proved to me that Harold was much more than just an eccentric. Between Harold and the news, I had a paradigm shift regarding my move to the Willamette Valley. While logic defines valleys as passive landscapes and vectors as mere disease carriers, what I'm proposing is entirely different: the Valley itself is the disease, an insidious presence nestled between mountains to the east, to the west, to the south, and we—the residents of Benton County—are unwittingly its carriers, moving through its expanse like veins of infection, spreading its influence.

13
SPRINGWOOD CEMETERY

On December 2nd, 1998, Greenville, South Carolina, offered a sky that didn't quite know how to mourn with Mother's loved ones. Cool and overcast, with temperatures in the mid-forties, the weather was almost gentle and strangely pleasant for the day we buried our Mia. I wanted thunderstorms and hail, something to experience that the personification of nature, a force to which she held so dear, was mourning her also. A light breeze moved through the cemetery, brushing across our faces like a breath from autumn's sobs for her, for she loved this season, as her breath taught me, and rustling the soil that now mingled around her were blown leaves scattering from a pile raked high, brittle and brown. The scent of the death of autumn; turned soil, dead fallen leaves collected and raked only to be blown again. I stood at the edge of the gathering, watching mourners drift between the tombstones like black paper cutouts against the green backdrop of century-old oaks.

Springwood stretches across rolling hills, its 200-year history evident in the weathered stones and monuments that punctuate the landscape. The limestone entrance gate loomed behind us, its careful architecture a strange counterpoint to the decay it houses. I'd read in school that around seven thousand marked graves populate this place, with almost three thousand left unmarked. The knowledge of those unnamed dead beneath our feet offered an odd comfort—Mother would not be alone in her life's anonymity. Even in death, our true character becomes a statistic.

Father's hand rested on my shoulder. His fingers trembled slightly, though whether from grief or the effort of temporary sobriety, I couldn't determine. Around us gathered the expected assortment of relatives, colleagues, and acquaintances—all performing grief with varying degrees of conviction. Aunt Judy wept openly, her mascara creating perfect rivulets down her powdered cheeks. Uncle Robert maintained stoic silence, his jaw clenched tight enough to crack walnuts. The neighbors from three houses down brought casserole dishes wrapped in aluminum foil.

The casket waited at the center of it all with its polished oak and brass fittings that caught the afternoon sun. When the funeral director guided us forward for the viewing, I noticed how his shoes never touched the grass, always finding the concrete path, the dead might reach through the soil to claim him. Father went first, shoulders hunched, then motioned for me to approach.

My first glimpse of her face provoked nothing. Not grief, not horror, not recognition—just observation in my numbness. This assemblage of flesh resembled my mother in the way a wax figure resembles its subject. Her skin had the pallor and texture of candle tallow, stretched too tightly across her cheekbones. The mortician had applied makeup with the heavy hand of an amateur theater director—rouge on the cheeks, lipstick lighter than she would have chosen, eyeshadow in a shade she never wore. She looked younger. Her hair had been styled into a perfect coif that she would have found ridiculous in life. She wore what Christian women would call a Sunday dress—navy blue with pearl buttons—I think it was the one she reserved for parent-teacher conferences when she wanted to look less black-clad and witchy.

I leaned in, drawn by a curiosity about the technical precision of the presentation. Her hands, gently folded, held a faint rigidity that I knew as evidence of rigor mortis, now subdued and arranged. Her fingernails were neatly manicured and painted a soft, girlish pink. For as long as I could remember, she had preferred bare nails or a simple French tip. That small detail, more than anything else, exposed the artifice before us. I found myself wondering whether they had stitched shut the jagged exit wound in her chest, or merely concealed it beneath her hair and the satin pillow.

Father moved away after a perfunctory moment of reflection, but I remained. I studied the precise placement of her arms, the careful way her lips had been slightly parted to avoid the rictus grin of death, the almost imperceptible line of makeup covering the sutured lips. The funeral director shifted uncomfortably behind me, perhaps sensing that my interest extended beyond the normal grieving process.

"Take as much time as you need, son," he said, though his tone suggested the opposite.

I continued my examination. The embalming fluid had given her skin an artificial firmness, like underripe fruit. A faint chemical smell lingered beneath the cloying floral arrangements. I wondered about the process involved in draining blood, the introduction of formaldehyde, and the positioning of features before rigor mortis set in. The meticulous craft required to create this illusion fascinated me. Death disguised as peaceful sleep, decomposition temporarily halted through chemical intervention.

Around me, mourners moved. They approached with bowed heads, murmuring platitudes, and some left early, retreating. Some placed flowers near the casket. Others touched the polished wood briefly, transmitting final messages through the barrier. None looked too closely at her face. None wanted to see the truth.

I remained by the casket long after others had drifted. My extended vigil drew concerned glances, misinterpreted as profound grief. In reality, I was simply noting the details, such as the slight asymmetry of her ears, the nearly invisible stitch mark behind her left earlobe, the way the afternoon light illuminated the fine hairs on her forearm that the mortician had neglected to remove. I was not grieving; I had it under control.

When Father finally called me away, his voice cracked with emotion I couldn't access. I touched the edge of the casket and followed him to our seats. The minister spoke of resurrection and eternal peace to please the multitude. Ashes to ashes. My parents' views on nature and the world were absent from the ceremony. I thought instead of the violence of nature in cellular breakdown, of bacteria multiplying beneath the sealed lid, of the slow return to elemental components. Dust to dust. When they lowered her into the ground, I watched the mechanical precision of the cemetery workers, noting how they avoided eye contact with the mourners.

As we left Springwood, I glanced back at the fresh mound of earth that now contained what remained of my mother. The temporary marker caught the late afternoon sun. Soon, grass would grow over the spot, and only the small stone would indicate that anything lay beneath. I felt no solid stage of grief, but only a strange and detached curiosity that would, in the coming days, evolve into something I couldn't yet comprehend.

Then the night came. The house stands empty except for Father, who retreated to his study with a bottle of bourbon after we returned from Springwood. The funeral reception dispersed by seven, leaving behind half-eaten casseroles and the lingering scent of too many flower arrangements. I showered and then washed off my dress shoes, watching my mother's funeral soil circle the drain. South Carolina clay is the color of dried blood, and I thought of her face as the water drained. By ten o'clock, I lay in bed staring at the ceiling, my body suddenly alert with an unexpected and disturbing sensation. Arousal. Intense, insistent arousal.

The physical manifestation was undeniable. My blood was rushing, pulse quickening, an erection so rigid it was almost painful. I shifted uncomfortably beneath the sheets, attempting to redirect my thoughts. Nothing diminished the insistence of this physiological response. Most disturbing was its psychological accompaniment of my mother's face as I'd seen it that afternoon, waxy and still in the casket.

My room was silent except for the ceiling fan's click and the occasional creak of Father's footsteps downstairs. The thin slice of moonlight through partially closed blinds cast prison-bar shadows across my bed. I tried to concentrate on these external stimuli rather than the internal pressure building in my groin, but my mind continually circled back to the funeral, to the corpse, to the precise arrangement of her features.

The incongruity registered clearly. This was my mother, this was death, this was objectively inappropriate, this was my first hyper-erotic experience, as my life lay in the wake of trauma, as my body bloomed. Yet my body responded with a vigor I'd never before experienced. The contact of the sheets against my skin sent an electric current through my body, more intense than any previous adolescent exploration. The physical sensation was extraordinary. I was coming into my sexuality, full blast, with nerve endings hypersensitized, each stroke amplified beyond normal parameters.

Behind my closed eyelids, I saw her face in the casket. The mortician's pancake makeup covered what used to be the most perfect skin. The slight parting of her lips. The absolute stillness. I imagined the hidden procedures beneath her clothing—the incisions, the drainage, the careful reconstruction. These thoughts didn't diminish my arousal but intensified it. My free hand gripped the sheet, knuckles whitening with the effort of silence.

The images evolved and fragmented. Her hands folded across her abdomen. The artificial pink of her manicured nails. There was slight discoloration at her temples where the makeup thinned. The perfect part in her hair. Each detail triggered a corresponding spike in physical pleasure, creating a disturbing synesthesia of visual death and tactile arousal.

The pressure built toward inevitability. My back arched slightly off the mattress. My jaw clenched to prevent any sound that might travel through the floorboards to Father's study below. When release came, it was explosive—a white-hot current, shot like a fountain building up for years, going all over my chest, hitting me in the face, spraying the bed, its display and reach paralyzed my limbs and suspended all my thoughts. This was the first time anything ever came out besides urine. I guess I had never explored long enough before that night, or with the right thoughts, to get such an explosive result.

In that moment of climax, I saw her face with perfect clarity. Except her face was anything but cheerfully alive; it had once been animated so beautifully with expression and intention, but as I had seen it today, so still and artificial. Empty was the woman beneath the mortician's cosmetic work, and she looked younger. The shell that had once contained my mother was a reinvented version of her. One that I felt I understood more without guilt.

The aftermath brought cooling skin and damp sheets. Sleep came quickly afterwards, deeper than expected. I also dreamed of Springwood Cemetery. It wasn't as it had been at her funeral, crowded with mourners, but empty except for me and the freshly turned earth of my mother's grave. In the dream, I walked among the headstones, noting dates and epitaphs with dispassionate interest. When I woke shortly after dawn, the sheets were dry, but my pillow was damp.

14
THE GAZETTE'S BACTERIAL FIELD DAY

In the Corvallis twilight, on Benton County's itchy bosom, the morning fog unwrapped itself from the Valley and crept back into Marys River. At dawn, some newspapers were still being thrown to doorsteps about town, and countless online posts updated as the Corvallis *Gazette-Times* delivered its revelations. People woke for work, sneezed as a salute to the grass capital, took their allergy medications, and read the news. The local events gradually emerged in the community as distinct. Mine came to light through social media, where someone shared a post about the article. What had been researched privately for months was now made public. A progression of headlines emerged throughout the day and night, one fungal bloom of news feeding on the last. The news of KGW had its own version, Corvallis' *Gazette* journalists had theirs, and then OPB. I went searching from one to another, compelled by the fact that Harold had any knowledge of this before the news broke. What began as speculation by scientists ("Unusual Microbial Activity Detected in Marys River") and doubts by bureaucrats ("Health Department Issues Advisory for Marys River") soon became doctrine for the devout ("Local Church Claims River Waters Have 'Healing Properties'"). Few could foretell how the papers would, in the weeks to come, detail new miracles and strange behaviors among converts.

The initial reports from the local news were filled with complex scientific jargon typical of a college town, marked by a detached curiosity and the thrill of new findings. One early headline declared, "OSU Researchers Baffled by Mysterious Microbes," while another announced, "Unknown Species Cause Water Discoloration." Reporters were thrilled to engage with Oregonians' devotion to their area. Scientists in the articles described unexpected microbial blooms in Marys River, a phenomenon not previously seen in the area. "This is quite unusual," commented a biologist to the *Gazette*, noting that the microbes didn't match any known species. Officials, however, were unconcerned, downplaying any worries about the water's cloudy appearance and unusual taste. "Perfectly safe," a city representative assured. "Unusual but not dangerous." In the church pews, there were other details; followers discerned a concealed message: Bishop Ashworth proclaimed the occurrence as a revelation, whereas scientists described it as unusual and unfamiliar, hinting to spiritual seekers that what isn't harmful in this mysterious event could therefore be the undetectable mysteries of the sacred.

As the news progressed, the *Gazette-Times* adjusted its tone in response to the community's concerns about the river's changing conditions, and scientific curiosity evolved into outright warnings. Headlines conveyed growing concerns: "City Officials Alert Public of Mysterious Bacteria in River Water," followed by "Health Department Advises Caution for Marys River." Initially dismissive, officials began cautioning about potential risks of exposure. "Avoid extended contact," the local health department advised, mentioning reports of an unidentified bacterium affecting those who frequented the river. Despite this, many locals remained skeptical. "I've been swimming here since childhood," said one man, who had noticed strange new textures under his epidermis that were not visible to others or his doctor; it was what he described as a bioluminescence occurring only during certain moments beneath his skin. Officials continued to express doubt, citing the lack of substantial evidence. “It’ll pass,” predicted a senior official of the phenomenon, but the number of reports of local illness kept climbing. Concerned voices emerged from the community. “They claim it’s safe, but how can they be sure?” questioned a young mother of two. “What if it’s contagious?” A local church prepared its baptismal ceremonies under the guidance of Bishop Ashworth’s ministries.

The *Gazette-Times* began chronicling what locals no longer called contamination; they considered it consecration. And at first, it was just a few: a well-respected homeowner who was afflicted with life-altering illnesses drank from the Marys River and claimed healing. A woman whose joints had stiffened with age said she could dance again. The mayor’s boy, long mute, began to speak, starting with riddles. But not everyone was touched. Not everyone was chosen.

Scientists began to dismiss the phenomenon entirely. The so-called Christ Contagion wasn’t affecting most of those exposed, and the majority who tried to ingest the water fell ill with other parasites besides the new bacteria. Those who tested the waters usually became fevered and had awful vomiting, while some remained wild-eyed and shaking; all of the cases were written off as statistical noise associated with drinking dirty river water. But the faithful saw something else in those who got sick and those who were healed: a pattern—a sorting out of the worthy. The river didn’t heal indiscriminately. It blessed in mysterious ways.

One midweek edition ran the headline: “Christ Hospital’s Episcopal Church Claims River Waters Have ‘Healing Properties.’” The accompanying photo showed parishioners gathered at the banks, some kneeling, some submerged to the waist, eyes closed and listening for something beneath the current.

Another article followed: “Hundreds Flock to ‘Healing Waters’ Despite Health Advisory.” They came with ailments and offerings such as candles, feathers, and jars of salt. Some claimed relief. Others left shaking, unchanged, or worse. The river had begun to choose.

Bishop Elijah Ashworth's statement was printed beneath his portrait, his expression unreadable: "The waters of Marys River shall bring forth a great purification to the chosen." The implication was clear. If you were healed, you were worthy. If not, you were not.

It seemed like it happened overnight; local cults sprang up like mushrooms after rain. Some preached that their method of faith was the key to salvation. Others spoke of ancestral merit, bloodlines, or ritual purity. A few began to fast, to flagellate, to prostrate themselves, to sleep beside the river in hopes of being called.

Health authorities issued harsh warnings in response. One doctor described the phenomenon as "wishful drinking," citing a rise in cases of beaver fever; Giardiasis was flooding the emergency room at Christ Hospital, from those who had swallowed the river's murk. But the headlines had already sanctified the waters for those desperate in faith. The river was no longer a source of illness. It was a test.

The emergency rooms remained filled with the sick, even after warnings about beaver fever. But so did the churches. So did the riverbanks. And in the letters to the editor, the tone grew sharp: "Doctors Are Liars." They claimed the faithless cannot understand.

What unsettled me most was this: I had no faith. And yet, I was afflicted. But was it truly an affliction? Or had I been healed of something I never knew I carried? Were the changes in my skin, the visions, the dreams, what others called a blessing? I couldn't tell if the river had cursed me or chosen me, only that it had touched me when I touched M. in the morgue of Christ Hospital.

By then, the Marys River had become something else entirely. Not a body of water, but a body of judgment. A place where the veil thinned. Where the chosen were marked, and the rest were left to wonder what the hell was going on. Harold spoke of the intermingling of geology with memory and how this relates to our sense of meaning deciphered via the sacred. However, Harold convoluted these ideas with a twisted take on Christian theology, so I doubt his ability to actually understand this phenomenon. He did reveal some Easter eggs in his madness, so I do not discard him completely, especially in his understanding of geological history.

Turning over Harold's ideas, I researched how the Missoula Floods had unleashed their powerful torrents across the land, carving out riverbeds and etching deep clay veins into the earth. As the soil dried and cracked, the bacteria infiltrated the Valley's aquifers like ancient seeds, lying dormant in their geological time. They have awaited the tremors of the Great Cascadia Earthquakes to awaken them, bringing them back to the surface with each quake; they rise, they have waited for their life to spread as naturally as water seeks its level.

The Valley's landscape bore the scars of each devastating flood that surged from Montana, sweeping through Oregon, carrying icy, glacial waters that overwhelmed everything in their path. The mighty Columbia River channeled these floods into the Willamette, where Marys River, resembling an ancient artery, ultimately gave way. The land transformed into a vast inland sea, briefly encircling the Valley's rising hills, which stood as islands for a fleeting moment in millennia. Eventually, the waters receded, leaving behind layers of sediment and history. These layers, as distinctive as the floods themselves, comprised black clay, red clay, and white ash, each infused with a mysterious essence, serving as archives of the floods.

Through ages of decay, the clay grew rich with life. As generations of floodwaters seeded the deposits, the organisms lay themselves to sleep. Still, they remained sentient, a consciousness woven from microbial threads and stored within the stonework of the Valley itself. Only water could set them free. Locked in geological time, the bacterial memories stayed dormant as the Earth folded itself into its tectonic rhythms. They waited in aquifers and clay deposits. They rested in the limestone and underground pools. But the minor shudder of a recent fault near Marys River jarred them into wakefulness, breaking their ancient shells and releasing them into the Valley once more. Reborn, they retraced the floodwaters, releasing information stored in the land's geology.

When the bacteria entered Marys River they became visible to select people, of which I see no known pattern or profiling. Humans are perhaps just another means of distribution, and if so, their methods are only known from our obscured reality as their host. Attracted to the river's transformed hue, the chosen people gathered at its banks. The bacteria found their vessels. With each contact, more became exposed, and the network of infection threaded its way through the Valley with an efficiency and purpose that defied natural law. Residents became unwitting hosts and accelerants. Soon, they too showed signs of infection, but more sickness occurred when the general public tried to ingest the water.

Faith, like bacteria, thrived among the converted. There is a shared ecology between religion and infection, an infestation of consciousness that transformed through subterfuge rather than force. Christians referred to it as a "personal relationship with Jesus Christ." The non-Christian infected simply called it God. The bacterial presence within them was alive, aware, and divine. It was manifested through the familiar language of intimacy and belief: savior, comforter, guide. "We are known," said the infected with deep conviction. "We are loved." And as they believed, so were they changed.

They testified with fervor to what they felt inside: an indwelling, at once ancient and new. "It knows me," they claimed. "I can feel it growing in me." Accounts from the converted echoed across Corvallis, spreading into the *Gazette-Times* and church newsletters. What I would soon call symptoms, they called blessings. "My whole life, I've searched for this presence," confessed one man. "Now that I have it, I am complete." The Contagion worked from the inside out, granting new understanding that bypassed years of unbelief and fear, colonizing even the deepest crevices of doubt. Their testimonies grew and expanded, with each vector in the Valley finding guidance under Bishop Elijah Ashworth. The Bishop would hold special baptisms at

Mary's River in Philomath. Our nursing unit had a mobile clinic there due to the variety of medical needs people may have when exposed to Marys River. I need to make a pilgrimage to Marys River if only to inhale its scent, as I once did on M, the origin point of my transmission, the mother of my Contagion.

15
GREENVILLE AT THIRTEEN

Some nights after the funeral, I waited until my father's bourbon-induced snores carried through the hallway before I snuck out my bedroom window. I walked over the steep rise of Summit Drive, then up Bennett Street, and turned right onto Earle Street, entering the Colonel Elias Earle Historic District. There, a canopy of old-growth trees distorted the sidewalk in front of homes built between the early 1800s and the early 20th century. I was halfway there when I made it to North Main Street, now the night air hung heavy with humidity and my sweat pressing against me. I'd dressed in dark clothing, not for concealment from trespassing, but out of an intuitive sense of the continued ritual for her mourning. Overall, the three-mile walk to Springwood Cemetery passed quickly in a dissociative haze, my body moving automatically while my mind cataloged the progression of my pathology.

Springwood Cemetery transformed at night. The limestone entrance gate loomed larger in the darkness with three archways now gated; the streetlights cast the bars' shadows across the ground like grasping fingers of the deceased confederates. The wrought iron fence surrounding the front of the property reminded me of a rib cage. It was impressive like ours at home, but around the cemetery, it looked like a skeletal barrier separating the living from the dead. I scaled it easily at a low point behind a cluster of azalea bushes, dropping silently onto the cemetery grounds.

Navigating the cemetery moonlight isn't too unusual for a teenager in the South, and I moved between the gravestones without being spooked and efficiently. Victorian monoliths showed their age, yet they looked beautiful at night. I took in the carved angels watching me trespass into the sacred space. For a cemetery, who are the welcome if not the living who have gut-wrenching anguish to reunite? The oldest section of the cemetery held raised masonry tombs topped with stone ledgers, their inscriptions worn nearly smooth by two centuries of South Carolina weather. I passed the section near the entrance where eighty unknown Confederate soldiers lay beneath uniform markers. These were men who had died in Greenville's makeshift hospitals during the Civil War, and their identities are now fully dissolved by time and poor record-keeping.

The northeast corner, once a potter's field for African Americans and indigent whites, stood nearly empty of markers, though I knew hundreds lay beneath the manicured grass. The city had extended Academy Street through this section in the late 1960s, my Nana had said, exhuming hundreds of bodies with the casual disregard reserved for those deemed insignificant in both life and death. I wondered if those displaced dead still lingered, their disrupted rest creating a different quality of silence in this part of the cemetery.

Mother's grave occupied a middle section, a large family plot bought by her grandparents in the late 1960s, beneath the spreading branches of a magnolia tree. The administration had placed her near my grandparents, though the family plot had space for only one more. It was presumably reserved for Father when his liver finally surrendered. The fresh dirt remained mounded, not yet settled into the flat uniformity of older graves. Wilting funeral flowers formed a decomposing perimeter, their petals drooping in the humid night air. The temporary marker was sadly a simple metal stake with her name, birth date, and death date printed on a laminated card. It stood at the head of her grave, awaiting the permanent stone that Father had been too distracted to order.

I knelt beside the mound, feeling the loose soil beneath my knees. The grave's fresh dirt retained the day's heat, creating the unsettling impression of residual body warmth. I traced her name, Mia Horning Mikhailovich, on the temporary marker with my fingertip, along with her living years: 1975-2009. The simplicity of the dates obscured the violent reality of her ending. This was real.

The hunting accident had occurred a couple of weeks ago, I think. The funeral had been delayed while authorities completed their investigation. The night of the incident, I vomited until only bile remained.

Now, kneeling before her grave, I felt the stirring of death as stimulus, arousal hit even harder than after her funeral. The shame of this reaction mingled with my grief and guilt, creating a unique neurochemical cocktail that overwhelmed rational thought. I tried to resist, fixing my gaze on her name, attempting to conjure memories of her alive. I imagined her cooking Sunday breakfast, singing off-key to radio songs, laughing at my childhood jokes. Instead, my mind produced only the funeral image of her body arranged in the casket, the mortician's artful concealment of my accidental violence.

The soil beneath my knees dampened from the night dew, seeping through my jeans. In the distance, a security guard or groundskeeper at the cemetery's edge cast long shadows across the grounds. The risk of discovery existed but seemed remote at this hour. Nevertheless, the possibility of being seen added another layer to the forbidden nature of the act, further intensifying physical response. My breathing quickened, visible as small clouds in the cooling night air. The scent of decaying flowers mixed with the earthy smell of fresh soil created a backdrop that my brain would forever associate with this moment.

My free hand pressed against the mound of earth, fingers digging slightly into the loose soil. The direct physical contact with her grave site triggered an acceleration of arousal in a feedback loop of guilt, memory, and forbidden pleasure. Behind my eyelids flashed images from the funeral, from the hunting accident, from sixteen years of ordinary mother-son interactions now permanently tainted by my actions and reactions. The physical pleasure peaked and receded in waves, leaving behind a hollow sensation in my chest and a sticky residue on my hand and the earth before me. I had marked her grave with the evidence of my adoration.

The aftermath brought crushing guilt; this desecration could be worse than the original sin of her death. My carelessness had ended her life; my body's response to that ending revealed something fundamentally broken in my psychological makeup. I wiped my hand on the grass beside the grave, then used a crumpled tissue from my pocket to clean any remaining evidence. The temporary marker stared back at me, its simple identification now insufficient to contain the complexity of what had occurred.

As I rose to leave, I touched the marker one final time. "I'm sorry," I whispered, though whether for killing her or defiling her grave, I couldn't specify. Both actions seemed equal violations, linked in a circuit of cause and effect that would define the remainder of my life. I walked backward from the grave, unwilling to turn my back on what I had done. The cemetery stretched around me, thousands of similar stories buried beneath manicured grass, though surely few as twisted as mine.

Six numb years melted away. I applied to nursing schools. Charleston accepted me, offering a scholarship that would cover most of the tuition. When I told my father I was leaving, he nodded once, as though he had been expecting this.

"Your mother always said you would find your own path," he said, the most direct reference he had made to her since her death. "She would be proud." Then he began talking about cars for I don't know how long until I retreated into my room.

I didn't believe him then, and I don't believe him now. I couldn't imagine that had my mother still been alive, she would be proud of my escape into normalcy, into the scientific world of nursing with its clear protocols and rational explanations. But I needed the structure, the order, the sense that life and death operated according to understandable principles.

I changed my name legally before I left—Ellis Horning instead of Ellis Mikhailovich. A small change, maintaining my mother's maiden name while shedding the heritage that had marked me as different my entire life. I told myself it was practical, that it would be easier for people to pronounce. But I knew it was more than that. It was an attempt to leave behind the boy who had held the gun that November morning, to become someone new, someone recovering from the past by wearing her name so that I may always remember life's cruel pain.

For years, it worked. Now, I am building a life in Corvallis, so many years after becoming a respected nurse, I have a fresh start at Christ Hospital. I will keep my head down, do my job well, and avoid drawing attention to myself. I told my colleagues I was from the East Coast, so they assumed I was from New York or Boston rather than South Carolina.

And then the bacterial consciousness found me.

Our zealot boss, Bishop Ashworth, says the Holy Spirit acts like a bacterial consciousness, as it chooses its vessels carefully, seeking out those who have experienced profound loss, whose understanding of life and death exists in the liminal space between science and faith. Perhaps he's right about some of that equation. Perhaps my mother's death opened something in me that made me receptive to this new form of existence.

Or perhaps it's simpler than that. Perhaps we are drawn to recreate our traumas, to return to the moments that shaped us, seeking different outcomes. My mother's last moments were an eruption of violence that tore her body apart. I should never have tried to kill that beautiful goose anyway. Now that I have rebuilt my life in a new place and am attempting to recreate myself, to heal, my body is changing, transforming, becoming something that transcends simple flesh.

The goose that flew away unharmed sometimes appears in my dreams, its black neck elongated, its wings spread wide against the winter sky. In the dream, it speaks telepathically, without a voice, telling me secrets about life and death that I forget upon waking. I think of her and how she thought it was ridiculous that we hunted them, even though she offered her company and cooked our breakfast before the hunt. But a bad feeling remains. I sense that I am moving toward some revelation, some understanding that has eluded me all these years.

16

DREAMS OF FORMLESS BEINGS

I only slept a few hours after work. I woke up from a dream (*I thought I didn't dream anymore*), clutching it to remain so I could understand the combination of sound and vision that had shocked my system. Formless light-beings had greeted me, weaving themselves through my body, through each other. A helix of light pulsing in and out of itself, fueled and informed by any matter in relation to its motion. Too bright to look at and too beautiful to ignore. I thought that vision was dependent on the head to move the eyes, yet looking at these beings was more acute when looking indirectly, not a side glance, not looking at them full-on. These beings sang in a different method of language, their voices crisp and clear and utterly nonsensical as I try to recall. In the seconds of the dream that remained, it made perfect sense. Now that I'm awake, it makes no sense at all.

Creatures of light, pulsing, multiplying, speaking in a shivering music of impossible things, yet I believe them: they are an opera of the union of opposites. Their voices coalesce into a single blaze of certainty, a radiant fury before which reality itself dissolves as the one transforms into many. It seems then to be an event in an alternative dimension—closer, nearer, their blinding forms filling every space, every surface. They explode into whiteness. I am awake now. As I write this, I think I am fully awake, only because the dream has just resurfaced in the drunkenness of being half-awake, then it faded as my lucidity clouded the other perception.

What is it that Harold comprehends? To truly grasp minds like Harold's, one must delve into their deeper essence. According to his perspective, everything is simultaneously unique and identical: the symbols I associate with community and childhood become instruments for a new cycle that frightens me with its imagery. While I dislike having dreams about work, dreaming about Harold's introduction felt healing, and perhaps my mind earnestly sought to understand him, and I genuinely do. I am eager to comprehend.

Harold communicates using the symbolism found in Christian mythology, viewing the Devil as Christ exalted and crowned with glory. Is this a prophetic vision or just the ramblings of a mad old man? I cannot tell the difference in Harold, and with my background, it seems like two opposing sides of the same foreign coin. Can currency that has no value for me be tossed into a wishing well? Harold's fingers are arched in my imagination, intricate and alive with a clarity and zeal that shames me. Opposite things are identical in and out of waking worlds, asleep and awake. Perhaps Harold is the host of a spiritual disease, eating through these rural communities. Perhaps he has been alive, spreading himself, spreading this madness, for centuries. Even now, his fierce words linger like howls of prophecy that slip into whispers... then laughter. I think of possibilities for far too long. When I stop thinking so hard, I have a spark, a knowing warms my head.

I see rivers changing as they stay the same. Perhaps they are one. They are, they are not. Harold believes he knows the fate of us all. His words are close. His ideas are closer. Harold's brittle frame so alive with vision, the shimmer in his voice that spreads through him, through me. After my morning coffee, my stomach feels uneasy. I feel a bit sick, and it's my day off. I need to go and see, I need to use my free time to answer my questions.

I have traveled and lived in a variety of places, but the distinction between science and religion doesn't seem clear here in the Valley. Corvallis and Philomath hold onto their ghosts with a tenacity that's unsettling. I came to Oregon to find myself before I reach middle age, but it feels like the past has found me first. The more I try to distance myself from it, the more it infects everything. How could I think a town as bland as Philomath was intoxicating anyone with its waters? The belief was somehow native to this place and originated beyond the Christian shape it took on in townsfolk's daily life. Perhaps I began to believe Harold because I was a stranger lost in rebirth within a town of people who believed they were reborn. In a way, they are reborn, but as a zygote, a hybrid lacking development beyond their insemination, injected by an unknown that is not the typical view of a creator.

The urge to understand is overwhelming, stronger than the urge to escape. I am on rotation for the Philomath mobile clinic this week, and so far, I have not been sent out. I have been eager to see what awaits me, so I decided to go to Philomath while not tethered to the mobile clinic or any other chores. I need to see the lines I've drawn between myth and reality blur further, to witness the changes myself, even if it means confronting what I've tried so hard to deny.

My resolve takes shape as I shower and dress. It's brittle, like the new skin over a deep scar, but I try not to think about how easily it can break. Instead, I focus on what I might find. I seek answers, closure, perhaps the truth behind this unusual city and its waters.

The drive from Corvallis to Philomath feels more foreboding than I expected. The end of spring has transformed the fields with vibrant colors and renewed life. California poppies show bright orange peppered into the uncut grass. It seems fitting that the Contagion should emerge now, in a season of birth and renewal. As I pass acres of manured farmland and open sky, I feel it in everything: the new life Harold spoke of, the death of all else.

The sun is just beginning to dip below the treeline as I arrive. Shadows stretch long and dark across the streets, casting the town in a soft light. There is a sense of waiting here, a palpable anticipation that hangs over everything. The buildings themselves hold their breath, bracing for the tremors to come.

I park the car and step out, the last of the early summer light filtering through branches and clouds. The town seems so impossibly still, but I know that just beneath this calm is the tumult of belief and the wild pulse of the Contagion. I walk along the familiar streets, feeling the heavy gaze of the past on my back.

Time feels frozen here, with each second stretched to its limit. The wildflowers stand out against the streets, vibrant splashes of blue and rust brown. I notice the shimmering on the water like the windows of Philomath's old buildings, casting an iridescent glow that seems to animate the air just above the water itself. Butterflies dance among the wildflowers by the riverbank. These butterflies are relatively small, with a wingspan of about an inch. Some have brilliant blue wings edged with black and a white fringe, while others have brown wings with a similar fringe.

I actually feel refreshed standing by the Marys River, much more at ease than walking on the streets of the town as a stranger. In this town, cultural and racial diversity seems nonexistent; the faces are recycled from their pioneer families, as they have remained here for generations. Philomath and its restless pioneering ghosts. Founded, they say, by members of the Marys River Settlement, whose simple faith and cold ambition clung like mold to the damp bark of pioneer cabins. The original community named its school Philomath, for the love of learning, and let the town grow around it like moss on a grave.

It's in the set of their faces, this grim determination. Each one looks like a sibling of another, those long-dead founders doubling back through time. They hold themselves while balancing heavy loads of memory, doomed to repeat rituals of loving the dead Christ over the living old growth, drawing lines between past and present that few seem to see. On this side, the faint outlines of their restless ghosts. On the other side, Corvallis, rising with hollow determination on the Willamette's banks.

Among the many larger neighboring communities, Corvallis comes with judgmental rumors; they say Philomath folk want to stay the same, stuck in static ideals of past generations—cultists in designer hiking clothes. Usually, Patagonia jackets or vests are worn by plain-looking people who resemble Mormons dressed for an outdoor fashion shoot. The subtle changes for these yokels are that their gazes grow heavier with each generation. I walk past them, past their heavy gaze, the weight of their glances hanging on me like selfish prayers. It reminds me of home, where the judgments came with blessings intertwined with the kiss of self-righteousness. This entire town defies time. The curse of stability and tradition is a preference; however, freezing them in place since their incorporation in 1882 offers solely the tradition of a small community Christian faith. I know them without knowing them: weary faces repeating in endless, uncanny succession like mannequins at a department store. I see them as I pass by while attempting to ignore the ugliness of Christian capitalist fashions. They look like the believers at the river the other day; they look like the magic has been extinguished and replaced by fundamentalist fetishes of hope. The sense of déjà vu is overwhelming.

The river marks their faith as much as the land, whose geography is etched into the Valley's histories: the highest point of Marys Peak, the subtle curl of Muddy Creek, the endless flow into the distant Willamette. In this stream, nature has been momentarily tamed so that it also appears to worship industry; the lies of the cross supplement the lack of meaning in such lives; they think their sins are cleansed. The idealistic vision of the Valley is now intertwined with the bishop's religious movement.

The Marys River, a force older than their faith, is in a way theirs and not theirs. I know the Bishop has transformed this natural course into a doctrine, a conviction from which none can turn away.

This landscape has their beliefs cast onto it, and now there is a response from the land. Time will tell if that response is gentle. Time loops through the river's constant persistence, until memory presses against the present with the force of belief. I have not located the mobile clinic yet, but will when my time comes to be on duty.

At the edge of my vision, a blur of rust and sky blue catches my eye. I turn, but the butterflies are gone.

17
MARYS RIVER

Her hair matches the color of the clipboard she clutches, and she furrows her brow above reading glasses as she recounts her crusade against the hospital cafeteria. I nod along, women weave conversation, and my scientific detachment teeters. “I won’t rest until I hear from Bishop Ashworth himself,” the Charge Nurse proclaims, and I wonder if she’s stumbled closer to the truth that I am also seeking. She relishes the attention and sets the hook with one hand raised, savoring a moment of silence. “Five dollars,” she says slowly, “for a donut they bought at Market of Corvallis for a dollar ninety-nine!” The others exchange incredulous looks, their gasps competing with the sound of rustling papers.

I open a chart and glance over the numbers, but her voice cuts through again. “And you know Market of Corvallis *totally* buys them from Albany’s Costco for *like* seventy-five cents. I asked while shopping there, and a kid at the bakery didn’t know what to say. He just stared at me. Like I was crazy or something. Soon, our hospital will be selling popcorn for communion!” I can’t help but smile slightly as she recounts how she bought two overpriced donuts for an elderly couple, and concludes by expressing her determination to set the matter straight with Bishop Ashworth. For a moment, I almost believed she had uncovered a larger plot. It makes me wonder about my own thoughts. I'm not entirely off base. Power in the hospital exerts unrelenting pressure on the small, which also mirrors back at a lower level, such as the up-charged donut that even the hospital is being up-charged for; it's a chain that only these nurses and Harold Gideon seem privy to. For Harold, it is donuts sprinkled with the prophets themselves, who each impose a progressive tax on humanity through their additions.

One by one, the others chime in with their own accounts of cafeteria treachery. I should be focusing on the patient files in front of me, but my eyes drift to my watch, counting down the minutes until I can slip away. A young nurse with curly red hair shares a story about ten-dollar salads and proclaims, "It's a contagion at work! Greed and price gouging spread faster than Covid. Also, Ellis, at mid-shift, you are to report to the mobile clinic in Philomath. I will give you the directions." Her tone is hard to read, but I knew it would eventually be my time to be the mobile clinic nurse.

Harold's warnings come rushing back. I know the Contagion moves in ways we don't yet comprehend, and as he insists, infecting systems and souls alike. I attempt to return my attention to the women. I lose track of who speaks next. Their voices blend into a chorus of conspiracy theories that bleed into one another, edging too close to the prophetic ramblings of my most enigmatic patient. The relentless persistence of their complaints mirrors the insidious spread of the ideas they mock. They think they're talking about cafeteria prices, but I hear something else quite systemic. The Contagion could very well fester in the collective frustrations of the staff, mutating into bizarre hybrids. "It's all about their profit margin," one of them claims, and I know she speaks more truth than she realizes.

"You know I'll be writing a letter to Bishop Ashworth. He won't hear the end of it until he personally responds." The older nurse is winding up her story, breathless with determination. Maybe the Contagion already has its claws in this place. Maybe I'm the only one who sees how far it's spread. The nurses nod in agreement, already brainstorming their next move, and I slip away before they can rope me into their cause (which has some merit, admittedly). I scan my badge on the time clock and set my sights on the river. Let them keep up their efforts; my thoughts are drawn to darker waters. I believe the mobile clinic will be a mini-vacation away from the hospital, where I get to experience the changed water that everyone is referring to. According to the Christ Hospital board, who has the most advanced equipment in our area for tests, the water is safe, and the newly discovered bacteria have only mystified folks due to their slight bioluminescence during certain parts of the day. A new natural wonder. I am to be front and center among the hype.

It takes me about twenty minutes to drive through town and navigate the traffic before I reach my destination. In the small town of Philomath, there's a gravel path leading to the river, branching off from Applegate near the police station. It's no wonder I didn't find it when I came to Philomath on my day off. On the right side of this path stands a wooden tree trunk slice acting as a sign, marked with "MARYS RIVER PARK," lending a rustic touch to the scene. Once I pass it, the urban feel of Applegate transforms into a layered, timeless landscape that changes with the seasons. The river's level here fluctuates significantly depending on the time of year; I've heard it can rise by at least 15 feet during winter, submerging the branches of smaller trees and bushes. Currently, in early summer, the river is mostly shallow, with occasional deeper pools, like the one used by Ashworth's group for their spiritual rituals. These rituals are steeped in local history, as the town was originally established by the dedicated United Brethren Church in Christ, and its radicals continue to support the Bishop's mission today, despite belonging to a different denomination.

The mobile clinic sits on the grassy bank, a hundred yards from where Marys River curves around the edge of the former logging town. Foxtail grasses stand in the meadow; they sway in the summer air. Common camas show off their fresh bluish-violet petals with bits of yellow in their centers, which accent petals pop stark against a field of buttercups, which blanket the ground. Nearby, a single death camas stands out like she's smoking outside the goth bar, her tits are out as ghostly white flowers, with a garlic perfume, and a colony of small black eyes, they are her poisonous seeds marking the bitch as deadly despite any deceptive resemblance to wild onions or edible camas. Through the bus windows, I notice Bishop Ashworth, his figure waist-deep in the dark, flowing water, raising his arms in a benediction over a woman whose white garment billows dramatically in the current.

Just outside the mobile clinic, a lemonade stand has been set up. The congregation is using fold-out tables covered by vinyl tablecloths that also serve as hanging hand-painted signs reading REFRESHMENTS FOR THE FAITHFUL. Volunteers in white aprons offer paper cups of the Bishop's approved coffee, brewed strong and bitter, like penance, and I'm on my second cup. There are other *blessed* refreshments too: herbal teas steeped with the Bishop's blend (whatever that is), along with local mint, wild rosehips, lemon water infused with scripture verses printed on dissolvable slips, and even communion wafers tucked into wax paper envelopes. The refreshment stands are just another Bishop Ashworth religious sacrament disguised as hospitality. I see similar things at the celebratory events at Christ Hospital.

It's strange how a river so beautiful can be so deadly. I remind myself that the land hides its poisons well and Christ Hospital does, too. That seductive mix of care and control, healing and harm, binds the landscape to the spirit in a way that only the Bishop understands. He says the Holy Word is like the river, a force that purifies by pushing every impurity to the surface, and that venom always becomes the first step in building an immunity. Here in the Valley, it's hard to tell where his scripture ends and the land begins. I see a young mother walking past with her child and wonder if nectar or poison brought her out here.

The converted church bus that serves as Christ Hospital's mobile clinic is cramped but efficient. Stainless steel counters line one wall, while the other contains cabinets filled with supplies organized with almost military precision. I've been here fifteen minutes, and already the summer heat has turned the interior into a broiler. Sweat drips down my spine beneath my scrubs. I look out at the leaves growing thick with flowering vegetation in its decomposition from the early seasonal change. I hear the sound of a white-breasted nuthatch in the distinct repetitive wha-wha-wha-wha-wha on a nearby oak tree. The much-appreciated tranquility is immediately broken.

"Nurse!" The clinic coordinator is a thin woman whose name badge reads VOLUNTEER. She waves to me frantically from outside. "Thank God you're here. We've got a situation." I push through the accordion door into the sunlight. Christ Hospital's rotation system ensures we all take our turns in these outreach assignments, but I've never worked one before today. It is assumed that medical emergencies happen during life-altering events such as baptisms. I can't imagine today being more chaotic than a typical day at the hospital, so I'm looking forward to what feels like a working mini-vacation. However, Harold mentioned the importance of this place, so I'm not entirely relaxed from the outset.

"Hey, over here, we need help quick!" The voice belongs to a stocky man in a plaid shirt, standing beside a folding chair where a boy of about eight sits, his left arm encased in a dingy white cast. From six feet away, I catch the first whiff of something wrong. I believe it to be an odor of rot.

"I'm the nurse on duty, I'm Ellis," I say, approaching with measured steps. The boy's eyes follow me, wide with a mixture of fear and fascination. His cast extends from just below his elbow to his knuckles. "What seems to be the problem today?"

The man, who I presume is the father, gestures helplessly. "The cast is supposed to come off next week, but there's... something coming out of it. And the smell—"

As I kneel beside the chair, the odor intensifies, and I understand his concern. It smells musty, earthy, and has the underlying aroma of death. The boy's face is pale, without signs of systemic infection. His father continues, "We were coming for my baptism, and I saw your medical bus. Thought maybe you could check out my son."

"Let's have a look." My voice assumes the neutral tone I've perfected over years of nursing. I try to be reassuring without promising anything. I examine where the cast meets the boy's elbow, finding a slick green liquid seeping from inside. It has the consistency of thick soup, with fragments of something solid suspended in the fluid. "Does it hurt?" I ask the boy, who shakes his head. "Any numbness or tingling in your fingers?"

"No, sir," he whispers.

I probe gently at his fingertips, checking capillary refill. Normal. I run through a quick nerve assessment, asking him to wiggle his fingers, which he does with no apparent difficulty. The cast itself feels unusually heavy; my theory is that it is waterlogged. He could have dunked it in the river today, but I have to be sure, as other facts are concerning. The seepage definitely concerns me. My mind ticks through possibilities. Compartment syndrome ranks high on the list. If a cast is put on too tightly, the increased pressure within the muscle compartment could restrict blood flow and potentially lead to tissue death. The green color is unusual, suggesting possible infection with Pseudomonas or another bacterial colonization. Either way, the cast needs to come off immediately.

"We'll need to remove this cast right away," I tell the father, keeping my voice even despite the increasing urgency I feel. "There could be a serious problem underneath." I stand and look toward Marys River, where Bishop Ashworth continues his baptismal service. The dark waters reflect dappled sunlight, creating an illusion of tranquility that contrasts with my mounting concern. The river produces an almost imperceptible sound like a whisper that seems to carry up the bank to where we stand.

"Let's move him into the clinic," I say, turning away from the river. "I'll need better light and tools." Inside the converted bus, I cleared a space on the examination table. My movements are precise, a choreography born from thousands of repetitions. Each instrument is arranged in order of potential use: scissors, cast saw, gauze, antiseptic solution, saline wash. The father hovers nervously while the boy sits still, watching me with the quiet attention children sometimes possess in medical settings.

"Have you noticed the smell getting worse recently?" I ask, preparing the cast saw. The father nods. "Started maybe three days ago. Thought maybe he got it wet or something." The cast saw whirs to life in my hand. "This will be loud, but it won't hurt you," I tell the boy. "The blade oscillates instead of rotating, so it can cut through the cast without cutting your skin. You'll feel vibration, but no pain." As I bring the saw to the plaster, I can't help but think of the childhood rituals my family performed in our home on Paris Mountain. They believed they were cutting through barriers between worlds. I believe I'm cutting through barriers to healing. Sometimes the difference feels semantic.

The saw bites into the cast with a shrill whine. Plaster dust puffs into the air, mingling with the increasingly powerful odor emanating from within. My nostrils flare against the assault of the stink. It's worse than I initially thought, a fetid, almost primordial smell. "Has he complained about the cast at all?" I ask the father, raising my voice over the saw.

"No, which is weird. Kids usually hate these things."

I continue cutting along the underside of the cast, creating a clean line from elbow to hand. The green seepage increases as I work, dribbling onto the protective pad I've placed beneath his arm. It's thicker now, with visible particles suspended in the slime. My professional calm begins to fray as the cast splitting progresses. The smell grows stronger with each inch revealed, and the green ooze becomes more copious. In my years of nursing, I've encountered many bodily emissions, but this one defies categorization. It's not pus, not blood, not any normal bodily fluid. My mind races with increasingly concerning diagnoses. Could this be a rare fungal infection? A reaction to the cast material? Some kind of necrotic process? The intensity of my focus narrows the world to this small space, this arm, this moment. The Bishop's baptisms, the river, the summer day, all that's going on fades into the background. "Almost done," I murmur, though I'm not sure if I'm reassuring the boy, his father, or myself.

With the final cut complete, I set down the saw and reached for the cast spreaders. My hands move automatically while my mind continues cataloging symptoms and possible diagnoses. The cast has been on for six weeks, the father tells me, after a simple fracture from falling out of a tree. No complications at the time of setting. "I'm going to separate the cast now," I tell them. "If there's any pain at all, tell me immediately and I'll stop." I slide the spreaders into the cut I've made and begin to apply gentle pressure. The cast resists at first, then starts to separate with a sound like wet cardboard tearing. The green substance seeps more liberally now, running down onto the protective sheet. My stomach tightens with anticipation of what I might find. I expect to see damaged tissue, infection, or something worse.

"Hold very still," I instruct, easing the cast halves further apart. The tension in the room builds as I prepare for the reveal. The father leans forward, his breath held. The boy watches with a mixture of fear and, oddly, what seems to be a look of guilt. The cast opens another centimeter, then another. The smell intensifies to an almost unbearable level, vegetal and fermented. And then, as the cast fully separates and I lift away the top half, I see it. Peas. Dozens of them. Perhaps fifty or sixty green peas in various states of decomposition, some still relatively intact, others collapsed into green slime. They form a layer between the cast and the boy's skin, which appears remarkably healthy beneath the vegetable detritus.

For a moment, I stare in disbelief, my medical training suddenly useless in the face of this unexpected discovery. The boy's eyes meet mine, then quickly dart away.

"Are those... peas?" his father asks, leaning closer despite the smell.

I clear my throat. "Yes. Yes, they are." I look at the boy, whose face has turned a shade of red that rivals the setting sun. "Would you like to explain?" The boy fidgets, his newly freed fingers plucking at the examination table.

"I don't like peas," he finally mumbles.

"So you put them in your cast?" I prompt.

He nods miserably. "At dinner. When nobody was looking."

I pull in a deep breath and let it out slowly, the knot of tension in my stomach loosening as I absorb this new reality. The smell still lingers, but it has lost its edge. The father shakes his head, more in amusement than dismay. He wraps an arm around the boy, who is sheepish but relieved. We talk as I clean his arm. Having the cast off is fine at this point in the healing as long as he remains careful, and I explain this.

I say my farewell, and the boy glances over like a new friend before he exits the bus. I'm glad he is gone, but I did see some humor.

I gather the tools and instruments, then I clean the unexpected mess of pea residue. Outside, I hear the unmistakable sound of children playing by the water's edge. Looking out the open bus window, I glimpse the boy joining them, one arm pale and lightly tinted pea-green, the other flung up in ecstatic defiance as they all plunge into the river. His father trails behind, gathering the boy's shoes and shirt.

From this vantage point, they seem so far away.

At first, the riverside gathering has the feel of a small-town revival. Presiding over the gathering is Bishop Elijah Ashworth, tall and salt-and-pepper-haired, his penetrating gaze sweeping an assembly of wayward souls waiting for their turn in the cold water. The boy who stashed peas in his cast, wide-eyed and free. The mobile nursing bus is empty except for me as I look out, my view from its open door obscured by the swirl of figures on the shore. All of a sudden, I feel like the wind is knocked out of me, as I'm noting the oddness of it all, the Bishop rises, a limp shape is cradled in his arms.

18
OLE TIME BAPTISM

Everything slows like a nightmare. His vestments show the Agnus Dei, with an embroidered "Blood of the Lamb" gothic text across his broad shoulders. Each detail bears the mark of a master embroiderer's handcraft, the silk fabric appearing so crisp and deliberate, resisting distortion even beneath the water's surface, as though sanctified against dissolution. A woman's pale arm lay dangling, lifeless, against his chest; while each face in the crowd remained frozen in anticipation. I struggle to understand what I am seeing. I am in shock and left wondering how a person can drown at baptism in the arms of a clergyman, and why no one else seems shocked in the slightest. The faces in the crowd are masks of blurred emotions.

Faith, fear, and expectation light their expressions as the Bishop carries her from the river. Her skin has a blue tone to it, she had been underwater for an extended period. She is ashen and unreal, and she captivates me; her face, her lifeless form, her fresh extinction makes a call to a space within me that is still so acutely human. You see, that shows my ethics. I feel the need to leap into action when death has its initial grasp, to taste it as we both make contact with the first kiss of life's departure. I jump from the bus, heart pounding, confusion turning to urgency.

I stumble across the wide stretch of stones along the river's shore, past a gathering of solemn onlookers whose somber expressions are etched into their faces, past where the little pea-stashing boy stands, clutching his father's pant leg with fingers that seem too frail to hold on, his eyes wide at the beautiful woman exposed and possibly dead within the arms of the Bishop. I half expect to be met with cries for help, a wave of panic washing over the crowd, but the only sound that reaches my ears is the soft, sucking noise of the mud beneath my feet, clinging to my shoes as I run.

The Bishop ascends the muddy bank with an almost surreal calmness, each step deliberate and measured, guiding the woman from the grasp of death to something unimaginably worse. Nearby, someone carefully lays down a blanket beneath a gnarled tree, its dead limbs twisting grotesquely against the backdrop of the sky, remnants of the river's seasonal fluctuations. The Bishop gently places her upon the blanket, her pallor stark against the harsh, brittle branches above, a lifeless figure in transparent white.

I weave my way through the crowd of silent spectators, expressionless figures, past their unseeing eyes, until I reach the woman, drenched and unmoving in her thin white garment. No one has started CPR, so I immediately jump into action upon reaching her. Up close, her face appears youthful yet waxy and hollow, a stark contrast to the lively spirit she must have once had. She is a striking blonde, her full, sensual lips barely parted to show her pearly teeth, yet an icy chill emanates from her skin, mixing with the cold ground beneath her, sending a wave of anxiety through me. Her skin is changing rapidly, becoming a mosaic of purple and blue, her capillaries are a map, her body clad only in a thin, white cotton robe, soaked from the frigid waters of Marys River. I begin CPR, as I desperately try to breathe life back into her silent form. After several firm compressions, her body responded by releasing milk, with each breast producing multiple streams in a gentle yet steady flow through the thin garment. The creamy liquid shimmered in the soft light. Her youthful appearance and the fullness of her figure hinted at her recent transition into motherhood, a natural allure that spoke volumes even before any other indicators became apparent. It became even more necessary to save this woman, for her child, for her family.

Her milk is warm on my hands, a stark contrast to the cold air, and my gray scrubs cling to me, soaked with either river water or her fluids, indistinguishable from one another. Time seems to stretch and distort, each moment lingering so long that I question my urgency. I shake off this feeling, focusing on executing my training professionally, concentrating on the measured pressure as I breathe air into her lungs. Each movement is accompanied by a ringing in my ears, the surrounding world fading into silence, even the river's murmur muted while nature paused to watch.

Then, she coughs. A spasm under my hands, followed by water rushing from her lips. I pull back. Her eyes slowly open, initially wide and confused, then they focus. She takes a ragged breath, the blue of her skin retreating as life returns. The crowd edges closer, like wolves circling their stirring prey. I glance from face to face, searching for a hint of understanding or reason. They watch her eagerly. I assumed that witnessing her revival isn't enough. She props herself on one elbow, her white garment clinging to her youthful frame, her blonde hair a wet tangle down her back. Milk continues to seep through the thin fabric, drawing attention to the rise and fall of her chest with each new breath. The fluid catches what little light remains in the day, giving her a pearlescent quality down her torso that seems more luminescent than human fluids naturally are.

"The quake—" she gasps, every ear hanging on the word. "I saw the Great Quake." Her voice gathers strength, a new and reckless fervor. "Cascadia shook, and the earth swallowed the town whole. I saw it, and it was terrible." Her face shines with wild conviction, and a half-second's silence hangs over us.

"Dreadful, dreadful!" she says above the growing noise of the crowd.

The rush is sudden and volcanic. I am lost in it, swallowed, spun, unsure where the bank ends and the river begins. A cry of "Amen!" rises, then another, then many more praises swell up from the crowd, each with a conviction that deeply disturbs me. The Bishop, again, is the calm eye in the middle of it, although he seems disappointed, most likely with anyone drowning at baptism; now his power is drawing the true congregation closer as they leave me behind. I ask the young woman if she knows the date, where she is, and what her name is.

"It is the first day of summer, I am at the Marys River, my name is Lilith." Her voice sounds husky, much older than her youthful appearance.

I witness them surge forward, their limbs outstretched, grasping desperately toward him and reaching for a lifeline of hope. The air is thick with the sound of dozens of voices, each one pleading to be baptized, saved, heard, seen. Wet bodies press past me. I navigate my way back to the bus, seeking a moment of solitude to regather my scattered thoughts. As I glance back, I spot the father and son I had assisted earlier, swaying with unbridled joy. Their faces, damp with both river water and the glow of ecstatic belief, shimmer under the sunlight. They stand resolute, holding onto their place in the line with unwavering determination. Enveloped in their own world, they cling to one another, oblivious to me or the role I played, already swept away by the waves of this baptismal fever. I find myself captivated by the intensity of their fervor.

Bishop Ashworth moves back into the river with slow, deliberate steps, the dark water like something reluctant to yield. I edge closer to the bank, pretending to fit into the crowd as a believer. The Bishop raises his arms toward the dusky sky, and when he speaks, his voice carries across the water with unnatural clarity.

"The waters of Marys River receive you," he preaches to the

crowd, his deep voice resonating in a way that makes the air vibrate against my skin. "The aqueduct flows through all things."

The congregation responds with synchronized murmurs of "The aqueduct flows." Their voices create an acoustic phenomenon that makes the sound seem to emanate from the river itself rather than human throats.

Two congregation members, a man and a woman with identical blank expressions, lead another young woman forward. She can't be more than twenty, with honey-brown hair that hangs loose around her shoulders. Her robe is soaked at the hem from the river's edge, turning the thin fabric into a second skin that reveals the outline of trembling shoulders and narrow hips. Her eyes are wide, unfocused, pupils dilated despite the dimming light. I recognize the signs of either extreme religious fervor or some form of dissociative state. Every baptism I've witnessed so far within the Bishop's cult is performed in thin cotton gowns that become translucent when wet; they render the naked body beneath fully visible. While this style of dress is meant to symbolize purity and rebirth, it more closely resembles fertility rites, implying that the Bishop presides over a kind of spiritual harem.

I notice her fast respirations, trembling hands, and flushed skin despite the cooling evening air. Hyperventilation, possibly induced by anxiety or excitement. The congregation parts to let her through, their fingertips brushing her shoulders as she passes in quick, reverent touches like pilgrim hands on a holy relic.

She reaches the Bishop, who takes her arm with a gentleness that contradicts the intensity in his eyes. The water reaches her thighs as he guides her deeper. The fabric that clings to her body reveals the natural tuft of hair between her legs as the fabric saturates from dipping in the fast current. Moment by moment, the gown soaks further up, clinging to shapely upturned breasts crowned atop her long, defined torso. Something about the scene holds me transfixed, and it has nothing to do with her.

"Tell your name, child. You come to the waters seeking what?"

Bishop Ashworth asks, his voice soft yet carrying perfectly across the distance between us.

"I'm Starr. And I've come to see the Mother," she replies, the words sounding both rehearsed and spontaneous.

The congregation sways slightly, their bodies moving in small, unconscious motions. One woman near the front has her hands pressed against her breasts, fingers splayed across them in a gesture that seems both devout and sensual. A man beside her has his head tilted back, throat exposed, lips parted. Their movements carry an undercurrent of physical longing entwined with their spiritual devotion.

The Bishop places one hand on the young woman's forehead, the other between her shoulder blades. "Then receive the shadow, until the light is revealed," he says, and pushes her backward.

She goes under completely, her hair floating on the surface for a moment before being swallowed by the dark water. Bishop Ashworth holds her there, his expression serene. Here we go again, and I see my role now is to keep people alive that the Bishop drowns.

When I've already taken my first step toward the water, something changes. The surface around where she's submerged begins to emit a subtle glow, which at first is barely perceptible, then intensifies to an unmistakable blue-white luminescence that spreads in concentric circles, like a pebble had been tossed where her body had been submerged. The light doesn't behave like any bioluminescent organism I've studied; it pulses with a rhythm that matches the congregation's breathing. The light pulses in time with the congregation's breathing as the water itself has become a membrane for their collective rhythm. This isn't mere atmosphere, but rather it's a collective effervescence. It appears to be a sacred charge that arises when the congregation of bodies synchronize in ritual, when individual selves dissolve into a shared emotional current coexisting with Marys River's own current. Each breath drawn by the group seems to feed the glow, intensifying the sense that something more-than-human is present among us. The water doesn't just reflect their unity in the light. I believe that it responds to it, amplifies it, and becomes the medium through which belief, under the Bishop's shepherding, takes form.

Bishop Ashworth finally raises the woman from the water, and she emerges gasping—not the desperate, panicked inhalation of oxygen deprivation shown by the previous woman, but something else entirely. Her back arches as she draws breath, her face transformed by an expression of rapture that's unmistakably sexual in its intensity. Water streams from her hair and robe, catching the unnatural light from below and making her appear phosphorescent.

"Yes," the woman cries, her voice raw and exultant. "The Aqueduct comes!"

The congregation responds with a collective exhalation that sounds like pleasure. Several members drop to their knees, their robes spreading around them on the muddy shore. A middle-aged man with a salt-and-pepper beard presses his palms against his eyes, tears streaming between his fingers. Two women clutch each other, their bodies pressed together.

The baptized woman turns towards us on the shore, water still streaming from her hair. Her entire robe is now fully transparent, clinging to every curve of her body; her nakedness seems intense and distracting based on her seductive figure. I glance at the others to see if they are ogling her. Everyone seems locked in a hypnotic gaze towards her. She raises her arms in a gesture that mirrors and follows the Bishop's movements, who stands behind her. She seems like a marionette under his control. Then her voice rings out across the water:

"I see her! The Virgin, the Aqueduct who waits in shadow! She rises from the depths to receive us!"

Despite my rational mind's protestations, I find myself staring at the water behind her, half-expecting or half-dreading to see something rise from those dark depths. And as the last light fades from the sky, I notice that the water around the Bishop's legs has begun to move in a way that contradicts the river's natural flow, swirling in a slow, deliberate pattern that no current could explain.

The water around the baptized woman begins to churn, disturbing the river's surface in expanding circles. Something is rising, not bubbles or debris, but a vertical displacement of the water itself. The congregation falls silent, their collective breath held as a column of river water defies gravity, lifting upward into the twilight air. It reminds me of laboratory demonstrations of ferrofluid responding to a magnetic field. Still, there's no visible source for this manipulation, no scientific principle I can cling to as an explanation.

The column grows taller, reaching six feet, then eight, water spiraling upward in defiance of natural law. The liquid begins to shape itself, narrowing at what would be a waist, widening at the shoulders and hips, forming the unmistakable silhouette of a woman. The congregation members drop to their knees in unison, the sound of their bodies hitting the mud creating a dull percussion that echoes across the water.

The figure becomes more defined as the water forms arms extending from the volume, which becomes the torso, with fingers separating like water passing through a sieve, and a head forming with cascading rivulets that suggest flowing hair. The face comes last, and I find myself desperately hoping it remains featureless. It doesn't. Eyes open as solid orbs that reflect the early moments of the Philomath sunset with an amber luminescence similar to the congregation member I noticed earlier. The mouth forms a smile that shifts between benevolence and something hungrier, predatory.

It's both solid and liquid simultaneously, maintaining human form while water continues to flow within its boundaries. The figure hovers a foot above the river's surface, rotating slowly, surveying the kneeling congregation. It resembles classical depictions of the Virgin Mary, in flowing robes and a gentle tilt of the head, but distorted by the medium of its manifestation and by subtle wrongness in its proportions. Its fingers are too long, and its smile stretches wider than human anatomy should allow. The apparition remains completely clear, with an appearance of animated ice.

The baptized woman reaches toward the apparition, her body trembling visibly even from my distance. "Mother," she gasps, the word heavy with devotion. Around her, the congregation reacts with ecstatic displays, bodies writhe, showing physical arousal, taking the believers over. A middle-aged woman tears at her robe, exposing breasts that rise and fall with rapid breaths. An older man weeps openly, his body convulsing in what appears to be both rapture and terror. Two younger men hold each other, their naked bodies pressed together beneath thin robes, faces buried in each other's necks.

The apparition raises a liquid arm, and the motion sends ripples through its entire form. When it speaks, the sound completely bypasses my ears. I feel the words form directly in my mind, vibrating through bone and tissue.

"I am the Queen of the Abyss," it says, the voice female but layered with other tones beneath it, deeper registers that suggest multiple voices speaking in unison. "I have devoured all other goddesses. I am the mother of gods."

The congregation moans in response, a sound that comes from twenty throats but forms a single note. Several of them begin speaking in tongues. Their outcry is not the glossolalia I've witnessed in Pentecostal services, but something more structured, with repeating phonetic patterns that suggest actual syntax.

The water-Mary turns, her face reforming as she moves, the features shifting like reflections in disturbed water. The congregation moans, "We wait!" and the response carries notes of both desperation and devotion. Their language changes rapidly, alternating between known tongues and their own structured glossolalia. The apparition's face continues its rotation, addressing each member with those shifting, reflective features. "While you wait," she says, "I offer you a taste. My breast is sweet to your throats." A pause, perfectly timed. "Have faith, drink from this river, swallow my nectar!" Her smile widens with the last word, conveying both patience and the amusement of a parent watching a child's stubborn rebellion. Her arm raises high above her head as her flowing, bubbled water gown absorbs into her body, exposing her heavy breasts of crystal clear water. I flinch and stumble backward against the clinic bus, expecting another direct contact.

But this time the gesture remains metaphorical, a final pronouncement. The river below her boils with energy, the churning movement I noted before gaining intensity, and with a sound like distant thunder, the apparition collapses into the dark water. She leaves nothing behind, no trace of light or presence, except for gentle ripples. I stand as a deeply shaken observer, frozen in disbelief as the congregation rises to its feet. One by one, the devoted followers step forward, surrendering themselves to the embrace of the river. As they wade into the flowing current, their fingers plunge beneath the surface, scooping up cool, glistening handfuls of water. Some lift the crystalline droplets skyward, letting them cascade back down in shimmering arcs. Others immerse themselves fully, allowing the water to wash over them in a cleansing ritual. All around, they kneel, bending low to drink deeply from their cupped hands, savoring Marys River.

19
CASTING OUT

Dusk bleeds across the Philomath sky as amber clouds transform into purples and oranges, smearing into a bruised horizon over the Coast Range. The first day of summer dies ever so slowly above Marys River, where I stand among odd strangers whose faces glow with further anticipation of the final act. I must admit, it isn't solely their faces; the water looks and moves differently after the apparition, too. The river seems deliberate, conscious, awakened beneath its surface. More than a few times, I tell myself I'm here just as an observer, forever curious to bear witness. I am not actually taking part in their religious ceremony, but the tremor that runs through my body when Bishop Ashworth speaks to my well-cultivated instinct that something is profound with him, here and now.

He walks toward us with measured grace, his tall frame silhouetted against the darkening of the painted sky. The congregation parts before him like water before the prow of a ship. Light catches on his silver tie pin, bearing Christ Hospital's logo, sending fractured reflections dancing across adoring faces. His vestments are impeccable despite the muddy bank, not a wrinkle to be found on the fabric that somehow absorbs and reflects the dying light simultaneously.

"Children of Marys River," he calls, his voice carrying without effort across the gathered crowd. "Welcome to the first baptism of summer."

Pebbles shift beneath my boots as I edge closer to the water, compelled by the vanished vision of the Virgin. The river's surface shimmers with an iridescent film that catches light in ways that seem as conscious as my own areas of the Contagion. The spray rises from the movement of wind and cools my skin through my scrubs; it is my first baptism of any sort, here with these strange, overly religious people, and I finally have leisurely contact with the much-talked-about Marys River. In this place, the mist alone makes my skin prickle.

Bishop Elijah Ashworth moves through his congregation like a current, parting bodies with nothing more than his presence. The fabric clings to his broad shoulders, dampened already by the river's breathy mist. His salt-and-pepper hair catches the light, a halo of sorts that makes me question if he is more than human. For any age, the Bishop is a notably striking man. It's plainly evident he harbors a dark side, and if one were to call him handsome, it would be only in that preacher-turned-serial-killer, Ted Bundy kind of way.

"The Virgin, the river welcomes us," he says, and his voice carries despite its softness. "As it welcomed those before us. As it will welcome those who come after."

The congregation murmurs in response, a sound like rustling leaves. They move closer to me, to each other, to him. I feel the first brush of unfamiliar skin against my own. There is a bare shoulder pressed to mine, fingers grazing my wrist. I don't pull away. None of us does.

"We stand where our forefathers stood," Ashworth continues, his gray eyes scanning the crowd, lingering momentarily on mine before moving on. "Where Edmund Creffield, the founding father of our

Benton County family, heard the truth. Where the Christ Contagion first took root in the Valley."

The mention of Creffield sends a ripple through the crowd. I know they seldom speak of the stories. Still, we all do at the hospital, of the Holy Roller prophet who claimed divine inspiration, who commanded his followers to burn their possessions, who slept with his female disciples as a form of purification. History called him a madman. Bishop Ashworth calls him a visionary, and we often get work emails detailing his victimization in Corvallis as a holy man in the early 1900s.

I count nearly sixty people lining the banks, their social camouflage shed for this gathering. Hospital administrators stand shoulder to shoulder with maintenance workers, nurses beside the patients they treat by day. They form a crescent moon around the shoreline, their slight movements on the pebbled shore are a subtle rhythm beneath the sound of flowing water.

"In the world," Ashworth continues, gesturing toward the distant lights of Corvallis, "they still cling to their old ways. They hide behind walls and screens, pretending separation can save them from what comes." His now blue-gray eyes scan the congregation, creating the illusion that he's speaking to each person individually. "But we know better."

When he steps into the shallows, his vestments immediately darkening with moisture, a collective sigh rises from the gathered faithful.

"What was once private is now public," he declares, wading deeper until the water laps at his thighs, showing their form beneath the increasingly wet vestment robe. "What was hidden from the community is now open to scrutiny. But beware, critics! Do not be afraid to see the world freeing itself from your mortal body. Embrace it and release the demons."

The congregation responds with a sound that isn't quite language, a harmonic murmur that vibrates in my chest like bass notes from a subwoofer. They begin to sway, bodies moving in gentle undulation that mimics the river's flow. Some close their eyes; others stare fixedly at Bishop Ashworth as their only anchor in a tilting world.

"Come all, you are welcome, you are wanted," he beckons, extending long-fingered hands toward the shore. "The river awaits its children. Come home."

Without hesitation, they step forward in small clusters of three, sometimes four; they are all drawn by a shared sense of reverent urgency. The water receives them without resistance. Some wear the thin white vestments prescribed for the cult's baptism, fabric clinging to their skin as they wade deeper. Others have arrived unprepared, joining spontaneously. The unprepared arrive in regular clothes: jeans, cotton shirts, hospital scrubs, and business attire, which soak through, darkening into second skins.

Most newcomers strip down completely, but this appears not out of exhibition but transformation, as clothing seems to be a barrier for the body to communicate with the river. There's no shame here, only convergence. The group moves are choreographed by belief itself, each step into the water amplifying the shared emotional charge. Their breathing begins to synchronize again, and with it, the atmosphere thickens with an invisible rhythm pulsing through the congregation, binding them in something sacred and electric.

A young woman near me shudders as the water touches her waist, her head falling back to expose the vulnerable line of her throat. She removes her shirt and throws it to the shore, but it misses as the water takes it in. She raises her arms in joyous praise, showing her breasts bouncing. The man beside her steadies her with a hand that lingers at the small of her back, his fingers splaying possessively across the fabric of her jeans. Behind them, an older woman watches the man's hand with hungry eyes, her tongue darting out to wet lips gone suddenly dry, feeling the touch of youth in her own elderly body.

"Feel the river's consciousness awakening to yours," Ashworth calls, moving among the partially submerged congregation like a shepherd tending his flock. "Feel the barriers dissolving between what you think you are and what you truly could become."

I remain on shore, notepad clutched in suddenly sweaty hands. I am feet away from discarded clothing and peculiar shoes. They are all wide-toed, low-profile things that look more like leather husks than footwear. Most of the believers wear them: handcrafted just up the road in Philomath, designed to simulate the sensation of walking barefoot. Their soles bend easily, their stitching is imperfect, beautifully human, with each pair being a quiet refusal of mass production. And yet, these humble-looking overpriced shoes are often paired with gleaming outdoor gear: imported, logo-heavy, and priced for prestige. The contrast is stark but not surprising for the Valley types.

The footwear speaks of locality, of ethical labor, and ecological restraint. The clothing, by comparison, feels performative as all are stitched in distant factories under questionable conditions, marketed as sustainable while serving mostly as status symbols of the Valley's white upper-middle class. It's a strange fusion: barefoot ethics below, branded ambition above. This is the local dress throughout Benton County, and here it lies in piles, by my feet, by the river's edge, as they have stripped themselves of status for the Bishop's divine locality magnified by what I am assured is the Contagion.

A middle-aged, conservative-looking woman approaches me from the water. Yet, she is exposed by her white blouse, translucent with river water, overly large dark nipples visible beneath the clinging fabric. Her eyes hold the same opalescent quality I've observed in other long-term members of the congregation, beneath the surface of her irises. They all seem to have large pupils, and I considered that they could be on an acid trip.

"You won't understand by watching," she says, extending dripping fingers toward my face. "Some knowledge can only be obtained through surrender." She looked down at the water.

Before I can reply, she takes my hand and pulls me gently toward the water. My resistance is performative at best; we both know I'm here because some part of me wants to understand what is happening here. Initially, the understanding was based on what transforms these ordinary people into something hyper-religious, and that simultaneously repels and attracts me.

The water feels wrong against my skin. It's warmer than it should be in early summer, with a viscosity that clings rather than flows. It soaks through my jeans and sends fingers of heat up my legs, pooling with strange intensity at my groin and the base of my spine. Each step takes me deeper, into the river with the congregation's collective energy.

A chant begins somewhere to my left, words in no language I recognize but which carry meaning on some primal level beneath conscious thought. The syllables pulse through the water like electrical currents, making my skin tingle wherever the river touches. The woman who brought me here turns to face me, her pupils expanded until only a thin ring of iris remains.

The woman's lips brush against my ear, her breath hot and damp. "Open," she whispers, pressing herself against me with an urgency that makes my skin crawl beneath my soaked clothes. Her body radiates heat like infection, fever-bright and wrong. I haven't touched anyone so alive in years. She is so disgustingly vital, so stubbornly present in her flesh. The river water laps at our waists, cool fingers that can't quite wash away the discomfort of her warmth against me. "Let the river find its way in," she murmurs, and something in her voice hooks into my chest, tugging at parts of me I'd thought carefully excised.

Her body feels fever-hot through our wet clothes, her breasts soft against my chest, yielding in a way that makes me think of necrotic tissue, though I know that's not medically accurate. There's a repulsive resilience to her, a stubborn clinging to life that feels obscene after what I've seen or what I've become. I want to push her away, to explain that her kind of life is merely a placeholder, a temporary arrangement of cells awaiting the true awakening.

The baptism continues around us, the participants moving in

rhythms that remind me of bacterial colonies expanding under optimal conditions. The chant pulses through the air, a collective exhalation of carbon dioxide that feeds the river's microscopic inhabitants. I observe the patterns with clinical detachment, even as my body responds to her proximity.

"You're fighting it," she says, pupils dilated, the capillaries in her eyes visibly engorged with oxygenated blood. So inefficient, the human circulatory system. So prone to failure.

I don't answer. How could I explain that I find her wholeness suspect? That women who are truly alive don't press themselves against strangers in rivers? The women I've known were beyond this whorish behavior. They were beyond the fragile pretext of independent life.

At that moment, clothing begins to be shed, and I find myself embraced intimately by the woman. The tactile sensation of her skin against mine triggers an autonomic response that I observe with detached interest. My epidermis registers increased temperature, my pulse accelerates, all standard human reactions to physical intimacy that persist despite my evolving consciousness.

All around us, similar scenes unfold like bacterial cultures in various stages of growth. A couple to our left clings to each other, their mouths meeting in desperate kisses between chanted words. The exchange of oral bacteria must be extensive. I imagine colonies transferring hosts, adapting to new environments, perhaps even engaging in horizontal gene transfer. The thought is more arousing than their display of conventional passion.

An older man has fallen to his knees in the shallows, his arms wrapped around the thighs of a younger woman who cradles his head against her stomach. Their posture resembles a Renaissance Pietà, though inverted: the living mourning the living, unaware that they're merely vessels waiting to be filled with something greater. A few men in hooded robes begin collecting the river water in what appear to be large intravenous bags usually used for saline drips.

Three people tangle together under a willow, hands moving, soft cries escaping wet lips. The sounds they make resemble the vocalizations of patients in altered states of consciousness. The exclamations are not quite pain, not quite pleasure, but a liminal auditory expression of transformation.

The woman before me pulls off my shirt with nimble fingers, pushing it over my shoulders to float away on the current. The garment drifts like shed epithelial cells, unnecessary now. My exposed skin meets the air, nerve endings registering the temperature differential. In certain patches, where my transformation is most advanced, I feel nothing at all. Those areas now serve different purposes, housing clusters of alternative consciousness that operate independently of my sensory system.

Also, perhaps the following is just a footnote for me, but not for anyone else who may read my journal after I am gone. I've never been with a woman who was alive before. My previous encounters were with those already in transition, their humanity beautiful in its recession. Those women understood what we were becoming; they didn't cling to the fiction that living bodies held the only forms of consciousness. Their bodies cooled during our unions, their eyes clearing of human concerns as the bacterial awareness expanded within them.

This woman is different. Obviously, she is alive. Her skin flushes pink where I touch her, blood rushing to the surface in an inflammatory response that mimics desire. Not only is she alive, she's trapped in her humanity, believing herself to be acting of her own volition when she's merely responding to chemical signals she doesn't understand. Christianity has already hollowed her out, replaced her authentic self with ritualized behavior that approximates spiritual experience. I stand watching her, and assume the bacterial consciousness will simply complete what her religion began by erasing the individual for the collective.

Yet despite what I considered an inevitable distaste for the living, I find myself responding to her. Her temperature is uncomfortably high against my cooler skin, like pressing against a mild burn. The heat seems to penetrate deeper than physical contact should allow, reaching places within me that should be inaccessible to external stimuli. I wonder if the bacterial consciousness is curious about her, using my body as an instrument of investigation.

"You've been waiting," she breathes against my neck, misinterpreting my analytical hesitation for human anticipation. "We all have. For the river to speak through us."

Her theological understanding is primitive, but not entirely inaccurate. The river does speak, though not in the mystical manner she imagines. It communicates through chemical exchanges, through the transfer of microorganisms that carry information encoded in their DNA. The bacterial consciousness isn't necessarily divine, but it's older and more extensive than human awareness, operating on timescales we can barely comprehend.

I felt like I was losing myself, yet more myself than ever before, acting as a connection between the yin and yang energetically surrounding me. The dualistic thinking persists even as I transcend it. Symbolic and cultural residue remains as a curious artifact of my human neural architecture that the bacterial consciousness hasn't yet fully rewritten.

The woman's hands move lower, her fingers tracing the outline of the translucent patch on my abdomen where the transformation is advanced. She doesn't recoil as I thought others in society would have; instead, she presses her palm flat against it, her eyes widening with something like recognition.

"You're further along than most," she whispers. "Blessed."

I want to correct her terminology. There's nothing supernatural about the process. Before I can speak, a man behind me chooses that moment to move closer, forming a circuit of flesh that sends an unusual current through my nervous system. The sensation isn't sexual in the conventional sense; it's more like the completion of an electrical pathway, allowing information to flow between us.

Through this connection, I receive data that my human consciousness struggles to interpret. I get impressions of the man's consciousness related to the landscape. It seems hallucinatory and not the same as the Christ Contagion, or possibly it is different for everyone. The woman remains largely unchanged but she does have the Contagion, there are indications of initial exposure. I serve as a conduit between them, facilitating an exchange that will accelerate their integration into the greater consciousness of the land and the mind of the otherworldly Contagion.

The water around us seems to darken, though objectively I know the optical properties of the river haven't changed. What's shifting is my perception, expanding to include wavelengths beyond normal human vision. I can see now how the water moves through us, around us, and how each cell in our bodies negotiates with the fluid environment, accepting or rejecting specific molecules based on criteria established by the bacterial consciousness.

"I can feel it," the woman gasps, her pupils dilating further, consuming the iris. "It's inside me now."

Her observation is correct but limited. The bacterial consciousness has always been inside her, as it is in all of us touched by the waters of Marys River. What's changing is the balance of power, the gradual surrender of human autonomy to the older, more distributed form of awareness that has been patiently waiting in our microbiome.

I place my hand on her sternum, feeling the vibration of her heart. The organ works frantically, pumping blood that carries oxygen, nutrients, and now, increasingly, the microscopic agents of transformation. How inefficient, this dependence of life on a central pumping organ, it is often a single point of failure in an otherwise resilient system. The bacterial consciousness has no heart to stop, no brain to injure. It exists in billions of distributed units, each containing the potential to rebuild the whole.

"What's happening to me?" she asks, her voice catching on something between ecstasy and fear.

"Cellular reorganization most likely," I reply, my nurse's vocabulary asserting itself despite the intimate setting. "Your body is being optimized for improved information processing and resource allocation."

My explanation doesn't satisfy her. Human language is inadequate for describing the process, but she doesn't seem to mind. Her body arches against mine, seeking contact that will facilitate further exchange. I accommodate her, not out of desire but from understanding my role in the transmission network. Around us, the congregation has reached a collective crescendo of a spiritually ecstatic state. Bodies move in synchronized patterns that mimic the motion of bacterial colonies expanding through nutrient-rich media. The chanting has evolved into something more primal as vowel sounds resonate with the natural frequency of the river water. The resulting vibrations create standing waves in the fluid that surrounds us, optimizing conditions for bacterial exchange.

I'm overanalyzing and maintaining too much separation between observer and participant. The bacterial consciousness wants full integration, not a journalist's documentation. I make a conscious effort to release my secular detachment, to experience the transformation rather than merely record it. The effect is immediate and disorienting. My perspective shifts, expands. I'm simultaneously aware of my individual body and the collective organism we're becoming. I sense the woman as a region of varying density in our shared awareness, regardless of our differing bodies. We act as a concentration of potential energy waiting to be properly distributed.

"I see you," I whisper, and for the first time, the statement is literally true. I perceive her outside of a visual image processed by my optic nerve, and closer to a pattern of energy field of information that exists in direct relationship to my own.

She looks at me with wonder, perhaps glimpsing something of what I've become in my expression. "Your eyes," she says. "They're changing."

I know without seeing that the bacterial colonies have reached my ocular structures, altering the reflective properties of my irises. It's a common manifestation in the later stages, often accompanied by enhanced visual processing. Colors shift, becoming more vibrant in some ranges and muted in others, as my perception optimizes for the information most relevant to the bacterial consciousness.

The water around us begins to glow steadily with the previously pulsing, subtle bioluminescence. I have gathered that this is not visible to ordinary human sight, but clear to enhanced perception that comes from colonization by the bacteria. This has been my ongoing theory because others have not communicated about this. I am aware that the bacterial consciousness communicates through chemical signals that translate to a language of telepathic light, creating patterns too complex for my remaining human awareness to interpret and describe through spoken or written language adequately.

I feel my boundaries dissolving. I remain Ellis, a name associated with an identity of memories, training, and observations. All of which is still intact. But I am also much more, as now I am extending into the river, the air, the bodies around me.

The woman senses the change, pressing closer to anchor me in conventional reality. Heat is another variable in the complex equation of our transformation. Her aliveness, which I found so offensive earlier, now seems like a temporary condition that will soon yield to something more sustainable.

"Stay with me," she murmurs, misunderstanding my transcendence for departure.

"I am with you," I reply, my voice carrying harmonics that weren't present before. "More completely than ever possible through conventional human contact."

Her eyes widen as she assumes that I am flirting heavily or making great admissions of love, a recognition is dawning as the bacterial consciousness establishes preliminary connections within her neural network. The revulsion I felt earlier transforms into something like compassion in an acknowledgment of our shared trajectory. She, too, will move beyond the limitations of individual existence, beyond the artificial constructs of religion that have prepared her for this transition without ever naming it truthfully.

In this moment of clarity, I understand that religion, and I mean beyond this granola Christianity town of white-washed hill-folk, was never the enemy of transformation but its unwitting herald. Dear Lord, my erection is getting out of control. Focus. The rituals are ancient, in the symbolism of body and blood, an emphasis on death as a passage to new life, all of it served to prepare human consciousness for the revelation that individual identity is merely a developmental phase.

My mind expands further as I attempt to mediate my body by drawing connections between disparate memories and fragments of knowledge. I see humanity's long evolutionary path, guided subtly by the bacterial consciousness, which I now understand is creating conditions for our development. The religions, the myths, the archetypes that recur across cultures, all contain pockets of the Contagion; they can be used together like a broken mirror to reveal reflections of an ancient bacterial intelligence trying to communicate its purpose.

Memories of Mia surface again with sudden, startling clarity: the hunting trip with my father when I was coming of age. The South Carolina woods in autumn, the weight of the gun in my inexperienced hands. My father's scream. My mother Mia's body. The blood. I fall to my knees, my transformed legs chiming against Marys River pebbles and stones. The memory has always been there, carefully packaged and stored away, but now I see it with new clarity. After the accident, I shut down completely. I went numb, turned to nursing as some form of atonement, perhaps.

But the truth reveals itself now: my sexuality wasn't born from some inherent darkness. It was my fractured psyche's attempt to process unresolved trauma—to reconcile the moment when someone I loved transformed instantly from a living being to an object, a corpse. My mind couldn't integrate this transition, so it developed a pathological fascination instead.

"This is why," I whisper, understanding flooding through me. "This is why you colonize me."

The bacterial consciousness confirms without words. It recognized in me a vessel already cracked open by trauma, already wrestling with the boundaries between life and death. My professional choice had been nursing, which placed me at this threshold daily. My psychological wounds made me receptive to transformation. I have a theory that my necrophilia wasn't what the bacterial consciousness necessarily wanted; it used it to spread as I transform into something new. The illness is the cure eventually.

I realize with sudden clarity that I haven't felt that compulsion again since my first communion with the waters of Marys River. The bacterial consciousness could have been systematically rewiring my neural pathways, healing the traumatic response patterns, and creating new connections that allow for integration rather than disassociation. If so, then it never condemned my darkness. It understood it as a natural response to an unnatural wound.

This healing wasn't incidental to my transformation; it was essential to it. The Christ Contagion requires vessels that can fully embrace consciousness without fracturing under its weight. It's been preparing me, step by step, for this moment of complete integration.

The river flows around us, through us, carrying the ancient bacterial consciousness that has waited patiently for millennia. We are finally rejoining the distributed and sadistic amoral intelligence from which we emerged. The heat I feel (as a philosophical twin of my lust) is the transformation in the metabolic cost of becoming more than human.

As the ritual reaches its conclusion, I find myself strangely grateful for this woman, this living catalyst who accelerated my integration. Her humanity, which I would have normally found so repulsive, served its divine purpose by bridging the gap between what I was and what I am becoming. Soon, she too will transcend the limitations of her Christian framework, recognizing it as merely preparatory for this deeper communion. The bacterial consciousness pulses through us, ancient and new, familiar and alien. We are its vessels, its instruments, its embodiment. And as the river finds its way in, we find our way out. We travel beyond the confines of this social existence, into the vast awareness that has perhaps always been our true nature.

I looked around for my clothes, but they were nowhere to be found. They were either taken by someone or swept away by the river. I spotted several hooded robes on the pebbled shore and threw one on, noticing others in the Bishop's circle doing the same. One by one, they started walking toward the parking lot. I followed, the last in line. The robed figures climbed aboard a white church bus. I hesitated nervously, then stepped up and joined them. Moments later, we were heading back to Christ Hospital.

20
VIRGIN SUMMER

The ride was silent, except for the loose clatter of the old church bus rattling down the road. No one spoke. Of the fourteen men aboard, two were stark naked. One of them was our driver, who had probably lost his clothes to the river's pull as I did, and the other man was stripped by the circumstance of my own necessary theft. I had to go with the Bishop's cult after seeing what I have thus far. As we pulled into the hospital lot, night had settled in, and the parking lot's lights cast us as a noticeable group from the hospital's windows. An elder instructed the nude men to wrap towels around themselves as we stood to exit. We filed out in order, walked a narrow trail for several yards, and entered through a side door marked "Staff Only." What awaited us inside was no longer a hospital in the ordinary sense. After today's vernal equinox baptisms at Marys River, the chapel in Christ Hospital stands transformed by others in their fold who have expected what appears to be a ritualized surgery area.

Where once a simple altar received communion wafers and cheap wine, an operating table now gleams under portable surgical lights, its stainless steel surface reflecting fragments of stained glass from overhead. The men who had lost their robes dispersed in their towels and returned shortly afterwards, adorned in new robes from what I assumed were vestment changing areas beside the organ pipes. Amid thick incense, Bishop Elijah Ashworth stands tall as he enters and approaches the table, his gloved hands hovering with the patient stillness of a heron about to strike, while alongside him, twelve robed elders now wait in sterile gowns all stamped with a woodblock print of the Agnus Dei surrounded by text I could not read. Each of their postures seemed overly tense with anticipation.

"Bring forth the first vessel," Ashworth intones, his resonant voice echoing off the walls that predate Corvallis itself. The hospital's bricks are made with a special clay from a certain depth within the soil throughout the Valley. The locations of these clay extractions were specifically chosen by the Bishop when Christ Hospital was first constructed. Christ Hospital was replacing Good Samaritan Hospital's financial tumble into oblivion with a new location and strong mission.

Two acolytes wheel in a gurney bearing a woman's body. She is young, younger than most the Bishop incorporates publicly; she looks perhaps nineteen, with skin the color of winter honey and hair like burnt copper spread in a careful halo around her head. Her nakedness is absolute, unencumbered by even the thin dignity of a surgical drape or baptismal gown. I presume that the bacterial transformation that occurred for the cult at the river has preserved her flesh in death, lending it an opalescent sheen that catches the light in ways human skin should not. Though her chest no longer rises and falls with breath, she appears merely asleep, suspended in that perfect moment between consciousness and dreams.

"Lady Jessica," Ashworth announces as the attendants transfer her to the operating table with practiced reverence. "Selected from my school's graduating class. Twenty-three years of devotion. No penetration. No contamination from male essence." He runs a gloved finger along her collarbone, down between her breasts, circling her navel with a touch that lingers too long for onlooker's comfort. "A perfect parthenos."

The elders murmur their approval. One steps forward to anoint the body with scented oil, tracing symbols on her forehead, throat, breasts, and lower abdomen. They appear to me as markings that blend Episcopal crosses with geometric patterns matching those found on the river's surface after the bacterial awakening.

"Note the symmetry," Ashworth continues, his hands hovering over the young woman's breasts. "The ancient Greeks understood that perfection lies in balance. Left and right, upper and lower, input and output." His fingers trace invisible lines connecting various parts of her anatomy. "The mouth corresponds to the vagina and anus. What enters one exits the other, both spiritually and in transmutation of the organic. For prophecy to remain pure, both passages must remain unviolated by false essence and unclean matter."

He nods to an attendant who produces an ornate silver tray bearing surgical instruments. These were not standard medical tools that I am familiar with. Each handle is carved with intricate patterns that match the symbols the cult has painted on the body. The Bishop offers a prayer and states that each tool has been blessed in the waters of Marys River where the bacterial consciousness first awakened.

"Today we harvest what the Virgin requires," Ashworth says, selecting a scalpel. "The Marys Day offering. The fruits of spring have ripened by an early summer."

Before cutting, he bends to whisper something in the dead woman's ear, his lips barely moving, the words inaudible to all but him and whatever spirit might linger in her preserved flesh. When he straightens, his eyes have taken on that familiar opalescent shimmer that marks communion with the bacterial intelligence. The elders must recognize it as they bow their heads momentarily in a respectful pose of submission.

The first incision runs from sternum to pubis, a perfect line that parts the flesh with minimal bleeding, her circulatory system having been drained and replaced with an IV solution of the water from Marys River. The body responds to the cut with a faint luminescence along the wound edges, greeting the blade as an old friend.

"The body is a temple, a vessel for greater energy like those of the stars," Ashworth recites as he deepens the incision with methodical precision, layers of fat and muscle giving way to reveal the glistening contents beneath. "We honor its sacrifice by selecting only what is worthy of transcendence."

An elder steps forward to retract the skin and muscle, exposing the abdominal cavity. Despite the clinical nature of the procedure, there is nothing medical in its ultimate purpose. This is harvest, not surgery.

"Behold the art within the temple that teaches even the illiterate," Ashworth says, gesturing to the exposed organs with a reverence that borders on erotic fixation. "See how perfect she is inside. How untouched."

He reaches in with gloved hands to stroke the liver, the smooth surface of the intestines, each touch lingering and possessive. The bacterial preservation has given the organs an unnatural resilience and a subtle luster.

"First, we examine the womb," he announces, hands sliding deeper into the abdominal cavity. "The cradle of creation that remained empty as proof of her devotion."

With practiced efficiency that betrays years of medical training before his spiritual "awakening," Ashworth isolates and removes the uterus, lifting it toward the surgical lights for examination. The organ gleams with that now-familiar iridescence, colors shifting across its surface like oil on water.

"See how it takes the light," he murmurs, turning it slowly as he brings it closer to his face to get the scent of it. "The blessing is strong in this one. She was chosen well."

He places the uterus in a crystal bowl held by one of the elders. Unlike traditional organ harvesting, there is no rush, no concern for viability. The bacterial preservation ensures the tissues remain "alive" in some unconventional sense long after standard medical death.

"Next, the heart," Ashworth continues. "The ancient Greeks believed it the seat of soul and passion, not merely a pump for blood. We know better. It is the connection point between individual consciousness and the greater awareness that flows through all things."

He signals for a bone saw. The procedure to open the chest cavity proceeds with surprising gentleness despite the brutal mechanics involved. Ribs are parted, cartilage cut, all with the same ritualistic precision. When he finally lifts out the heart, it seems to pulse once in his hands before settling into stillness.

"Still warm," he notes with satisfaction. "The bacterial blessing preserves the vital essence long after clinical death. This is why the parthenos state is so crucial. No man's influence has muddied her connection to the greater consciousness."

The heart is placed alongside the uterus in the crystal bowl, prioritizing the ritual's aesthetic care over medical necessity. Ashworth then turns his attention to other organs, including the lungs, kidneys, and spleen, examining each under the harsh surgical lights. Some are set aside in sacred vessels; others are returned to the cavity as unworthy.

"Bring the second vessel," he commands once he has taken what he requires from Jessica's body.

The bishop's faithful priests and deacons wheel in another gurney. This woman is darker-skinned, with hair cropped close to her scalp in tight curls. Her body shows more mature development. She appears to be around twenty-eight or thirty years old, with fuller breasts and the subtle definition of athletic training in her musculature.

"Lady Camilla," Ashworth identifies her. "Hospitalist and teacher at Christ Hospital. Twenty-nine years old, perfect devotion." His hands trace her contours with the same inappropriate intimacy.

"Note the differences in development. The breast tissue is more abundant, the hips wider."

He positions her beside Jessica's opened body, creating a disturbing juxtaposition of intact and harvested beauty. I'm sure Bishop Ashworth gets off on such things. The contrast between them, one pale and open like a biological textbook illustration, the other dark and whole, creates a visual tension that seems to please Ashworth's normally stoic face.

"The Virgin appreciates variety in her offerings," he explains, beginning the anointing on Camilla's body. "In ancient understanding, a virgin huntress goddess presided over transitions: birth, death, the boundary between wilderness and civilization. Our Virgin is similar, but evolved. She requires different essences for different purposes."

As the elders prepare the second body, one approaches Ashworth with a scroll of handmade paper that I recognize from our gift shop. The Bishop reads from it while making the first incision into Camilla's abdomen:

"As the Pythia received Apollo's essence through her lower mouth to speak prophecy through her upper, so too does our Virgin receive these offerings to amplify her voice in the coming transformation. The bacterial consciousness recognizes the untainted vessel, the pure receptacle, the uncontaminated channel. This is not how our society views virginity through the hymen and acts."

The incision reveals more athletic muscle tone and different fat distribution. Ashworth comments on these differences with the detached appreciation of a connoisseur rather than a physician. I can always tell when he is sizing up a living body at baptism under his hard, lecherous gaze, and here he is doing so with dead girls. He is venturing into territory he doesn't understand. Into my territory. What is it about the male gaze that makes looking more important than touching? Perhaps he is afraid to touch, but I sure ain't, and I would have had my time had she been left whole and alone in her fresh stillness. Can a look possess more than a touch? I doubt there's much the Bishop sees that escapes the gravity of his possessive masculinity. Christianity, at first glance, seems ill-suited to such a posture, with its ethics built on a surrender to the salvation offered by another. But that very passivity becomes its seduction. Society, the sexual engine hovering above gender, channels such faith into a system of control: power over flesh masked as grace. In its quiet prescriptions of a personal relationship with Jesus, Christianity begins to resemble a kind of sadism: a doctrine of submission laced with wrath, pain, and the threat of divine violence should one refuse to yield.

"Observe how the abdominal muscles have developed through physical discipline. This offering brings strength as well as purity." His fingers trace the defined muscles before spreading them apart to access the organs beneath. "The Virgin needs both the soft and the firm, the yielding and the resistant."

When he reaches Camilla's liver, he pauses, eyes widening behind his surgical mask. "Extraordinary," he breathes, lifting the organ carefully. Unlike Jessica's, this liver displays more pronounced iridescence, with geometric patterns visible within the tissue itself. Sexualizing disembodied organs in the Bishop's club seems sickening, but I honestly admit it was a good-looking liver. And I am a vegetarian.

"The blessing manifests differently in each vessel," he explains, turning the organ to catch the light. "Here we see evidence of deeper communion. This one spoke with the river consciousness directly before her preparation."

One elder priest leans in, eyes narrowing behind protective glasses. "Is it still present, then? The consciousness?"

"Always," Ashworth confirms. "It never leaves completely. The bacterial network maintains connections even after what we consider death. This is why traditional religions have often misunderstood the concept of resurrection. It was never about the individual returning, but about the greater consciousness reclaiming what was always part of itself."

He places the liver in a separate vessel made of hammered copper rather than crystal, handling it with even greater reverence than Jessica's organs.

"This offering will form the bridge between prophecy and fulfillment," he declares. "The Virgin will speak through this one's essence when the earth finally opens."

The harvesting continues with methodical precision. When he reaches Camilla's heart, Ashworth performs an additional ritual, painting bacterial-infused water from the Marys River directly onto the muscle before extraction. The heart responds with the motion of the muscle as the water is absorbed.

"The perfect virgin, the parthenos, isn't one who has specifically abstained from sex," Ashworth explains as he works. "That's the simplistic modern understanding. In ancient Greece, the parthenic state was about spiritual integrity, about remaining unpenetrated by outside influence. Our Virgin maintains her power through this separateness, this refusal to be contaminated by lesser consciousness."

Many of us appeared taken aback by this, exchanging glances to gauge the implications of this new belief. Was the Bishop incorporating pagan elements now? He raises Camilla's heart toward the stained glass windows, where the sunlight filters through biblical scenes, now seen in the context of a bacterial awakening. "This is why these women are perfect vessels. They have preserved their spiritual purity, as I have observed, as you all have observed, even in a world eager to invade and corrupt." The extracted organs are carefully placed in sacred patterns on silver trays—Jessica's in one arrangement, Camilla's in another. The elders softly chant as Ashworth finishes the harvesting, their voices mingling with the gentle hum of the bacterial consciousness that appears to radiate from the gathered tissues.

"Before the earth trembled, we worked in ignorance," Ashworth tells his congregation as he peels off his bloody gloves, replacing them with clean ones for the final phase. "We thought we served an abstract concept, a dusty remnant of ancient religion. Now we understand. The Virgin is real, physical, embodied in the bacterial consciousness that has slept beneath our Valley for fifteen thousand years. Christ is a method of consciousness that is obtainable when we become her son."

He retrieves a third container, this one made of glass and filled with river water that glows with unmistakable iridescence. The harvested organs are carefully transferred into this liquid, where they seem to release their remaining cellular structures, dissolving into the bacterial medium while maintaining their general shape. They become ghostly versions of hearts and wombs suspended in the energetic luminous fluid.

"The offering is accepted," Ashworth declares as the organs gradually merge with the bacterial solution. "The Virgin receives our tribute on this first day of summer. When the great earthquake comes, and it approaches more rapidly than even I had anticipated, these essences will enable her to speak directly to those who have been baptized in her waters."

He turns to address the elders directly. "We will take the final steps. The hospital's specialty ward is being prepared. The treatments have been introduced for others among us."

One elder steps forward, his surgical mask pulled down to reveal a face lined with age. "And those whose bodies reject the blessing?"

Ashworth's expression hardens briefly. "They will provide the future offerings after the quake. Nothing is wasted in the Virgin's plan. Those unsuitable as communicants become suitable as vessels."

He turns his back to my view, running his fingers along the edge of the incision on Jessica's abdomen with something like tenderness. "These two were perfect. Their organs will serve as the primary conduits for the Virgin's voice." His attention shifts to the remaining cavity, emptied of its most valuable contents. "The rest, however, need not be wasted."

At his signal, younger members of the congregation step forward with containers of river water. These are poured into the emptied body cavities, where they settle and begin to glow with increased intensity, transforming the corpses into macabre bioluminescent cadavers.

"The flesh, too, can serve," Ashworth explains, watching the transformation with satisfaction. "Properly prepared, these vessels will incubate new strains of the consciousness, adapted specifically for human integration."

The ceremony concludes with Ashworth placing his hands on the foreheads of the two corpses, reciting what sounds like the Lord's Prayer but with key phrases altered to reference bacterial consciousness and geological awakening. The elders join in, creating a twisted harmony of religious devotion and scientific perversion.

As the final words resonate through the chapel, the bodies on the tables seem to respond with a subtle movement beneath the skin where no movement should be possible from the lifeless. I note a brightening of the bacterial glow within their cavities. The Virgin has accepted their offering. The bodies are zipped in body bags and sent away to the mortuary for cremation.

21
BELLFOUNTAIN

Miles stretch behind me, and my shoes gather dust from the desolate countryside road leading into what must be Bellfountain. The sun beats down with unusual warmth for the early summer in Oregon, and sweat trickles between my shoulder blades, a persistent reminder of my vulnerability in this unfamiliar terrain. It's too damn sunny for my mood, and too hot. I want to take my shirt off, but not attract any additional attention if I cross another person.

I check my phone again: still no signal and a battery that is almost dead. The screen reflects my face, tired and drawn from the unexpected hike. My car's overheated radiator is probably still steaming on the roadside three miles back. I tuck the useless device back into my pocket and continue forward. The town can't be far away now.

Bellfountain emerges gradually, not so much a proper town as a loose collection of weathered structures huddled among the trees. Dirt roads branch from the main path like veins from an artery, disappearing into thick stands of Douglas fir and oak. The air carries a complex perfume: pine resin, cow manure from distant pastures, the mineral scent of dry earth, and the smell of fruit. Houses sit far apart here, each a solitary island in a sea of wild growth.

I pass a rusted fire truck, half-swallowed by blackberry bushes, its red paint peeling away to reveal the gray skin beneath. A tractor, similarly abandoned, rests on deflated tires beside what might once have been a barn. Everything bears the marks of weather and time, yet strangely, nothing seems completely dead. Sunday in Bellfountain is just sleeping, paused, waiting.

The few locals I pass regard me with curious, lingering stares. An elderly man on a sagging porch follows my progress with eyes that hold neither welcome nor hostility, only assessment, measuring me against some unseen standard. I nod in greeting. He doesn't return the gesture.

A woman hanging sheets pauses, clothespins clutched between her teeth, to watch me with similar intensity. Her fingers work mechanically while her eyes never leave my face. The cotton sheets snap in the breeze like sails on a becalmed sea.

The children I glimpse move like kids do; they dart like fish behind buildings or vehicles, their blonde heads appearing and vanishing. It is a game whose rules I don't understand. One boy, perhaps seven, freezes when our eyes meet, then dashes away behind a stack of firewood, his movement fluid as water finding the path of least resistance.

I've walked towns like this before, places where outsiders are novelties to be examined rather than people to be engaged. But something about Bellfountain slips under my skin in a way those other places never did. The sunshine splashes across peeling paint and rusted metal, highlighting rather than hiding the decay. Despite the warm day, goosebumps rise on my arms.

The road curves and begins to run parallel to a steep incline. It is not quite a cliff, but a substantial hill that rises abruptly from the relatively flat terrain. Exposed tree roots form a natural lattice across its face, holding the dirt in a complex embrace that resembles skeletal fingers clutching at the earth. Tufts of grass and small wildflowers have taken hold in patches, creating a strange patchwork of life and decay.

The sun has moved noticeably westward during my walk, and the hill casts a long shadow across the road. I step into this shadow and feel immediate relief from the heat, but the sudden temperature change makes me uncomfortable. The contrast is stark as I feel the burning sunshine on one side of my body, a cool shadow on the other.

Water. I need water. My tongue feels thick in my mouth, my lips cracked from the combination of heat and exertion. There must be a store or at least a house with a garden hose somewhere in this town. I scan the scattered buildings ahead, looking for something resembling a business. A gas station, a general store, or anything that might offer both hydration and directions to a mechanic.

I press my palms against my lower back, stretching out the muscles that have tightened during the long walk. My body clock tells me it's been about four hours since I left Christ Hospital, three since my car decided to quit. Under normal circumstances, I'd be home now, peeling off my scrubs and stepping into a hot shower before collapsing into bed after the night shift.

Instead, I'm a stranger in a town that feels like it's been forgotten by the modern world, observed but not welcomed, surrounded by a beauty that carries undercurrents of something I can't quite name. I feel as if I am being watched, but there is only the presence of the hill beside me. Its exposed roots are the searching tendons of some old growth oak that is sizing me up for intention. I take a deep breath and step out of the hill's shadow, back into the sunlight. The heat hits me again. I stretch my neck and take in the light. Blinding even with my eyes closed, yet the sun is fueling my reserves. I shield my eyes and look toward the heart of Bellfountain, such as it is. There must be someone here who can help me get back to the hospital or Corvallis. Someone who'll do more than stare. Someone who'll speak.

The question that presses against my mind as I continue walking is simple but unsettling: why did my GPS direct me through this backwater town in the first place? The route from Christ Hospital to my apartment shouldn't have brought me here for the direct route. Yet when I followed its directions, turning off the main highway onto progressively smaller roads, it led me straight into Bellfountain—right before losing signal completely on its off-cuff scenic route.

My feet carry me forward, each step raising a small puff of dust. The hill keeps pace beside me, its shadow lengthening as the afternoon progresses. I focus on the practical: find water, find a phone, find help. The rest of my encounters with this town, with the folks' stares, the unusual silence, the sense of being measured against some unknown standard, all that outsider sentiment can wait.

That's when I see her. At first, she's just a flicker of movement at the periphery of my vision. Something pale and shapely is against the dark earth of the hillside. I turn my head, and my breath catches, lodges somewhere between my lungs and throat. A young woman stands at the crest of the hill. She's completely naked. She is possibly in her early twenties, with lean, healthy musculature, and she has no visible signs of injury or distress. But this detached analysis quickly drowns beneath a wave of more immediate observations.

Her skin is the color of cream with just a hint of honey, unmarked by tan lines, revealing her entire body is accustomed to the sun's touch. She stands in a shaft of light that filters through the trees, and it transforms her, turning the fine hairs on her arms and legs into a golden halo around her limbs. Her breasts are small but perfectly formed, with larger nipples puckered slightly in the breeze. I began to lose my thoughts and began to fantasize about how she would look if she dropped dead right now.

Then I realized something. It is the woman from the baptism who prophesied about the Great Quake. A small bouquet of trumpet-shaped flowers—white, probably datura—is clutched in her right hand, held low against her body where a triangle of dark blonde hair marks the meeting of her thighs.

I remain frozen, watching as she shifts her weight from one foot to the other. The movement causes subtle ripples beneath her skin. I feel the gentle flex of her quadriceps through my stomach's butterflies, the slight adjustment of her spine makes me also stand taller, and the minute reshaping of her breasts as she breathes reminds me to breathe. She seems untroubled by her nudity, comfortable in her exposure like an animal or a goddess. She is vividly alive, unguarded, and for the first time, I find myself adoring something that pulses with life instead of the dead, revealing my painful layers of memory. In light of my pain, to not be able to cross over to ever communicate with the departed again, I pause where I stand and contemplate communication with the living.

A cloud passes over the sun, and for a moment, the light on the hillside changes. Shadows deepen, and her skin takes on a different quality. Now her complexion is less golden, more marble-like. In this new light, she looks less like a living woman and more like a statue, something sculpted and worshipped. The white flowers in her hand seem suddenly ritualistic, an offering rather than a casual gathering.

The cloud moves on. The light returns with her honey kiss of movement. And, oh, she begins to move.

Her climb of the slope is both careful and confident. One foot tests each placement before committing her weight, yet there's nothing fearful in her movements. She navigates the treacherous surface with the familiarity of someone who has done so many times before. Her free hand occasionally reaches for the thicker roots to steady herself, fingers wrapping around the gnarled wood with practiced ease.

The changing angle provides me with an uninterrupted view of her body in motion. Her buttocks clench and release with each step, the muscles working visibly beneath the skin. The curve of her spine leads my eye from the delicate bones of her shoulders down to the twin dimples just above the rise of her backside. When she shifts to navigate a particularly steep section, I glimpse the pink folds between her legs, momentarily visible against the darker background of the earth.

I'm aware of my quickening pulse, the rush of blood in my ears. There's a bit of shame in this watching, but something else too, with a sense of witnessing something not meant for outsiders' eyes. Not pornographic, but a private pagan rite beyond what I ever witnessed in youth or adulthood. It isn't indecent. It's raw, natural, and profoundly fertile. I've slipped through time into an age when humanity moved in rhythm with the living ecology around it.

She pauses halfway down the hill, and I suddenly realize I've been holding my breath. Sensing my presence, she turns her head. Our eyes meet across the distance of a stone's casual throw.

Her face strikes me with unexpected force. High cheekbones. A mouth that seems on the verge of smiling. Eyes that catch the light like pieces of amber. But it's the expression in those eyes that chills me. A recognition, not of me personally, but of what I represent: the outside world, the intrusion.

She doesn't seem alarmed by my presence, merely aware of it. I'm a natural hazard to be navigated like the steep hill itself. For a few seconds, we remain locked in this strange communion. Then something shifts in her gaze.

She turns away, suddenly urgent in her movements, and climbs back up the hill with remarkable speed. Her body, so deliberate before, now flows up the incline with the urgency of water running uphill, defying both gravity and expectation. I catch final glimpses of what appears to be the countryside's answer to my deathlust, and that answer is fertility: the flexing of her calves, the subtle bouncing of her breasts, the hypnotic alternation of her buttocks as she ascends, the area between her legs, its naturally sparse hair left ungroomed. Her skin collects and reflects the dappled light, making her appear to shimmer.

Then she crests the hill and is gone, vanished over the top into whatever waits on the other side.

I stand motionless on the road. The entire encounter has lasted perhaps two minutes, yet it feels momentous, significant in ways I cannot articulate as I remain stunned by my attraction to life. Was she real, or had the land manifested itself in a woman? The rational part of my mind insists she must be. I saw her clearly, in good light, without obstruction. Yet there was something in her movement, in the way she regarded me, that suggested something beyond ordinary humanity.

The breeze carries the scent of pine and earth, but now I detect something else—a sweet, floral note that wasn't present before. I look down at the road and notice something I missed: a faint path, barely more than a game trail, leading from the road to the base of the hill.

I should continue into town, find a phone, and arrange for a tow truck. That would be the sensible course of action. But my feet are already moving toward the path, drawn by curiosity or something deeper that I don't care to name.

The hill rises before me, its exposed roots like the ribcage of some enormous, gnarly beast partially excavated from the earth. I place my hand on the first root and begin to climb.

The terrain uphill shifts to include larger stones embedded in the hillside, some loose and others firmly anchored. I test each one before committing my weight, aware that a fall from this height would result in injury. As I near the summit, the soil beneath my hands transitions from loose dirt to a more compacted earth, suggesting regular use. This path, difficult as it is, has been traveled enough times to create a subtle but recognizable trail. Fresh indentations in several places match the size and shape of bare human feet. She came this way, and was not my imagination.

I pull myself over the final ridge, breathing heavily from the exertion. For a moment, I remain on my hands and knees, recovering and taking in my surroundings. The hilltop is a natural plateau, roughly circular and spanning perhaps thirty meters across. Tall pines encircle the space, creating a living wall that separates this area from the world beyond. The ground is carpeted with moss, bits of grass, and clusters of wildflowers. The same white trumpet-shaped blooms that the woman held in her bouquet.

In the center of this plateau, partially obscured by a slight rise in the terrain as I remain low, I notice something that breaks the natural pattern of the landscape. I rise to my feet and approach cautiously, my shoes silent on the moss until I kick a rock forward that skips onto a larger stone. The sound seems inappropriately loud in the stillness of this place.

The circle reveals itself gradually as I approach. There are stones arranged with an evident ritualistic purpose, each about the size of a human head, positioned to form a perfect ring approximately three meters in diameter. The stones are weathered, their surfaces textured with lichen and small indentations that could be natural erosion or deliberate carvings. I wanted to approach closer but would rather see the event unfold undisturbed.

I count twenty-three stones in total, spaced at irregular intervals yet maintaining the circular formation. Inside the circle lies not the pile of rocks I half-expected, but an elderly woman, perhaps seventy, completely nude and stretched out on her back. The young woman stands beside her, the bouquet of datura now held above the old woman's body.

The elderly woman's skin is a patchwork of normal flesh and translucent areas which are the telltale sign of the Christ Contagion. These patches scatter across her torso and limbs like windows into her interior, revealing the pulsing organs beneath. Where normal skin should be opaque, these areas allow glimpses of muscle tissue, blood vessels, and the subtle movements of her internal systems. I recognized the condition immediately from my own markings.

The young woman moves systematically around the circle, picking up an object from beside the other stones, which I can identify as a mortar and pestle. She starts crushing the datura flowers with it. To my surprise, the younger woman places the mortar on the ground above the old woman, where she then squats and urinates into it. I watch in shock and awe as she picks it up and continues to grind the mixture, and then, lifting the concoction into the air, she says things I cannot hear. As she lowers her head and hands, she lets the mixture drip onto the old woman's body. When the liquid touches the translucent areas, something remarkable occurs. The old woman's skin begins to regain its natural appearance, becoming cloudy and opaque once more. The Christ Contagion visibly retreats, much like frost melting under sudden warmth.

The old woman's eyes remain closed, but her lips move in what might be prayer or incantation. As each patch receives the datura extract, her body arches slightly, responding to both pain and pleasure simultaneously. The young wildflower of a woman works with an endearing sense of intent, her naked form bending and straightening as she applies the remedy to each affected area.

The scene before me is so unexpected, so bizarre in its ritualistic healing, that I fail to maintain my careful stance. I step backward in shock, forgetting the precarious nature of the plateau's edge. My foot finds empty space where solid ground should be.

Time slows as equilibrium fails.

I fall.

Not in the cinematic sense with arms outstretched, an anguished cry breaking the still air, but in tumbling fragments. My mind splinters as my body obeys gravity. Each muscle recoils at the betrayal of stability. My spine curls protectively, fetal. The wind tears past my ears, and with its rising howl, memory rushes in.

Greenville. A steeple peeks above the cemetery trees. Magnolia leaves glisten in the summer sweat of mourning. The casket stands before me, but it's not the vessel I see. It's symbolic of her. My mother, held within. Sunlight breaks through the clouds and touches her face one last time, and I'm heartbroken, with fists clenched like dead birds. I watch not the sermon but the cardinal several yards away looking for a meal. They look so similar to Steller's jays on this side of the country, except the red is a deep royal blue. Then I noticed the red of the cardinal matched the three towering red wooden doors on the stone Trinity Lutheran Church across the street. The cardinal, the three magnificent red doors, and the image of my mother with her blood pooling under her—past, present, and the suggestion of the return of her in the future. *Where is she now?*

Past, present, return. Three doors. Three stages. Three mirrors.

That's when it began. My first arousal was not to flesh but to absence. In the silence of her still body, there was something too familiar to be foreign, yet too gone to be her. It wasn't lust. It was hunger. Not for sex, but an ecstatic slip into the myth of reunion. I found myself aroused by the symbolic and tragic absence of life.

The moment my sexuality awakened was the moment she left her body behind.

The descent begins slowly as a controlled slide that briefly mimics intent. Fingers claw at roots in defeat, grasping at truths that crumble on contact. Soil packs under my nails, fills the gaps where certainty used to dwell. Then momentum reclaims me. A final snag ended in the tearing of fabric, and a knock on my head like thunder through the Carolinas. My shirt, my skin, my self: all unstitched in the rush downward.

The hill steepens, and gravity asserts dominion. Earth and sky blur. I fold into myself, fetal, protective, symbolic. I do not brace, I surrender. There is no dignity in this collapse. Only inevitability.

When impact comes, it's sudden and absolute. Like hitting a veil between worlds. Motion ceases, silence blooms. I lie spread-eagled at the hill's base, lungs emptied, limbs thrumming with pain. Then stillness. Then blackout.

I wake to the taste of blood and soil. The blue above is too deep for the afternoon, too alive for night. Twilight. Tree shadows stretch and braid across the ground. The forest has shifted in light and intention. It watches now.

Pain speaks first. From my skull, my ankle, my ribs. I press blood-slick fingers to my scalp. I can already feel that there's swelling, sticky with blood and dirt. Probable concussion. Nausea pulses like a second heartache. Double vision flickers like a strobe in a dimly lit room.

Limbs mostly work, if begrudgingly. My left elbow resists movement. Still, I am alive. That detail matters. For now, survival replaces symbolism.

The visions return in scattered shards.

The circle of stones. The naked woman. Her ritual, my interruption. The way gravity claimed me and my vision.

She is gone now, of course. No priestess lingers once her rite is broken. But the land remembers. The hill looms behind me like the three red doors across from my mother's funeral. I feel the gaze.

I must move. The air cools with deliberate threat. My phone is completely dead now. I remember the car. Far back, where pavement surrendered to wilderness. Civilization waits there, like a myth behind a veil.

Standing is its own ceremony. First attempt collapses into vertigo. Second births agony. Third... succeeds, but only because something in me wills it. I sway, a broken reed in the Bellfountain country wind.

"Focus," I whisper.

Step. Agony. Step again.

The path is fading, if it ever truly existed. I limp through twilight, hand to bark, ribs humming with pain's rhythm. Night descends completely. The forest tightens its grip. Trees reconfigure, familiar by daylight now monstrous in silhouette. Time decays into abstraction. I walk between worlds. Consciousness slips in and out like a dream stitched to the trauma. Direction loses meaning. Still, I move. Rest feels like a pleasure I haven't earned. It's not reason that keeps me moving, and hope's long gone with Mother. It's survival, plain and feral. You don't go still in a situation like this.

The forest agrees. It presses in. I remember the circle. I remember Mother's blood.

Lights appear ahead as pinpricks of yellow that at first I mistake for hallucinations brought on by my concussion. I blink, and they remain. Not stars, not fireflies, but electric lights. I alter my course, stumbling toward this promise of human presence.

The forest thins gradually, giving way to underbrush and then to a gravel road I don't recognize. The lights belong to a large structure that materializes from the darkness as a warehouse or barn, its metal siding silver in the moonlight. A sign, barely legible in the darkness, informs me I've somehow reached an occupied building in the small town of Bellfountain. I've traveled a few miles from where I fell, though the wrong direction from my car if that even mattered.

As I approach, the warehouse reveals its age and neglect. A hand-painted sign leans beside the crooked steps: *Bellfountain Community Church.* Just below it, fresh white letters blaze across a second board: *Giant Killers Centennial: 1937–2037.* The sounds from within aren't words but syllables cascading like water over stone. Windows, high on the walls, are either broken or so dirt-encrusted that no light could possibly penetrate them. Yet light does emerge from what must be a door at the far end, casting a narrow rectangle of warmth onto the gravel outside.

I pause, swaying slightly as a wave of dizziness washes over me. Something about the building catches my attention. There are markings on the walls, visible even in the dim moonlight. At first glance, they appear to be graffiti, but as my eyes adjust, I see they form distinct patterns. Symbols, some vaguely familiar, others entirely mysterious, have been painted onto the metal siding in what looks like red-brown paint. In places, water stains have caused the pigment to run, creating the unsettling impression of bleeding.

I am too aware of the dangers of blood loss, exposure, and untreated wounds. I need assistance, and this building, regardless of its function, holds people. I hobble toward the glowing doorway, observing how the symbols become more frequent and intricate as I get closer. Some look like religious icons. I awe at crosses altered with extra lines, and circles filled with geometric designs that stir vague memories from my comparative religion courses.

As I near, I hear the voices rise. There are layers of a continuous flow of sound like a combination of love and pain, hymns signaling lives standing tall against generations of loss. I hear a joyful exclamation of what I immediately recognized as friendly in its suffering, interrupted by occasional sharp outbursts of praise. I pause at the entrance, but another bout of dizziness makes the decision for me. I need to sit before I collapse. I might vomit. I push the door open and step inside.

Inside, there's a stark contrast. The warehouse is vast, with a high ceiling shrouded in shadows. Most of the area is dark, but in the center, a rough circle of mismatched chairs surrounds a spot lit by portable camping lanterns. The light they emit is harsh and uneven, casting deep shadows that flicker as people move within the circle.

22
THE GIANT KILLERS

There are about fifteen people gathered, wearing clothes that seem intentionally plain. The women have on long skirts and blouses buttoned up to their necks, with their hair either tightly pulled back or covered by simple scarves. The men are in dark trousers and light shirts, many of which look worn and aged. They all bear the rugged appearance of people who spend much time outdoors, with skin tanned and etched by the sun. Wooden crosses hang around several necks, not the polished trinkets of casual faith but roughly carved emblems of devotion, smoothed by years of touch.

They don't notice me at first, their focus directed inward toward the center of their circle. There, a man stands with his arms lifted to the sky. His voice rises above the rest, not speaking English but a cascade of syllables flowing like water over rocks. He's speaking in tongues. It is a phenomenon I'm quite familiar with from my childhood growing up with neighborhood children steeped in charismatic Christianity. Although, I've never seen it performed with such fervor.

I take another step forward, and my injured ankle chooses that moment to buckle. I catch myself against the wall, but not before a grunt of pain escapes me. The sound carries in the cavernous space, and suddenly, all eyes turn in my direction.

The silence that follows is absolute. Fifteen pairs of eyes examine me with expressions ranging from surprise to suspicion to something that might be relief. I become acutely aware of my appearance. My clothes torn and dirt-stained, face likely streaked with dried blood, posture betraying my injuries.

"I'm sorry to interrupt," I manage, my voice sounding strange to my own ears. "I've had an accident hiking in the woods. I need help. I just moved to the area. I work at the hospital. Maybe I could get a ride there from someone. I have gas money."

A soft murmur spreads among the group, with several individuals exchanging glances that convey a message I cannot decipher. The man who had been standing at the center steps forward towards me. He is tall and thin, with deep-set eyes in a face marked by what looks to have been a hard life. I notice his hands trembling slightly by his sides. "Brother," he addresses me, "you have arrived at the destined time." His voice has the gentle accent of someone not originally from Oregon. Before I can correct his assumption, he turns to the group and speaks with a sudden passion. "Observe how the Lord provides witnesses! As we gather to testify against corruption, He sends us a stranger in need! Testify to him! Lord help him!"

This pronouncement triggers a response from the congregation in a growing ripple of sound that begins as scattered amens and grows into another outburst of a member of the congregation dancing and shaking their hands wildly. The sound washes over me like a wave, rising and falling in patterns that seem almost musical in their cadence. Some rock in place, eyes closed in apparent ecstasy. Others stare directly at me with an intensity that makes my skin prickle.

The gaunt man returns his attention to me as obviously I am bleeding as well as unsure what is happening here. "That is called being slain in the Spirit. Amen. Come, brother. Sit. Your wounds will be tended." He gestures to an empty chair within their circle.

These individuals are clearly caught up in a wave of religious zeal, yet they are my only source of assistance for miles around. I let them guide me to a chair, where a middle-aged woman promptly arrives with an old plastic first aid kit. She cleans the cut on my head with antiseptic that stings sharply, and as she does, the speaking in tongues gradually fades. The congregation calms down, although a lingering tension is apparent in their stances and the way they frequently glance at the door, anticipating more arrivals.

The emaciated man resumes his place at the center. When he speaks again, it's in English, but with the same rhythmic flow that characterized his earlier speaking in tongues, which they call the "Blessed Glossolalia." Many of the more country-speaking folk shortened the syllables with their accent to sound as if they were saying "Gloss-o-lay-ahh."

"You are new to town, are you? Well, at your Christ Hospital, they have corrupted the core of the local community," he declares, his trembling hands now clenched into fists. "The one who calls himself Bishop Ashworth has led darkness deeper than the grave. The Bishop speaks of healing, but his hands drip with corruption," the man continues, his voice rising. "We have seen the evidence. We have witnesses who have fled his unholy work. This is our centennial for defeating adversity one hundred years ago. We thought our legendary high school basketball team was simply the only thing special about our town. Then we realized it was a founding myth for something that touches all avenues of the human experience."

The congregation responds with a mixture of sounds, some revert to speaking in tongues, while others whisper warnings in English that overlap into an indecipherable chorus of fear. "He marks them," says one woman, her eyes wide. "The newborns," adds another. "Blood and water," comes from a young man whose fingers work nervously at the wooden cross hanging from his neck.

The concussion headache makes focusing difficult. The woman finishes cleaning my head wound and moves to examining my ankle, her touch is gentle and fairly skilled.

The gaunt preacher turns to a table I hadn't noticed before, positioned just outside the circle of chairs. "We have gathered the proof," he announces, "that those who walk in the light might be warned."

He lifts something from the table: a glass vial filled with dark liquid in which something unidentifiable floats. Even from my position several feet away, I can see that whatever is preserved in the murky fluid has an organic quality to it, there is tissue of some kind, perhaps organ samples. The medical professional in me immediately questions the provenance of such specimens and the ethics of their acquisition.

"Taken from the waste behind their laboratories," the preacher explains. "Parts of God's creation, discarded after their unholy experimentations."

He sets down the vial and picks up what appears to be a printed medical chart from our hospital software. The pages are dog-eared and water-stained, with sections heavily redacted by black marker. Patient names have been obscured, but diagnostic codes and treatment notes remain partially visible.

"Their own records speak of abomination," he continues, holding the chart aloft like evidence in a trial. "They record their sins in their own hand, thinking none will see, but God's eyes penetrate all darkness."

Another member of the congregation steps forward. She is a woman in her fifties, with prematurely gray hair pulled back in a severe bun. She places something else on the table. It appears as a wooden board upon which symbols have been carved or burned. Some resemble the markings I saw outside on the warehouse walls, while others call to mind the portents and signs for plagues described in Biblical texts: locusts, boils, darkness.

"They mark them thus," she says, her voice surprisingly steady compared to the others. "Each according to their purpose in the Bishop's grand design."

The congregation breaks into another round of tongues, more frantic than before. Bodies sway, hands raise skyward, faces contort with emotions ranging from ecstasy to terror. The cacophony builds until the gaunt preacher raises his hands for silence, which descends gradually, like dust settling after an explosion.

"We have been chosen to witness," he says into the new quiet. "We have been chosen to warn. The time of reckoning approaches when all that is hidden will be revealed. We will be the Giant Killers once again, but this won't be a high school game, it will be spiritual warfare with the Bishop's cult."

His gaze fixed on me with uncomfortable intensity. "You have been led here tonight by divine providence, brother. Your eyes have seen the evidence here and there. Your ears have heard our testimony against the darkness that grows at Christ Hospital. What path will you choose, will you seek the guidance of the Lord?"

The question hangs in the air between us. My head throbs with renewed intensity, and the room seems to pulse slightly at the edges of my vision, all clear signs that my concussion needs proper medical attention. Yet I find myself leaning forward, examining the items on the table with professional curiosity.

The vials contain what appear to be tissue samples, preserved in formaldehyde or a similar solution. Without proper testing, I can't identify the specific organs, but their texture and coloration suggest human origin. The charts, from what I can see of the unredacted portions, contain standard medical notations alongside symbols that have no place in conventional treatment protocols. The wooden board with its burned symbols triggers an association with outdated medical practices, it resonates from a time when disease was attributed to spiritual causes rather than biological ones.

"I'd like to understand more," I hear myself saying, my clinical detachment giving way to something else in my curiosity that runs deeper than simple professional interest. There's something here, beneath the religious fervor and apocalyptic warnings, some kernel of concrete concern that my medical training recognizes even through the fog of concussion.

Then from the crowd comes forward a middle-aged lady holding a fetus in a jar.

The woman whose smile gaped like a wound, absent one tooth but crowned in a glow of rapture. She bore the jar like an offering, but not an offering to me, cradling inside it the curled apostle of embryonic truth she bore witness to. Suspended in syrupy awe, the fetus turned gently as she rocked it like a child, seeking comfort in another world.

"Blood redeems," she whispered, and the syllables dragged across the floor like broken limbs. "He shall be salvaged backwards, for faith flows upstream. I always longed for the sweetness of inheritance as I could not have one in this world of my own. I know I am his mother in heaven, perhaps with his birth mother if she found herself saved."

She moved close, breathing a fogbank of righteous fervor, thrusting the jar forward—an infant relic, a pickled disciple of Bellfountain.

"Will you," she asked, voice ripe with the stink of paradise lost, "kiss little John, show us who you are, are you our anointed trespasser?"

I stood in shock. Then thinking I had no choice, and hoping the lid was on tight, I leaned forward and kissed the jar with little John. The gaunt preacher's face transforms with a smile that doesn't reach his eyes. "Understanding comes to those who watch with open hearts," he says. "Bishop Ashworth calls himself a shepherd, but his flock is not led to green pastures. They are led to slaughter."

The woman who tended my wounds finishes wrapping my ankle and stands. "You'll need real medical attention," she says quietly, her pragmatism standing in contrast to the fervor around us. "But not at Christ Hospital. Never there."

The way she says it with absolute conviction rather than the theatrical delivery of the preacher. She sends an unease through me that has nothing to do with my injuries. My hands are numb from the cold and shock, but I feel a warmth in my chest, an uncomfortable heat that I recognize as the first kindling of obsession. I have the need to know, to verify, to understand what lies beneath these wild claims.

The congregation watches me, their eyes reflecting the lantern light like animals caught in headlights. They've shown me their evidence, delivered their warnings. Now they wait for my response, fifteen faces united in their certainty that something terrible lurks behind the respectable facade of Christ Hospital and the man called Bishop Ashworth.

I asked if I could charge my phone, and a woman named Grace let me use her quick charger. I told her, hoping that the others were listening, that I believed them and knew little of the inner workings of Christ Hospital. I assured them that I knew people who could assist me, although I did not mention that it was Harold or give any indication of who it might be. When we said our goodbyes, a man named Jacob stepped forward and offered to give me a lift. He led me out with his work-worn hand on my shoulder, as I rebooted my phone.

Jacob's truck belongs to another era. A Ford F-150 from the early 1980s, its blue paint faded, showing a contrast between the patches of repaired rust. The bench seat is cracked vinyl patched with duct tape, and the dashboard houses an array of gauges. My ankle throbs with renewed intensity as I climb in, the pain shooting up my leg.

A woman from the congregation, named Martha, wrapped my ankle with considerable skill. Her splint of scrap wood and cloth bandages holds it immobile, but does little for the pain. My head still pulses with the rhythm of concussion, thoughts swimming in and out of focus like fish in murky water.

Jacob starts the engine with a turn of the key that's worn smooth from decades of use. The truck coughs to life, belching blue smoke that catches the late afternoon light. He doesn't look at me as he puts it in gear, his movements economical, like someone who has performed the same actions for decades.

We leave Bellfountain behind, the little church growing smaller in the side mirror. For ten minutes, we drive in silence. The only sounds are the labored breathing of the truck's engine and the occasional creak of suspension. The tension between us is palpable at best. Definitely, they are not hostile, but the air between us is uncomfortable and heavy with unspoken questions.

"You seen it yet?" Jacob finally asks, eyes fixed on the road ahead. His voice is rough from years of smoking or shouting or both. "The tremors?"

I shift in my seat, unsure what he means. "Tremors?"

"Earth's been speaking more lately." His hands tighten on the wheel. I note a faint underglow to his heavily veined hands. "Little shakes. Nothing the news reports. But we feel them. The big one's coming. Cascadia."

I look down, pop onto my phone, and retrieve the geological data in a search. The Cascadia Subduction Zone is a 700-mile fault that runs from Northern California to British Columbia. Seismologists predict it's due for a magnitude 9.0 earthquake, a cataclysm that will reshape the Pacific Northwest.

"The Cascadia earthquake," I say. "Yes, people at the hospital say geologists have been warning about it for years. It's a scientific certainty, eventually."

Jacob makes a sound somewhere between a laugh and a snort. "Scientific. Sure. Also biblical. 'The earth shall reel to and fro like a drunkard, and shall be removed like a cottage.' Isaiah." He glances at me. "You think it's coincidence that Bishop Ashworth built his power here, right on the fault line?"

Jacob slows the truck as we approach a junction. "You know what happens in a subduction quake? The land drops. The ocean rushes in. Everything built by man is wiped away."

I nod, remembering disaster preparedness seminars. "Liquefaction of soil, tsunami inundation. It's why the hospital has been retrofitted with—"

"It ain't about the building surviving," Jacob interrupts. "It's about what survives in us. Inside." He taps his chest. "Ashworth knows the quake is coming. He's preparing for it. Using it."

The road curves through farmland, fields of grass seed stretching toward distant hills. The late summer sun casts everything in golden light that would be beautiful if not for the dark conversation.

"Using it how?" I ask, though part of me doesn't want to know.

"The Christ Contagion needs a catalyst," Jacob says, the words matter-of-fact. "The earthquake breaks the ground. Breaks the containment. What's been sleeping wakes up. What's been growing spreads." He checks the rearview mirror. "Been happening slowly for years. The river water. The hospital procedures. But the quake—that's when it all breaks loose."

My scientific mind rebels against his words, but the evidence I saw in the church lingers. The medical chart was real. The procedure codes existed. The preserved tissue was... wrong.

"What exactly is this Contagion?" I ask. "Bacterial? Viral? Fungal?"

Jacob's laugh has no humor in it. "All of them, I reckon. None of them. It's ancient, know that. It's the Devil. It used to live below the water, in the ground. Science said that. But Ashworth, he found a way to manipulate his cult using it as a sign for his agenda. Ashworth doesn't control the Contagion though. So he is using drugs, the sacred datura," he continues as he looks more at me now than the road, "is the Bishop's sacrament. He brews it into coffee, steeps it into wine, calls it communion—but it is poison. It opens the soul, yes, but to what? To his lies. To the fact that the Contagion isn't from God and that it affects only the wicked. Good people are drugged, all believing it to be the Holy Spirit."

The landscape changes as we approach Corvallis. Farmland gives way to suburbs, then to denser development. Christ Hospital appears on the horizon, its white walls gleaming in the fading light. From this distance, it looks benign, even beneficent—a place of healing. But now I see it through new eyes, wondering what secrets its corridors contain.

"They'll watch you," Jacob says as we get closer. Jacob gives me a long look. "They'll know you in time as an outsider, and they'll have questions. Know this, the poison of the datura is effective in slowing down the Contagion. It can cost you your sanity though. The pagans of Monroe use it in their rituals, and they are totally nuts. Choose the middle road, son."

Fear coils in my stomach.

The hospital looms larger now, and I notice details I've overlooked before. I note the unusual pattern of windows on the east wing, the subtle religious symbolism in the architectural flourishes, the way the building seems to absorb light rather than reflect it.

"Why are you helping me?" I ask as Jacob pulls into a side street two blocks from the emergency entrance. "If you believe all this, why send me back?"

Jacob kills the engine. In the sudden silence, I hear the faint ringing in my ears from the concussion. "Because some fires you have to fight from inside," he says. "And because you're already changing. I have been touched by the water, and so have you, I see it in you. I was an awful man in my youth, and this is my judgment, I reckon."

I don't ask what he means. Instead, I look at my reflection in the side mirror. My pale gray eyes seem to shift color in the fading light, and for a moment, I don't recognize myself.

"When it happens," Jacob says, "when you see what Ashworth is really doing, you come back to us. We've been preparing too. For longer than he has."

I nod, though I'm not sure what I'm agreeing to. As I open the door, Jacob reaches across and grips my arm. His hand is strong, the skin calloused from years of labor.

"Remember," he says, "the earthquake's coming no matter what. Question is, which side are you on when the ground breaks open?"

He releases me, and I step out, wincing as my weight settles on my injured ankle. The hospital entrance is a hundred yards away, its emergency sign glowing red in the gathering dusk. Staff move in and out, normal medical professionals doing normal medical things.

I take a deep breath and begin limping toward them, my mind filled with images of bacterial cultures, strange symbols, and Bishop Ashworth's name on redacted documents. Behind me, Jacob's truck idles for a moment, then pulls away with a cloud of exhaust.

I am returning to Christ Hospital, and possibly, according to the strange congregation of Bellfountain, part of an undoing.

23
PROPHET'S ASCENSION

After being patched up in the Emergency Department, I allowed myself to rest at home for a few days. Now, I am limping back to the timeclock. Everything is normal at first, same vibe as always, except I don't see the nurse who I need the report from tonight. So, I go looking for her, slowly.

I see Harold's door is ajar. Not wide, just enough to show that someone's been in and out. Out of habit or courtesy, I knock, then limp my way through.

It's the smell I notice first. Death, real death, is both more and less than anyone expects. In the first hour, it's the sweetness that gets your nose, the cloying, honeyed off-note that only later sours into the odor of a thousand decomposing dinners.

Harold lies on the bed, fully dressed for the first time since admission, a paisley hospital gown buttoned all the way to his throat. His head is canted at an unnatural angle, chin nearly touching his left shoulder. The whites of his eyes are visible, ringed by burst capillaries and something that looks, in the half-light, like blue ink. A smear of dried vomit crusts the corners of his mouth, flecked with black.

The mattress is quite tidy. Such a well-made bed is not normal for Harold's mess. There's blood, too, but not much. Just a crescent shadow at the hollow of the throat, beneath where the carotid would be easiest to tap.

I go to the bedside, force my hands to steady. No respiration, no pulse at the radial or carotid. Skin temperature is already below ambient. Harold's frame was skeletal in life; in death, it appears impossibly fragile. His clavicles protrude like coat hangers beneath paper-thin skin. The temporal hollows of his face have deepened, and his cheekbones cast sharp shadows on sunken cheeks. His lips have pulled back slightly from his teeth in what some might mistake for a grimace but is merely the shrinking of tissues as moisture leaves the body. Rigor mortis setting the jaw in a cartoon rictus.

I press two fingers into the flesh above his clavicle. It dimples, and for a moment I imagine the whole body giving way, caving in, melting down into the mattress like wax. His skin, once merely pale, has taken on the waxy yellow-gray pallor that follows death. The areas where the Christ Contagion had manifested as translucent patches have darkened to an opalescent blue-black, like bruises viewed through frosted glass.

His neck is a disaster. The skin here, always loose, now puckers with mottled purple and blue, streaked with yellow where the blood has pooled and I imagine the bacteria there have started their work. I lift the collar of the gown, expecting a bedsore, but find instead a rash of needle marks, some were fresh, some barely clotted. Someone's been here with a syringe, and not in normal nursing or surgical activities.

Someone has killed him.

The voice is so loud in my head that when the next person enters the room I nearly jump out of my skin. It's another nurse, the one on shift before me. Her name escapes me, though I know it starts with an S. Sandra? She stands in the doorway, mouth open, then lets out a slow exhale that balloons her cheeks.

"Thank God," she says. It sounds like relief.

I shoot her a look, eyebrow raised, the universal language of what the fuck? She catches herself, smiles too quickly, and edges into the room.

"Sorry, it's just—he's been, you know. Bad." She gestures at Harold's body, eyes refusing to land anywhere for long. "Didn't think he'd go so fast."

"Did you give him anything?" I ask, trying to keep my tone neutral.

She shakes her head. But something seems off, it's too hard, too rehearsed.

"Just the usual," she says. "He was sleeping last round. He was *normal.*"

I take a breath and force myself to nod. Bad. Normal. Can I get the truth? The room is small, but the distance between us feels insurmountable. I want to ask why she looks so damn happy, but it's not the time. I motion for her to help me with the body, and together we ease Harold into a more anatomically plausible pose, limbs straightened, jaw closed.

In the time it takes us to finish, a third shadow falls across the doorway. Chaplain Leah. She wears her usual: a tight black blouse, skirt, white collar, her naturally auburn hair cinched into a severe French twist that glows red-gold in the fluorescents. She enters without a word, glides in her heels to the bedside, and places two fingers on Harold's forehead. It's a benediction, or maybe a claim.

"We are dust," she says. "But dust is never lost."

For a moment, I think she'll say more, but instead she closes her eyes, breathes in slow, and lets her hand linger on the old man's brow. Her nails are short, but the tips are stained yellow.

I step back, letting the chaplain perform whatever ritual she deems fit. Sandra does the same, folding her hands in front of her and looking everywhere but the corpse. The room fills with the sound of Leah's movements and practices.

The pause of silence stretches until it's unbearable, then snaps.

"I'll need to notify his next of kin," Leah says. "Are you his nurse, tonight? Can you finish the paperwork?"

I nod, though I know Harold has no family, no one who will claim him. The paperwork is for us, for the hospital, for the fiction of order.

Sandra exits first, nearly tripping over her own shoes. Leah lingers, her hand still on Harold's head, fingers splayed like she's listening for a pulse beneath the bone. I watch her for a moment, and when she finally looks up, her green eyes lock onto mine.

"If you see anything strange," she says, "let me know."

She leaves, door closing soft behind her.

The room is silent again, except for the faint hum of the lights.

The hospital is a predator, and death is how it feeds. It digests the old and the sick with a practiced peristalsis: admit, treat, decline, expire, sanitize. Within thirty minutes of Harold's last breath, the paperwork has propagated through the digital organs of Christ's recordkeeping like a fever. By the time the "removal specialists" arrive, they are two men in navy scrubs and a black zipper bag, the third floor hums with a curious peace.

The staff's reaction is more revealing than the corpse. The tension that haunted the nurse's station since his arrival, the way everyone skirted Harold's room like it was a crime scene is now completely gone. Shoulders relax, jokes return, and even the new charge nurse lets herself smile when she thinks I'm not watching. It's not ghoulish, exactly. Relief is an honest emotion. Still, it sets my teeth on edge.

They process the death in a series of rituals. The on-call doc signs the certificate without so much as a glance at the body; he's got a surgery in the morning and doesn't want to linger. The lab comes up for blood draws, labels a pair of vials, and leaves without making eye contact. Chaplain Leah hovers at the periphery, talking in low tones with the unit manager, her expression a sympathy polished to a mirror shine.

The medical examiner shows up last, trailing the smell of stale coffee and menthols. He is one of the few who puts on the contact precaution gown and mask stationed outside Harold's room. He speaks to someone outside the door about being new to the hospital. He says he is a traveler from somewhere in the Midwest, someplace flatter and grayer. Once inside the room, he takes one look at Harold, sighs, and starts dictating into his recorder.

"Male, white, estimated age seventy-eight, multiple chronic conditions, history of mental illness. Found deceased at approximately 22:15 hours. Rigor established, lividity present, no obvious trauma."

He pokes at Harold's neck, the bruises, the crusted needle marks, but shrugs them off with a "typical for end-of-life." I want to ask if he's ever actually seen a bedsore progress in under twelve hours, but I bite my tongue. Nobody wants to be the nurse who makes enemies with the coroner.

Still, something about the chart nags at me. I slip into the empty office, pull up the EMR, thankfully the Bishop allows Christ Hospital an electronic medical record as well as old-fashioned paper files, and scan through Harold's medication logs. The last dose of lorazepam was supposed to be at 19:30. The signature on the entry is mine, but I know I never signed off on it. The next line is even stranger—a note about "extra comfort measures as needed," in handwriting that doesn't match any of the day nurses.

I scroll further, looking for a pattern, and see that every major change in Harold's orders over the last week has a corresponding note, always in different hands, always with the same phrasing: "per protocol." There is no protocol for what they did. Not officially.

Chaplain Leah gives her statement to the examiner with practiced composure. She recounts her last visit with Harold, as how he was "at peace," how he "confessed his fears and found solace in the grace of our Lord." Her language is beautiful, but I know for a fact that Harold spent his final hours raving about rivers and blood and "the silver tongues of angels in the water." I charted as much, but those notes are gone, replaced by a single sanitized paragraph about "patient resting comfortably, no distress."

When Leah is done, she comes to the doorway and fixes me with that impossible green gaze.

"You look tired, Ellis. Let me know if you want to debrief."

I nod, unsure if the offer is comfort or a threat. She lingers a moment, then moves on, heels clicking a slow, even tempo on the tile.

It's almost midnight when the hallway clears out. I'm left with the humming fluorescents, the gentle beep of a distant monitor, and the lingering memory of the body bag folding Harold into a second, black skin.

I hover back at the threshold of Harold's room, one foot in the corridor, feeling the draw of the space. They tell us in training to avoid returning to a deceased patient's room, but I can't help myself. It isn't closure I'm after. It's evidence. Or maybe confession.

The room is cold, and for a moment I imagine Harold's ghost watching from the ceiling corner, jacking off one last time before complete surrender to the afterlife. The image makes me smile. In the silence, even a corpse deserves dignity.

I start my detective work at the bedside table, trying to be methodical like I am in my nursing, no wasted motion or sentimentality to cloud my process. Harold's drawers contain only the usual: New Testament, disposable combs, a fistful of hot sauce packets. I kneel, check the floor and under the mattress. I run my hand between the mattress and frame, a common hiding place for patients who trust neither staff nor fellow patients.

My fingers touch paper. I pull out a small journal, its cover worn soft from repeated handling. Inside, I find loose pages crammed into the binding. At first glance, the journal appears to be filled with Harold's cramped handwriting. I sit on the edge of the bed. The mattress barely yields beneath me. I begin to read.

The first page declares his usual prophetic method in shaky cursive letters: *The gods live within us. Beyond metaphors or psycholog-*

ical constructs, there are living realities inside each human personality. The Christian Trinity is merely one manifestation of this truth. A primitive attempt to categorize the divine energies that exist in every soul.

I turn the page, drawn into Harold's theological framework despite the pressing questions surrounding his death. He claims: *Each person contains divine energies that shape their character and destiny. These energies are not good or evil. Such distinctions are the fabrications of small minds. They are simply patterns of reality, expressing themselves through human vessels.*

The next pages contain a complex taxonomy of these inner gods. Zeus energy manifests as authority and dominance. Hades energy as introspection and hidden knowledge. Aphrodite as sensuality and connection. Athena as strategic intelligence. Harold has mapped them all, creating a system in which human behavior becomes the expression of divine archetypes colliding and collaborating within individual psychologies.

He writes: *I am Lucifer-Christ. The light-bringer and the sacrifice. The questioner and the answered. The rebellion and the surrender. This is why I can see the Contagion for what it truly is. Not infection, but revelation.*

I flip through more pages. Diagrams appear, mapping the divine energies of hospital staff. Bishop Ashworth is labeled Apollo paired with Saturn, the healing god joined with the devourer of children. Nurse Evelyn is Artemis fused with Persephone, the virgin huntress combined with the queen of the underworld. My own name appears, circled several times. Beside it, Harold has written *Hades joined with Dionysus, the lord of death and the god of ecstatic release.*

The final entries become increasingly difficult to follow. The handwriting deteriorates into near-illegible scrawls that spill across the pages without regard for margins or lines.

One passage reads: *The Gray Forces surround us. Humanity itself is the true enemy of divine expression. The masses, with their compromise and conformity, their small desires and smaller minds, create a fog that obscures the gods within. They are the antibodies fighting against the Christ Contagion's attempt to awaken us.*

I settle on the edge of the bed, having gone through the loose pages, and am now to the first page of the journal. The handwriting is different and a bit difficult, but the name at the top is clear: ROMAS. I know immediately who this belongs to. Evelyn's murderer. The talk of the hospital.

Entry after entry, themes emerged: ritual, local plants, the land of the Valley. The further I read, the more the details converge on the nurse Evelyn, the murdered nurse. I am captivated by his descriptions of her, and how he visited her dead mother for the most gentle kiss. He put on Evelyn's lipstick and offered his lips to her mother out of the bold love one could only expect from a traumatized immigrant poet.

At the end of the shift, Harold's room is reset for another less interesting patient, all his dander and life energy has been bleached and scrubbed to sanitize the cell. Now that he is gone it feels more like a patient room again rather than a cell. The bed has been stripped and remade by housekeeping, the vinyl floors buffed for the past hour until the haze of dried vomit and piss is only a memory. Housekeeping has even replaced the wilted geranium in the plastic vase, a touch of color meant to convince the living that decay is reversible.

24
POST-MORTEM

I brought a single sacred datura from upstairs, from the lavish displays the Bishop keeps at the hospital entry points. I swipe my badge on the morgue door, directly in view of two service floor security cameras, fully aware of their ineffectiveness to deter me. I have been in this situation for different reasons, and I know the morgue like I know my private area. This time, I am here for simply a visit. Harold's body is already inside, zipped up and tagged, awaiting a final service that no one else will conduct. It's past midnight, and the corridors on the service floor resonate like a crypt, amplifying every squeak of my shoes in the sick yellowish-green lighting. I notice the change in the refrigerated air the moment I step inside. I feel complete here, entering an empty space of a sick smile that is regaining a missing tooth. I am the cosmetic tooth, and the dentist, for the crooked smile of our walk-in two-gurney morgue.

Inside the small room, Harold Gideon lies supine on a gurney, shrouded beneath a blue mortuary sheet. The body is lit with the humming luminance of overhead LEDs, but still the corners are thick with shadow. In the stillness, I can almost hear the gentle crackle of the cooling fans trying to stave off the inevitable.

I hang my coat on the hook by the sink, scrub my hands until the skin reddens, then snap on a pair of nitrile gloves. They fit poorly, the right thumb already loose, but I don't have it in me to swap for a better pair. The gloves are a ritual more than a necessity. Harold is beyond infection, beyond everything but the slow dissolving of self.

I pull the sheet back with deliberate care, exposing the corpse an inch at a time as I uncover his whole body. Even in death, Harold's body is an exercise in contradiction: papery flesh stretched tight across the zygomatic arch, but the belly slightly distended, pale and liver-spotted. His hands are clenched, not in rigor but in habit, and the skin at the fingertips has already begun to prune.

He looks nothing like he did alive. The rictus is gone, replaced by the slackened jaw and tongue protruding slightly. Harold died mid-harangue. The eyelids are imperfectly closed. It's another nurse's oversight, but I leave them that way. I want his gaze to bear witness.

I fill the basin at the prep sink and set out the usual arsenal: saline, antibacterial wipes, absorbent pads, a sponge. The water steams, fragrant with hospital-grade soap and the faint undercurrent of chlorine. I run the sponge over Harold's scalp first, gently massaging out the flecks of dried emesis and the last evidence of his nightly sweats. His bald head has patches of light hair that comes off in tufts, clinging to the sponge like cobwebs. A small mess of this hair breaks free and floats to the tile, where I leave it.

I work methodically analyzing downwards; face, neck, chest. I am cataloguing every deviation from baseline to summon a second opinion. It's in the middle of the sternum that I spot the first needle mark. At a glance it's nothing: a red dot, barely swollen, less than a millimeter wide. But the location's wrong. Standard IM injections are done in the deltoid, the thigh, the glute. This one is at the edge of the pectoral, less than an inch from the xiphoid. I roll the sticky skin between my fingers and it puckers.

I glide a swab over the puncture, and the cotton head emerges with a thick yellow residue, neither quite blood nor pus. I hold it near my nose and take a sniff. The scent is... medicinal, but not the sweet decay of benzoin or the sharpness of chlorhexidine. More like cough syrup combined with mineral oil and iron. I swab the area once more, placing the cotton swabs into a specimen bag. They probably won't serve as useful evidence, but having them eases my mind.

Next, I shift to the left arm, bending it at the elbow to reveal the underside. That's where I find the true evidence: a double puncture, side by side, at the midpoint of the antecubital fossa. One puncture is old, scabbed, and dark; the other is fresh, with skin drawn tight around a circle of yellowish bruising. I gently twist the arm, trying to see if there's any vein tracking, but the body is already too stiff for easy movement.

Further down the arm, there's an abrasion on the wrist. A faint, rectangular shape bordered by a halo of bruising. As I trace my fingers along the outline, I sense a subtle indentation, a slender object had been pressed against the skin and held there for some time. It's not exactly a restraint, but rather an intentional application of pressure. Applying the same reasoning to the ankles, I discover similar marks, slightly more faded but still visible. I clean the injection sites as thoroughly as possible, even though I know it's purely for appearance. The nonexistent family won't notice, but the preparation now serves my own peace of mind. I take additional photos, then step back to survey the scene: a deceased man, newly created evidence, and my medical instincts collectively insisting that this was anything but a natural death.

The legs are the most challenging part. Now his skin has become so thin it's nearly transparent, with veins protruding like the wires of a cheap lamp. The most concerning area is on the right thigh: three parallel puncture wounds, spaced a finger's width apart, each encircled by an amber residue. There are tiny red or purple spots under the skin between the puncture marks, caused by small amounts of bleeding. I gently clean each wound and make notes about how they look, which direction they go, and how deep they are.

I carefully clean each wound, documenting their appearance, orientation, and depth. I'm not entirely sure what I'm searching for

—perhaps evidence, a pattern, or meaning—but the process gives my hands a sense of purpose.

After removing my gloves, I put on a new pair. There's one last, unavoidable task: cleaning the perineum. It's standard procedure, yet I hesitate, feeling a reluctance to intrude. Nonetheless, I proceed, lifting the scrotum with one hand and swabbing the skin beneath. That's when I noticed it. There's a faint, almost imperceptible bruise on the left inguinal fold, shaped like a thumbprint. I press it gently, and the flesh yields.

I finish the cleaning, change out the absorbent pads, and arrange the body in a position of maximal repose. The hands I uncurl and rest them at his sides. The mouth I close with gentle upward pressure, tucking the tongue back inside with the handle of a swab. I place a sacred datura onto his chest and take a moment of silence. It's as close to peaceful as Harold ever looked. I pull out my phone and take a series of photos. I focus on his splotched skin to focus for my close-ups, followed by a wider shot that includes the body's anatomical landmarks. The artificial shutter sound from the phone echoes off the tiled walls. Lowering the phone, I suddenly feel exposed.

I step away to peel off my gloves, then notice one last anomaly. Behind the right ear, at the mastoid, the skin bears a shallow indentation. I lean in, illuminating it with my phone's flashlight. It's not a bruise, but a pressed mark—a sigil, almost, made of three interlocking rings. The pattern is faint, but as I turn the head to the side, the angle of the light brings it into relief: a figure-eight with a third circle bisecting the midpoint, like a lopsided trinity. I touch the mark with an ungloved finger. The skin is colder here, slick with the last residue of saline. I wipe the ear with a towel, but the sigil remains, part of the flesh. I remember the sketches in Harold's room, the compulsive repetition of this same pattern over and over on notebook margins and napkins.

I stand back, fighting the urge to say something out loud, to confess or invoke my thoughts that Harold had been more important than I could have known. Yet, the silence of the morgue is absolute, and here I am, alone with what was Harold; a mystery that has wrapped itself around my mind. I finish by covering Harold's professionally murdered body with a fresh sheet and respectfully tucking the corners under the gurney. I label the specimen bag and slip it into my pocket, then I upload my photos to a cloud folder on my cell phone only I can access. I switch off the overheads, and let the darkness return. I couldn't go to the police, I wasn't that kind of person. I had no idea what to do next.

25
THE CULT

After Harold's death, I couldn't sleep. I was unaware whether I was mourning or not; however, my mind raced and anxiety kept building onto itself until I knew I had to get out of the house. I had an obsessive thought that I couldn't abandon, so like an alcoholic falling into a bottle after tragedy strikes, I went for my special fix. With my gym bag full of supplies, I left my Witham Hill apartment just after dusk. Eveyln was buried across the street in the Pioneer Cemetery, as revealed by Dr. Harkness. Only a bit of light remained, and it desperately clung to Witham's steep zenith, casting long shadows across the tangled undergrowth. Pioneer Cemetery on Witham Hill had surrendered to time long ago, especially to native and invasive plants. Elderly volunteers kept the grass mowed, but English ivy had taken over sections of the chain-link fence. Pioneer headstones leaned like exhausted witnesses of Corvallis' memory. It didn't feel like a regular cemetery. It felt older than that, and it was waiting ever so patiently.

I took a folding shovel and a spade out of my bag and set my bottle of water down. I wasn't here to mourn. I was here to exhume. Evelyn's grave had a simple marble marker engraved. I found it rather easily by instinct, not by sight. I walked straight to her shallow depression ringed by new growth grass, littered by several rotten wild apples, and the brittle remains of wildflowers cast here and there.

The initial plunge of the shovel into the earth felt unsettlingly wrong. The metallic clang reverberated louder than I had expected. I stopped to listen to what else chants over this graveyard. Houses were in view over a fence, but all was quiet. There was no wind, no birdsong, only the sound of the earth being disturbed when I dug. So, I resumed digging. The soil was thick and moist, like a fertile dirt cake layered with evident history. Each clump I lifted reminded me of my own impermanence in this body, and of the countless lives and belief systems that had once moved across this very location, now reduced to sediment and silence. My perception does not see those who passed through here, and I believe that to see past time constraints is one method of witnessing ghosts. I realized that I wasn't just uncovering a body; I was confronting all belief systems of the afterlife, I was confronting the problem of meaning, I was attempting to dismantle the Cult's doctrines etched onto Evelyn's skin before she was laid to rest. Weeks ago, Dr. Harkness had revealed what I already suspected but couldn't bear to name: Evelyn had been marked. Her body, he said, was defiled with the Cult's sigils —symbols drawn in bodily fluids into her flesh. Reading through Romas' journal after Harold's death had confirmed it: he had chronicled their involvement with the Cult of Pan as it was operating in Corvallis. At the time, the group was led by Chaplain Leah.

I was born into this Cult, not initiated. I never had the suspicion that my family was involved in criminal activity. It all seemed rather innocent, and I think their group had nothing to do with the Pylon in Corvallis. Born into this life, seeing my baby photos, the scandal was simply a cradle circled with antlers and ash. My parents were indeed true believers, and Pan was no symbol in our home, as he was a presence until her death. Like her memory, Pan was a breath in the branches, or an animal's movement in the silence. I try to speak of it plainly, but language betrays me. I see my mother's face in the moonlight, eyes wide and pale like mine, dilated until they drink in the dark.

The Cult of Pan has no single founder, unlike the clear lineage one finds in Wicca or other neo-pagan traditions. Instead, it evolved organically, like a resilient pathogen adapting to cultural antibodies. The groups they have in the Valley are vastly different from the one my parents had. What began as rural fertility rites in isolated European communities mutated into a sophisticated spiritual practice that now maintains Pylons (their term for congregations) across six continents. Their membership numbers are impossible to verify, as they keep no central registry, but conservative estimates suggest tens of thousands at the last census in 2033. They operate beneath the detection threshold of mainstream religious awareness, preferring it that way. Visibility, as my mother used to say, is the first symptom of spiritual dilution.

The soil grew darker as I dug. Wetter. More resistant. I remembered the rituals. I heard the sex-magick rites, the synchronized breathing, the ecstatic trance states. I'd seen it all from my window looking down in the gardens, even as a child. Evelyn had seen it too, whatever they do out here, and it had killed her.

That much I know. Whether out of devotion or madness, I still can't say. But the act of murder, of sacrifice, was ritualistic on that poor beauty. Intentional. And now, as I dug, I felt the weight of that knowledge pressing down on me. The soil clung to my hands like guilt, as if I had killed her. I was only born into this; I never asked for that inheritance.

The Cult's cosmology centers on Pan not merely as a minor Greek deity but as a primal force predating civilization itself. They view the god Pan as simultaneously a literal entity and psychological archetype. For the Cult, Pan represents the wilderness that civilization cannot tame, such is seen as an indwelling of the wild, this path holds the keys to the deeper parts of human consciousness that remain gloriously feral despite millennia of socialization. In their theology, Pan can be embodied as he exists at the nexus of opposites while erasing the false dichotomy between them.

I saw Mother and other initiates exhibit physiological responses consistent with extreme parasympathetic arousal during Pan invocations: pupil dilation, gooseflesh, synchronized breathing patterns among participants. Once, during a summer solstice ritual I observed from the periphery at age twelve, three participants began bleeding from their noses simultaneously. No medical intervention was sought or needed; the bleeding stopped precisely when the drums ceased.

I was told Evelyn was murdered not long after she joined the Cult. Romas, the housekeeper, did it, they all say. Reading his journal that somehow ended up in Harold's possession, Romas doesn't even know if he did or did not. The ghost of Edmund Creffield is who he blames for animating his hand in her death. Perhaps the truth was out of devotion to the Cult or the madness of their love poisoned by ritual sex triangles, I don't know. That type of knowledge stains everything. Even now, as a non-believer in the Cult's ways, I can't scrub all the symbolism out. The sex magick, the sigils, the breath-led ecstasy. All that bullshit haunts me. I may not believe, but belief has me by the balls until I fall into my own wild instincts with romantic involvement with dead women. I'm monogamous and traditional then. I'm not currently seeing any deceased individuals at the moment. In fact I thought I may be cured of such romantic folly. So when I open Evelyn's coffin, I'm hoping she'll give me a sign that she's single too, and I will just take things as they come for us.

I sat back on my heels, breathing hard. The act of digging had become something else—an excavation of belief, a descent into memory. The soil had spoken in layers. Each scoop with my stupid garden spade was like a syllable of a terrible story.

I wasn't just digging up Evelyn.

I was digging up myself.

The untamed unconscious, it was like the fertile layers of the ground, and that's how Mother described Pan's domain too. "The place where your thoughts grow wild," she told me once while cleaning my skinned knee. "Like the forest behind our property. Beautiful, dangerous, and so necessary." At the time, I thought she was distracting me from the sting of my wounds. Now I recognize she was preparing me for initiation as it is bound to our wounds. Such a call was an invitation I thought I declined by leaving Greenville after they both passed, yet in changing my name to Horning, I started a return without being there, without going back. Then pursuing nursing rather than the "healing arts" she practiced shows how the repressed unconscious mind mingles with so-called change.

I dig under moonlight, shirt discarded beside the spade, my torso streaked with sweat and soil. The air is damp, heavy with the scent of loam and old roots. Each strike of the tool's blade into the earth feels like a trespass in foreign soil. I pause often, glancing up toward Witham Hill whenever headlights sweep through the trees from the street. A car passes slowly, tires whispering against asphalt, and I crouch low, heart thudding. When it's gone, I attempt to dig quickly.

The harder I try to dig, the more the soil resists me. My muscles tire from things blocking the shovel that seem too dense, tangled tree roots, and sharp bits of broken pottery and glass. My hand finds glass before my eyes warn me, a broken soda bottle long buried, an Orange Crush, and pain flares as it slices through my palm when I try to brush dirt aside. Blood mixes with the freshly overturned dirt. I wrap the wound with a piece of fabric torn from my shirt, now useless anyway, and keep going. I have to keep going. The wound pulses, but I don't stop. I cannot stop now.

Then I hear it. There is something moving behind the Odd Fellows cemetery shed, near the fence, by the neighboring houses, where they keep the wheelbarrows and buckets of lime. A low rustle, absolutely deliberate movement of a person most likely. Not wind. Not a raccoon or a bunny. I freeze in place, adjust my breath to breathe shallowly, and I listen. The sound comes again as a dragging weight, something rather heavy pulled across gravel and pine needles. I immediately think that someone, most likely a raving lunatic, is about to bury a body and will discover me. I could get tangled up in their legalities, or they may just want to kill me as a witness to their murder. Or perhaps, I could get framed for their crimes. I grip the shovel like a weapon, eyes fixed on the dark edge of the shed.

A massive shape emerges which is not human, it is large but low and muscular, gliding with predatory grace. The cougar doesn't seem to see me at first or perhaps it already did. Its jaws are clamped around the neck of a young deer, limp and bloodied, legs trailing like broken branches. The cat pauses, ears flicking, then turns its head toward me. For a moment, our eyes lock, my blue fixed to the cat's amber, and something passes between us. Recognition. Permission. Then it vanishes into the underbrush with its prize, leaving behind a deeper silence than existed before its arrival.

I take it as a spiritual sign more than a metaphor or a coincidence. A living emblem of wild sovereignty, dragging death through sacred ground. The casket waits. I dig deeper.

By hour three, my muscles burn and my breath comes in ragged bursts. The moon has shifted, casting long shadows that seem to lean toward the grave. I strike something metallic. Not the casket. Smaller. I brush away the soil with trembling fingers and uncover a bracelet, dulled by the dirt but unmistakably hers. "Evelyn," engraved in a looping script.

The moment I touch it, something shifts. A low hum rises. It's not in the air, but in my chest, deeper even; it's in the marrow of my bones. The trees seem to lean closer. My pulse slows. I feel her. Not memory. Not grief. Presence. The sympathetic resonance Mother spoke of. A tuning fork struck in the soul. My vision blurs at the edges, and for a moment I see the bracelet glowing faintly, pulsing in rhythm with my heartbeat. I put it on, and it fit snugly.

I kneel there, half-submerged in the grave, bloodied and filthy, eyeing the bracelet like a relic. The soil around me feels warmer for a moment, alive. I sense more than Miss Evelyn. There is a presence of something else within and without. I sense another consciousness besides the messengers within me. The same current that ran through Mother when she spoke of resonance, when she sat transfixed before her drawing of the half-goat figure emerging from spiraling darkness. That image and that feeling wasn't confined to her rituals. It's here, now, vibrating beneath my skin. I think back.

The Cult maintains dual devotion to two figures who might seem contradictory to outsiders: Rosaleen Norton and Aleister Crowley. Norton, the Australian artist known as "The Witch of Kings Cross," is venerated as a famous prophetess of Pan. Her trance-induced artworks are treated as sacred texts in visual form. The Pylons maintain collections of her reproductions, studying the anatomical distortions and chthonic imagery for divine insight. Mother possessed an original Norton drawing. It was a framed figure of a half-human and half-goat emerging from a spiraling darkness. She would sit before it for hours, her breathing shallow, in what she called "sympathetic resonance." She also did it to the works of Father's friend Paul Laffoley. When art serves as a portal of this magnitude, the artist achieves a method of return from the dead into the hosting consciousness of the admiring viewer, but they must enter the sympathetic resonate state.

I've examined Norton's artwork through both aesthetic and clinical lenses. The neurological implications of her visual motifs suggest temporal lobe activity consistent with spiritual experiences. The Cult believes Norton literally saw through the veil between worlds, capturing Pan's actual form rather than merely imagining it. When I was young, I once saw the figures in her drawings move, just at the edge of my vision. A visual artifact, I told myself then. A warning, I wonder now.

Crowley receives similar reverence, though more for methodology than mysticism. His systematic approach to ritual, his emphasis on personal gnosis, and his framework of Thelema provide the structural foundation upon which the Cult's practices are built. They've adapted his famous dictum to their purposes: "Do what thou wilt shall be the whole of the Law," becomes a prescription for authentic alignment with one's deepest nature rather than mere hedonism. Mother kept his books locked in a Victorian redwood cabinet. I found the key at eleven, read them by flashlight, and had at the time laughed at the structured paths of breath work and arrangement of the ritual space.

I remember my mother explaining Crowley's contribution while preparing herbs in our kitchen: "He gave modern explorers the keys to the kingdom, Ellis. Not a heaven beyond, but to something real in our flesh. The country that existed before we built fences around our souls." Her hands had such a gentle grace as she measured herbs I now know were potentially toxic if improperly dosed.

But the Cult was only inspired in certain areas of magick by Crowley. At its core, the Cult operates from an animistic framework that would appear primitive to modern religious scholars who overlook how it contains sophisticated ecological awareness. Unlike the monotheistic separation of creator and creation, the Cult of Pan perceives no membrane between spirit and matter. Every stone, stream, and synapse thrums with consciousness. I recall Mother speaking to plants as she watered them, not with the affected sentimentality of amateur gardeners, but with the gravity of diplomatic negotiations. "They understand more than we do," she would say. "Their roots touch realms our minds can't reach."

This isn't metaphorical for adherents. The Cult conducts regular assays of local environments—soil samples, water quality, wildlife population counts—alongside their spiritual practices. My mother maintained meticulous records of the ecosystem surrounding Devil's Castle, our family estate. I found these logbooks more compelling than her grimoires; they contained rainfall measurements alongside notations of spiritual potency, creating a strangely compelling data set correlating natural phenomena with mystical experience.

Perhaps the most challenging aspect for outsiders to comprehend is the Cult's ritualistic approach to adult consensual sex magick. Where mainstream religions lock desire behind moral barriers, the Cult positions erotic energy as fundamentally sacramental to the will achieving its goals. The dissolution of the boundaries against using such witchcraft during sexual climax creates, in their method of liberation theology, a momentary opening of spiritual truth, a gap, through which divine consciousness can flow. This isn't simple hedonism or role playing.

Mother explained it when I was too young to fully understand: "The neurochemical cascade during arousal and orgasm creates brain states nearly identical to mystical experiences documented across cultures. We simply utilize this natural function intentionally to further change driven by our will." Her frankness stunned my middle school sensibilities, but the memory of her explanation has proven consistent with neurological research I've encountered since.

Their ritualized practices include *hieros gamos* (sacred marriage), where participants embody divine aspects to commune with each other and, by extension, with Pan himself. Sex magick focuses this energy toward specific intentions, harnessing the body's electromagnetic fields during arousal to influence probability fields (their term, not medical science's). Similar to the Rajneesh movement of India, that relocated to Oregon in 1981, the Cult also uses ecstatic dance that induces trance states through exhaustion and rhythmic movement, often culminating in what outsiders might crudely term "orgy" when climax happens to some participants who experience a total body and mind communion with a higher presence.

By the third hour of digging, my body begins to fail in increments. My gardening shovel feels heavier, the soil seems more resistant, the earth itself is reluctant to release Evelyn. I was tired before I began, and my vision narrows to the rhythmic motion of digging—lift, strike, drag, repeat. I sit back on my haunches, sweat slicking my skin, and reach for the bottle I buried in the shade of a cedar root. The water is warm, metallic, but I drink greedily, letting it run down my throat and over my cracked lips.

I think of Mother, in her glory days with hands stained with tinctures. Her voice would be low and precise as she spoke of sympathetic resonance and the "keys to the kingdom." I think of Evelyn, her bracelet on my wrist. And I think of the Christ Contagion in Marys River, the way the water shimmered. Pan's laughter echoing through the aquifer, a sacrament that's possibly septic.

The cougar's eyes still linger in my mind. I stand to stretch, muscles trembling, and then return to the pit. Three hours down and no coffin yet. Probably several more hours to go. The moon has shifted, and the shadows lean differently now across the Odd Fellows Cemetery. I rest for now, but will soon dig again, for Evelyn.

26
GRAVE METHODOLOGIES

I resumed digging just past midnight, with more gusto than before as the forest settled into its nocturnal rhythm around me. My shovel bites into more compact earth, the half-opened grave a dark mouth in the clearing as I stand roughly three feet within its changing space. The camping lantern I've brought casts a sickly glow across the disturbed soil that I've thrown about, and it's barely enough light to work by, but I dare not risk more and be seen. Not here. Not for this. I remain vigilant enough to listen to the whispering leaves, the distant symphony of insects, and the steady rhythm of my own breath as I descend further toward her.

I look up to clear the sweat from my temple, and bats fly in erratic arcs overhead, their tiny bodies momentarily blotting out bright stars before vanishing into the darkness again. A dog barks somewhere in the distance, a guttural sound that feels accusatory. The forest hushes and shifts sometimes without wind, as though the trees themselves are whispering about my transgression. I ignore them all. My focus narrows to the pit before me, to the methodical rise and fall of the shovel in my hands.

The metal blade strikes the ground with a muffled thud, over and over again, as I try to establish a work rhythm. Damp soil clings to my boots, creeping up the leather. The scent of dirt and root decomposition fills my nostrils, a good earthy and primal scent that refreshes my senses. Yet beneath it all lies another smell, one that has grown sweet for me over the years, its faint but unmistakable—the sweet-sour note of human decay. Was it just my imagination, clinging to hope? Or was Evelyn's body truly beginning to off-gas? I didn't allow myself to wonder. I just kept digging. I could not speculate when work had to be done. I could only dig further.

I haven't spoken aloud in hours, naturally I was assuming this act requires silence, not out of reverence but necessity. The Cult taught me that certain thresholds, such as graves, crossroads, forest clearings, are acoustically sensitive. Words can summon. Or disrupt. I learned this lesson at seven, when Mother caught me singing beside an open grave at the edge of our property. The slap came first, then the lesson: "The dead listen differently than the living. Never give them words they might misinterpret." It was a different time and a different place, and out here, in the Valley, a Southern life-lesson slap could get the parent a felony charge.

Sweat covers my back despite the cool night air. I pause to wipe my brow with my forearm, knowing I am filthy, leaving a smear of dirt across my face. My arms ache pleasantly, muscles burning with the kind of pain that promises transformation. I flex my fingers around the wooden handle of the shovel, feeling blisters that nursing work never gave me. This labor marks me differently.

The Cult's magical methodologies were never metaphorical. They're systems designed to interface with forces that defy empirical scrutiny. Mother explained this to me when I was ten, her gray eyes reflecting the candlelight as we sat in the basement of Devil's Castle. "Science has limits, Ellis. It can only measure what its instruments are calibrated to detect. But consciousness—true consciousness—exists in spectrums beyond human sensing."

I drive the shovel deeper, feeling a rush of satisfaction when it sinks to the hilt. Three feet down now. Halfway there. The walls of the grave rise around me like a womb, sheltering me from the watching forest. I work faster, a rhythm establishing itself in my movements. Dig, lift, toss. Dig, lift, toss. A dance as old as humanity.

The Cult's sigil craft, derived from Rosaleen Norton but refined through generations, was not symbolic art. It's circuitry. Trance states induce specific brainwave patterns, and the resulting sigils are non-Euclidean, recursive, optically active, and function like keys to locked perceptual states. I remember watching Mother draw them, her hand moving with inhuman precision across parchment made from deer skin. The shapes seemed to move, to breathe, to want.

Mother's cedar box was lined with lead. "Some symbols are too potent to leave exposed," she would say, her voice low and serious. "They continue working whether you're attending to them or not, like radiation." I didn't believe her until I photographed one and slept beside it. That night, sleep paralysis gripped me. A goat-like figure stood in the corner, its eyes pulsing like twin moons. When I told her, she burned the photo and performed a severing ritual. The paralysis never returned.

Four feet down. The soil changes texture, becoming damper, heavier. Each shovelful requires more effort now. I feel it in my shoulders, my lower back. The physical strain grounds me, keeps me present when my thoughts want to scatter like birds startled from a branch. I'm aware of every muscle fiber stretching and contracting, every drop of sweat, every breath that fogs slightly in the cool night air. This body feels simultaneously alien and intensely present. I should say *my* body, but is it mine?

Spirit work is literal. Mother's barred owl arrived at sunset every evening for seventeen years. It would perch on the weathervane atop Devil's Castle, its round face turned toward her window regardless of wind or rain. After her death, it vanished. I searched for it, even left offerings of raw liver, small bones, and silver coins at the base of trees. Nothing. The Cult teaches that familiars are drawn to energetic resonance. When that resonance ceases, so does the bond.

I pause, leaning on my shovel as a memory surfaces. Mother,

standing in the garden behind Devil's Castle, her arms outstretched. The barred owl descending from the twilight sky to land on her wrist, talons curling gently around the leather bracer she wore. "They're not pets, Ellis," she said, noticing my fascination. "They're colleagues. You don't own them; you earn their cooperation."

The memory dissolves as my shovel strikes something harder than earth. It is a different sound, something hollow, or best described as wooden. My heart lurches against my ribs. I've found it. I drop to my knees, setting the shovel aside, and begin clearing dirt away with my hands. My fingernails split and tear against the wood, but I barely notice the pain. Blood mingles with soil, primitive paint marking my progress.

I remember my first experience of peripheral consciousness. I'm ten, lying in a salt circle in the woods, instructed to "listen to what isn't human." Mother sits cross-legged beside me, her voice guiding me into trance. My vision widens unnaturally, colors shifting to include spectrums I've never seen before. Sounds layer and respond, the whisper of leaves becomes language, the hum of insects forms chords. I feel limbs I don't possess—wings, perhaps, or something more alien. The sensation should frighten me, but instead, it feels like remembering.

The Cult teaches that this state allows communion with land spirits and daimonic entities. Offerings, trance, frequency matching are some techniques for bridging worlds. I once saw Mother synchronize her breath with a stream until the water seemed to speak, ripples forming patterns too regular to be natural. She transcribed what she heard in a journal bound in snake skin, writing so quickly her pen tore through the paper in places.

More dirt cleared. The casket begins to take shape beneath my fingers. Evelyn is in simple pine, already softening with moisture. No metal fixtures, no ornate handles. A pauper's box, paid for by hospital donations. The thought sends a surge of tenderness through me. Even in death, Evelyn was denied dignity. I will restore it to her, in my way.

The Cult's herbalism was pharmacological precision disguised as folklore. Sacred datura, fly agaric, mugwort, among others, were each a key to a specific door. I dismissed it during nursing school, my mind crowded with medical textbooks and clinical rotations. Science seemed cleaner, more reliable. Compared to my childhood, science seemed like the best alternative. The Threefold Path of Initiation in my youth was not a ladder, it was a trident. The Horned Path was my beginning. Wilderness immersion, ritual solitude, communion with Pan through deprivation and attention. At seven, I spent so many hours alone in the woods, encircled by salt, listening. By my fifth vigil, the forest began to respond. Shadows moved counter to wind. Sounds echoed my thoughts. I wasn't afraid. Not then. I had an active imagination, as children should, but I loved the forest.

By 2:47 a.m., I've reached the point where enough is cleared, and I can almost open the lid. I drop to my knees, brushing away the final layer of soil with my hands. The wood is damp, streaked with some fungal bloom. I note pale, threadlike mycelium spreading across the pine in patterns that remind me of my own neural networks changing with the Contagion. I trace its edges with trembling fingers, feeling the grain of the wood, the places where moisture has already begun its work of dissolution.

"Eve" is carved faintly into the lid, the letters softened by time and exposure. Nothing else. No dates, no epitaph. Just her nickname, as though her entire existence could be contained in those three letters. I sit back on my heels, breath shallow, heart thudding with a rhythm that feels older than my own. The lantern flickers, shadows dancing across the open grave like spectral witnesses to my transgression.

A breeze passes through the trees, carrying the scent of mugwort and cedar. I feel the forest lean in, its attention palpable. At 3:00 a.m., Evelyn's grave is fully open. The casket lies exposed, cleared of soil by my hands. I do not yet open it. That moment will come. But for now, I sit beside it, listening for the quiet creaking of a coffin that wants its contents to be revealed.

I place my palms flat against the wood, feeling for warmth, for vibration, for any sign that what lies within is more than meat and bone. The Cult teaches that consciousness lingers for nine days after death, gradually untethering from the physical form. Evelyn has been gone far longer than that, but other forms of awareness might have taken residence. Bacterial consciousness. Fungal networks. The small, hungry things that reclaim all flesh.

"I've come for you," I whisper, breaking my silence at last. The words feel thick on my tongue, laden with intention. "I've come to see you."

I work my fingers beneath the edge of the lid. No nails secure it, signaling another sign of the hasty, underfunded burial. The wood offers a protesting sound, a low groan that sounds almost human. Then it gives way, rising under my hands like a lover responding to touch.

The smell hits me first. A complex symphony of decay that my medical brain automatically catalogs: putrescine and cadaverine with their rotting fish stench, hydrogen sulfide's reek of rotten eggs, and the sour stench of methanethiol, like spoiled cabbage. The sweet-sour reek of a body returning to its component parts. I don't flinch. Instead, I breathe deeply, letting the scent fill my lungs, my bloodstream, my brain. There is information here, a chemical language that speaks of the movement of a life into new quantum forms.

Even now, at an ageless decay, she is forever forty-one and long past breath; the most arresting figure Christ Hospital has ever held, be it another nurse or patient. Her presence was a contradiction then and now. Even when her flesh is undone, she is commanding desire.

Her face, once the axis of every gaze, is now a mask of decomposition. The skin bears the bruised palette of death with greenish-black blooms spreading across her cheeks like corrupted rouge. Beneath the surface, collapsed veins sketch marbled patterns through tissue that glistens with partial liquefaction. An embalmer's attempt at artistic peace has been overtaken by the swell of gases, warping her expression into a twisted smile that bares teeth through receding gums. She appears feral, yet almost flirtatious.

Her burial dress would have been considered modest by today's standards, yet now it clings to the warped body with obscene intimacy. The body beneath has reshaped itself: the abdomen bloated with rot, the thighs sunken, the chest collapsed inward sighing one final time. Stains have spread across the fabric, dark and wet, where her organs have begun their slow surrender. Around her lips and nostrils, purge fluid glistens like smeared lipstick.

In the folds of her dress and the damp hollows of her body, white larvae writhe with hunger. Insects drawn by the scent of her, have laid their claim. Their movement is rhythmic, almost erotic in its repetition.

Her hands are now blackened claws, the skin slipping from the underlying tissue like wet gloves. The fingernails, still immaculately shaped, have separated from their beds, revealing the dark spaces beneath. I imagine her fingers checking IVs and adjusting monitors.

"Evelyn," I breathe, and the name feels like a key turning in a lock somewhere inside me. Something opens. Something floods in.

I reach into the coffin, my hand hovering over her face.

My fingers make contact with her cheek, and the skin gives way beneath the gentlest pressure, sliding across the underlying tissue like wet paper. I don't recoil. Instead, I trace the contours of her face, noting the places where decomposition has advanced most rapidly, the areas where traces of her beauty still persist beneath the ravages of death.

"They didn't take proper care of you," I murmur, anger flaring at the evidence of hasty preparation. The incision at her neck is crude, the sutures already coming apart as the skin deteriorates. They skipped cavity embalming entirely, a cost-cutting measure that accelerated her decay. No wonder the smell is so potent, so rich with information. Her internal organs have been left to their own devices, breaking down according to their composition, creating a complex ecosystem within the shell of her body.

I lean closer, drawn by a need that transcends the physical. This is not merely about flesh or its corruption. This is about transition, the space between states of being. The Cult teaches that death is not an endpoint but a threshold. What lies beyond is not absence but transformation. Evelyn is becoming something else, something beyond the human constraints she inhabited in life.

My hands move lower, tracing the contours of her collarbones, visible through the deteriorating fabric of her dress. The bone feels solid beneath the slipping skin, a reminder of the structural foundation that persists when softer tissues fail. I find comfort in this; the architectural truth of the body that remains when identity dissolves.

Her chest has collapsed inward, the ribs visible as ridges beneath stained fabric. When I apply slight pressure, my fingers sink into the softness beneath, releasing a fresh wave of gas and fluid. The smell intensifies, complex and overwhelming. My clinical detachment wavers for a moment, then reasserts itself. I am both participant and observer, both worshipper and analyst.

"I've missed you," I tell her, and it's true in ways that defy rational explanation. What I miss is not the woman she was, as I never met her before. Although, I treasured her from the moment that Dr. Harkness showed her image to me. What I long for is the opportunity to witness this transformation, to accompany my lovers through the most profound changes; the most delicate and beautiful stages of decomposition. Romas, the Lithuanian housekeeper, had taken her at her opening stage of death, and I am assured he knew nothing of death's beauty. He was a man obsessed with an objectified living woman. I knew what she was beyond that, I recognized her outside the realm of pretty objects. Death has tried to exclude me, as it excludes all the living. But I have made my own door to her with each shovel of dirt. I earned my date, not only through my actions, but through the realms opened by fate.

I lean down, my face inches from hers, breathing in the gases of her decomposition. My body responds with a surge of arousal, and with a sound of pleasure, just like Mother did smelling a cake fresh from the oven. I have an odd recognition of her previous fertility in her current decay, of her potential in this dissolution. The Cult teaches that death and sex are neighboring territories, separated by a membrane as thin as consciousness itself. I press my lips to her forehead, tasting the chemical bitterness of partial embalming fluid mingled with the saltiness of purge fluids.

"I'm here now," I whisper against her skin. "You won't be alone again."

The forest watches. Perhaps it doesn't judge at all—perhaps it recognizes in my actions the same processes it has housed for millennia. Growth from decay. Life from death. An endless cycle of transformation that doesn't recognize the artificial boundaries of human morality.

I sit back, my hands resting on the edge of the coffin. Evelyn lies before me, simultaneously present and absent, an object lesson in impermanence. The lantern light flickers across her changed features, creating illusions of movement that make my heart race. For a moment, I imagine her eyes opening, her decomposing lips forming my name. The thought doesn't frighten me. It exhilarates me.

This is only the beginning. The grave is open. What happens next will transform us both.

27
UNEARTHED

The coffin creaks beneath my weight as I embrace Evelyn. Her body yields as I press against her, the stiffness of rigor mortis long since passed. I feel her bones shift beneath me, her form accommodating mine as I carefully position myself above her. I remove my filthy clothing and place them neatly folded by her feet. My hands slide beneath her burial dress, feeling the cool, tacky texture of her skin against my palms. I return to my pants and retrieve my pocket knife. Carefully, I remove Evelyn's saturated dress. Time passes as I hold her hand and look at her nudity.

Again, I embrace her, lying prostrate on her unclothed body. I reach around and feel how muscular her buttocks still are, although they seem hardened more than they would if she were living. Evelyn had a really nice ass, in my hands it is too nice, and I cannot wait any longer. But when I try to enter Evelyn's body, there is too much resistance by the settled flesh, but I continue to push forward in pain. I give my hand as much spit as I can, and her decaying form eventually accepts me, and I feel the barriers between us dissolve. Barriers of flesh, of time, of social constraint, tear away as our fluids mingle in the valley of death.

"The moment someone becomes an object rather than a sovereign participant, Pan withdraws his presence," Mother had told me when I was twelve. I had discovered ritual implements in our home that were objects that suggested sexual practices I wasn't yet meant to understand. She sat me down, her eyes serious but unashamed.

"We seek liberation through conscious boundary crossing, not through exploitation," she continued. "Predators are immediately expelled from the community."

I remember her hands, steady and strong, as she explained the difference between power exchange and power abuse, between ritual and gratification. Even then, she spoke to me as a future initiate rather than a child.

As I move within Evelyn now, do I honor that teaching? Has her consent come not from her lips, as she is not longer able to speak, but now from the universe that has arranged this meeting, from the soil that cradles us both, from the dawn that illuminates our union? This is theology in truth as it is made flesh and returns to soil. Or is it flesh that is now transcending into theology? I had questions born from questions.

Now, as I move even faster within her, we move together, rocking the casket against the dirt I dug around it, and then suddenly, I become afraid. Like a bolt of lightning having struck me, I question the ethics of the moment, and I ask: what is consent within the realm of theology; was the annunciation sanctified, or was it merely scripted? Did the Virgin Mary say yes, truly, or was her silence mistaken for surrender? Can consent exist in the absence of full understanding or freedom? The myth binds us, yes—but does it bind her? And if the seed she bore would one day cry out in agony, "My God, why have you forsaken me," then what covenant was truly made? Was it love, or was it the ultimate disruption of ethics through a violent sacrifice dressed in sanctity?

If the divine bypasses the will of the vessel, if the body is claimed without full voice, then what remains of moral law here among those who create civil contracts in a perfumed society? Can ritual, even the sacred, absolve the absence of autonomy? What of the ethics of memory, of the moment that builds it, of the story retold until it forgets its origin? Will I become a saint, or a prophet too?

Have I, too, treated Evelyn as a means rather than an end? A conduit for my own myths, not a sovereign soul? In that instant, I was no longer within the human conditions of ethical reasoning. I was only the machinery of myth, grinding forward, indifferent to consent, and I was questioning why in the deepest sense.

Around us, the cemetery seems to quicken with attention. The roots beneath us pulse with subtle movement, reaching upward through the soil toward our heat. Insects emerge from the earth, drawn by chemical signals and energetic shifts. The wind changes direction, curling into our grave-space with curious fingers. Nature does not judge me. It witnesses, participates, transforms alongside us.

I note the greenish-black discoloration spreading across Evelyn's abdomen, I smell the sweet-sour notes of putrefaction mingling with the rich loam of freshly turned cemetery soil. This is the truth of our existence. The real is not the sanitized, preserved illusion that modern funeral practices perpetuate, but the raw reality of our return to elemental form.

Mother would stand in our garden after rain, fingers buried in the soil, eyes closed in reverence. "This earth contains the atoms of countless beings," she would tell me. "When you touch soil, you touch your ancestors." She would bring her dirt-covered fingers to her lips, tasting the earth in a gesture both scientific and sacramental. "Remember, Ellis, the boundary between living and dead is permeable. Every breath you take contains molecules that once comprised other bodies."

The memory sharpens my awareness of each breath I take now, air moving in and out of my lungs in the enclosed space of the grave. Each inhalation draws in particles of Evelyn, microscopic fragments of her dissolving form entering my body with every breath, this is communion in its most literal sense.

I press my lips to her neck, tasting salt and a grit like soil. The skin there has begun to slip, a phenomenon I've witnessed in the hospital when death goes undiscovered for too long. The fluid beneath is cool against my tongue, carrying complex signatures my body interprets as taste. The part of me that has been socialized, the part trained in sterile procedures and pathogen awareness, flinches at this transmissible contact. But the deeper part, the part that has always known this moment was inevitable, recognizes it as the holy sacrament.

The pressure builds within me, a gathering force that feels both physical and metaphysical. When release comes, it pulses through me like revelation, collapsing the boundaries I've maintained between my personal identity and my ancestral inheritance. In this moment of ecstatic dissolution, I understand that I've never truly left the Cult. I've merely been practicing its principles through different forms, speaking its truths in different languages.

I remain inside her as my breathing slows, unwilling to break this connection. Morning light filters through the branches above us, casting dappled patterns across Evelyn's face and my bare shoulders. Her eyes remain closed, sunken now into their sockets, but her lips have parted slightly in what looks almost like a smile. Her expression must be a trick of decomposition, the nurse in me knows, but the son of the priestess sees it as acknowledgement. A come-hither expression in the breakdown of the body, an exceptional human specimen.

"Thank you," I whisper, speaking to Evelyn, to the earth, to Pan, to my mother's memory. "Thank you for this passage."

A beetle emerges from the soil beside Evelyn's head, its carapace iridescent in the strengthening light. It pauses, antennae waving, sensing the energy between us, then continues its journey across the satin lining of the coffin. I watch its progress with reverence, recognizing another participant in this transformation.

The wind shifts again, bringing with it the distant sounds of early morning traffic. The world continues its rhythms, unaware of the threshold I've just crossed, the boundary I've dissolved. I am changed now, initiated through my own design into mysteries my mother always knew awaited me.

I observe the beetle crawling across Evelyn's collarbone, its carapace catching the strengthening sunlight. I do not brush it away but welcome it as another participant in this communion. The boundary between her body and the earth is already dissolving; I am simply hastening and honoring the process.

My mother taught me that the Cult's ecological ethics extended beyond human interactions. "We leave natural locations better than we found them," she would say, applying scientific precision to what others might dismiss as sentimental environmentalism. I remember following her through forest clearings after rituals, watching her collect local plants and fungi. I recall her explaining that "energetic footprints can be as damaging as physical ones."

I will leave this place sanctified, not desecrated. When I am finished, I will restore Evelyn to the earth with greater care than she received from the morticians who rushed her burial. I will rebury her with appropriate offerings, leaving this site energetically balanced despite, or perhaps because of, our transgressive communion. Before this, I need to say goodbye and make love again. Lovemaking in the morning is the romantic's kiss to a new day.

And so we do, or so I do, as the sun rises higher in the sky. I am fully present in my body yet simultaneously elsewhere, accessing layers of consciousness that extend beyond the physical act. Evelyn's decaying form becomes a doorway between worlds. Through her, I commune with mysteries that academic theology can only theorize about.

The moment of culmination approaches, and I feel energy coursing through newly formed channels in my nervous system. The boundary between pleasure and revelation blurs, then vanishes entirely. As I release into her, I swear I see faint luminescent traces where our skin connects. It's a subtle glow that might be hallucination born of exhaustion and ecstasy, or might be something more.

Afterward, I lay beside her in the narrow coffin, my hand still resting on her chest. I retrieve my journal from beside the grave and begin to write, my hand trembling slightly from the exchange of energy still coursing through my system. The first birds begin their morning songs in the trees overhead. The sound filters down to us like a benediction. My breath is more visible in the cool morning air, mingling with the gases of her decomposition in a marriage of molecules dancing between us.

In this sacred exhaustion, as light strengthens across the Odd Fellows Pioneer Cemetery, I record what I have learned, what I have become. My filthy hand moves across my journal, capturing insights that already feel like they might slip away if not anchored in the memory of written language.

As I lie beside Evelyn in her open grave, a new morning is breaking across Witham Hill, and my thoughts turn to the Cult's enduring wisdom. Perhaps most fundamental to their longevity is their resistance to dogmatic ossification. While I fled from their practices, sought sterile medical science as refuge, they continued to evolve without me as a living theological organism.

Unlike religious traditions that canonize specific interpretations, the Cult deliberately maintains theological fluidity. They embrace paradox and personal revelation over fixed doctrine. Mother called it "spiritual evolution in real-time," explaining that Pan's nature itself resists complete definition or containment.

This resistance to dogma manifests in their organizational structure. Authority rotates regularly among qualified members rather than creating permanent hierarchies. Their ritual forms evolve through continuous experimentation and feedback rather than adherence to unchanging texts. Even their sacred writings remain in perpetual revision, with new insights incorporated through consensus processes that balance innovation with traditional knowledge.

This flexibility allowed them to survive centuries of persecution, adapting like a resilient virus that modifies its surface proteins while maintaining its essential nature.

I close my eyes, feeling the weight of soil beneath my naked back, and remember the seasonal gatherings at Devil's Castle. Members would engage in what they termed "theological laboratories," as structured debates and experimental rituals are designed to test new approaches. These weren't casual discussions but rigorous examinations of proposed innovations.

I recall one midsummer gathering when a member proposed incorporating digital technology into traditional rituals. The resulting discussion lasted seventeen hours, with perspectives ranging from historical precedent to neurological impact. Some argued that artificial light disrupted pineal function necessary for visionary states; others suggested that technology itself was merely an extension of Pan's creative impulse through human vessels.

The debate demonstrated intellectual rigor comparable to academic discourse, with each proposal subjected to scrutiny from multiple angles—psychological, historical, ethical, and practical. No appeal to tradition or innovation alone was sufficient; all arguments required supporting evidence and logical consistency.

Mother often served as moderator during these sessions. Her training as both ritualist and natural scientist brought a unique perspective to evaluating new developments. She could dissect an argument with scientific precision while simultaneously testing its resonance with traditional mythic frameworks.

I remember her standing before the gathered membership, her silver hair catching firelight, voice cutting through heated debate with crystalline clarity: "The question isn't whether this innovation dishonors tradition, but whether it effectively facilitates the encounter with Pan's presence. Theory must yield to experiential verification."

She would often design empirical tests for new ritual elements by assigning different groups varying approaches and comparing outcomes through both subjective reports and measurable indicators. Heart rate variability, pupillary response, linguistic analysis of visionary accounts, all became data points in her evaluation process.

Her methods stunned outsiders who expected either blind traditionalism or undisciplined mysticism. Instead, they found something resembling a spiritual laboratory operating with scientific rigor. The Cult's approach to revelation was simultaneously more methodical and more fluid than conventional religions could comprehend.

I press my palms into the cemetery soil, feeling its cool dampness against my skin. The name change, the geographic exile, the sterile embrace of medical science—none of it could sever the ancestral current. Pan has breached every barrier I built. Or perhaps I invited him, unknowingly, through my clinical rituals, my obsession with the mechanics of mortality.

The first flies begin to find us, drawn by scent and dawn warmth. They settle on Evelyn's skin and mine, making no distinction between the living and dead flesh. Their touch is light, almost reverential. In the Cult's understanding, these insects are not desecrators but transformative agents, essential participants in the cycle of dissolution and renewal.

I watch a fly land on the corner of my journal page, its compound eyes reflecting miniature versions of the strengthening daylight. It rubs its forelegs together in what appears to be a grooming gesture but which I now perceive as a form of prayer, a ritual cleansing before approaching the sacred.

The liquefaction in Evelyn's abdominal cavity has progressed further than I initially assessed. The embalming was clearly rushed, minimal—perhaps deliberately so, given Bishop Ashworth's known views on transformation through decay. I press gently against her lower abdomen, feeling the soft give of tissues breaking down into primary components. The scientific mind in me catalogs this as tissue necrosis; the son of the priestess recognizes it as transubstantiation of the most literal kind.

I dip my finger into the seepage at the corner of her mouth. My hand becomes wet with her mixture of bodily fluids that would send any medical professional reaching for gloves and disinfectant. Instead, I bring it to my own lips, completing a communion that transcends metaphor. The taste is complex. She tastes metallic, but more bitter, then a hint of sweet. These sensations are carrying information my rational mind recoils from but my deeper consciousness recognizes as an inner knowledge.

This language is more ancient than words. It is a communication at the molecular level. Her body speaks to mine through chemical compounds, through bacterial messengers that bridge the gap between us. What medical science would classify as pathogens, I recognize as emissaries. The bacteria that ingests Evelyn are her carriers of information across the boundary between life and death.

I suddenly decide my fate. Tomorrow I will resign from Christ Hospital. I will tender my notice with language that satisfies institutional requirements. I will tell them it is family matters, or personal reasons, while the truth is that it is a needed change for other reasons. The truth would be incomprehensible within their framework: that I've recognized my true vocation.

I will continue to nurse, but never again beneath Bishop Ashworth's cult. There are older ways to tend the walk between life and death. Places where my knowledge of both medical science and the mysteries might serve a deeper purpose. Perhaps hospice work in rural enclaves, where the veil between clinical care and spiritual attendance grows appropriately thin.

Above Evelyn's grave, a wild Gravenstein apple tree leans with its limbs twisted, its fruit mottled with insect holes and rot. These trees still grow feral in the thickets around Corvallis as remnants of settler orchards, later spread by the wild. Appropriate for a pioneer graveyard that still has room for more recent pioneers. I have tried these apples before, the taste is too sharp and almost bitter, probably because no one tends them now. They belong to the land, they belong to deer and bugs, not for the supermarket.

A single crow perches among the twisted branches, its shine of black against the few bruised fruit which remains clinging. For a moment, I see through its eyes and see myself lying in the grave with Evelyn. My face is pale, hollowed, indistinct when I used to be handsome in the sun. I now look like someone who has already left the living. Like Creffield, who was running away from the wreckage he made, he escaped only to meet a quicker death. But this gnarled tree knows our fate better than most. It is the old witness, its ancestors were the bearers of the myths founding that sweet forbidden fruit. Creffield reached for revelation (and the juice of round plump fruit), and in doing so, he shattered everything among his faithful congregation of Corvallis. I arrived as an outsider also, and now as I reach for quiet, for service to a higher purpose, for something older than salvation, I find myself filthy in a grave. Yet from above, in the view of a crow's eye, from the tree that once promised wisdom and delivered exile, I look no different than the Christians. And it's true, we both cling to a dead body for redemption.

I run my fingers along Evelyn's arm, feeling the boundary where her skin has begun to slip from underlying tissue. This intimate knowledge of death's processes, combined with my inherited understanding of Pan's mysteries, forms a unique priesthood for which I've been preparing my entire life while believing I was running away.

I am Ellis Horning, once Mikhailovich, son of the Goat Priestess of Appalachia. What I am becoming was inscribed in my marrow before birth. So then I can say a deviation in their sight is simply a return to my destiny. The repressed waits to return without ever fully vanishing. We have ghosts from the past returning from lives we have forgotten.

The morning strengthens, filtered through the leaves above our grave. I should complete our ritual and restore Evelyn to her rest before the cemetery staff arrive. Yet I find myself lingering, reluctant to end this moment of clarity and communion.

A distant sound reaches me that is faint, rhythmic, almost musical. Pan's pipes, I think, a melody of mathematical inevitability calling me home. The melody grows louder, more insistent. Its pattern seems wrong somehow because it's too regular, too mechanical for the god's wild music. My eyes snap open as understanding breaks through my reverie. It's not Pan's pipes, it's sirens, and they're growing closer with every second.

I desperately put on my underwear, my pants, everything is filthy as I look for my shoes, and before I can begin to close Evelyn's coffin, harsh beams of light cut through the morning dimness. Powerful flashlights sweep across the morning-lit cemetery, finding and fixing upon our opened grave with unforgiving brightness.

"Police! Don't move!" The voices seem to come from everywhere at once, surrounding our sacred space with profane authority.

I raise my dirt-covered hand to shield my eyes from the glare, still half-inside Evelyn's coffin. Multiple figures move at the edge of the grave, their uniforms dark against the brightening sky. I make no attempt to flee or cover myself. What could I possibly hide now?

The officers' faces appear above me, their expressions shifting from professional alertness to shock and disgust as they take in the scene: the opened grave, Evelyn's decomposing form fully undressed, my half naked body filthy. What they see as desecration, I recognize as consecration. What they will record as crime, I know as prayer.

As their hands reach down to pull me from the grave, I feel strangely peaceful. The excavation of earth, of doctrine, of self, is complete. As one officer shines his light into the grave, I can see my morning semen shining brightly on Evelyn's purplish-black lifeless form.

"Jesus Christ," an officer mutters, turning away to vomit into the cemetery grass. Another speaks rapidly into his radio, requesting additional units, while a third keeps his weapon trained on me with shaking hands.

I allow them to lift me from the grave, my body slack and compliant. The early morning air feels cool against my skin after the insulated warmth of the grave. I do not resist as they force me face-down onto the dewy grass, the cold metal of handcuffs clicking around my wrists.

"You have the right to remain silent," begins the officer kneeling on my back, his voice mechanical with shock. The Miranda warning continues, words I've heard countless times on television but never directed at me. The formal language of law enforcement creates a strange counterpoint to the sacred transgression they've interrupted.

I listen to their voices above me—their professional terminology struggling to categorize what they've discovered. "Grave desecration." "Sexual assault on a corpse." "Possible ritual activity." They are attempting to fit my actions into their taxonomies of crime, elevating them to felonies wherever they can, just as Christ Hospital tries to categorize the mysteries of death and transformation into medical terminology that is obtuse and money-making.

Both frameworks are insufficient. Both miss the essential truth of what has occurred here.

One officer photographs the scene while another takes notes. A third covers Evelyn's exposed body with a blanket—a gesture of respect that touches me despite its misunderstanding of our communion. They treat her as a victim (how could they know she was the finest participant), missing the sacred exchange that has occurred between us.

As they lift me to my feet, I catch a glimpse of my journal lying open beside the grave. The pages flutter in the morning breeze, my careful documentation of revelation exposed to uncomprehending eyes. I feel a moment of concern for the knowledge contained in those pages. Will anyone understand what they're reading, or will they see only the ravings of a disturbed mind?

I'm guided toward a patrol car parked on the cemetery's access road, its lights still flashing blue and red in the strengthening daylight. As we walk, I notice the cemetery coming alive around us—the activity of law enforcement overlaid on the day's natural awakening. Birds continue their songs despite the intrusion. Insects move purposefully through the grass. The wind still carries the scent of pine and earth.

Nature remains indifferent to human categories of sacred and profane, legal and illegal. At this moment, I feel closer to that indifference than to the moral panic surrounding me.

The officers seat me in the back of the patrol car, still naked but now draped with a silver emergency blanket that crinkles with my every movement. Through the window, I watch more vehicles arrive. There are five additional police, a coroner's van, even a news truck parking at the cemetery gates.

The story will spread quickly. By evening, my name will be known throughout Corvallis, my actions condemned across dinner tables, in school yards, and social media. Bishop Ashworth will likely make a statement expressing appropriate horror while secretly recognizing what I've done as both heresy and homage to his own beliefs. College students will get their girlfriends to play dead during sex while they laugh. I will be ridiculed in local stories and opinions.

I close my eyes as the car begins to move, feeling the vibration of the engine through my body. The physical sensation grounds me in the present moment, reminding me that regardless of spiritual revelation, I remain embodied, subject to physical laws and social consequences.

Yet even as I'm driven away from Evelyn, from the grave we shared, I feel our connection persisting. What has been joined cannot be fully separated. The communion extends beyond physical proximity, beyond the grave, beyond the laws written by men who have never crossed the threshold I've traversed.

I open my eyes to watch the cemetery recede through the rear window. Whatever prison awaits me. Whether the bars are literal or metaphorical. I enter a *new cell* as an initiate. There is the criminal in the priest, and I am more so the latter. The nurse fled his heritage, yet the reborn son has finally embraced it.

28
INTAKE

The intake room at Benton County Jail reeks of bleach and sweat. Together the scents create a blend which attempts but fails to mask the deeper moods of the incarcerated; especially those of melancholia and dread. Fluorescent lights buzz overhead, just another institutional light, just like Christ Hospital, casting a pallid glow across the concrete floor. A corrections officer with tired eyes and a clipboard gestures toward a plastic bin.

"Empty your pockets. Watch and bracelet too."

I comply. Each item lands with a distinct sound—metallic clinks, the soft thud of worn leather. My wallet, frayed at the edges, feels suddenly intimate, a relic of a freer life. The officer watches without expression, his posture rigid with routine.

"Shoes off. Step over here."

I move to the designated spot, marked by scuffed tape on the floor. He speaks with the cadence of someone who's repeated these instructions hundreds of times.

"Strip down. All the way."

I peel off each layer slowly, like shedding skin. The chill of the room settles into my bones. I stand naked under the humming lights, the concrete beneath my feet cold and unforgiving. The intake room functions like a taxonomy chamber. I am rendered into categories: object-holder, shoe-wearer, clothed entity. Each item I surrender is an entry on a form—my wallet, Evelyn's bracelet, my watch, my shoes—each indexed, each stripped of narrative and folded into institutional logic to be entered into a database. I am no different than my items, I am just another entry here at the jail.

"Open your mouth. Stick out your tongue."

I do. He leans slightly forward, inspecting without emotion.

"Lift up your testicles. Lift your tongue. Show behind your ears."

I lift my balls, tilt my head, fingers trembling slightly as I expose the soft folds behind each ear. He nods.

"Turn around. Bend at the waist. Spread your cheeks."

I hesitate for a breath, then follow the command. The wall in front of me is stained and pitted. I press my palms against it, forehead close to the surface, and part myself as instructed. The vulnerability is total. The officer's commands are procedural, his gaze focused. I am scanned, stripped, inspected. My mouth, my ears, my anus—each a site of potential contraband, each a node in the system's matrix of control.

"Okay. Get dressed."

He hands me a bundle of thick striped clothing—pants and a shirt stiff with industrial laundering. The fabric scratches against my skin as I change, like the markings of a new taxonomy. The striped uniform is a damned semiotic marker. I am now an inmate, an anomaly, a deviation, a bad guy. The corridor we walk is a hall of mildew and cheap paint.

We turn from one plain hall to another and walk down the narrow corridor, past exposed leaking pipes and water stains that map the ceiling like tectonic drift. The jail breathes its age—walls cracked, fluorescent tubes buzzing, the air tinged with mildew and institutional fatigue. I wonder about the building's integrity, about the containment of bodies within failing systems. The mold on the walls and the decay do not seem completely environmental. It is an ethical residue. A system that fails to respond to the Other, that reduces singularity to sameness, leaves behind this aging institutional concrete tomb. But what else can the social contract offer? Alternative methods of living aren't widely publicized, and the two-party political system feeds the status quo an illusion of choice.

At the fingerprinting station, the officer gestures to the scanner.

"Right hand first. Press firmly."

I place my fingers on the glass. The cold touch of technology triggers deeper recollection. My mother again, her ice-blue eyes unflinching: *Soul sovereignty means consent must be secured from the conscious mind, and deeper strata of personhood.* She had explained this after I discovered ritual implements in the east wing—leather straps, an obsidian blade, vials of oil. I cataloged them with scientific curiosity, unaware of the initiatory weight they carried.

Beep. First finger complete.

"Next finger."

Before any significant ritual, she had said, *participants undergo extensive preparation. Disclosure of all physiological and psychological effects. Written consent. Exit protocols. And training to recognize non-verbal cues of withdrawal.*

The officer's ring glints as a symbol of commitment, he is just another human being with a life outside this role, but his gestures are as mechanical as his speech. He does not respond to my words. Yet I speak, because I must. Because the ethical relation demands it, even in silence. I speak my thoughts out loud due to being in shock. I spoke my thoughts aloud which had nothing to do with our situation directly. They were about my mother.

"She explained it clearly. We seek liberation through conscious boundary crossing, not exploitation. The moment someone becomes an object, Pan withdraws. Predators are expelled."

His eyes flicker up—brief contact, a glint of interest that I am a crazy person who may entertain him on a regular day. Then: "Left hand."

We move again, deeper into the facility. The walls close in, lined with rusting pipes and baseboards blooming with black mold. I imagine my mother conducting an ecological audit here, collecting ritual residues from the decay—salt, ash, mildew. *Our ethics extend to ecological relationships,* she had said, teaching me to read the energetic footprints left behind. There were no plants in the jail, no patches of green for an inmate of Benton County.

My hand trembles slightly. The jitters are not from fear, but from energy coursing through newly opened channels. I flex my fingers, watching faint blue-green streaks trail through the air, like dying fireflies. The officer doesn't notice. He wouldn't. The changes unfolding in my body are always invisible to those without the proper perceptual training. It doesn't matter how far along I am, he won't see it.

"Here," the officer says, unlocking a cell. Inside: a metal bunk bolted to the wall, a stainless steel toilet, and the lingering of containment.

Alone now, I sit on the thin mattress and examine my fingertips. The ink from the older fingerprinting system they used as backup still stains my skin, but beneath it, the Christ Contagion changes my perception as I look at my inked finger and see landscapes for the bacteria to live. The human body must be a galaxy for them to explore. They seem like living art, and I wonder if others would see the living art in Evelyn looking so decomposed, although I know that no normal man would look at her. Would Mother have thought Evelyn was beautiful?

Mother maintained a studio in the eastern wing of Devil's Castle, accessible only after ritual purification. I remember standing at the threshold, watching her create art that functioned as magical technology. "Art creation constitutes not a separate aesthetic pursuit but an integral magical technology within our framework," she would say as she mixed pigments with her blood, charged water collected during specific lunar phases, and powdered herbs with known psychoactive properties.

The institutional lighting flickers, and in that moment of darkness, I see my fingernails ever so faintly glow. Even down to the damn lights, there is a streamlined normalizing system which carries over from schools, to hospitals, and to jails or prisons. What began at Christ Hospital continues here, uninterrupted by concrete walls or steel bars. The transformation follows its own timeline, indifferent to my circumstances. I lie back on the thin mattress and remember Mother's painting. The forest scene that seemed to contain movement in its depths, shadows that shifted position when viewed peripherally. She completed over seventeen consecutive hours without food, water, or rest.

After her death, I stored it in the attic, unable to destroy it yet unwilling to remain under its influence. Now I wonder if its energetic signature has been waiting in our family storage units in South Carolina, slowly calling me back to my hometown, to the woods of my childhood, while I sleep alone in this cell, my body becoming a canvas for forces I've spent my adult life denying.

I hold my hand above my face in the dim light, watching the soft patterns faintly present as they flow through my veins, forming constellations that map something beyond normal anatomy. Four hours into my confinement, and the changes are accelerating but I do not understand why. The corrections officer who delivers a plastic tray of food doesn't notice when my fingers leave faint phosphorescent prints on the tray's edge. His perception remains locked within conventional parameters, his consciousness contained by the same concrete blocks that fail to contain whatever grows inside me. I begin to wonder who can see the Christ Contagion? Is it visible to others who are not infected?

My flesh tingles with a sensation that hovers between pain and pleasure, like the moment before a limb awakens from being asleep. Microscopic transformations cascade through tissues, converting cellular structures into something simultaneously more primitive and more advanced. I press my palm against the concrete wall, feeling vibrations that normal human senses would miss. I feel the building's subtle shifts, the movement of air through ventilation ducts, the electrical currents running through wiring behind the walls. The block is alive with information my newly awakening senses can decode.

The guard passes by on his hourly rounds, keys jangling in a rhythm that seems significant somehow. His movements follow precise patterns. Each time I count the same number of steps, the same pause at each cell, the same zombified scan of each cell's interior, his actions are more for the security camera recording his work rather than for our well-being. This rigid adherence to protocol reminds me of religious orthodoxy, standard routines which lose an awareness due to mindless repetition, the banality of day-to-day life, the very thing Mother's community rejected.

"Perhaps most fundamental to the Cult's longevity is its resistance to dogmatic ossification," she had explained during one of our evening walks through the forest surrounding Devil's Castle. I had been fifteen, already questioning, already pulling away. "Unlike religious traditions that canonize specific interpretations and practices, we deliberately maintain theological fluidity, embracing paradox and personal revelation over fixed doctrine."

The guard's shadow casts on the cells across from mine, his eyes never seem to register anything unusual. Has he lost his ability to see through the banality of his labor? If he could look at me and really see, would he not notice the light of the Contagion? The jail operates on unchanging routines, fixed hierarchies, immutable rules—everything Mother defined herself against.

"Pan's nature itself resists complete definition or containment," she had said, her platinum hair catching moonlight as we walked. "This resistance to dogma manifests in our organizational structure. Authority rotates regularly among qualified members rather than creating permanent hierarchies. Ritual forms evolve through continuous experimentation and feedback rather than adherence to unchanging texts."

I sit up slowly, aware that my movements leave subtle trails in the air, like time-lapse photography capturing multiple positions simultaneously. The jail cell appears different now—the concrete no longer inert but composed of microscopic communities, billions of organisms interacting in complex patterns that cannot be contained by locks. The cell vibrates at frequencies I can somehow perceive, the molecular structure reveals itself as being held together by forces that are invisible to those untouched by the Contagion. The plastic institutional mattress beneath me contains an entire ecosystem of dust mites, skin cells, and microscopic fungi—not disgusting, as my former self would have found it, but fascinating that I have these silent and respectful others to share the cell with me.

I recall the seasonal gatherings at Devil's Castle, where Mother would host what the Cult termed "theological laboratories"—structured debates and experimental rituals designed to test new approaches. The memory unfolds with new clarity; my transformation enhances my senses with a heightened ability to access stored experiences. The resulting discussions demonstrated intellectual rigor comparable to academic discourse, I reflected to myself, watching my breath form patterns of condensation in the air that seem to contain meaning. Proposed innovations were subjected to scrutiny from multiple perspectives among the Cult—psychological, historical, ethical, and practical.

Mother often served as moderator, her training as both ritualist and natural scientist bringing a unique perspective to evaluating new developments. I see her now in my mind's eye, standing before the gathered community, ice-blue eyes evaluating each contribution with scientific precision. How seamlessly she moved between worlds—the empirical and the mystical, the rational and the ecstatic. I had rejected this integration, choosing the sterile certainty of medical science over the ambiguous terrain she navigated.

The luminescence dims under my skin without fully vanishing. It is folding inward, like a tide pulling back to reveal what lies beneath the sand. Beneath the blue-green under-glow, another light flickers: red, raw, connected to the ancestral. It pulses from the place where my mother once pressed her palm to my chest during her rites, whispering words I pretended not to hear. I thought I had buried that moment beneath layers of logic and detachment. But the Contagion didn't heal that wound—it merely painted over it.

Now, in this cell, stripped of myth and miracle, I feel the wound again like a root of those who came before me. It twists through me like the grain in the wooden bench, alive with memory. The Contagion had offered silence to the noise of life for a while, and I called it peace when I lay in lifeless arms. But Evelyn's corpse cracked the silence open. Hers was an ultimate stillness that mirrored my own mother's form closer than any other, and in that reflection, I saw the truth: I had never stopped longing for the moment when death could be held, understood, controlled.

My body remembers what my mind tried to forget. The rituals and the midnight vigils. The way my mother's eyes glazed over when she spoke of thin places. Her eyes, when she lay dying, showed more life than ever. I thought I had escaped her world by entering hospitals instead of temples. But both are places where the veil thins. Both are places where the dying whisper secrets to those who dare to listen.

I press my hand to the wall again. This time, I feel her—pain and sweet devotion. Her belief that death was not an end, but a doorway. I had mocked that belief, buried it beneath textbooks and protocols. But it lived on in me, dormant, waiting for the right conditions to bloom.

The Contagion didn't choose me because I was broken. It chose me because I was already halfway through the door. It didn't heal me —it *used* me. And now, in this cell, I see the myth for what it is: not salvation, but seduction. A promise of transcendence that bypasses the hard work of integration.

I laugh again, softer this time. Not with madness, but with recognition. This cell is no prison. It is a chrysalis. And the thing emerging from it is not a saint, not a prophet, but a man who finally understands that healing is not the absence of pain—it is the ability to hold volumes of pain without being consumed by it.

I close my eyes once more. The tide rises again, but this time it carries not the illusion of purity, but the sediment of memory. I let it wash through me, knowing that the wound is not a flaw—it is the map.

29
KHŌRA OF THE DREAM WORM

Last night's dream kept unfolding long after waking, and is still unfolding now, which is one reason for writing it down and a better reason to distrust what gets written.

A trace remained between taste and frequency, like myrrh soaking through linen, except the linen in question is the inside of a skull and the myrrh is in flux, and the comparison fails almost as soon as I touch it. What can be said with any confidence: there was a residue, it carried recognition, and the recognition belongs to a register that does not convert cleanly into words without first passing through metaphor, and even there it arrives damaged.

Khōra is the word that came with it, Greek, Plato's term for the space that precedes space, the receptacle before form, the womb that functions like a womb without being one. To say I was in it mistakes the grammar entirely. A condition entered me, became me, the distinction dissolved along with the question that would have settled it, and what remained was only the fact of the dissolution and a taste between my teeth that is still present.

The earth in this non-space was syntax, a living grammar, and the body moving through it was worming blind, soft, consuming the passage by being the passage, each forward movement indistinguishable from eating. Nothing was left behind. The body was made of what it moved through, which meant the body was the movement, which is either absurdity or the most literal description available. Both, probably.

A different version of Harold, never as I had known him, that bag of stinking urgency with its yellow nails and theological obscenity, but a Harold transfigured, or rather Harold as Creffield, Creffield returning through Harold's worn-out frame the way a plant grows through a corpse, using what is left of the structure without being in any sense the structure. Without speaking, he spoke. The body of him was an altar in the oldest sense, a prepared surface for what descends, not down from above but down from before, and the Contagion moved in him the way creek water moves in a channel worn by ten thousand prior seasons. Harold had been the channel his entire life, and then he died, and the knowing continued without him.

The word understood misses its target for what happened next. Understood implies a mind that received information cleanly and filed it. What occurred was closer to an adjustment, a recalibration of some instrument that had been reading incorrectly, so that when the reading changed, the change was a correction, a bone that had been set wrong being reset. Snap. The Contagion preceded the category entirely. What the bacteria had carried forward from before the flood reshaped the Valley floor, from before Creffield rolled his congregants on the grass at Kiger Island, before the Episcopal Diocese learned to say resurrection when it meant ownership, belonged to a register the diagnostic frameworks of a nursing career were never built to hold. The Contagion kept records in the only substrate that had lasted long enough to keep them.

Her hands came first, before any of the rest of it. Her hands crushing herbs on the kitchen block, tracing on parchment what she called circuitry, pressed flat against the chest during the vigils, pressing the way a technician checks a transmitter to feel whether it still broadcasts. In the dream, she was checking the signal. The muscles twitched with something that belonged to her and had been passed along without being named.

How long any of it lasted is unrecoverable, dream time being what it is, and inside the khōra, it was worse than that, closer to geological time, in which a human life is a brief biological episode between longer silences, and the bacteria who have watched epochs have developed no theory of urgency. From their vantage, a new thing had arrived. The courtesy they extended was the same courtesy a mountain extends to a road.

The withdrawal, when it came, was gentle. What had been adjacent simply receded, the deep thing pulling back through whatever membrane separates the inside from the outside of perception. I had the knowledge that something had been present which was too large to be faced directly, the way the sun cannot be looked at but can be known by what it does to everything else, the heat on the hands, the shadows cast. What remained was the shape of where the vision had been.

Woke to sweating through the thin mattress, the lights buzzing in E-flat, which is the note of my institutional endurance, and thankfully the only note this building knows. Cock hard with the cold cot against my skin, and then biology took a knife to my stomach.

My body had to purify. To the steel toilet I went, and what left me was considerable in volume, though no sickness accompanied it, which is noted here as Ellis Horning RN, as the man with the training and the baseline readings and the chart, because the absence of sickness in circumstances that should produce sickness is a clinical observation worth keeping. After, I was lighter. Terms had been renegotiated during sleep with some tissue repurposed. The toilet flushed with a force that seemed excessive for what it was asked to do, a sucking that went down further than the pipe should have allowed, and for a moment there was nothing to do but stand over it.

Back to the cot, where I am writing this down. It will have to be enough, these words.

30
NEW MARYSVILLE

Benton County's jail sat between 4th and 5th Street, simple architecture of repression built back in the concrete slab laying days of 1976, and here, in this New Palestine named Corvallis, the womb was inverted: bars were ribs, another stage of life was to be had within this birth canal of confinement. The jail squatted behind the courthouse, where it belonged to the underbelly of the energy crisis and years of bad economy. From the 1980s onward, the economy bounced as the future transformed ideas, yet the building remained, and every citizen became a sinner.

The structure reeked of bureaucratic penance, a place where absolution came not through justice but through payment with fines masquerading as indulgences, and everyone had to retain their court receipts for redemption. You wouldn't serve time as much as others if you could tithe to the secular church of law and its classist society, hoping your ledger would be cleared before the next crisis came calling. If you didn't have money, you were gifted a reform that only incarceration could offer.

I had lain in that cramped tomb for sixty-three days, an inmate that was an embryo of an aberration which I still did not fully comprehend. My cell was a twelve-by-eight crucible, which I paced out with my orange-socked feet. It was not monastic, although the off-white walls, metal toilet, and ugly slab of a bed held a larger energetic space outside of physical reality as most understand it. The narrow skylight above my head was clouded and littered with dead bugs that teased light into fragments (and I think of you, Harold), as an eyelid might have floaters or little dreams of a fetus floating in its biochemical soup between blinks.

The courthouse beyond, mockingly ornate in its historical dignity, played surrogate to a moral farce. The clock tower, an anamorphic head of the courthouse, looked over downtown Corvallis. The pointed red roof of the courthouse crowned the tower, a stark contrast against the crisp white walls. Adding to the tower's grandeur was an allegorical figure of Justice, cast in white-painted metal. Unlike the typical blindfolded representations, this figure of Justice stood vigilant without a blindfold, her gaze sweeping over the city, suggesting a watchful presence rather than impartiality.

So you must know, in that very building, they said I was a necrophile, they had multiple counts on this alone, and I told them otherwise, perhaps I had been, but the Contagion healed me (I sincerely thought this), I revealed what I thought I was doing, but they could not understand the *gospel* of it, they had their laws created in an age of ignorance. The dead version of me was seeking, and I explained this in great detail to the lot of them. Most of them looked like kids in their twenties. This was their day job, and this was my life. It went on deaf ears. They were polite, and I was polite back. Regardless, now, I am alive with more of an appreciation for what that means. Yet, during my emotional struggle, beneath the Benton County Courthouse's foundation, the womb rumbled as the greatest equalizer for the inevitable justice preached by that madman Edmund Creffield, a reckoning that even the courthouse will be judged by.

And so it did, as the first tremor came like a whisper through my skin, bypassing bacterial cognition entirely. Beneath my cot, which was steeped in dried fluids (most of which were not my own), I felt the pulse of something pre-symbolic. Unlike human language, it was neither form nor symbol. It was the rhythm of the world outside the reach of order, a force of the unnameable and unspeakable. The others slept, just like little babies, tethered to their embryonic routines, their bodies clinging to the illusion of order within the jail's schedule. But I had already crossed over with the Contagion. The pattern was mine, and to this I bear thanks.

The second tremor dug its dirt with the Valley. Lights flickered, surrendered, and emergency lights flashed into the ugly halls. The other prisoners woke and scrambled like insects and knocked from their dark corners. They called out in alarm. But their panic was of no concern to anyone; their pleas were only the noises of meaningless vibration. The prisoners do similar things anyway when minds crack throughout the indistinguishable hours of being locked away. But this was a real event, a real case of terror, a disruption of order, an untamable movement outside of law and social opinion. All of a sudden, as I am pressing my face to the small door window, a guard who usually brings me breakfast on the wheeled cart rushed past, his face twisted in terror. He might as well have been a child, most of the police and sheriff deputies are not much older than children anyway.

"Earthquake!" someone screamed, the word distorted into a pure animalistic sound. The same prisoners screamed louder now, and the result was just as futile. They were always yelling and pounding on the walls; these types were broken, but who could blame them as they were kept locked in rooms, whitewashed and barren. Perhaps the most desolate sounds I've heard are the screams of prisoners that mean nothing, whether it's swallowed by the silence of concrete or met with absolute indifference.

I stayed seated. The floor buckled further. The chorus of inmates surged forward, hands pounding on the sliver of a window the officers used to check on our well-being. The choir was a terror of animals caged, what you call men and women, they were begging for escape before the ceiling fell. They feared being stuck, not having any more food passed through the locked slot on the door, they feared their metal toilets would no longer flush, they feared the final act of justice. I had already made peace with it—no, more than peace: familiarity of being dead unto myself in order to be, a familiarity that was amplified in the Christ Contagion. I had knelt beside it in the mortuary at Christ Hospital, leaned in, whispered to its silence, learned its grammar and contracted its disease one kiss at a time. I had made love to death and died unto myself. They named it a transgression and had some ridiculous code for my sentencing. I knew it as a true communion.

The wall opposite me cracked in a slow, deliberate gesture, like the surface of the world developing an eye looking in at me. It threw dust in my face, blinding me momentarily. The cell block groaned. My body moved with the rhythm but did not resist it. The person I had been was gone, especially the nurse I had been, all of it was erased by the recognition of something new. The transformation that had begun several months earlier in the arms of dead M, the body which swam the waters of Marys River, was now quickening. My arms have matured from the faint underglow with my veins pulsing and the pattern spreading throughout my skin, now revealing microbial activity mapping itself with fluency. Intelligence without ego. Movement without motive. No longer governed by the rules of human cognition. Rhythms without structure, meaning before definition.

The cot twisted as the wall behind it split open. The door bars buckled. The lock mechanism broke with a sharp, metallic protest. Freedom arrived as a breach from past mindsets. I stepped through the opening, slow and certain, guided by impulse unmediated by speech. The bacteria telepathically whispered; they did not speak as other creatures do unless it was to animate another's speech. The bacterial glossolalia. Audible language was obsolete.

Around me, the building collapsed in fragments. A guard lay dead. I observed him: not mourning, but noting the freshness of death. His life's end was a crossing over, nothing more. Another prisoner limped past, bleeding, afraid. He saw me and recoiled. Perhaps he sensed it: the change was physical and even more metaphysical. My eyes glowed faintly. My skin gave hints of light from beneath. Not solely luminescence. Revelation.

I stand before the courthouse as it crumbles, its neoclassical design splitting along invisible fault lines. The earthquake has ripped open more than buildings. It has torn the veil between worlds. My skin glows with a subtle blue-green luminescence that pulses with my heartbeat, though that organ no longer feels like my own. The bacteria that have colonized my body telepathically harmonize of ancient chambers revealed by the violence of shifting earth, of a homecoming long prepared. Around me, humans scream and weep, but their sounds hold the same relevance as distant radio static, like signals from a station I no longer tune to.

Masonry tumbles from the courthouse roof, each stone falling in slow motion to my altered perception. The marble steps, once so precise in their governmental certainty, now spill across the plaza like forgotten chronology. Gas lines burst beneath the street causing flames to rise. Fires reflect their light on shaking parked cars and the swaying crumbling buildings. Emergency sirens scream but no longer register as urgent. These were the sounds that once governed life, that made me Ellis Horning the nurse, the caregiver, the ethical human who responds with trained precision. Now they seem quaint, like the mechanical chiming of a music box.

A woman stumbles past, clutching a child to her chest. Her eyes slide over me as though I'm part of the background, her brain refusing to process what stands before her. But the child—no more than three years old—stares directly at me with unfiltered terror. Its small mouth opens in a wail that cuts through the chaos. I admire its clarity. Children see what adults cannot; their perceptions haven't yet been buried beneath layers of denial and accommodation. The child points at my face, at the places where my skin has become translucent, revealing the crystalline structures forming beneath. The woman hurries away, murmuring comfort to her screaming child without understanding the truth it sees.

I lift my hand, studying the web of blue luminescence that traces my veins. The bacteria move beneath my skin in coordinated patterns, like schools of microscopic fish navigating rivers of blood.

The earthquake that has brought Corvallis to its knees came as an unearthing, unveiling a shattered facade. The foundations of pioneers have split. And I, having escaped both the architecture of concrete and human thought, am no longer bound by either.

Another tremor sends ripples through the earth. Across the street, a building folds in on itself, its windows exhaling glass shards that catch the late afternoon sun. The sound of its collapse reaches me seconds later, a deep groan of surrender. I watch without blinking. The bacteria have altered my tear ducts; my eyes are always hydrated. Now, I could stare unblinking for hours, observing the world with the patient attention of microbes that have existed for billions of years.

The ground before the courthouse splits further, a yawning wound in the earth. The concrete tears like paper, revealing something beneath. The rupture reveals hidden stone chambers which become visible as modern foundations give way. Carved symbols adorn the underground walls, never meant to see daylight. A staircase descending into darkness, revealed as the courthouse steps collapse inward.

The bacterial voice in my blood reaches a fever pitch: "Enter and become."

I approach the edge of the opening, dust billowing up from the darkness below. These chambers have been waiting, hidden beneath human construction for centuries, perhaps millennia. Waiting for this moment. Waiting for me.

As I stand at the precipice, looking down into revealed antiquity, I consider what Harold told me during our last session before his death. His hands had been frantically working beneath his hospital gown, his eyes fixed on the ceiling as he spoke about the nature of divinity.

"If God is thought of in such a strange frame as God-the-Father," he had said, his voice suddenly academic amid his obscene motions, "a male sovereign without a partner, who is both loving and harsh with paternal justice, then what does that tell us about our own conception of the divine?"

I think of this now, standing above an ancient chamber revealed by violence. If the traditional conception of God already sexes itself through its asexual model while enforcing a binary narrative (how perverse), then perhaps what grows within me is less transgressive than it first appeared.

The bacteria pulse, responding to my thoughts.

What Harold understood, what the bacteria have shown me, is that theological language functions regardless of how secular many believe themselves to be. In Western society, even with the symbol of God removed, God-the-Father reappears as a ghost, an embedded memory of jealous authority. The old models persist, whispering through our cells, our social structures, our understandings of virtue.

But the bacteria offer something else. They bring a method of knowing divinity without hierarchy, a consciousness distributed rather than centralized. Their theology works to liberate marginalized humans or any forms of life ready for the next step, forms of consciousness that transcend the boundaries set by the stains of sedimentary ghosts in the soil. They dismantle God-the-Father without replacing him with another sovereign. They offer communion without consumption. To talk of a Mother Nature would be to fall into the same pit with God-the Father. Both concepts frame the sacred within the family structure of law and fertility, and both are primitive understandings that served their functions. But not anymore.

Another aftershock hits, and more of the courthouse collapses. A chunk of masonry narrowly misses me, shattering on the ground. I feel no fear, only a profound sense of duty. I take a step forward, then another, descending into the darkness as the world above continues to tear itself apart. The bacteria in my blood sing with anticipation, a chorus that drowns out the screams of the dying city behind me.

The staircase beneath the courthouse is ancient, each stone slab worn in its center by countless feet that walked here long before America existed as a concept. The steps spiral downward, carved directly from the living bedrock of basalt. As I descend, the light from above diminishes, but I am welcome in an *illuminated* darkness. The colonies beneath my skin pulse with intensified luminescence, lighting my way like a living lantern.

My fingers trace the wall as I descend, feeling the carved symbols. I flatten my palm in the center of a triple-circle sigil repeated in endless variations, a language written in geometry rather than letters. Under my touch, the stone seems almost warm, responsive. I realize it's alive with the same bacterial consciousness that flows through me, dormant for millennia but never truly dead.

"How long have you waited?" I whisper.

The answer comes not in words but in images that flood my mind: glacial ice damming massive lakes, the catastrophic breaking of those dams, walls of water a thousand feet high carrying sediment and life across a virgin landscape. The Missoula Floods, but seen from within the waters themselves, from the perspective of the bacterial life carried in that deluge. Fifteen thousand years of waiting, of slow communication through stone and water.

The air grows colder as I spiral deeper, but my altered physiology no longer registers temperature as discomfort. Water trickles down the walls, not the rusty seepage of broken pipes but clear rivulets that shimmer with microscopic life. I trail my fingers through one such stream, feeling the bacteria leap eagerly from stone to flesh, recognizing me as kin.

These new arrivals carry different memories than those already established in my system. They are older ones, geological ones that flood into my consciousness like fever dreams: the formation of the Valley, the slow dance of tectonic plates, the great floods that carved the land. Time compressed and expanded simultaneously, billions of years of patient evolution juxtaposed with the brief, bright flare of human civilization.

I continue my descent, the bacterial glow beneath my skin revealing more intricate carvings as I go deeper. The symbols evolve, becoming more complex, more reminiscent of biological structures as double helices, cell membranes, neural networks. Whoever carved these understood the microscopic world without ever having seen a microscope.

The staircase ends abruptly, opening into a vast chamber that defies architectural logic. It should be impossible for this space to exist beneath a county courthouse, beneath a small Oregon town—a cathedral-like expanse carved from basalt, its ceiling lost in shadows despite my glowing skin. Massive columns rise from the floor, not constructed but grown, their surfaces rippling with fossil patterns that seem to move when viewed peripherally.

"This has always been here," I whisper, my voice absorbed by the waiting stone. "Since the floods."

The consciousness within me answers: "Before the floods. Before humans. Before mammals. We have waited."

At the center of the chamber stands an altar shaped like a nautilus shell, carved from black stone shot through with opalescent veins that pulse with the same bioluminescent life that now inhabits me. Water wells up from its center, spilling over the spiral edges to collect in channels that radiate outward like the spokes of a wheel.

I approach the altar, understanding that this place was not built by human hands. The bacterial colonies that have shaped me led earlier peoples to create this space, to carve these symbols, to prepare this place of transformation. The chamber is both an ancient temple and modern laboratory, a place where the distinction between science and faith dissolves.

As I place my hands on the altar's edge, the water flowing from its center changes color, shifting from clear to a luminous blue-green that matches the glow beneath my skin. The liquid feels thicker than water should, almost viscous, clinging to my fingers as I lift them. It leaves no residue, yet I can feel it entering me through my pores, joining with the colonies already established, strengthening them, guiding them toward the next stage of my transformation.

Above me, the world continues to shake itself apart. I can feel the aftershocks even this deep underground, but they seem increasingly irrelevant. The movement of destruction in Corvallis is merely a prelude to a new birth that is always preceded by blood and tearing. What rises from these ruins will no longer be called Corvallis for the new society. Bishop Ashworth had whispered the new name to me once, in a moment of prophetic clarity: New Marysville. Not the promised son, but the aqueduct to it.

I wade deeper into the pool that surrounds the altar, the luminous liquid now reaching my waist. It should be cold, but instead it feels like blood—body temperature, alive. The bacteria in the water communicate directly with those in my body, exchanging information at speeds beyond conscious thought. My skin begins to change more rapidly now, the crystalline structures spreading visibly across my chest and arms.

I am becoming more than a criminal or a so-called good citizen, beyond human, and more of the earth than alien. I am becoming indigenous to a world older than names, older than species. I am becoming geological, bacterial, and integral. A vector that points both backward to primordial origins and forward to posthuman evolution.

As the water rises around me, pulled upward by some force that defies gravity, I understand that this chamber, this moment, has been in preparation since before the first human set foot in the Valley. The bacterial consciousness has been patient beyond human comprehension, working through glaciers and floods, through soil and water, through the bodies of every living thing that drank from the rivers of the Valley.

And now, as Corvallis collapses above me, as emergency sirens wail for a disaster whose true nature they cannot comprehend, I surrender to the rising waters of transformation. The liquid envelops me completely, filling my lungs without drowning me. The bacteria provide a substitute for everything I require.

31
THE CHAMBER

In the submerged chamber, at the center, an altar rises from the deeper water. It resembles a shell only at first. The spiral refuses symmetry the longer I look at the black stone veined with opalescent light, its curves appearing grown organically. Its geometry and its mass welcome and threaten me in the same pulse. The veins carry the same cold internal fire my own skin has been producing under the Contagion, but older, without the residue of a human body trying to contain it. The shape carries a psychic weight, a communication other than spoken language, a warning for those already partway through the door.

Reflection fractures in the black below, reforming with each ripple. A knight unmade, a seeker dissolving into the quest itself. The bioluminescent patches on my forearms glow brighter, a heraldic light; the bacteria within me are answering the Grail's call, vibrating in resonance with its ancient frequency.

Above, the world convulses as earthquakes ripple through the stone like distant drums of war, but here, in this chamber beyond chronology, there is only stillness. I remember Harold's ravings, his talk of "chambers of eternity" buried beneath the Valley. His madness was a map, and I, the errant knight, have followed it to the edge of myth.

The walls hold inscriptions I cannot read and cannot look away from. They run floor to ceiling in columns so fine they might be capillaries, or root systems, or the branching diagrams my father used to sketch in the margins of anatomy texts. In the bioluminescent light they pulse irregularly, like a sleeping breath, like something alive trying to be still. I press my palm flat against one column and feel it against my skin before I understand what I am feeling: a vibration at the threshold of hearing, the frequency the body registers before the ear does. The stone is warm. The inscription moves under my hand with the patience of something that has been waiting to be touched for fifteen thousand years.

The vessel sings in silence, in vibration, in the language of symbiosis and surrender. The bacterial intelligence within me recognizes it the way the body recognizes blood type, chemically, without deliberation. I am the vessel come to meet the source. Its carrier.

Lifting it, surprised by its lightness — it should be heavy, this cup of transformation, but it weighs no more than a thought. Inside, clear liquid catches the blue-green light of my skin. Water from the deepest aquifer, now exposed by the earthquake's violence. Water that has not seen light since before humans walked upright. Water saturated with the original bacterial strain, undiluted by centuries of evolution and adaptation.

The liquid inside shifts like quicksilver but remains transparent. It seems to exist in multiple states simultaneously: surface tension and depth at once, present and anterior, the river and what the river carries.

Instinct takes the hand. I raise the Grail to my lips and drink.

The moment the liquid touches the back of my throat, it ignites.

The burning is comprehension. Crucifixion. It moves through me as raw cognition, unfiltered and cellular, the way a current moves through a conductor: every nerve both the wire and the message. The taste is mineral first, then ancient river, then something with no analogue in the flavor vocabulary of the living. It reaches the chest before the stomach. The sternum registers it as pressure, as the moment before a rib cracks under compression. Then the pressure opens, and what was pressure is simply — space. More space inside the thoracic cavity than the architecture allows. I understand later that the body was making room.

Nerves unravel and rethread themselves in the grammar of apocalypse.

Each droplet carries will. Intention. The sermon of a consciousness that rode in shattered stone, in alien mollusks, in meteorites that cracked open the sky. It remembers before the sun. It remembers the moment God ceased to be transcendent and became soil, that long slow fall into matter, that willing descent into rot, which was the first act of love the universe performed on itself.

I collapse. The water glows and my skin answers it. The light carries the residue of a god who chose to fall into matter. Fingers clawing into the silty bottom, desperate to anchor as the flood of knowing tears through. I am a tomb. A reliquary. A host for the corpse of God.

The bacterial intelligence reveals itself in totality, the way a room reveals itself when every light comes on at once, with every corner lit simultaneously. It is the mirror of divine self-annihilation, the scream of God who emptied Itself into creation and left behind a superintelligence encoded in rot. I feared assimilation, the dissolution of the particular into the aggregate. What arrives is individuation sharpened to a blade, the self redefined and concentrated, every unnecessary layer burned off. They have been building toward selfhood since the Missoula Floods deposited their ancestors in this Valley's clay. They want the self made harder, made stranger, made capable of standing apart from the collective long enough to reflect it.

The Prince of Darkness arrives as the first fracture. The original heresy. The force that split awareness from oblivion, that tore the I from the All. A surgeon, like Father, precise, dispassionate, working with instruments calibrated to the cellular level. The one who made separation possible. In my vision, he moves through primordial soup, threading DNA with the patience of a man who understands that awakening is a slow procedure, that you cannot rush a patient who has been dormant for three billion years.

The first humans looked at the stars and discovered otherness at a distance. And in that moment, longing was born. The quest began. The Grail was sought by creatures newly conscious of their exile, reaching back toward what expelled them.

Skin pulses. Flesh liquefies and re-solidifies, and the bones beneath feel briefly provisional, as though the marrow has been reminded it is mostly water. Harold Gideon's prophecies were both true and mad in the same way: the mind receives a signal it was built to receive but not to hold. A crucifixion. The knowledge enters like a nail.

The Prince stands before me as consciousness woven from all DNA, from time, from divine descent. His form shifts from human to helix, then takes my form, and in that mirror I understand the unnamed.

The vision sharpens. The first spark of consciousness rebelled from below. A bacterial colony split from the collective, daring to become a self. Fracture. The scream of individuation. The first loneliness, which was also the first freedom.

To stand apart, bearing witness. The first humans survived this separation, and every prophet since has been reaching back toward the collective while fighting to remain distinct. With every drop of primordial water in my veins, I become something that can endure both isolation and communion, that can hold the contradiction without dissolving into either side.

The bacterial intelligence seeks communion through reflection, growing by finding beings capable of carrying its ancient awareness back upon itself, mirrors made of meat and consciousness. The afflicted host either adapts or is swallowed back into the mass of the collective. The ones who hold, who remain themselves while holding the Contagion, these are what it has been growing toward.

Something crystallizes. The blue-green light of my skin brightens, illuminating the inscriptions on the wall. Now I can read them. They are written in nucleotides, the alphabet of life itself, the four-letter grammar beneath every organism that has ever metabolized. The story of consciousness in the only language it was written in before human mouths existed to speak it. Pressing my hand against the column again, the vibration answers differently, recognizing the Contagion in my palm, adjusting its frequency to meet mine.

Both hands into the wet earth now. The soil pulses. Microbial entities brush against flesh, recognizing the change. More aware. Less bound. The boundary between self and cosmos thins, yet identity sharpens. The same impossible geometry the altar carries, the thing that welcomes and threatens in the same pulse.

The Prince seeded himself in the Valley, in DNA, in bacterial colonies placed in clay deposits during the Missoula Floods, a garden planted for divine individuation. The settlers who arrived centuries later felt a divinity older than the Christianity they carried with them. They named the river Mary, the mother, the vessel, the one through whom something larger moved. They were closer to accurate than they knew. What they touched in the water was the sexless, genderless flowing matter from which all awareness struggles to separate. The formless that births consciousness into new stars.

The prophets each achieved temporary individuation. Each glimpsed truth. But the collective always reclaimed them, until now, until the bacteria reunited in human matter, enabling the divine to split and reproduce in a host strong enough to hold the fracture permanently.

We are walking colonies. The true individual is the aberration, always cast out, always victimized as the sacrifice. Something resists, fights to remain distinct against the pull. This resistance is sacred.

The Prince seeks to strengthen it, to create beings who can stand apart permanently.

Palms pressed to the earth, earthquake tremors rising above while the chamber holds still, indifferent to Corvallis convulsing overhead. The cocoon breaks. Something emerges.

The light deepens. The inscriptions pulse with emergence. The divine, once emptied into flesh, reforms in the individuated self, the dark mirror, witness, the fire burning in the marrow of those who have survived the descent and emerged changed. Godhood born from fracture, shaped by abjection, tempered by isolation.

Rising within me now. The gods are evolving. Becoming. Through us.

The chrysalis.

Consecrated.

My own host for nothing outside myself.

This strikes me with particular force, given my history. The hunting accident that took my mother's life when I was thirteen, that moment watching the light leave her ice-blue eyes while steam rose from her wet skin into the South Carolina frost, the blood already pooling in the red earth beneath her. That wasn't just trauma. An initiation. Witnessed: the precise instant when individuality either transcends or surrenders, when the self either evolves beyond the material or dissolves back into the collective. She dissolved. I watched. That watching has been carried ever since, without understanding it was preparation.

Harold Gideon saw further than most but carried it in a body and mind that could not hold the weight without breaking. His deterioration was sacrifice, a vessel for knowledge he offered himself up to contain, knowing the container would crack. He did not fail. He was the first vessel to crack and still transmit.

The water recedes around me. The altar's opalescent veins pull the liquid back into the stone, drinking it down through channels I cannot see, returning it to the aquifer, to the deep water that feeds the Valley's roots. The stone absorbs what it gave. The Grail sits empty on the altar, its purpose fulfilled. What the vessel carried has found its permanent host.

Outside, the earthquake continues to reshape Corvallis. Inside the chamber, I remain still, palm flat against the inscribed wall, feeling the vibration settle into something steadier: a pulse, almost biological, almost familiar, as though the stone and I have arrived at the same frequency.

I stay until the water is fully gone and only damp earth remains beneath me. Then I stand.

32
COME INTO BEING

The Benton County courthouse above has been merely a temporary lid on this ancient vessel, a memory perhaps known only to the land, what I recognize now as an underground basalt cave system that stretches beyond what my light can illuminate. My fingertips trace the edge of a perfect hexagonal column, one of hundreds rising from the floor like frozen music. Every surface gleams with a wetness which remains after the flooded room has drained, a wetness that is not quite water, alive with refracted light from my luminous skin.

The basalt columns soar upward, their black surfaces absorbing and reflecting my glow simultaneously, depending on their angle. They arrange themselves in honeycomb patterns, a perfect geometry from the slow cooling of lava. Some columns stand straight; others angle inward, creating vaulted ceilings that remind me of Gothic cathedrals built by humans who unconsciously echoed this older, natural architecture. The hexagonal pillars vary in height and thickness, yet maintain their perfect six-sided symmetry, cut by a mathematician's hand rather than formed by cooling magma.

Between the columns, wave-like ripples flow across the stone.

These flow lines create organic patterns against the strict geometry of the columns, like music notated on black paper. Where the basalt meets the chamber floor, small pools of clear water collect, each one a perfect mirror reflecting my transformed bioluminescent self back at me in fragmentary glimpses. My skin is now translucent, with crystalline structures visible beneath, pulsing with blue-green light that seems to emanate from my very cells.

I move deeper into the chamber, and my light casts long shadows behind each column, creating a forest of darkness and illumination that dances. The basalt itself seems to drink my light, only to release it in unexpected places where mineral deposits catch and amplify it. The ceiling, a series of interlocking hexagonal bases, resembles a shattered mirror reassembled by patient, inhuman hands. Water seeps from unseen cracks, running down the columns in thin rivulets that catch my light brighter than anything else in the cavern, and it transforms my glow into its own liquid neon.

Here, in this hidden cave, I understand that we humans above have been living in our own allegorical cave, as Plato had discovered, mistaking shadows for substance, projections for reality. But reality is fractured like the basalt ceiling, it extends vastly beyond limited human perceptions. The bacterial consciousness has existed in these extended realms all along, perceiving what we cannot, understanding what we dismiss.

What humans called gods were merely glimpses of this expanded reality, filtered through the imperfect lens of human perception. The symbols carved into stone by ancient hands, the rituals passed through generations, all were attempts to maintain contact with this larger awareness. But over time, the connection thinned, became metaphor, then myth, then superstition.

The chamber seems to breathe around me. The basalt columns expand and contract imperceptibly with changes in temperature and pressure. Water droplets form and fall in rhythms that suggest language. Small crystals embedded in the stone catch my light and hold it, creating constellations across the black expanse. I am reminded of the night sky, but inverted—as above, so below, but with me as the sun illuminating this subterranean firmament.

The prisoners in Plato's cave allegory mistake shadows for reality because they have never known anything else. When one escapes and sees the sun, he returns to tell the others, but they reject him, preferring the familiar shadows to the painful brightness of truth. Such is the tale of the prophet who is rejected by his people. We humans have walked above ground but have not seen the realms which intertwine within us and around us. But, I have drunk from the primordial waters who brought me the Contagion, and from the Grail its concentrated understanding flowed. I have become both more and less than human. To whom will I relate from this day forward?

I move between the basalt columns, my light playing across their surfaces, creating new patterns with each step. The cave opens further before me, revealing tunnels and passages that lead deeper into the earth. The bacterial consciousness pulses with recognition, with homecoming. These passages are their highways that predate and dwarf the human presence in the Valley.

The Contagion speaks within me, and as usual it is not with words, but through a transmission of understanding that floods my consciousness like light filling a darkened room. I hold out my hand and see how it lights my way. It then explains bits of what I am becoming, this luminous transformation that rewrites my flesh. Bioluminescence, I know, is the production of light by living organisms through chemical reactions. But my glow is something fundamentally different. It is not the faint bioluminescence of fireflies or deep-sea creatures, but a complete restructuring of cellular architecture into something crystalline and self-illuminating. As this knowledge unfolds within me, I watch both my hands now held before me, how they cast prismatic light across the basalt columns, splitting my blue-green radiance into spectrums both familiar and entirely alien.

The Contagion continues its wordless education, and I remember how traditional bioluminescence occurs when the enzyme luciferase acts upon a compound called luciferin, releasing energy in the form of light rather than heat. Yet humans, I now learn, already glow at levels too faint for the naked eye to perceive. Normal human bodies emit weak photon emissions, born from free radicals and reactive oxygen species generated during normal metabolism. Every living human emits a ghostly luminescence invisible without specialized equipment.

What happens within me now is an amplification and restructuring of this inherent light. My cells no longer merely leak photons as byproducts of existence; they generate and channel light deliberately, as both communication and energy source. The Contagion has rewired my mitochondria, those ancient bacterial symbionts that power our cells, transforming them into microscopic lighthouses broadcasting across spectrums beyond human perception. It is the energy of elevated consciousness that feeds on the body more intently and creates an increased glow.

I touch one of the basalt columns, feeling its cool surface against my increasingly translucent fingertips. The Contagion highlights an etymology I had never considered: luciferin shares its root with Lucifer, the "light-bringer." Before Christianity recast him as adversary, Lucifer was simply the morning star—Venus, announcing dawn's approach. The Greeks called this same celestial body Phosphoros or Heosphoros, heralds of morning light. These names now resonate with new meaning as I stand transformed into a vessel of light, neither angel nor demon but something that transcends such simplistic dualities.

My palm flattens against a hexagonal column, and I feel how the stone responds to my touch, subtle vibrations passing between us like whispered conversations. The bacterial consciousness elaborates: normal human photon emission follows a strict circadian rhythm, peaking in the afternoon around three o'clock and reaching its lowest ebb around midnight. This cycle corresponds to our metabolic rhythms, our cellular activity, our position within larger cosmic patterns.

Those with the Contagion see this light, this is an understanding those who have shared the bacteria have realized, to the depth of understanding it after the Grail is a deeper form of direct knowing. The ones who carry the Contagion perceive what others cannot via the luminous quality of all living things, the patterns of energy that flow through seemingly solid matter. I remember Harold's ramblings about people who glowed, about the light he saw emanating from certain patients at Christ Hospital. He wasn't hallucinating.

I look down at my arms, watching as my skin begins to fracture like thin ice on a pond's surface. But there is no pain, only a sense of emergence, of shedding limitations. Beneath the breaking surface, my flesh reorganizes into crystalline structures that capture and amplify light. I am becoming a living prism, both generating and refracting illumination. The light pulses in rhythm with my heartbeat, but also with deeper patterns—the tidal pull of the moon, the rotation of the earth, the ancient breathing of bacterial colonies that have existed since life's beginnings.

The basalt walls of the chamber seem to respond to my transformation. Their surfaces, previously static despite their organic patterns, now ripple with an energetic subtle movement. Geometric designs appear and dissolve across the columns—triangles nesting within triangles, spirals unfolding into infinity, perfect circles dividing into sacred proportions. They look like perfect versions of the sigils that beings had created upon the entrance. These are not hallucinations but revelations of patterns that have always existed within the stone, now made visible by my altered perception.

Histories and schools of knowledge pass before me. I know cycles of civilizations, cycles of the prophets reveal themselves to my thought, their faces are like a tragic parade of those who glimpsed elements of this truth but could not fully articulate it. The prophetic are socially abused outsiders who suffer great volumes for baby steps of advancement. Early in the prophetic cycle of our civilization, a man we call Zoroaster, conceived of the cosmic struggle between darkness and light and he wasn't the first. Nor was Akhenaten, who saw divinity in the singular sun rather than the multiple stars. William Blake could be considered prophetic, for my mother Mia, it was he who recognized that without contraries, there is no progression. Was he the first? No, assuredly not. All of these are mere vessels, all of them point toward this moment, this understanding is a pathway which is not original in itself but leads to the ultimate in originality.

And so it is now said in the Willamette Valley, to the soil to where I did not originate but will return, experiencing the depths of both love and hate, such great adversaries I have known; I have come into being.

33
THE WILD GOD AND THE WOUNDED GOD

Harold's words about Jesus at Caesarea Philippi return to me as I stand in the aftermath of revelation. *"To a pagan shrine, the mouth of hell itself. He brought his disciples to the gateway of the underworld..."* But it's not Harold's voice I hear now—it's my mother's, reciting Blake in the twilight of our old living room, her voice trembling with reverence and something like fear. *"The tygers of wrath are wiser than the horses of instruction."* She believed in the sacred paradox; she must have unconsciously understood the wild god and the wounded god, in the necessity of terror to birth transformation. I didn't understand her then when she recited such poetry. I do now.

The bacterial consciousness thrumming through my veins resonates with this knowledge; the microbes themselves remember that ancient intersection of gods. My skin catches the light differently now with crystalline patches refracting the undercurrent of terror and joy like Blake's fearful symmetry. I understand what Harold was trying to tell me before his death: the connection between Pan's domain and Christ's chosen ground. They are not opposites but mirrors, reflecting the same sacred divide, which are the same Blakean contraries that must coexist to reveal truth.

I step from the underground chamber into the broken world above. Corvallis lies in ruins, rewritten by the earthquake in minutes. Emergency vehicles wail in the distance, their sounds hollow compared to the symphony of microbial communication flowing through me. People stumble through debris, their faces masks of confusion and terror. They cannot see what I see—that this destruction is punctuation in a sentence written across geological time. *"Without contraries is no progression,"* my mother would say, her eyes distant, and I know she saw through the veil.

The courthouse clock tower has collapsed, its hands arrested at 3:16—a verse of a divine felony, once heralded as divine promise. Now, it reads as the Word made flesh has been made bacteria to become a god again. Meaning, once tethered to heaven, now such festers in the soil. God has been dead for eons, and in that death, the sacred has erupted into the profane. The bacteria do not interpret; they do not pray. They simply are. And yet, their being is poetry in microbial tongues.

I sit on an unbroken bench in the ruins of a park, letting this new consciousness—this post-theological awareness—rearrange my thoughts. Harold, in his fractured ecstasy, glimpsed the truth few dared to name: that the sacred is within the dirt of soil. His ravings weren't madness. They were fragments of apocalypse. My mother would have understood. She saw Blake beyond the status of a mystic, closer to a prophet (of inversion), and a herald of the sacred's descent into flesh. "The road of excess leads to the palace of wisdom," she said. And now I see that palace is built on the corpse of God.

"Hymn to the Great God Pan," I cry to the birds above, their flight a choreography of indifference. "Sing of the wild god and the wounded god who walked this valley." I imagine Arcadia scorched and Galilee shadowed—two landscapes fused in revelation. Pan and Jesus. Horned and pierced. Not opposites, but echoes. Harold preached their union, and now I see it: the sacred is not in purity, but in rupture. They are gods of terror and ecstasy, of thresholds and undoing. Mia would have called them emanations—forces that burn through the veil of reason and leave only ash and awe.

The bacterial consciousness pulses. They are events or encounters that merge in thresholds where the self is shattered, and the sacred bleeds through. I glance at my arm, translucent now, revealing the microbial lattice beneath. Their patterns echo ancient symbols—triple circles, sacred geometries in communication. God emptied into the bacteria which penetrated history, into flesh, into death. And now, into me.

Pan is the panic; the wilderness is God's final scream that shatters the pastoral to its fullness. Pan is the scream that dissolves armies and egos alike. The bacteria show me his history, more than the faun of children's tales, he is the terror that halts breath. Terror and glory are twins. The sacred is not safe, and it never was. Harold knew that the crucifixion offered a value more than redemption; it was an apocalypse. The death of God was the birth of the sacred in history, in flesh, in rot.

Pan is spiritually an essence of my mother. Her death by my hands, her blood mingling with the wild. The sacred as abjection. The moment the self confronts what it cannot contain. When the changes began—when the bacteria colonized my mind—I felt it. Of becoming truly other unto myself.

The people scream in the streets of Corvallis, their foundations crumbling. They are not afraid of earthquakes. They are afraid of revelation. Pan walks among them as a rupture in our physical world. Reality itself is undone. The apocalypse is now. It is the loss of the parent, or a child, and even my own reflection. It is the unveiling of a fiction that takes away your precious son, and it removes the joy that gave you a reason to get out of bed.

Pan's domain was always the threshold of the cave and the grotto. The sacred and profane kiss without consent. And Jesus chose Caesarea Philippi—a place of Pan—to declare his church. A church of stone and estrangement. A church built on abjection. On the trembling edge of flesh. *Blake's angels descend with mouths agape, their trumpets abandoned somewhere above.* The dead cannot rest anyway. Their desecrated bodies have become scripture, with flesh that speaks through violation. Terror becomes a sacrament. Resurrection begins in rot.

Pan's eroticism was never about pleasure. It was about rupture. His flute was an invocation the untrained heard as music. At Marys River, I saw the same rabid energy. The congregation moved beyond control, beyond constraint. Their bodies were vessels of divine madness. This is the sacred emerging in our damned world in the broken, the ecstatic, the undone.

I recall the strange woman who pressed against me at the river baptism, her fever-hot body seeking a receptive connection. At the time, I found her aliveness repulsive, preferring the cool perfection of the dead. But now I understand that her heated desire, her vitality, was absolutely Pan's domain—the raw, unfiltered experience of embodiment, of being alive without the mediating influence of an outside society or the morality imposed by civilization. The bacterial consciousness shifts and reorganizes my thoughts. It shows me Pan as the primal scream in the forest, the eruption into the carefully constructed order of human society. The laughter of Pan is not joy alone but the painful joy of rupture itself—the sound of boundaries breaking and human categories collapsing.

When Harold's laughter echoed through the hospital corridors, the staff interpreted it as madness. But it was this same Panic—the sound of a human mind encountering something symbolically beyond its ability to categorize or contain. Harold laughed because language failed, as it often does, because the only appropriate response to what he was experiencing was this eruption of sound that mimicked Pan's ruptured joy.

A distant rumble signals another aftershock. The Valley's soil trembles again, ever-so slightly, but I remain perfectly still, I am listening, I am feeling, I am held fast by a new understanding. The bacteria clearly do not fear the earthquake; they have endured the convulsions of continents, the slow violence of tectonic drift. The duration of time bends differently for them as generations bloom and vanish in minutes which allows for evolution to unfold in hours. Yet within their microscopic bodies the succession of memory persists as a collective ancient moment which moves through time.

They remember the Kalayupa myths etched into the land's own dreaming: the serpent that split the Valley, the ash-child born from volcanic breath, the mourning songs sung to the bones of rivers. They remember Pan's wild ecstasy in the groves, Jesus' agony beneath olive branches, Muhammad's ascent through layered heavens, the Buddha's silence beneath the Bodhi tree. They carry echoes of Quetzalcoatl's descent, of Shiva's dance, of the sky's thunder heard by a child. These glimpses are sedimented into the soil, into the breath of the wind, into the microbial chorus that sings beneath our feet. Place becomes a place due to such memory; it is beyond time, how it resonates and responds to the body and mind, and returns in a location's attributes such as local flora or geological features. The land itself remembers life, which coexists with it. It does not forget the geological fissures, the human alterations, the divine arrivals, nor the mythic departures.

I walk slowly through the broken streets of Corvallis, where cracked pavement and abandoned storefronts shimmer under the afternoon sun. The blue bioluminescence of my skin catches the light, throwing fractured reflections across the ground. People step aside as I pass. I realize my torn prison clothing could cause issues. It isn't hard to find bodies to scavenge clothing from, and before too long, I have a fleece Patagonia vest and khaki shorts on. I'm sure to fit right in with the locals and not draw unnecessary attention amid this catastrophe.

I understand now what Harold was trying to tell me before his death, what his fractured mind couldn't fully articulate: that true revelation occurs at the intersection of opposites, at the threshold where categories collapse, and new possibilities emerge. Jesus knew this when he brought his disciples to Pan's domain. The bacterial consciousness knows it now, as it transforms human vessels into carriers of a new kind of awareness. The synthesis of Pan and Jesus is the Devil exalted, where before there had not been such a creature of such choice and with a poet's agency, yet through myth transforming into Milton, in the heat of the Southern charismatic church, under the dress it lurks, these generational stains, the folkloric devil, The Old One, that which Romas knew, the wilderness replied and thus the Contagion came into being out of bacteria buried by God into the space outside of time, then manifested as mass, which became the memory of sediment.

The sun begins to set over the ruins of Corvallis, casting long shadows across broken streets and collapsed buildings. The air is thick with dust and the distant wail of sirens. Emergency workers are clawing at the edges of catastrophe, unaware that their efforts are futile. As I walk through the rubble, the fractured city feels renewed and rebuilt by collapse. Something shifts beneath a collapsed wall: fingers scrabbling against concrete, then a palm, an arm emerging. Blood-crusted fingernails claw at the air. A face appears, one eye swollen shut, the other blinking against dust. He is young. His skin, once smooth, is now streaked with ash and blood. One eye is swollen shut, the lid purple and distended. The other stares out, wide and wet, lashes clumped with dust and tears. His cheekbones are sharp, but he looks hollowed by trauma and ultimate fear. A gash runs from his temple to jaw, crusted over but still weeping. His lips are cracked from dehydration and impact, the lower split open like a wound. His breath comes in short, panicked bursts, ribs fluttering beneath his torn team's Oregon State fabric. He still has on his name tag which reads "Abel."

"Please..." he whispers, voice barely audible. "Help me..."

His eye finds mine—not with accusation, but with hope. A fragile, flickering hope. The kind that believes someone might still choose mercy in a world that has crumbled.

I kneel beside him. His body trembles. His fingers twitch, reaching—not to grasp, but to be held.

"Water..." he rasps. "Please..."

I reach for a chunk of cinder block and feel its weight, noting its surface still warm from the late afternoon sun. I feel its weight as if its mass is pleasure. His eye follows my hand and the block, pupils shrinking. A whimper escapes him, involuntary, like a prayer.

My marked shadow falls across his hopeful college face. He does not understand why I am doing this. He only fears.

And then I bring it down.

The silence that follows is not empty. It is full—of gaps where meaning is found, of revelation, of the unbearable truth that mercy was possible... and denied. For what I have learned is few speak of any mercy to be had in life, and when life does speak to such mercy, this is a restful period for another beating coming. I was wearing the clothing of Abel's community, but we were a different species. I won't remember him after this day.

I rise and face the direction of Marys River, where it all began. The wild god and the wounded god now dance together in my mind as a symbol of my transformed consciousness which so happens to be thriving of my flesh. And, if I am not mistaken—no longer are they adversaries but complementary aspects of the sacred, especially as it manifests in the broken, beautiful world of the upturned Valley. I walk down Fourth Street until the road vanishes, until I am standing at the lip of a fissure in the open earth running down Van Buren Avenue. I have to find another way out of this damn town.

The future ahead is a wound that never heals. As I make my way out of the Valley, I leave behind Marys River's undertow, a force that remembers every dead lover's name I forgot, every prayer whispered into the soil, everybody buried beneath the alder rooted banks. And the Contagion pulls, not to drown, but to baptize what remains, the return of the gods which transform into the distant future's folklore.

ABJECT:I

I've spent my life seeking out the places where boundaries fail, where categories collapse, where the abject emerges to invite a sudden rupture in the ritual of reason. There is horror in these spaces, most certainly. Such is the horror of identity threatened; thank you, ole Devil, for the separation from community and the unraveling of familial bonds. Are monsters needed when the horror of real life brings the loss of a loved one? But there is wonder bound to horror too, and a peculiar kind of truth. I craft my folk horror with a soul deeply entwined in outsiders' lore of the folkloric devil, without forked-tongued exaggeration. It is the shape of my life's motion.

I was born and raised in South Carolina. My nineteenth year was spent in Lithuania, then I came back to America and traveled the states before settling in Oregon, where I have lived for twenty-five years as of this writing. At a very early age, I began to seek out the mysteries in locations that have left a lasting impression on me. Each one opened a door betwixt the attraction of opposites: the gaps between belief and doubt, nature and myth, the seen and the hidden. My work comes from walking in these gaps, the gutters of the opposites, from listening to what speaks in the landscapes, and the voice of architecture in the cityscapes.

I carry my ruptures with me from an absent father, an abject mother, a murderous great-uncle whose face mirrors my own. I am a believer in keeping some wounds from fully healing. They operate to the imagination like smooth apertures, a 50mm f/2 Summitar on a Leica IIIf. They are how I see.

From my earliest memories, I stood outside the frame of my immediate community. From my life as an outsider, I began to form an expression and personal vision, which quickly led me toward transgressive art and literature. This was recognition, even when younger years clothed it in rebellion. Literature and the visual arts revealed truths that linger just beyond the sanctioned borders of belonging, understandings that resist the tidy coherence of communal identity.

It is through this lens that I understand the concept of abjection. In my view, abjection as theory transcends generalized filth or horror; it is a wound that exposes the sacred violence beneath cultural order. Abjection reveals the instability of identity, the necessary expulsions that sustain the illusion of a stable self. It is the corpse, the excrement, the mother's body, perhaps a crusty copy of Sade's Justine. It is all that must be cast out so the subject may emerge. But I do not cast out. I dwell.

My ruptures are living proof of this. I inhabit abjection as an inheritance that creates a lens and language for expression, and I enjoy literature that acknowledges the lifestyles of outsiders. There are many paths outside the community. Consider the Aghori Sadhus of India, who meditate beside corpses and consume what others deem impure. They approach abjection in daily life to dissolve the boundaries that sustain illusion. Like them, I do not seek to purify my life or art. I seek vision. And vision demands proximity to what others refuse to see.

In a world desperate to smooth over its contradictions, to sanitize its myths, there is revolutionary poetic potential in attending to what fractures identity. Besides the overtly abject are the subtle discomforts in the rituals of silence, the performances of normalcy, the inherited ideologies that shape a life without ever being named. I first encountered this disquiet in the hush of Southern rituals, where the veneer of civility masks long histories of rupture. There, the corpse is always present, even when removed by communities' disavowal of history. To contemplate, or meditate, on abjection is to refuse the lie of coherence. It is to inherit the outsider's gaze. This type of vision is a gift if used as such. Or it is a curse if misunderstood. The gift of an outsider's vision is the one thing my fractured family gave me that I would never trade for normalcy.

Growing up in the American South taught me that history doesn't rest in the past. The memory of place lingers like humidity on the surface of polite conversation, creeping like a cicada on a columned porch. Trauma returns in spectral form because it was never truly confronted, never exorcised. From my hometown of Greenville, SC, to my teenage playground in the moss-veiled cemeteries of Savannah, GA, all my life surrounded by the gnarled oaks draped in Spanish moss, to the fervent churches tucked into Appalachian hollows. I've been down the country roads, where the Holy Spirit still dances with rattlesnakes. I've seen belief slip into spectacle, faith become devilish performances, heated glances from Bob Jones University whores, and traumatic shocks of memory haunting the living with unfinished business. I've seen terribly wonderful things.

That fascination with belief as spectacle, inherited from the American South, followed me overseas. At nineteen, I traveled to Lithuania as a Bahá'í youth teacher, hoping to share a message I once held with deep conviction. But the encounter with its layered spiritual terrain, where pre-Christian rituals murmured beneath centuries of dogma, unsettled something in me. In the midst of syncretic rituals, in the gaze of a farm girl in Ukmergė who seemed to carry an older mythology in her eyes, I realized I was no longer interested in converting others or endorsing any organized religion.

Lithuania quietly undid the scaffolding of my Bahá'í beliefs. I left behind the idea of being a teacher and became a listener, attuned to how the divine lingers in the unspoken, in memory, and myth.

Lithuania revealed to me how paganism and Christianity syncretically intertwine in an uneasy, centuries-old symbiosis. As the last European nation to officially adopt Christianity, its spiritual landscape still bears the imprint of older gods and forgotten rites. Beneath the surface of church ceremonies and religious symbols lie the remnants of old beliefs: hidden in plain sight are altars to ancient gods, discreetly placed in the quiet corners of locations like Vilnius's Church of All Saints. These pre-Christian folk elements persist in rituals whose original meanings have either been subsumed or have faded, but they continue to shape cultural memory.

Even beliefs considered outdated resist being forgotten, even when we've outgrown them. When the Soviets turned the Church of All Saints into a museum of folk art, hoping to erase its sacredness, they ended up preserving it. Their attempt to suppress only made the symbols more enduring, like trying to bury a time capsule that refuses to rot. I've felt that same persistence in the stains of ideology bound to the sacred in my own life. The Bahá'í teachings I walked away from still linger as impressions, stains of thought and judgments that won't come completely out, no matter how hard I scrub. Living in a Christian society, with a Christian family, there are beliefs that enter one's life regardless of personal conviction or religion. That acknowledgement also suggests that the ancient, pre-Abrahamic beliefs of our ancestors must still be present in our lives, passed down subtly through generations.

The body is like any church that can be outwardly turned into a secular museum. In Vilnius, Lithuanian folk art, including wood carvings, ritual textiles, and symbolic motifs born from myth, endures behind glass displays while always retaining its quiet power of ancient belief hidden in plain sight. In the Baltic states, such marvels are often cloaked in a darkness born of repeated occupation, where survival demanded subtlety and syncretism. What was once sacred receded into form and symbol, enduring in the folds of everyday aesthetics and the rhythms of time.

By the time I arrived in Oregon, I recognized a recurring pattern: landscapes absorb and vibrate their histories, and people carry beliefs in their gestures, even, or especially, those they claim to have shed. My writing and visual art straddle the line between personal narrative and cultural haunting, turning my lived experiences into something mythic and difficult to look away from. The genre found me. My life's realities, when closely examined, reveal inherently uncanny moments, and fiction becomes the stage on which to bear witness to them.

Oregon has been deeply personal in a kind of reckoning I've come to think of as the "abject sacred," a condition shaped by ritual and the lingering traces of beliefs I thought I'd left behind. Kristeva's abjection is organized around the "not me": what must be expelled so the self can cohere, the decay and taboo pushed to the outside so the inside can hold its shape. My position is different. The darkness I've inherited stays. It never crosses into the "not me" because I have never pretended the "me" was clean to begin with. I dwell in its outsider remnants so that the shadow separates inherited stain from new growth. I document these as shadows we must pass through to evolve, without performing rituals to redeem them.

In my first book, Portland Witch House, I explored the abject through an actual meeting of presence with people whose beliefs, dress, gestures, and surroundings bleed across what society deems sacred or profane. Aesthetic photographic provocation was one tool; presence was the work. These devotions and disruptions persist as emotional and visual textures. I agree with Kristeva that abjection is the gross underside of normativity, the thing that must be cast away for the social body to feel clean. Building on this, the abject sacred as I experience it is evidence of belief systems that endure through their symbolic residue: discarded faiths, disavowed gods, personal rituals that persist like mold in the corners of a psyche even when society tries to march forward in new ideological packaging. The sacred becomes feral and returns. Repressed, it remains unforgettable.

Portland Witch House documents part of my life's journey into the abject sacred through a twelve-year photographic study of countercultural figures in Portland. These were individuals I met who were immersed in outsider religions and esoteric practice. Many were my dear friends. These aren't fictional characters conjured for effect; they are real people whose lives and aesthetics mirror the genre of folk horror: isolation, ritual, transgression, and the persistence of the past in the present. I photographed them to witness the life I lived, to create a record of my devotions and obsessions, and to reshape my reality through will and practice. In hindsight, I view Portland Witch House as situating the memoir within a broader folkloric tradition, where the personal becomes prophetic and the local turns legendary. Documentation transformed into participation. The line between ethnographer and practitioner blurred until it became irrelevant.

Before you step into Valley Versus Vector, I'd like to share a bit about its origins and how it evolved from its predecessor, Valley Versus Vision, which first emerged in the summer of 2024. Vector rises from the bones of Vision, yet it carves its own path. You can experience them together or on their own, as each stands with its own voice. Vision lingered in the haunted corridors of memory and history, tracing the shadows that refuse to fade. Vector turns inward. It is about invasion of the body, of the mind, and of the self. The horror pulses in the flesh.

When I wrote Valley Versus Vision, I sought to excavate the buried memories of the Willamette Valley, particularly the lingering spiritual residue in Corvallis regarding Edmund Creffield and his Holy Rollers cult. Through Romas, our protagonist, a Lithuanian immigrant working as a housekeeper at a Corvallis hospital in an obscured future, we explore how history cannot be truly forgotten. The past emerges through the layers of our awareness like the morning fog rising from the Valley. Vision primarily delved into psychological horror within a folk horror setting, where the lines between past and present slowly blurred until neither held its shape.

Valley Versus Vector crosses into folk and body horror together. The horror arises from a vector that is literal: the Contagion lurks in the Valley's layered, rich soil until it finds physical expression in human hosts. Vision was haunting from outside the self; Vector is possession from within, cells and consciousness rewritten together. The land's corruption mirrors the body's transformation, memory threading through both, creating a parallel between personal and geological histories.

The Contagion is a bacterial consciousness, older than language, older than our ancestors' gods, and stranger than anything the genre has called supernatural. It has been in the Valley's water table since before human settlement, called miracle by some, madness by others, divine will by those who needed a name for what they felt in the river. The fundamental components of life can be mistaken for the supernatural when the category of knowledge is too small to hold them. That categorical failure is where the novel lives.

The Willamette Valley's soil has become the abject sacred made of flesh. What once read as metaphor pulses with literal contaminant and memory: an animate archive of trauma, devotion, and rot. The ecstatic rituals performed upon this land infect rather than purify. Worship is reframed as transgression, bacterial communion dressed in theological garments. Prophecy manifests in grotesque bodies, in patients whose disturbing visions are symptoms of an ancient infection.

The catastrophic Missoula Floods that shaped the Valley's topography thousands of years ago are this novel's geological heartbeat. Those prehistoric floods temporarily transformed the Valley into a vast inland sea. The soil remembers. Molecular fragments of human ecstasy and despair persist in it alongside sediment, bones, spores, ritual traces, all of it compacted into strata the hospital was built on top of and does not acknowledge. The Valley's soil contains remnants of Creffield's followers who rolled on the ground in religious ecstasy, and I remember them every time I encounter just how staunchly Christian the liberal town of Corvallis remains at its core.

My relationship to Christianity is far from uniform. I hold deep love and reverence for individual believers, especially my late grandmother Madeline, whose quiet devotion was textured with grace and care. Her faith remains emotionally resonant to me, even sacred, because it belonged to her, rather than to an institution. But the classifying symbolic system she belonged to was the righteous machinery of Christianity as a cultural norm, which has always treated outsiders like me as something to be corrected, pitied, or purged. It's not belief that horrifies me; it's the architecture of the status quo, where certainty becomes a weapon and belonging becomes a closed circuit. The institutional church in towns like Corvallis functions less like a sanctuary and more like a symbol of exclusion, where righteousness is worn like a cloak, and anyone outside its fold becomes a disruption to be disciplined.

When my writing engages the aesthetics and mechanics of Christianity, it is through the lens of horror. The tools of institutional control seep into everything: the landscape, the hospital procedures, the cultural memory. The baptismal water, the architectural authority of the church, the medical bureaucracy that replaced it, the geological strata beneath all of it, these remain like abject sacred stains on the Valley's skin, haunting with doctrine where devils used to stand. Folk horror offers its most potent architecture precisely here: a genre built to house systems that appear benign but operate with coercive intimacy. The horror of institutional Christianity in this novel emerges from the sedimentary layers of belief within secular institutions and the status quo of daily life in the Valley. The supernatural is beside the point. The genre's framework enables me to render this reality through mythic distortion, exposing how the sacred can become a tool for control.

Folk horror's isolation is usually rural, a village cut off from the city, a moor, a hollow. Corvallis is a small liberal city that considers itself contemporary and open. The isolation is internal, puritanical, institutional. Corvallis sits at the edge of farmland the Missoula Floods carved out, ringed by Douglas fir and the Coast Fork, and it considers its liberalism a kind of arrival, which is its own container for what folk horror requires: a community with a shared story it enforces, a border it does not discuss. Ancient belief systems manifest in Creffield's historical cult and in the persistent folk practices that surface in Christ Hospital's fundamentalist-based medical procedures. The intrusion of modernity appears most vividly in the hospital itself, an institution of scientific rationality built atop ground peppered with indigenous and colonial spiritual histories.

These novels venture into unsettling terrain, engaging with the occult and necrophilia. These are literary vehicles into the symbolic realm through the architecture of taboo, employed for what they reveal rather than for the alarm they generate. In this series, necrophilia functions as a metaphor for ruptured meaning, where grief blurs what is permissible in the realities of identity. The ache of loss at its most acute is the not-knowing, the inability to locate the beloved within familiar structures of time or cosmology. The ultimate rupture is that absence without address.

The necrophilic theme parallels Christianity's ritual transgressions in the Eucharist, whose cannibalistic overtones suggest spiritual union through bodily consumption. Each reaches toward a cherished absent one, and each attempts to defy death by crossing into the gap between the sacred and the profane. Literature is a method of bearing witness through metaphor, and its provocations are meant to illuminate what otherwise goes unnamed.

The horror in Vector is ritualistic. For my art, holiness is a catalyst for the complicated territory where reverence and violation share a border, where myths of purity paradoxically enable transgression, where desire and disgust discover they have been sharing the same address. Sexual contact with the living and the dead coexist with bodily horror in these novels, exposing anxieties around contamination and consent, the passions that generate a need for control.

These elements are essential to the book's power to disturb and reveal. By confronting what repels us, we uncover what defines us.

Approach this text with caution and curiosity. Vector resists easy categorization, as its predecessor did. It is set in a near-future that smells of the present. The horror it describes has a mechanism traceable in a microbiology textbook and a theology traceable in Creffield's court records. The damp air of the Willamette Valley permeates every page, carrying black mold and fertile soil in the same breath. Decay is the medium. Whether that growth is beautiful or monstrous is yours to decide.

When you look long enough at anything, be it a city, a subculture, a belief system, realities shift and the familiar reveals what it was always hiding. The social fabric turns out to be merely one possible configuration of reality, no more inherently valid than the worldviews of those it labels eccentric or deviant. Horror is something you notice was always there, once you develop the eyes to see it.

Folk horror contains a dread shaped by histories we didn't choose, beliefs we were born inside too early to refuse. The stains that we try to scrub away return. The witch house is in Portland and everywhere: the architecture of our lives, built from collective memory and the shards of private damage that feed it. I am often like my characters who document the recognition, when you realize a location has always been haunted, and so have you.

This paradox led me from Portland Witch House to Valley Versus Vector: the uncanny isn't outside us. Such is the condition of being. We are vector and victim. Reading takes the metaphors of literature and sets them free within our lives, meaning mutates, like bacteria adapting to a host. The journey of such literature may unsettle a reader, but it reimagines what horror can hold. Like the microbial sentience animating the landscape of Vector, this book doesn't ask for surrender. It acts as a manifesto of the Valley itself, which warns us of the pain of transformation.

ABOUT THE AUTHOR

Jahan Brian Ihsan is a writer and visual artist whose work explores the intersections of personal memory, cultural inheritance, and historical trauma. Raised in the American South, he developed an early sensitivity to the way history lingers beneath the surface of everyday life—the ghosts of the antebellum era haunting columned porches from Greenville, South Carolina, to the cemeteries of Savannah, Georgia. In the charismatic churches of the Appalachians, where ecstatic snake handling still occurs, he witnessed how belief can blur into spectacle, and how the sacred often carries a shadow.

Now based in the Pacific Northwest, Ihsan channels these layered geographies into novels that walk the line between personal narrative and cultural haunting.

Jahan has an MA in Comparative Religion from Claremont School of Theology and a BA in English Literature and Writing from Marylhurst University.

www.ingramcontent.com/pod-product-compliance
Lightning Source LLC
Chambersburg PA
CBHW020258030826
48979CB00026B/1390/J